"My wife, Jane Petach Hanks, was the only registered nurse for the Flying Tigers during the war. She and I both think Louis Stannard's **China Diaries** is the most interesting book we have read of that era in that we **actually lived** so much of what the fictional character Anna relates in her diaries. It was one of the most exciting times in history and through Louis's characters, he rekindles our interest in that period reminding us of the impact we actually had on the war. Louis is historically accurate at all times."

—Captain Fletcher Hanks
Vice-President-Historian, CNAC (Chinese National Aviation Corporation)

"What a wonderful book! It's rare for me to pick up a book that I just can't put down, but this was one."

—Captain Steven Dixon, Polar Air Cargo

CHINA DIARIES

CHINA DIARIES

A novel

Louis Stannard

iUniverse, Inc.
New York Lincoln Shanghai

CHINA DIARIES
A novel

iUniverse books may be ordered through booksellers or by contacting:

iUniverse
2021 Pine Lake Road, Suite 100
Lincoln, NE 68512
www.iuniverse.com
1-800-Authors (1-800-288-4677)

ISBN: 0-595-32600-5 (pbk)
ISBN: 0-595-66652-3 (cloth)

Printed in the United States of America

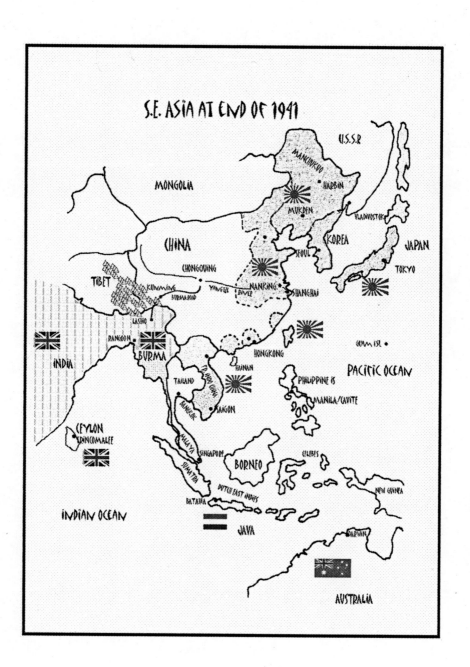

S.E. ASIA AT END OF 1941

C ONTENTS

▼

BOOK I

BOOK II

BOOK I

CHAPTER 1

▼

TRANS ARTIC AIRLINES
FLIGHT 401

Anchorage to Hong Kong
November, 1994

Captain Stephen Cannon couldn't get his mind off of the China Diaries. Ever since the phone call and then the meeting with Charlie Fat, nothing in his life had been the same. First, it was those guys in New York and then being tailed by them back to his home in Maryland, then the burglary, his computer and the letter. Now this trip to Hong Kong—it was all connected with the China Diaries.

He felt the autopilot enter a slight turn as they went past their waypoint. Through his headset, he heard Hal, the co-pilot, begin to transmit their position to oceanic control. With the position report in progress, and the 747 freighter steady on the next leg to Hong Kong, his mind pushed the play button for the recorder in his head, and the events of the last weeks again came to the forefront of his consciousness.

"Hello: Mr. Stephen Cannon?"

If it wasn't for the educated diction and slight oriental accent, he would have assumed it just another one of those targeted sales calls and slammed the receiver down. He had long ago lost the last remnants of civility when those interruptions came at home.

"Yes, this is Stephen Cannon."

"My name is Charlie Fat. I am a student from Hong Kong, and I'm here studying law at NYU."

Stephen remembered his first reaction. He thought the guy was selling magazines or soliciting for some sort of cause or something. Uncharacteristically, he didn't hang up.

"Yes, what can I do for you?"

"Excuse me for asking this question, sir, I just want to make sure I am speaking to the right person before going on. Mr. Cannon, was your mother's maiden name Anna Boreisha?"

For a moment, Stephen just stood there with the receiver to his ear. A thousand sequestered emotions flooded his senses. How would some stranger know his mother's name? She'd been gone for over fifty years! The little he knew about her was from his grandparents and the China Diaries.

"Mr. Cannon…Are you still there?"

"Ah…yes…please excuse me…is it Mr. Fat?"

"Yes sir, Charlie Fat."

"Mr. Fat…I'm sorry, this call took me by surprise. Yes, my mother's maiden name was Anna Boreisha, but she has been missing since World War II…1943, to be exact."

"Mr. Cannon, my great-uncle has just been allowed to immigrate from the People's Republic of China to Hong Kong where he is now living with my grandfather. My great-uncle, Cheng is his name, believes that your mother was instrumental in helping he and his family escape from the Japanese when they sacked the city of Nanking in late 1937."

For longer than it should have taken to reply, Stephen stood staring at a design in the wallpaper that he had never noticed before.

"Nanking Mr. Fat?…I don't know what to say! My mother's name is, or was, Anna Boreisha, but she grew up in Shanghai. She was a so-called White Russian; her family were émigrés. I guess it's possible she was in Nanking…but let me think. No, her journals didn't begin until just before Pearl Harbor was bombed in 1941. I don't recall any mention of Nanking, but if she did, it was just in passing."

"Journals…did you say journals, Mr. Cannon?"

"Yes, I call them the China Diaries. They were my parent's personal journals from the days just before the war began."

"The reason I asked, Mr. Cannon, is my great-uncle brought what he thinks is a Russian Army map case with him to Hong Kong. He says it belonged to your mother. It contained some film, a military medal of some sort, and yes, some journals...Mr. Cannon, are you still there?"

"Yeah...ah yes Mr. Fat...sorry, this is all so unexpected."

"Sir, my great-uncle must have been very taken in by your mother. While he was living in the PRC, he had no opportunity to try to find her. He speaks no English, and still, as soon as he arrived in Hong Kong, he asked my grandfather to get in touch with me here in the States, and see if I could locate her or some family member."

CHAPTER 2

▼

THE CHINA DIARIES

At home in Maryland
October, 1994

Stunned by the unexpected call, Stephen hung up the telephone, walked to the window of his home and looked out over the Chesapeake Bay.

After a moment of reflection, he went to the attic of the home left to him by his grandparents. He found his mother's old leather Gladstone, dusted it off, and took it back down to his study. He cleared a spot on his desk and set the bag down. The ancient leather case was cracked with age. Inside was an eclectic assortment of ledgers and journals held together with the old leather straps he used to carry his schoolbooks with in the fifties.

It had been more than thirty years since Stephen had last read the China Diaries. He thought the memories of his parents, of his mother's abandonment, were behind him, and here it was again.

The physical attributes of the diaries varied. Their selection seemed a function of whatever was available at the time. Some were leather, and some were composition books; others were ledgers, like his dad's logbooks. They even had a smell about them that suggested a former time. For Stephen, the China Diaries held his only memories of his parents. Without the diaries, his parents' history would have been lost to time. They didn't tell of their entire lives, only a short period, but they were all he had. He looked at them with a feeling of reverence. They were his only connection with the past.

Stephen reasoned the other ones, the diaries Charlie Fat's uncle held in China, could complement the diaries in his possession and reveal the truth. Since he could remember, he had harbored a certainty that his mother abandoned him to his grandparents just after he was born, but he had always clung to the hope that was not true. He almost feared the journals would confirm her abandonment.

Stephen couldn't help but reflect that every time he read the diaries he was involved in a kind of family voyeurism. Not only did these diaries tell what went on in their everyday lives, but also gave the reader insight about their feelings, passions, desires and even their sex lives. It was a peculiar feeling. Most children learned of their parents the normal way—from being their child—not him! Everything he had learned came from the China Diaries and his grandparents' accounts that faded from memory with every year since their death.

Unlike his mother, Stephen's father kept a diary as part of his personal flight log. Rather than a typical rectangular pilot's log, though, his father kept his flight particulars in a canvas bound, ruled ledger. Along with the required information: date, from, to and kinds of flight time; his dad kept a journal. Since they were sequential, Stephen knew he had all of them—at least up until the time he returned to China. His entries were informal, but through his writing, you could still get a very good idea of the soul of the man—how he considered events in his life. His writing captured the essence of not only what was going on during a trip, but in his life. Sometimes he drew a map, or he illustrated a particular scene with a drawing or a photograph. Very un-like a typical pilot's flight log, Stephen thought.

Anna, on the other hand was a formal diarist. Her interest in photography was evident as black and white, sepia and occasional color photographs complemented her entries throughout the journals. Anna's writing style made her entries come alive. You could almost put yourself in the world she described. It was her *other* entries that bothered him. Anna also put to journal thoughts and events for her eyes only. When reading these, Stephen felt he was treading deeply into her most private world—a place no one but she belonged. It was through those intensely personal entries that Stephen developed the notion that his mother left him and returned to China to satisfy those carnal descriptions so implicit in her diaries.

Stephen never understood why his mother's journals did not begin until the last few months of 1941 and continued only until she disappeared in late 1942. It was just about the time Anna met his father. His mother was born in 1918; that made her about twenty-three when her diaries began. Her writing style suggested one long accustomed to the discipline of journal writing, and Stephen reasoned that the ones in his possession were only part of a collection. Now, after Fat's call, he was sure of it.

Stephen sat down at his desk, unfastened the book strap and began to re-read the China Diaries.

C H A P T E R   3

▼

CHARLIE FAT

Queens, N.Y.
October, 1994

Charlie Fat rented a room from a family in Queens. It was inexpensive, near the rail-line and convenient to NYU. He had some time the following Saturday and suggested they meet at a Chinese restaurant not far from where he lived. Stephen knew the place. It wasn't far from his "commuter pad," and JFK, the home base for his employer, Trans Artic Airlines. Stephen was one of the thousands of airline pilots who commuted rather than live in or around New York. He had become as familiar with Queens as his home town of Annapolis.

After passing through the northbound EZ-pass tollbooth on the Delaware Bridge, Stephen put his two-year old Honda on cruise control, fell into the flow of traffic at about the same five miles-per-hour over the speed limit as the other traffic and began to think of the events of the last days.

He broke the date with Charlene tonight and rescheduled for his return. No great loss, he thought. It, like all the rest wasn't going anywhere except down hill.

Then there was China. There was no doubt that he would go to Hong Kong and meet Charlie's great uncle. The day after Charlie's phone call, he applied for, and received, his annual one-month's vacation. It would begin in two weeks and he would fly as a non-paid relief pilot, round trip to Hong Kong on one of his company's cargo flights. There, Stephen would meet Charlie's great uncle, hear his story and collect the mysterious map case and its contents that might explain his mother's disappearance. It was just last night he had spoken to the student, but it seemed much longer.

Lost in his thoughts about the China Diaries the drive went by quickly, broken only by the imperatives of finding the correct EZ-pass lane. Stephen got to the restaurant a little before noon.

The Chinese restaurant they had decided on was typical. There were no frills. The tables had wide white paper coverings, soy sauce, napkin dispensers and nothing else. The chairs were covered with a shiny red plastic. There was a row of booths with the same seat coverings against one wall. Stephen decided the few pictures on the wall had to be of China. There were the usual steam tables with almost warm varieties of Chinese food of questionable age. The lighting was neon. A few colorful lanterns hung from the ceiling, but they must have been only for effect, as they had no bulbs. He took a seat facing the door so he could see the student when he came in.

A waiter came to take his order. He was wearing a white dress shirt with no tie and black trousers. Stephen explained he was expecting someone else and asked for two menus and water.

Charlie Fat was easy to spot as he came through the door of the restaurant. He had told Stephen he would be wearing a plaid sports coat. Coat or no coat, he was easy to identify as there were so few customers. Stephen laughed to himself. Mr. Fat did not look anything like his namesake. He was very slender—so slender, his clothes hung on him like a scarecrow. He was of medium height, wore glasses, was impeccably groomed and had medium length hair parted down one side. He looked studious.

Stephen stood to greet him. "Mr. Fat? I'm Stephen Cannon." He extended his hand and smiled.

After introductions, Charlie said, "It is a pleasure to make the acquaintance of the son of a woman so prominent in my great uncle's memories."

Stephen said, "Mr. Fat, I can't tell you how much I appreciate your taking the time and effort to find me. It's a most amazing story—like a resurrection of a family member from the past. As I told you on the telephone, I have no idea what ever happened to my mother. All I know is she returned to China in late '42...that's the last thing anyone knew of her until your phone call. I'm hoping the journals in your great uncle's possession will shed some light on her disappearance."

Stephen took his seat facing the door. Charlie Fat sat opposite him in the booth. No sooner had they sat down than he noticed two middle-aged oriental men walk into the restaurant. Both wore cheap grey suits and sunglasses—definitely not students. In that it was a Chinese restaurant Stephen doubted he would have even taken notice except for the fact they were obviously looking for someone.

Charlie had his back to the door so the men did not immediately recognize him. He turned to see the object of Stephen's attention. After a quick glance he turned back to face Stephen. He seemed distracted and took a sip of his water.

Charlie Fat forced a smile and said, "Those two guys are my shadows. They are Japanese. I don't know which group they belong to, but I didn't think they would be following me today."

Stephen said, "Shadows…groups? What do you mean, Mr. Fat?"

Before he could answer, the waiter came to take their order. To avoid distraction, Stephen suggested they order from the menu rather than from the steam tables.

When the waiter left Charlie said, "I belong to a world organization interested in seeing that the Japanese Government and their citizens admit the role they had in slaughtering and barbarically imprisoning thousands of Chinese and Allies in World War Two. We want a national apology. Maybe you know this, but unlike the Germans, the Japanese have paid almost nothing in reparations while the Germans have paid over 14 billion dollars. Along with their admission of guilt, we are also interested in reparations for the surviving victims and their families. Many in our organization are like me. We are relatives of Japanese victims."

"Don't you think it's a little late for this sort of thing, Mr. Fat?"

"Please—call me Charlie, Mr. Cannon, and no, it's not too long. It's something that has to be done, not only for us, but to show the world that murder and barbarism will never be tolerated."

"Charlie, you know as well as I that it goes on every day."

"Yes sir, unfortunately it does, and seldom does anyone do anything to stop it. We have to keep trying, though. If you don't expose the atrocities and perpetrators of the past, what hope can there be for dealing with similar episodes in the future?"

"You have a good cause, Charlie. In all honesty, though, it doesn't seem to me that the world has learned very much. Look at Bosnia, Rwanda, the Congo—Iraq! No…in my opinion these things just aren't high enough on the world's priority list."

"You aren't alone. Except for their victims: older Chinese, Asians, some remaining veterans and especially ex-Japanese POW's…almost no one is aware of, or cares what happened. Awareness of the Holocaust is different, you know."

"Yeah, everyone knows about the Holocaust," said Stephen.

"You're right! The Jews have done a good job of making everyone know what happened. Their reasoning is sound. Keep reminding everyone and maybe it won't happen again. I only wish we could be as effective."

"Why can't your group make the same argument, Charlie?"

"They're trying, but don't even come close."

Charlie's two shadows sat at a table on the other side of the restaurant. One ordered something from the waiter, and the other began writing in a note pad.

Charlie continued, "You know, there are some Japanese who agree with our efforts but they are in a minority. They are out there, though. Actually, most Japanese don't have the slightest idea of what their countrymen did to precipitate and prosecute the war. There is almost no mention of Japan's responsibility for the war in Japanese schoolbooks. It is all part of a national psyche that says—'If we don't talk or write about it, we have no guilt in the matter.' Worse, there are these right-wing guys who refuse to admit that any of it ever happened at all. Mr. Cannon—these groups want to re-write history!"

Charlie motioned over his shoulder with his thumb.

"These guys shadowing me belong to one of those groups, but I don't know which one. They are, to say the least, pro-active in stopping any effort to reveal the truth. They want to suppress or discredit anything written about their war crimes."

Stephen could see that Charlie was warming to his subject.

Charlie continued, "When I called you, I told you your mother and my great uncle, Cheng…they were in Nanking together."

"Yeah, I was going to ask you about that."

"Did you ever read, or hear about the 'rape of Nanking'…or anything about the millions of Chinese they killed in the late thirties?"

Stephen said, "Nanking…yeah, I read something about Nanking. It was really bad, wasn't it?"

"Yes, very bad! Did you know your mother was there when it happened?"

"No…not until you told me on the telephone. You said that she and your great-uncle left there together. Were they there during that time…the time of the so-called rape?"

"Yes—both of them. My great-uncle and his family lived on a sampan. They made their living on the Yangtze. The sampan was their livelihood: home, business…everything."

"How did my mother figure in their lives?"

"Keep in mind I got everything I know by long distance from Hong Kong— from an excitable great-uncle I've never met. From what I have been able to piece together, your mother helped uncle Cheng and his whole family get away from the massacre at Nanking…how, I don't know. I am sure you will hear the story when you meet him. You are going to meet him, right?"

"Yes: I'm taking some vacation and flying over there on one of my company's regular flights."

"Regardless of the reason, Mr. Cannon, he was quite taken with your mother. According to him, she saved their lives. It was the reason he insisted I do anything possible to find her or any of her relatives."

He smiled and said, "In a Chinese family, you don't turn down a request from a great-uncle!"

"I'm glad you didn't. How did you find me, Charlie?"

"My great-uncle knew that your mother was an employee of the Chinese National Airline Corporation during the war. After the war, he went to CNAC and asked if anyone knew her. Almost everyone remembered her well. She must have been very popular with them. They said she married an American pilot from the Pan American Airline Company and returned to the States with him. One of the Chinese pilots remembered the American's name was Cannon, and that they went to his home in Maryland. While he was in the PRC, my great-uncle wasn't able to do anything. As soon as he got out, he called me, gave me the information, and the rest wasn't very hard. I did some searching on the internet, made some phone calls and found you in Maryland, and here we are."

"Yeah, that was my father all right; I never knew either one of them, but that's another story."

"What happened to her when she returned to China?"

"I don't know; my grandparents tried to find out from the Chinese airline she worked for, but they didn't know either."

"What about your father," asked Charlie?

"He was killed flying a Gooney Bird over 'The Hump'."

"Gooney Bird?"

"Yeah…That was the nick name for a DC–3. Good airplane for the time but really not enough performance for the high mountains and terrible weather…they frequently overloaded them trying to get war supplies into China; a lot of guys got killed doing it, including my father."

"I'm sorry, Mr. Cannon."

"It was a long time ago, Charlie."

Charlie changed the subject.

"Did you know if you were a prisoner of war with the Japanese during World War Two, your likelihood of dying in captivity was seven times greater than had you been a POW under the Germans?"

"No…I had no idea!"

"Yes, Mr. Cannon. About the only Americans aware of that are the few survivors left who were Japanese POWs…the lucky ones who survived. You know the Japanese routinely executed prisoners, don't you? If they didn't do that, they either worked or starved them to death."

Stephen said, "Yeah, it was really horrible. So…what's your group plan to do about it, what's your goal, Charlie? Today most people have no idea of what you are talking about. Seems to me your organization would just be perceived as a bunch of malcontents trying to stir up old resentments against the Japanese."

Charlie said, "That's certainly part of the problem, Mr. Cannon. Time and lack of education is definitely one of our enemies. With the help of the Marshall Plan, the Japanese have become one of the most stable democracies on earth. Everyone admires their achievements and respects them as a nation and a people, and we do not want to detract from that at all. However, the same could be said of Germany except for one big difference; the Germans, as a government and as a people have said, 'I am sorry' and they have said it in a way the rest of the world understands. They have paid billions in compensation to Nazi victims and continue to do so."

Charlie continued, "The big difference, Mr. Cannon, is because of postwar politics, the Japanese have gotten a collective pass! No national apology, no reparations to speak of…nothing. There have been a few books and movies but almost nothing about the atrocities, or what happened in China before Pearl Harbor. It's just not right, Mr. Cannon! Our organization believes it is necessary to expose all occasions of crimes against humanity so that the world is aware that it is an ever present danger."

Charlie paused a moment and took a sip of his water. Over Charlie's shoulder, Stephen noticed that one of their observers had taken a small camera from a shoulder bag he was carrying. He fiddled with it a second, raised the camera to his eye, and in extending his arm to take their picture exposed intricate tattoos on both wrist and arms. They disappeared under his stretched shirt and jacket sleeves.

Charlie saw the reflection of the flash and turned around in time to see one of his shadows glowering at him and putting the camera away.

Stephen asked, "Charlie, I'm sure they don't want a picture of your back. Do you think they might have some interest in me?"

"Mr. Cannon, some of these guys can be dangerous! They have been brain-washed to think that any effort to reveal their atrocities during the war is an attempt to denigrate their country, and that of course is not true. So far, at least in this country, they have limited their efforts to collecting information about their detractors and trying to discredit anything they might say about them. Lately, however, they have been more aggressive…intimidation…that sort of thing. Unfortunately, they have seen us together and I wouldn't be surprised if they take more than a passing interest in you. Mr. Cannon…these guys are zeal-ots!"

"Seriously, Charlie: why would they be interested in me?"

"Paranoia maybe…hard to say; maybe they will leave you alone."

While they finished their lunch, their shadows walked out of the restaurant. Through the Chinese calligraphy on the restaurant's front window Stephen could see the two lingering by a lamppost just outside. Stephen explained to Charlie more about his vacation and the arrangements he was making for meeting Cheng in Hong Kong.

Stephen paid the check and before they departed, he pressed three one hundred dollar bills in Charlie's hand. The student protested but Stephen insisted that he take it to help cover all of the cost for long distance and mailings to and from Hong Kong not to mention the cost he had already incurred tracking him down. He promised when he returned from Hong Kong he would call, and he would tell Charlie what he had found out.

Stephen and Charlie walked out front where the two men were still standing between the streetlight and the restaurant. They did not move, and Charlie and Stephen had to step into the street to go around. Charlie walked with Stephen to his car a little over a block away. Stephen looked back and noticed the man with the camera tailing them about a half block behind. As Stephen opened the door to his car, he saw the camera guy take another picture—this time using a tele-photo lens.

Stephen said, "Well, it's a safe bet they know what kind of car I drive." The two shook hands and Stephen left.

CHAPTER 4

▼

THE BURGLARY

Maryland
October, 1994

On the drive back to Maryland Stephen couldn't be sure, but he thought he might have been followed. Every time he went through the EZ-pass tollgate, he would lose the same Ford Taurus as they struggled through the normal lanes.

It was two days later when it happened. Stephen was coming home from the supermarket and saw two men wearing warm ups running from his house. They jumped in a Ford Taurus and sped off before he could get anything more than a description of the car. The lock on the old farmhouse door had been sprung damaging the wooden frame. Firsthand accounts of burglary victims ran through his head. "Violated," "raped," were the words that were always used. Perfect descriptions, he thought, as he walked into the ransacked house.

He dropped the groceries on the kitchen table and went to his study. His computer was on, and after a cursory inspection, he determined his meager passwords had kept the interlopers out of his desktop. All of his data discs were missing. Just as bad, the address book he kept on top of his desk was gone, and the contents of his file cabinet were strewn all over the study floor.

All the pieces fell into place when he saw the empty, "To file" box. It was there that he had left a copy of the letter to Cheng Fat, in Hong Kong.

Stephen called Charlie Fat. An answering machine asked him to leave his message. He explained about the burglary, told him about the missing letter and asked Charlie to call.

Stephen called Fred Botts, the local Sheriff. The two of them had grown up together in the same small town on the Chesapeake, so Fred knew the local gossip of his mother's disappearance during the war. Bott's father and Zachary, Stephen's grandfather, had been good friends. Stephen told Fred the story of Charlie's great uncle, his mother and Fat's organization. He told them how the right-wing Japanese organization Charlie described might be implicated. He gave Fred Charlie's telephone number in Queens should he need more information.

In a couple of hours, Charlie called back and suggested the Ultra Nationalists would be particularly incensed about any new information regarding Nanking. They would do anything to suppress first hand accounts on what happened there. He reiterated the fact that they had a worldwide reach and cautioned Stephen to be careful now that they knew about the missing China Diaries and his great-uncle Cheng.

When Fred left, Stephen gave the latest woman in his life a call. Charlene was more than an O.K. woman. They had dated off and on for about six months when his schedule and mood dictated. He asked if she would have dinner with him at Maria's, in Annapolis. At dinner there was only stilted conversation—small talk about mutual acquaintances, what was playing at the movies. He didn't mention anything about Fat's phone call or the break in, only that he had had business in New York.

He could feel it coming. He had gone through it many times before with all the others. The expected ultimatum came shortly after the first glass of Chardonnay. Charlene uttered the words that made adolescent men in adult suits quiver with fear. She wanted a relationship! It was as natural as the sun coming up in the morning. She crafted her declaration better than most, but the meaning was just the same. He was convinced by now that it was him and not her or all of the others.

For several years now, Stephen had given it a lot of thought. Almost all of his friends were married, or at least had been at one time or another. He was candid enough to realize that in the best of circumstances marriage was a difficult proposition. For a pilot it was more than difficult. For the International pilot, divorce statistics dictated almost impossible odds.

It was no mystery. Ask any pilot's wife. They were gone—sometimes for weeks on end. If there were children, they lived for more than half of every month without a father. Some wives adapted; others loved the freedom; most hated the separation. When their husbands finally did come home, their bodies had accumulated fatigue from crossing dozens of time zones. Most didn't know it but they were mentally and physically exhausted. Many didn't fully recover even after a long vacation, and most had to retire before they ever realized how bad they had felt during their international flying career. Naturally, the wives wanted to do things they deferred while their flier was away—parties, theater, social events, going out to dinner. It was the last thing the pilot wanted to do. He was a physical zombie and wanted nothing more than to zonk out and recuperate as well as possible before the next trip.

At least in the beginning, most potential mates didn't see it that way. They saw the international pilot's life as glamorous and exciting. They had all heard rumors of the high salaries earned by the pilots of the big jets. Most had visions of traveling with their husbands to exotic lands on free passes.

Still, many had good marriages. Stephen really did want a relationship. He wanted a family and he wanted children, but every time closeness suggested more than sleeping together he had an inner panic that it couldn't last—he found himself looking for excuses, no, any way out—anything except commit! Why couldn't he love someone beyond the confines of a bedroom? Charlene was only the latest in a string of many that didn't work out. She was intelligent, beautiful—the sex was great; he even enjoyed her company—at least to a point, and then he wanted to be alone.

For sometime now, he wondered if it had something to do with being raised by his grandparents rather than his father and mother. It wasn't a good argument though. His dad's parents were great; they had loved him as if their own, and it certainly wasn't the first time a kid was raised by grandparents. He did know one thing for sure—he could never quite shake the feeling that his mother had abandoned him and maybe that was the reason—if he didn't commit, there was no possibility of being abandoned again.

He had always assumed that both of his parents had died in the war but somehow his mother dying in the war just didn't cut it. Dads yes! Tragically, dads died far too often in war, but what about their mothers? How was it that it was only *his* mom that returned to China leaving him alone? When he was older, his grandparents told Stephen more of his parents. It was only when he was an adult, however, that they gave him the China Diaries and he got the *rest of the story*.

"Hey Stephen…You O.K.," asked Hal.

The co-pilot's remark brought him out of his reverie and back to the cockpit of his 747.

"Yeah, don't worry Hal; I'm still in the loop…just trying to work out a few things."

In the moonlight he could see wisps of cirrus flitting by as over a half million pounds of airplane shuttered in the light turbulence of the jet stream. Except for the cirrus, all the clouds were many thousands of feet below them. He made a mental note to check the Kai Tak weather. The monsoon season was effectively over but he wasn't thrilled about the forecast at Hong Kong.

The recorder in his head started playing again, and he recalled his mother's journal entry. It was the same month and almost identical weather, except instead of flying from New York to Hong Kong via Anchorage, his mother was flying from Chongqing to Hong Kong. The big difference was it was 1941, and she was flying over Japanese occupied China in a DC–2.

CHAPTER 5

▼

ANNA

Chongqing to Hong Kong
19 November, 1941

Arnaud DeRuffe sat in club seating on the DC–2 facing the rear of the aircraft. He liked club seating because he could observe the other passengers. Most everyone was asleep except the object of his present interest. He had noticed this beauty in the CNAC departure facility at Chongqing and suspected she was Russian. In this part of the world most of the beautiful ones were. She was saying goodbye to a distinguished looking gentleman, perhaps in his fifties. From their mutual demeanor, he did not think they were intimate…probably just business associates or friends. The woman seemed to have a perpetual half-smile and DeRuffe wondered if it was real or affected. He also wondered why she was going to Hong Kong. American connections? Probably…most Russians had few if any connections in Chongqing and certainly not Hong Kong. Americans that flew generally had many.

DeRuffe regarded the woman. With the exception of the reading light that highlighted her features, the aircraft was dark. She was writing. All the other passengers were asleep. At the direction of the Captain, everyone had their window shade pulled down. Just as well, he thought. He didn't want his employer's barbarians seeing the light and shooting them down, now, did he?

Fleeting recognition flashed through his memory and as soon as it came, it was gone. The thought waned and DeRuffe resumed his surreptitious examination of this intriguing person. Young, not like his sixteen year old whores in Shanghai and Chongqing, but probably no older than twenty-three or twenty-four. Her hair was rather short and straight with a lustrous sheen…none of those tight curls affected by so many women these days. Also, she did not wear one of those silly hats slavishly worn by Western Women simply because it was "in." This woman appeared to be one of the few who set her own fashion.

He was behind her when they boarded the aircraft. It was one of those brown winter days in China. Heavy grey clouds blew in low over the riverside airport and threatened rain, or sleet. The wind made it seem colder than it actually was and whipped the dust into swirling vortices as the passengers boarded the twin-engine airliner. Even so, she wore no overcoat, only a white traveling suit with a short waistcoat with those oversized shoulder pads. Maybe it was suitable for Hong Kong but certainly not central China in winter. White gloves completed her ensemble. Nice, but they concealed any rings she might be wearing, and DeRuffe really did want to know her marital status. An elegant suit but foolish, he thought…there is almost no way to keep such an outfit clean while traveling in China. Typical for Americans, but not the poor fucking Russians!

As the object of his attention climbed the folding stairs of the DC–2, she held her hand at her side to keep the cold wind from blowing her loose fitting skirt too high. Luckily, the steep stair allowed the dress to raise just enough to show very nice legs. Before she sat down, DeRuffe noted an athletic figure that suggested sport or a regular physical regimen. Unfortunately, the seat in front of her was in the way and he couldn't see her legs now. She was still writing and had taken the white silk or cotton gloves off, but now it was too dark to see if she was wearing a wedding band. It didn't matter; he would check again when they disembarked.

DeRuffe was a connoisseur of beautiful women. He collected them for personal as well as professional purposes. He considered them objects to be coveted and hoarded, as others coveted money, art and precious commodities. Many émigrés were the daughters of former White Russian nobility. They were used to being at the top of their society. As daughters of destitute families who escaped the Bolsheviks with nothing more than what they could wear or carry, these girls almost always found themselves caught up in the hostess, show girl or brothel trap…a trap that he himself had set more than once. For his purposes, that made harvesting them easy, as most would do *anything* to escape their impoverished circumstances. The special ones managed to "be kept," or find "suitable arrangements," and this one was very special. The ugly ones were doomed. Perhaps this rare jewel was married or had somehow escaped. What a shame that would be. Damn the gloves and darkness! If not married, DeRuffe wondered how she had managed to escape the traps other Russian girls could not. Maybe she hadn't! Perhaps she was a kept woman flying to Hong Kong to meet her benefactor. The thought intrigued him. If that were the case, he wondered who the lucky man was…probably a Taipan, Western magnate or such. Émigré women did not travel, except on rare occasions and that was usually to escape somewhere. With no passport and no citizenship, no country in the world wanted them except maybe the Bolsheviks. DeRuffe laughed at his own wit. They would take them just long enough to line them up against a wall and shoot them. The poor goddamned Russians…they had no status at all in Chinese or even expatriate society.

He regarded her face again. All of her focus was absorbed in whatever she was writing, and he was sure she did not suspect she was being observed. The sheen of her hair in the reading light intrigued him…almost like an Oriental's, he thought. It was cut almost like a man's, but longer, framing her exquisite face. It looked very good on her. The shape of her eyebrows contributed to her overall different, yes fascinating look. They were thick, lustrous, and complemented her other features. They looked almost sculpted describing a high, distinct arch, tapering to a very thin line at the temples. The eyes were brown, intelligent, and rather large. The cheekbones were high with subtle definition. Her mouth and sensuous lips portrayed the half-smile he had noticed before. She was still just slightly amused at the world. Because of the seat, he could only see a portion of one breast. Ample, he thought, complementing the rest of her sculpted body. He would have to check in with the Japanese barber tomorrow morning. Maybe he could tell him more about his fascinating traveler.

Anna's Journal
Chongqing to Hong Kong
1941, 20 November
Alex left San Francisco for Hong Kong today!

I have my face pressed against the window, as I never tire of seeing this beautiful land from the air. This evening, the air is smooth, and the sun is just setting below a low cloud layer highlighting a mosaic of flooded rice paddies all the way to the horizon. All of the reading lights in the aircraft are off except mine. In a couple of minutes, we will be in the clouds, and in a half hour, it will be dark.

Captain Sharp has had our running lights off since takeoff, and he has directed everyone to close their window shades. He doesn't want another Kweilen tragedy. Poor Captain Woods. After being attacked by fighters, he was only just able to force land Kweilen, one of our DC–2's, in a river. When the passengers and crew attempted to swim to safety, they were strafed unmercifully. Only Woods and two passengers survived. Since then, CNAC has been operating exclusively at night. Damned those barbarians!

After those events, I thought the world would have recoiled in disgust and demanded the Japanese be held accountable. Nothing has happened. The world continued as if Manchuria, Shanghai, Nanking, Kweilen and the murder of millions of Chinese were grist for Reuters and the news wires for a couple of days, a collective gasp, a sigh, and then forgotten until the next news flash.

Even though Japan is no longer a member, China protested again to the League of Nations but to no avail. Perhaps my little package from McHugh on the Japanese medical unit activities in Manchuria will change some minds. If only I had my journals from the Yangtze and Nanking, they might help too. Probably not! No one seems to care what the Japanese or those horrible Nazis do. (I must be careful what I write should this fall into the wrong hands!)

Captain Sharp is our pilot tonight. He has a reputation as being one of our best. I showed an interest in how they landed when the weather was bad and Charlie invited me to sit on the jump seat in the cockpit and observe the instrument approach into Hong Kong; clever me! Alex tried to explain to me how this is done but I didn't fully understand. Now I will get to see it first hand. Up until these procedures were developed pilots had no safe way to land in inclement weather.

Mr. Bond saw me off in Chongqing. Not only is he a mentor and a fine manager, he has repeatedly demonstrated his farsightedness. He is one of the few who has the ability to analyze events, see where they will lead and then act on his assessment. Recently, he directed that all of our pilots be qualified in instrument approach procedures. If he had not, we would not be flying at all right now. Thank God, the Japanese seldom fly at night or in weather. If they did, I think that would shut CNAC down for good.

I worry about my parents constantly. They are still in Shanghai living under Japanese occupation, and here I am, hundreds of miles away, working for CNAC, living comfortably in Hong Kong, and unable to help. I simply must find a way to get them out of there!

Oh yes, my Papa! This journal writing—it's all because of him! Oh, how many times I called him a martinet when he made me read all of those English and Chinese newspapers for "my subject for the day." He insisted I pick out the one article that stood out above the others, research what was said, and every day write down my thoughts, perceptions and interpretations in my journal and then report to him on truth behind the article. "This discipline," he said, "would teach me to think, write and to learn English and Chinese, all at the same time." Later, he made me do the same thing with the Japanese publications.

As much as I hated it, I now realize that without Papa's imposed education, I would not have this position with CNAC. After Billy, who knows what I might have done. Like so many Russian girls, for the few years my youth would permit, I would probably still be working for Hovans or someone like him and probably end up like poor Tanya. The truth is, without the language skills, the best I could hope for is work as a showgirl or a hostess in one of the clubs. The dichotomy for me is that except for my languages and Papa's education I would still be in Shanghai with my parents.

Continued—I must have fallen asleep. It is past midnight and we must be well over Japanese occupied China by now. I wonder what they think when they hear our engines from the ground? Only two more hours until Hong Kong.

I read today that the last of the marines left Shanghai on the U.S.S. Harrison. It will be the first time my old city is without marines since 1927. The article made me think about Billy for the first time in ages. He was such a lovely male and such an abysmal man. In retrospect, the education he gave me could have been a very painful experience if indeed I had learned it elsewhere. I still have a soft spot in my heart for him even after the way he treated me; I still wonder sometimes how he is getting on.

The article said the marines were headed for the Philippines. Should the Japanese start something Billy should at least be safe there because of the large military presence.

I often think of the role Mr. Bond sees CNAC playing in China's development. Even before this undeclared war with the Japanese the largest single obstacles to China's social and economic development was transportation within the country. She has always had good seaports and rivers but far too few roads and railroads to the interior.

There was little air travel at all until CNAC began operations in 1928. When I first started to work for the airline in 1936, they had three major routes covering much of China. Look at us now! Besides Hong Kong, and limited service to Indochina, the only air routes left are to Kunming, in far Western Yunnan province. From Kunming, we provide the last air link westward over the mountains to Lashio, Rangoon and Burma, or the more dangerous "Hump Route," to Assam, in India. Should the Japanese close the Burma Road, as Mr. Bond suspects, CNAC will be more important than ever. Now with all the ports, major roads and rail transportation *closed or threatened, CNAC is the last rapid link from the interior of China to the outside world. We must survive if China is to have a chance.*

The one bright star on the horizon for China has been the arrival of the American Volunteer Group. The AVG is a group of American fighter pilots detached from elements of U.S. forces. They have volunteered to fly as mercenaries for the Chinese.

Two of their airplanes were in Chongqing today. The pilots have painted a shark's mouth on the nose of the planes giving them a distinctive look. The press has taken to calling them the "Flying Tigers." They are still training and should be a formidable force against the Japanese once they are operational.

Their commander, Colonel Claire Chennault, flew one of them from Kunming yesterday. I had the opportunity to meet him as he was speaking with Mr. Bond about a shipment. The Colonel was very worried about the acute shortage of spare parts. He said it is crucial they get tires and other spares for their fighters as soon as possible. Without the tires, he doubts that the AVG will be able to put a plane in the air in another month. Remarkably, the Colonel is having the spares flown out from the United States. They are supposed to arrive on the Hong Kong Clipper, on December 6; Mr. Bond has directed me to help expedite the shipment along to the AVG as soon as it arrives.

I have been so busy with CNAC (and Colonel McHugh) lately that I have not been able to journal for some time. With this almost 800-mile night flight, it gives me some time to catch up with all the wonderful things happening in my life.

Last week I was meeting the Clipper from Manila when I had the good fortune to meet Mr. Alexander Cannon, a most remarkable flight officer.

One of our passengers had left her camera aboard and I ran back to retrieve it for her while she was still engaged with immigration formalities. I had just stepped through the door of the Clipper as Mr. Cannon was trying to leave. It was one of those rare moments when you are transfixed and can't think of appropriate words. We both stopped and just stared at each other. I felt very strange—very much like the first time I saw Billy at the Far East Cabaret. I believe me blooshed. (I think that is the English word for turning red when something embarrasses you) More often than not, it is the other way around; I can remember many occasions where I have caused men to bloosh...not Mr. Cannon! I really cannot explain it. He is not the most handsome man I have ever met, not even as handsome as Billy, but nevertheless, different. What is it with me and American men? It is probably because I have been influenced by so many movies where the hero was an American. Somehow, he seems to exude character—an inner strength I have not seen in many men. He wants so much excel in his flying career and break from the life his father wants him to pursue. He wants to be his own person, and I really think he will do it.

Alex is very tall, even taller than I am. The first time he spoke to me, it was as if we were two characters in a play and he was speaking from a script. He said, "I had no idea Pan Am had Russian Princesses in their employ."

I remember saying, "See how wrong you were! I really am a Russian Princess, but no one else in the world seems to care except you!"

He still thinks I was joking, and I'm not about to tell him that I really am (or at least was) a princess.

I knew he was interested by the way he found an excuse to help me find Ms. Caitlen's camera. The rest of his colleagues were waiting for him in customs, and here he was speaking with me. We had to leave the seaplane base separately, so he asked to see me again before he returned to San Francisco. I pretended to be busier than I actually was and told him he might try to reach me at Pan Am's office, in the Peninsula hotel.

We met for the afternoon tea dance at the Pen. He asked me if Princesses were allowed to dance, and I told him only with Princes. Perhaps I am attempting to make more of something than warranted, but I do enjoy his company.

He told me of his family who live in the state of Maryland. Their home is near a small town called Annapolis. I later looked in my atlas and found that Annapolis is not far from Washington, DC.

Alex explained that his father was a Congressman. That makes him a member of the United States Government, who together with his elected colleagues represent the people from their districts and propose laws to the Federal Government for them to consider—such a far cry from what goes on here in China and my poor Russia!

I continued to ask more questions of Alex regarding his education and how he became interested in aviation as a career. I found it fascinating that his interest began as a boy, just as mine began when I was still in my teens. He told me of how he and his father would sail to the nearby town of Baltimore and visit the Martin Aviation factory. How interesting it is to find Alex flying Martin Clippers not so many years later.

His interest in aviation attracted him to apply to the United States Naval Academy. It too is not far from where his family lives. After he graduated from the Academy, he served his country by flying naval airplanes. His father wants him to follow in his footsteps as a politician, but Alex wants to continue to fly.

There did not seem to be enough time that lovely afternoon to find out as much as I wanted to know about Alexander Cannon. In turn, he was just as interested in asking about me—my family, Shanghai and how I came to work for CNAC. He seemed particularly interested in how I acquired my languages, and was surprised to find I learned most from the journal disciplines Papa insisted on while I growing up.

Alex (I think I will call him Alex now) was particularly interested in how my parents were faring under Japanese occupation in Shanghai. We spoke for some time about how I might possibly get them to Hong Kong, but for the present, that seems impossible.

After tea, the dance ensemble began, and I was not surprised to find that my new Prince was an excellent dancer. The musicians played none of the modern dance music Alex was used to in America, and he was surprised when I told him there were many clubs in Hong Kong and in Shanghai that played only American swing and Jazz.

After tea, we went to Eddie's, an English Pub nearby the Peninsula and had a lovely dinner. It was still early, and afterwards, we went to a club that played American swing. At the club he said was considering a change to Pan Am's Cavite base, outside of Manila, where his airline seniority would allow him to fly as a first officer, and in a year, maybe even as captain. (Wouldn't it be amusing if he and Billy were to meet?) He suggested he would be able to see me often and wondered what I thought of that. I told him I would like that very much, and I meant it. It was a wonderful evening.

Alex escorted me home and we agreed to meet again his next time through. He left for San Francisco the next day but is due to return on November 26. Then, he will be in Hong Kong until the December 8. He kissed me for the first time and I can still remember the amazing sensations it sent through my whole body. After Billy, I did not invite him in. I needed some time to consider why he affects me as he does.

Enough for now. That sleazy character in club seating is staring at me again. He thinks I haven't noticed! I don't remember his name, but I could never forget such a face. It was with Hovans, at the Far East Cabaret, in Shanghai—must have been late '36 or early '37. I'd never forget that sickly complexion. I'll pretend I'm sleeping for a while. Maybe he will lose interest and go to sleep. I want to be rested to observe the instrument approach and landing.

It was the departure lounge in Chongqing, when she had noticed the foppish guy in the Pongee suit. Anna closed her eyes and recalled the scene. She had been speaking with Bond just before boarding, and she was receiving last minute instructions from her boss on the best way to handle passengers transiting from the Clipper to CNAC. Her observer had a mustache, long sideburns, was very thin and almost as tall as Anna. He had a poor complexion and wore one of those Chinese versions of a Panama Suit that only looked good on certain types of guys. He wasn't one of them.

Anna was used to having men look at her with more than casual interest, but this one fell into the category of those she loathed. Rather than the usual looks of appreciation for a woman, this one was the type that undressed them with their eyes. His next wholesome thought would be his first, she thought. He thought he was being discreet, but she had long ago learned to spot those who paid more than passing interest, especially since she started being a courier for Colonel McHugh.

She closed her eyes and again tried to sleep, but couldn't keep from thinking about her mother and father. Writing in her journal always brought them to mind. For the hundredth time she wondered how they were fairing under the Japanese occupation. A vignette of the drunken Japanese soldiers at Ginling College flitted before her closed eyes. She wondered if those girls had been able to put it behind them by now or if they had even survived—probably not! It all seemed so long ago. She hadn't thought about it for a such a long time now. She reasoned it was her musings and that character in club seating that brought back the horrible memories.

Anna came abruptly awake to find him staring again. He tried to avert his eyes but it was too late. She knew he had more than a casual interest in a female traveler. She closed her eyes again and tried visualizing the movements and postures of Cheng Tu's Taijiquan exercises to take her mind off of the loathsome traveler. It always helped.

It seemed she had slept only minutes when Charlie Sharp shook her gently by the arm. She woke from an un-restful sleep. It was time for their approach into Hong Kong.

Anna knew there were mountains on all sides of the Kai Tak airport. All she knew of the instrument approaches they used was what she had heard from the pilots. They were procedures that allowed the pilots to navigate their aircraft down between the mountains and maneuver safely for landing.

The airplane and cockpit were in total darkness. The only light was from the soft glow from the instrument background lighting. Sharp climbed back into the Captain's chair. He helped Anna with the jump seat and gave her a drawing depicting the procedure the co-pilot would be flying into Hong Kong. Even though the southwest monsoon was effectively over, they were in solid cloud.

The radio operator was busy with the new radio equipment from Telefunken. He gave Anna a headset and adjusted the volume. From pilot's conversations, she knew that everything depended on listening intently to signals from a radio transmitter on the ground. A comfortable volume and a clear signal were essential.

Sharp said, "Anna, that dash-dot you are hearing is the Morse letter 'N'".

He pointed to the drawing and showed her the "N" quadrant on both sides of the radio transmitter and said, "Tommy will hold the airplane's heading we are on now until that Morse "N" you are hearing begins to blend with the dot-dash "A" on the other side of the inbound course. That means we are approaching the inbound leg of the Kai Tak beacon. If he didn't turn on course and kept the same heading, we would fly through the course and the continuous "on the beam" tone would change to the Morse letter "A" meaning we were on the other side of the course—understand?"

"So when we are 'on the beam,' like the new slang phrase, the dash-dot of the "N" and the dot-dash of the "A" cancel each other out and we get a continuous tone—is that right?"

"Yeah, you got it—just listen and watch the heading Tommy flies and you will get the idea."

Anna listened intently. Everything began to make sense. They flew at an altitude above the mountains. Suddenly there was no tone, and she said, "The tone...it's gone!"

Charlie said, "That was the 'cone of silence'. When you didn't hear anything, we were right over the beacon. Now, Tommy is turning to the outbound leg. He's flying at a constant speed for a specific time. That corresponds to a safe distance to begin our let down. We're over Kowloon Bay now. As long as he keeps 'on the beam,' it keeps us over the water and away from the mountains. At the end of his time, Tommy will execute a course reversal, what we call the 'procedure turn,' reverse course, and let down to what we have determined as our approach minimums. If we break out of the undercast, we land. If we don't, we execute this missed approach procedure and climb back up to a safe altitude—get it?"

Anna watched the co-pilot maneuver the airplane on instruments. They were still in clouds when the Tommy increased the engine's revolutions and lowered the landing gear. She felt slightly heavier in her seat and heard the whine of the hydraulic system. The aircraft ballooned slightly as final flaps were set. Tommy was concentrating on flying a heading that kept a constant tone in his head set.

She watched the altimeter as it continued to un-wind when suddenly they broke out of the clouds. Kai Tak airport was straight ahead. The thrum of the engines changed just as the co-pilot eased the throttles back for landing. In seconds, the Douglas's tires gave a gentle bark and they were back home in Hong Kong.

Before stopping at customs and immigrations to check on the man in the Pongee suit Anna checked in at operations to see if the *Hong Kong Clipper* was on time for tomorrow's scheduled arrival. The Chinese duty officer greeted Anna and said with a look of mock curiosity.

"Miss Anna, the Clipper is not due until tomorrow afternoon, at 15:20, as usual...so why you checking so early for the arrivals?"

Anna's half-smile turned to a full-fledged grin. She replied with an exaggerated Russian accent and said, "Eeeht ees impossible for a poor Russian girl to have a private life around theeze place! You people have spies everywhere and I can't even keep a leetle deener rendezvous from you." The clerk laughed and said he would call her at her apartment if the Clipper was delayed.

Anna stopped by the customs desk where she saw Mr. Panama Suit clearing formalities. Unseen, she sidled up to her customs friend and told him of her concerns about the man. He knew Anna and gladly gave her the information.

The customs agent said, "The man's passport and his landing card records his name as Arnaud DeRuffe—he's a French National. List his permanent address as Chongqing and occupation as businessman. He will be in Hong Kong for one day; he is booked on the next Clipper to the United States."

November, 1994

Trans Artic flight 401
Anchorage to Hong Kong

Stephen saw movement out of the corner of his eye. He saw Hal shift in his seat and reach to tune the single side band radio to the weather frequency. A glance at the Inertial Navigation System showed they were approaching the 170-west position.

That simple task! It took him only seconds, he thought, and the new "glass cockpits" did it with digital electronics and colored pictures! In his dad's time, not more than a hundred people in the world could find an airplane's position over the ocean, and most of them were pilots with Pan Am. It took a navigator working full time just to figure out where they were. Then, it took a highly trained radio operator using Morse code to send that position to their company. While they were doing that, a flight engineer had to adjust a myriad array of controls to keep those large radial engines running to get them where they wanted to go.

Regardless of his musings, Stephen unconsciously scanned the instruments assuring himself that Hal and the big Boeing's automation were not only doing the work of seven crewmembers of his fathers day, but doing it at eight, rather than two-miles-a-minute. It wasn't long until his thoughts drifted back to the China Diaries and an entry by his father that so well characterized the differences between flying then and today.

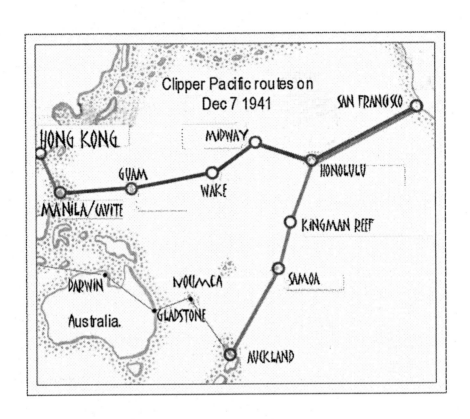

Clipper Pacific routes on
Dec 7 1941

HONG KONG

MIDWAY

SAN FRANCISCO

GUAM

WAKE

HONOLULU

MANILA/CAVITE

KINGMAN REEF

DARWIN

NOUMEA

SAMOA

Australia.

GLADSTONE

AUCKLAND

C H A P T E R   6

▼

ALEX CANNON

At home—Oakland, CA
18 November, 1941

Alex's journal

> Since Hong Kong, Anna Boreisha is seldom from my thoughts. The good
> news is that tomorrow it is off to my new base at Cavite. There, I will be
> closer to this amazing woman and within a year have a shot at Captain.
>
> The bad news is, I have to break it off with Tracy tonight. Soon, I will have
> to tell my parents. Added to that, my last trip out of Treasure Island will be
> with Captain Neville Brewster, God's curse on aviation!

Oakland, *Enroute to Treasure Island sea plane base*
19 November, 1941

Except for the white naval looking "wheel hat" sitting on the back seat with his
leather suitcase and flight bag, a casual observer would have looked at the navy
trousers, white shirt and navy tie and guessed the young man was just another
businessman on his way to work in San Francisco rather than a Pan Am crewmember, in uniform, on his way to cross the Pacific. If the observer were a
woman, only the most discreet could maintain a comportment of no interest.
Most would have dropped their normal subterfuge and simply stared, or as many
did, fussed with their hair, blushed, or even flirted. Normally, the not quite thirty
young man carried a natural smile and a composure unaffected by the almost
hero status the media had bestowed on the men in his profession. Today was different. A slightly furrowed brow and a face fixed in concentration betrayed a preoccupation with something.

His thoughts were still on last night when Pan American Second Officer Alex
Cannon slowed for the tollbooth on the Oakland Bay Bridge. The politicians
said just a few more years and no more tollbooths—the bridge would be paid for!
Yeah…right, he thought. Two cars away from the booth Alex noticed "Old Phil"
was on duty. The toll taker knew just about all the Pan Am crewmembers who
commuted from the East Bay.

Phil recognized Alex as one of the Clipper pilots that regularly traveled the
bridge from the Oakland side to Pan Am's new Treasure Island flyingboat base.
The newspapers and radio stations had elevated the crews to near celebrity status

as indeed they were. Pan Am's aviation pioneers had done something no one else could even come close to doing. They had blasted landing bases from coral reefs across the Pacific and were the first in the world to fly routine commercial flights from the United States to the Orient.

"Morning Mr. Cannon...off to the Orient today?"

"Morning, Phil! Yeah, but this time it's one way. I'm being transferred to our Manila base, at Cavite. This will be my last flight out of Treasure Island for awhile."

"Well, I'll miss seeing you Mr. Cannon...you being one of my regulars and all. Now you watch out for them uppity Japs...ya hear? The Tribune says ain't no telling what them fellers is up too, so you watch out for em real careful like Mr. Cannon!"

"Thanks, Phil...the company has been keeping an eye out, and I'm sure they wouldn't be moving me out there if they thought there was any danger."

"Well just you mind what happened to Earhart and Noonan! You can't tell me it weren't them Japs!"

"Yeah Phil...I'll watch out. See you when I get back this way!"

Alex accelerated his 1938 Ford coupe into the fast lane of the Oakland Bridge and compartmentalized Phil's comments in the back of his mind. Even though his thoughts were occupied with the blow he delivered to Tracy Summers last night, the seaman in him, honed by years of sailing, couldn't help but notice the moderate northwest wind that was blowing against the ebb tide on the bay. If the wind and wave stayed like this, he thought, it would help the fuel laden Martin get on the step for takeoff—any choppier though, it could be a tough bash. He left himself plenty of time for his pre-flight duties today. Damn! Captain Neville Brewster was in command today. Instead of being the amalgam that brought a crew together, the word was, he was one of those that could have everybody ready to kill him before they even got off the water.

He had taken Tracy to dinner and the movies last night. They had seen the *Maltese Falcon* with Humphrey Bogart, and had dinner at Sloan's. He would never cease to be amazed at a woman's perceptiveness. It was like a sixth sense. Soon after he had picked her up Tracy's body language told him that she sensed he was holding back. He knew he was transparent and had never been very good at keeping that kind of a secret. Alex kept it to himself all through the movie and waited until after dinner to tell her. Then it was out. He was transferring to the Cavite base, near Manila, in the Philippines, so he could upgrade to captain sooner. Worse, he broke off the engagement and told her about Anna. It was the only honest thing to do, but damned—maybe he shouldn't have been such a boy scout. It would have been so much easier on both of them if he had just not said anything about Anna. In his way of thinking, though, it would have been dishonest not to do so. At least he left no illusions. He had no idea if Anna, living half way round the world in Hong Kong, had any feelings for him at all. He thought so, but at least Tracy would not be wondering if there was a future with him. Damn—the truth was a hard thing to deal with sometimes!

Worse, now he was going to have to tell his parents. He and Tracy Summers had met at one of the numerous social gatherings way back when he was still a "Middy" at the Academy. It wasn't long until the two of them became *an item*. She was smart, pretty and as far as both sets of parents were concerned, they made the perfect couple.

Tracy was the daughter of a prominent family in Zachary Cannon's Congressional District. Over the years, the two families had become good friends. Not only did they socialize together, but the Summers had also been supporters of Zachary's political ambitions. Throughout their courtship both families just assumed the two of them would eventually be married. So did Tracy, and up until now Alex had just gone along with it. Meeting Anna in Hong Kong had changed all that. After last night, he had no choice but to tell his parent's back in Maryland. It was too late for a phone call, so it would have to be a letter, probably from Honolulu or Hong Kong.

After Annapolis, Alex went to Pensacola for flight training. His performance was upper third. His reports suggested, "Midshipman Cannon would make a very capable officer if he learned to keep his fiery temper in check." To help in that regard, his academic advisor directed him to join the boxing team. In that venue, he left an excellent record of wins—usually by knockout or TKO. Nothing was recorded with regard to whether the sport curbed or exacerbated his temper.

Alex excelled at Pensacola. He complemented a natural piloting ability with a thorough technical background guaranteeing a fleet assignment on graduation. It was with the fleet that he learned the intricacies of naval air operations as a fighter pilot. As much as Alex liked the Navy, he was even more intrigued by progress being made in commercial aviation: especially transoceanic air transportation. Since he could remember, he had watched the disparate airlines of the world fighting for dominance in the fledgling industry. It was Pan American, though, that was emerging as the leader in international aviation. It was Pan American that was turning coral atolls into refueling bases and steppingstones across the Pacific. It was Pan American that was turning the dream of long range, over ocean travel into a reality. Captains Ed Musick and Charles Lindbergh, both pilots with Pan Am, became his idols. It was natural, then, that as soon as his Navy tour was completed, he applied for, and was accepted by, Pan Am as one of their entry-level pilots.

Normal progression was to start a pilot as a navigator where the candidate learned the art of long range over water navigation including the embryonic science of in-flight celestial navigation. Aviation topics were not the only things the entry-level aviators had to learn. They already knew how to fly, or they would not have been hired in the first place. Alex's good record, military flying and Naval Academy engineering background made him just the kind of pilot the new Pan Am was looking for. Now, he and the rest of the new pilots had to learn to fly *Pan Am's way*. Besides night and instrument flying techniques they had to learn everything from first aid, bending a line to an anchor, and setting that anchor from a flying boat. If they were successful in the preliminaries, they progressed to the normal flying boat maneuvers of takeoff, landing, docking, sailing, picking up moorings, water navigation in currents and mooring to name a few; a knowledge of world wide buoyage and ship navigation aids was a must.

When a pilot's seniority permitted he progressed to the rank of co-pilot, and if progression were normal, to captain. Each step required months and even years completing a curriculum designed by Andre Priester. Priester was a Dutchman by nationality and an experienced aviation manager. Juan Trippe, Pan Am's founder, hand picked Priester to insure that their pilots were the best and safest in the world. After correspondence courses that gave the pilot a grasp of the subject matter, Priester's stringent curriculum required more ground school followed by exhaustive in-flight training and then rigorous flight checks to make sure the candidate had acquired the skills he had set up as Pan Am's standard. Many pilots never did and were terminated. When qualified, the new captain obtained the exalted title of Master of Ocean Flying Boats.

Flight engineers and radio operators had their own curriculum. They advanced through their own disciplines. Only in extraordinary cases did they ever become pilots.

Every crewmember had to go through the same rigorous standards except for a few who were flying boat captains before Priester set up the curriculum and the stringent standards. These few had "grandfather rights," and were exempt because of their *experience*. Captain Neville S. Brewster was one of those. Alex and many others thought the policy a big mistake.

It was common knowledge that Brewster commanded by fear and bluster. He was a big guy and used his size to intimidate subordinates. He had been reported a couple of times for actually reaching across the cockpit and punching a co-pilot.

In that he had few verbal or leadership skills, it was his way of giving emphasis to an order. So far, he had gotten away with it, and fortunately, there were not many like him left. Captains like Brewster were rapidly becoming anachronisms found at the more senior bases. Treasure Island was one of those bases, and he was well known to the crews that had to fly with him.

Alex knew he was a better pilot than most. Like most junior pilots, he was impatient with the seniority system even though he knew it was necessary. If a pilot were otherwise qualified, he still could not "upgrade" until there was a vacancy. If then, he had been a pilot longer than others equally qualified, he would get the "bid" for the open position. Cavite was a junior base and would afford Alex his opportunity. Four more legs, Alex thought…then Cavite, long layovers in Hong Kong with Anna and no more Brewsters!

CHAPTER 7

▼

THE NAVIGATION
NIGHTMARE

Clipper flight 801
19 November, 1941

The curved off ramp to Treasure Island always afforded a panoramic view of the flying boat base. Today there were several Clippers "on the hard," in various stages of maintenance. Others were at their piers tugging at their dock lines. His ship, the *Philippine Clipper*, was moored to the number one departure dock being readied for the weeklong flight to Singapore. It was one of the M–130's, built by Martin, the normal ship for the run.

Joe Mellon had just pulled into the parking lot in front of him. Joe was the co-pilot, or first officer for today's flight and was busy taking bags out of his car. When he saw Alex pull up he walked over to his coupe and said, "Hey Alex...you up for two and a half weeks of Brewster?"

Alex remembered his father's admonition. "Unless you have something positive to say about someone, keep your mouth shut."

"Hi Joe...can't say I've ever had the pleasure but sure looks like I'm going to find out about him first hand! Anyhow, I'm just one way...I've got a Cavite bid!"

Joe laughed, "Well, you Pettit and Hunt are at least back at your stations. We poor co-pilots are sitting right beside that eight ball...right where he can reach across and punch you."

"So I've heard...does he really do that?"

"Yeah…he does. It's hard to explain. Kind of like the bully back in grade school whacking someone to let them know who the top dog was."

"Jeez! That's hard to imagine…imagine! Wonder how he gets by all the screening?"

Joe said, "When he started, there was no screening…everything was about fly-ing time, and he had a lot of it. Best I can guess it's because he's part of Priester's chosen few…some day it's gonna catch up with not only him, but the company too!"

The two flight officers walked into the operations office; they said hello to the dispatchers and other clerks on duty and began their pre-flight preparations.

Alex opened his flight case, with both hands reached in, and carefully with-drew a small-hinged wooden box. From the box, he took his chronometer and a small log he kept in the case by the pocket-watch sized timepiece. He laid those two most important items next to the time hack radio and flipped on the switch. WWV was the official time of the US government's Bureau of Standards that transmitted its signal by powerful long-range radio heard round the world. The tick and beep of the time signal gave navigators an exact time so that they could set their chronometers to the same time in Greenwich England. An exact Green-wich Mean Time, or GMT, was and is the basis of all celestial navigation. Exact time was extremely important as only a five-second difference could result in a one-mile error in a line of position. Alex noted the difference between what his timepiece read and GMT. He jotted it down in his little note book and noted his time piece had gained exactly 12 seconds in the four days since he last checked. That gave a rate of three seconds a day. With that information, Alex was confi-dent of the exact GMT even if he could not get a WWV time hack over the next couple of weeks.

After checking his bubble octant for accuracy Alex went through the double swinging doors to the meteorological office and said hello to the duty met officer. He studied the horizontal weather depiction and winds aloft while the weather officer briefed him on what to expect along their route. Knowing the winds and weather Alex went back to the planning room and plotted a "least time track" to Pearl Harbor. They gave no consideration to air traffic as very few aircraft in the world even had the capability to fly between the West Coast and Hawaii. They would be the only airplane in the sky. After checking the forecast winds, Alex pre-pared a flight plan and projected a flight time of twenty one hours and thirty five minutes…twenty minutes over the schedule.

John Pettit, the first flight engineer, came into the planning room and handed Alex their fuel load and the Clipper's fuel burn figures for this, the longest leg in the Pan Am system. "Read and weep Alex...Only three passengers and the mail. The rest is fuel bringing us up to max takeoff gross weight. Can't wait till we have enough Boeings for this run...might even be able to carry some revenue besides mail on this leg."

Alex said, "Hang on John and I'll give you a copy of the flight plan so you can figure the burns on it for your howgozit."

John took the flight plan and headed for the Clipper dock just as Captain Neville Brewster came through the planning room door. He ignored the flight engineer when he said good afternoon. He looked over Alex's shoulder at the course he had plotted on his chart but said nothing. When Alex saw him standing there, he stood up to introduce himself and said, "Hello Captain Brewster, my name is Alex Cannon."

Brewster was tall...taller than Alex. He was a powerfully built gruff looking man who at first glance reminded him of Lon Chaney, except taller. He did not look Alex in the eyes and ignored his outstretched hand. He had very close-cropped, almost white hair, and one of those complexions that suggested a bad case of acne as a youth. Large hands with huge knuckles complemented the long, almost gorilla-like arms that hung from his broad shoulders.

Still not looking at Alex, Neville Brewster said, "How long?"

"A little over schedule, skipper...twenty one hours and thirty five minutes."

Brewster only grunted, turned and left the planning room.

I hope his flying is better than his personality, Alex thought.

He gathered up his charts and equipment and walked out of operations on his way to the docks. He had to push very hard on the door against the now very brisk wind from the northwest. He looked upwind toward the open water and wasn't surprised that the small waves he had seen crossing the bridge now sported white caps and the characteristic short steep waves of wind blowing against the tide on San Francisco bay.

As he turned from the operations building to the dock, he saw the *Philippine Clipper* rocking majestically at the passenger boarding dock. After all this time he was still struck with her beautiful lines as she seemed to strain at her moorings ready to take passengers and mail across the Pacific to the Far East and China.

Alex noticed a young woman and two men pacing up and down in front of the Pan Am passenger departure lounge. The woman looked familiar and seemed not to be with either of the two men. Instead, she seemed interested in the activities of the flight, maintenance and service crews swarming over the flying boat. The two other male passengers had their backs bent to brisk wind, each smoking a cigarette and seemingly lost in their own thoughts as they paced the dock.

Men in white coveralls with Pan Am in large blue letters sewn across the back were just finishing the process of loading tons of aviation gasoline. Others, similarly dressed, were loading mailbags through the open hatches in the fuselage. Spray from the building waves splashed against the pilings sending water over the boarding dock.

Alex walked down the dock to the service platform and climbed up the steps to the entrance door on the front of the fuselage. He set his suitcase in the baggage compartment, said hello to Ricky Parraga, the purser, and climbed the ladder to the flight deck. As he reached the top of the ladder, he noticed that Tom Paine, the radio operator and Joe Mellon, the first officer, were already busy with their pre-flight duties. Farther aft, up between the wings, and looking forward and down on the rest of the flight crew, John Pettit, the flight engineer, was finishing his preparations for engine start. As he set his flight bag and octant down at the navigation station, he noticed the captain's seat was vacant. It was twenty minutes before scheduled departure.

Alex forgot about Brewster and completed is own pre-flight duties. As he plugged his headset into the ships intercom system, he heard the rest of the crew reciting the Before Starting Engines checklist. He had just finished checking that all of his reference books were aboard and up to date when Joe Mellon called on the interphone and asked, "Anybody seen the skipper back there?"

Alex looked at his wristwatch and saw it was four minutes to scheduled departure. He squeezed the interphone button and said, "I'll check and see if he's down in the cabin, Joe."

Just as he was ready to climb down the flight deck ladder, Captain Brewster came through the hatch, removed his coat and hat hanging, hung them on a hook for that purpose, went forward and climbed into the captain's seat. Without saying anything and before putting on his headset and seatbelt he gave the signal to cast off lines. The mooring launch was still maneuvering to assist the undocking maneuver when Brewster barked, "Start the engines!"

Joe Mellon was nonplussed at Neville Brewster's command. He held the still un-finished part of the pre-start checklist in his hand and said, "Captain! We're drifting toward the leeward dock...don't you want to let the launch hook on before starting?"

"God Dammit!...If I wanted the launch hooked on, I would have called for it now, wouldn't I...Now start the engines!" Even though Brewster wasn't on interphone, everyone could hear the exchange between the two pilots.

John, the flight engineer knew they had begun to drift, and knew they would have no steerage until they had engine power. He repeated the command to anyone listening and began starting all four engines in sequence. The big Martin, with no way on and no launch for a tow had already begun to drift toward the leeward docks.

Roger Kent, the third officer, was standing at his station in the nose hatch. He watched helplessly as the Pan Am launch tried to maneuver in front of the drifting Clipper while still keeping clear of the whirling propellers. A launch crewmember held a single line in two separate coils, one in each hand. When the launch coxswain maneuvered as close as he dared, the crewman expertly threw the coil to Roger who caught it in his outstretched arms and quickly made it fast to the Samson post on the nose of the airplane. Just before the Clipper drifted into the adjacent dock, the launch was able to take a strain on the line and tow the seaplane clear of the docks and to the takeoff area.

The launch had only towed them a short distance when Brewster gave the order to cast off. Brewster was on interphone now and just as the last engine was started, he called for "max power!" Roger Kent was still in the process of closing the nose hatch. None of the required preparatory checklist had been run.

As soon as the engines came up to full power the Clipper's hull began to protest with the terrific pounding in the short chop and freshening wind. As the flying boat gathered speed, the pounding increased to the point the airplane shook with every wave. From his position, Alex saw the entire ship was being engulfed in salt spray from Brewster's self-induced gale.

Acceleration was far slower than normal. The fuel-laden flying boat was at the maximum allowable takeoff gross weight and could not gather enough speed through the impeding short steep waves to plane, or *get on the step*.

Everyone aboard knew that no flying boat could takeoff without first getting on the step. The attempted takeoff went on for another agonizing thirty seconds with tremendous bashing and no appreciable increase in speed. Suddenly, all power came off, and the nose of the *Philippine Clipper* buried in the waves up to the cockpit windows. Brewster had aborted the takeoff.

Without waiting, Alex pressed the talk switch on his interphone and said, "Captain Brewster, Alex here…over behind Treasure and the bridge supports the waves are almost flat in the lee of the island. Probably give us a much better takeoff run from there."

Before Neville Brewster could respond, Third Officer Roger Kent called up from the nose station and said, "Captain, Roger here…looks like we might have sprung a plate. We're taking on some water down here!"

Brewster came on the interphone and said, "OK, ah…yeah, it's pretty rough so get the pumps going. We're gonna taxi down in the lee of Treasure and try it from there. Let me know how much water we're making!"

With no warning, there was a deafening roar from engines one and two. The flying boat lurched abruptly to port as Brewster used differential power to blast the Clipper through the wind in an abrupt right turn. Just as the port, upwind wing turned through the wind; a sudden gust lifted it burying the starboard sea wing in the water. With the turn down wind, completed the Clipper righted itself and the motion was much better as Brewster made for the sheltered water.

As Brewster continued to *sail* into the lee of Treasure Island and the bridge supports Alex was wondering what the passengers must be thinking. As if reading his thoughts, Ricky Parraga, the steward, stuck his head up the flight deck ladder and yelled, "What in the hell is going on up there? The passengers are scared shitless!"

Before anyone could respond to Parraga's question, Al Hunt, the off duty Flight Engineer, pulled off his head set and said to no one in particular, "That stupid son of a bitch has just forced about a ton of salt water over the whole airplane and through all four engines. If we don't get a fresh water wash down or a helluva rain shower, we're gonna have to trash em all! In a week, there won't be anything left out there but a mass of corrosion."

Parraga had his answer, but before he could return to the passenger cabin, the Clipper lurched to starboard and again turned into the wind. As soon as they straightened out, and with no warning from the pilots, all four engines again went to maximum power backfiring in protest from the salt water cold soaking and the abrupt power change. Brewster had begun another takeoff in the smoother water he had failed to notice before. Alex noted the time and punched his stopwatch to clock the takeoff run. Anything over fifty seconds usually signaled abnormal acceleration and that something was wrong. This time the Martin rose on the step just before they came out from under the lee of the island and bridge supports into the rougher water. In that they were now skimming along the wave tops, the short steep chop had much less effect than before. With each passing second the pounding became less as the Martin's wings lifted the hull, and the Clipper morphed from boat to flying machine.

After the takeoff, there was none of the usual banter on interphone. No one spoke to each other. Only Roger Kent called and declared he had the bilge pumped dry. Everybody was lost in their own thoughts, as they had to anticipate another two weeks with this buffoon.

It was just after 4 p.m. in San Francisco when the Clipper turned west toward the Golden Gate Bridge. Alex noted the time and looked pensively at the city, the bridge and the receding coastline. With his transfer to Cavite, he had no idea when he might glimpse these vistas again. His thoughts turned to Hong Kong and Anna as the airplane was enveloped in the low clouds of Northern California's early winter. They would not see land again for more than twenty-one hours.

In a few minutes, the flying boat broke through the stratocumulus cloud deck and into the brilliance of the late afternoon sun. They leveled off at 6500 feet as their initial cruise altitude just skimming along the tops of the silvery clouds. Flying just above the cloud tops was one of the most beautiful and satisfying sensations of flight. Not only were the cloud tops beautiful, but it gave one a real awareness of the airplanes speed.

Since Hawaii was more or less in the same direction as the setting sun, Alex knew he would have a long time to shoot it before setting. As long as it was in sight he would be able to get valuable speed line information—or how fast the Martin was traveling over the water. The very strong radio signal from San Francisco's radio transmitter would provide them with their course line, the other part of the navigation problem.

San Francisco to Honolulu was the longest over water route segment of all Pan American routes. Once they left, there was no place to land except the open ocean until they reached the Hawaiian Islands. An open ocean landing was the least desirable, but only option, should anything necessitate a landing enroute. It was with that in mind that Pan Am designed procedures to insure they had enough fuel to go to a point on their route, about half way corrected for wind, lose an engine and then either continue or return with sufficient fuel to effect a safe landing. This point along their route was called the PSR, or point of safe return. There was another point called the PNR, or point of no return. That was the point where the crew lost their option to return as there was insufficient fuel.

Shortly after the *Philippine Clipper* leveled off, Captain Brewster came back to the flight deck. He put on his coat and hat and said he was going to the off duty rest station in the rear of the airplane. Third Officer Roger Kent mumbled hello and went forward to sit in the captain's seat as the relief pilot. Brewster paused at the stairs, looked at Alex and said, "I'll tell you the same thing I told Mellon. I need to get some sleep and be fresh for the landing at Pearl! Wake me only if something goes wrong. And...What's your name?"

"Alex Cannon, sir."

Brewster continued, "Yeah, Cannon—I don't want you putting anything in that navigation log about that little bit of water we took on during the take-off...you hear?"

Alex said, "Captain, if we don't mention it in the maintenance log they won't be able to fix it."

Brewster said, "Nothing in any logs, damn it!" He turned and shouted up to the flight engineer.

"You hear that Pettit? I'll tell them what they need to know in Pearl to fix it. You two understand what I'm telling you?"

Pettit didn't respond. Alex looked directly at Brewster and said, "Yeah Captain, I understand exactly what you are telling me."

Brewster didn't respond, but turned and went down the access ladder.

As soon as the crew knew Brewster was off the flight deck, the interphone began to come alive, just a little at first and then as a crew working as a cohesive unit with a common goal. Tom Paine, the radio operator, said the signal from San Francisco was strong and should provide a good course line until out of range. Alex noted Tom's report in his navigation log.

Until Pan Am's Hugo Leuteritz developed long range direction finding equipment it had been impossible to consistently fly the oceans safely solely by celestial navigation. When there was cloud cover, a navigator could not see the stars, moon and planets, and without those celestial bodies it was impossible to fix the airplanes position without radio signals extending far out over the oceans.

The engines thrummed hypnotically in the background as John Pettit made minute adjustments to the propellers RPM. Alex thought all the pilots would have to do the first four hours or so was simply: *stay on the beam*. His task would be to cross the course line with a sun shot to determine if the speed over the ground was the same as on the flight plan. If the forecast assumptions in the flight plan were correct, his part would be routine.

Things started to go wrong a little over one hour after takeoff. The sun was still above the horizon. Alex had just come back from the flight deck where he took a sun shot with his octant. He looked at his flight log and rechecked his calculations. He corrected his sight for octant error and their height above the water, converted the observation to a line of position, and plotted it on his chart. At first, he didn't believe his math, but he had taken two shots to make sure his observations were correct. If those shots were right, the distance run in the last hour was only 78 miles and even with the significant forecast headwind, the Clipper should have flown 98 miles! He thought about the captain asleep in the rear of the airplane. He wasn't about to wake him yet. No telling how that jerk would respond.

Alex called on the interphone to Joe and Roger at the pilot stations, "Hey you guys, did one of you drop the anchor during takeoff?"

"Waadaya mean, wise ass?"

"From my sun shots we are going to be 19 minutes behind at the next position. If I'm not completely screwed up our ground speed is only 68 knots right now," Alex said.

Joe called down, "You out partying last night Alex?"

"Hey John!" Alex called to the flight engineer. "How about getting me some fuel figures for 02:25 GMT."

"Yeah Alex, will do."

Joe Mellon called from the cockpit, "Hey Alex, we were about to call you! Look how the heading has cranked around just to keep on the Frisco beam. Compare that with the heading you pre-comped on the flight plan. Your pre-flight heading isn't even close anymore."

Roger Kent added, "Looks like we've got some hellacious winds that are nothing like those forecast. The flight plan and the weather picture we got in Frisco just doesn't jive at all with what we're seeing."

Alex finished calculating the 125-degree west fix for their next position. He checked both chronometers to see if the time he used for his sun shots were still valid. They read within one second of each other. Then he made sure he had used the right date and time for extracting data from the almanac. That too was O.K. Alex paused for a moment and tapped his pencil on the chart in thought. After a moment, he took his parallel rules, drew the wind triangle on the chart and picked off the actual wind with his dividers. He didn't like the wind vector he saw.

Alex stood and stretched. He looked at his watch and decided he would take a break before confirming the numbers. He called on the interphone and said, "Alex here...I'm going to take a walk guys. Be back in a minute." He took off his headset, put on his uniform jacket, went down the ladder, through the galley and opened the door to the main cabin and a different world.

Alex always tried to close the compartment door as quietly as possible. He did not want to disturb the passengers when entering the lounge.

Gone was the roar of the engines just over his head in the crew compartment. Gone too were the technical complexities of radios, engine controls, gauges and dials. In the noise-muffled cabin only a rhythmic drone remained. He had entered a world of urbane elegance; it was the best that air travel could provide in 1941.

Lounge chairs were fixed in club style, facing each other and separated by coffee tables. Most of the cabin was in a more or less art deco style with a lot of aluminum and leather trim. The two male passengers were in animated conversation gesturing with their hands for emphasis. Playing cards and cocktails were on the tables in front of them. Unlike the flight deck, conversation was carried on in a normal voice due to the extensive soundproofing. The female passenger Alex had seen at the Treasure Island dock was young, perhaps in her mid twenties. She was reading a fashion magazine. At first, she only looked at him over the top of magazine as she flipped a page. Pretty, Alex thought, but not what Alex would consider beautiful. She affected a permanent wave that seemed to be so popular with many women those days.

The purser had just finished serving a round of drinks. On his way back to the galley to help the steward with dinner he paused by Alex and said, "We will begin the dinner service shortly Alex, how's the weather look?"

"Looks fine right now Ricky, just lots of wind…looks like a long night."

"OK, keep me advised and we'll get started as soon as they finish their drinks. We won't start making up the berths till later."

Alex asked, "The captain still asleep back there?"

"I suppose so…haven't seen him since level off."

Ricky Parraga continued towards the galley. The two male passengers only nodded in their acknowledgement of his presence and continued their conversation. As he passed by towards the rear of the aircraft the young woman said, "Say Captain, How's things going up there…you birds got this ship on the beam?"

Again, as at the terminal, recognition flickered through Alex's memory as the woman looked up still thumbing through the magazine in her lap. As she spoke, she let the magazine fall back onto the table and began to smooth hair that didn't need smoothing. Alex paused to acknowledge her comment.

He said, "Yes Ma'am…things are going fine. I'm not the captain, though. My name is Alex. I'm the navigation officer."

"Well Captain, you couldn't have proven it by me. When we left Frisco, I thought we were in a submarine instead of an airplane," said the woman.

"Yes ma'am…the wind was really kicking up the waves back there."

"You don't recognize me, do ya Captain," asked the woman?

"You do look familiar ma'am, but I just can't quite place your face."

"Well, waddaya know...that's a change...most guys know who I am. Name's Bonny Belinda...I've done a couple of movies and I'm giving myself a vacation to Hong Kong."

Bonny Belinda went on to explaining, more than necessary Alex thought, what movies she had been in, how a producer was chasing her and how she was taking this trip to "get him out of her hair." The unmistakable message of "I'm available" was coming across loud and clear. This was not the first time he had received such messages. This time, though, it made him uncomfortable. It wasn't Bonnie Belinda; she would make a delightful distraction on the many *layovers* they would have between here and Hong Kong. Although strictly against company policy of fraternization with passengers, it would have given him something to think about other than coping with Brewster until he changed crews at Manila's Cavite base. It's just that now he felt somehow committed to a Russian girl he hardly knew—he had to make sure this woman got the message that he wasn't in play.

"Well, I hope you enjoy your vacation, Ms. Belinda. Please let Mr. Montagna or Mr. Parraga know if there is anything at all you need to make your trip more comfortable."

As he was about to continue his walk through the cabin, Bonnie Belinda said, "Say, Captain: whaddaya think about all that fuss in the papers about the Japanese...is there anything to what they say?"

"I really am no expert, Ms. Belinda...I know everyone is keeping a close eye on what's going on...I'm sure it won't affect your vacation."

The smile left Bonnie Belinda's face as Alex turned and continued through the cabin. The two gentlemen were still in conversation and Alex only nodded acknowledgement as he returned to the flight deck.

Just before sunset, Alex again took the octant to the cockpit and asked the pilots to shoot the sun so he could check his last ground speed calculation. Roger's seat was in the best position so he took the shot and handed the octant back to Alex being careful not to move the vernier on the delicate instrument. Before he left, Alex asked them to note the exact time the lower limb of the sun touched the horizon, just before sun down.

In a short time, Roger called and Alex "hacked," or noted the exact time. Correcting the pilot's sighting of sun down for the Clipper's altitude, he verified the last octant shots he had just taken. He read the altitude from the vernier scale, calculated the intercept and plotted the line of position on his chart. He cross-checked that plot with the sun down fix, and they both agreed. With the last sun shot he was also able to cross check the accuracy of the ships compasses. The second sun shot confirmed the bad news of the first. He looked at the plot and again tapped his pencil on the table. He was confident of his calculations, and it didn't look good.

John called down his fuel remaining figures to Alex and said, "Let me know the damage when you finish the numbers Alex."

The howgozit was nothing more than a graphical illustration of estimated, versus actual, fuel burned at a given position. Alex stepped away from his navigation table and handed the howgozit and the flight plan to Joe Mellon and Roger Kent. "Read and weep guys! Tell John when you get a chance."

Joe turned around in his seat, looked at Alex and said, "You sure of your shots Alex?"

"Yeah, Joe…they came out the same as Roger's shot and the sun set fix. I saw how far the sun's speed line put us behind flight plan and checked to see if I had screwed up. The second one gave us the same dope as the first, so then I checked the sights and my chronometers. Both checked with sunset—both are right on! With the heading you have been flying to stay on the beam, I calculated the wind to be 260 degrees at 65 knots rather than what the flight plan said."

"O.K. Alex…have you told Brewster yet?"

Alex said, "No, he's still asleep…didn't want to wake him. We have several hours to go to the PSR. If the trend continues, we've still got plenty of time to wake him. Maybe the wind will slack off a bit before then. I'll let you know if it changes."

"Yeah, keep us posted Alex! Remember the sprung plate on takeoff. Sure wouldn't want to be making an open sea ocean landing with *Captain Smoothie* at the controls."

In about a half an hour, Alex noticed the first few wisps of clouds going past the window. "Great," he thought, "just great!"

If ocean navigators were unable to see celestial bodies or cross radio bearings to determine their position they were left only with the art of estimating their ground speed and drift by observing the ocean below them. If this was impossible, they were left with only one option and that was to point the airplane toward their destination based on their pre-flight calculations.

It wasn't bumpy yet, but he knew it would affect the steward's job of serving dinner. Worse, he thought, Brewster doesn't know yet. In the next 15 minutes, they were in solid cloud.

Over nine hours had elapsed since takeoff. Brewster had slept almost the entire way. No one wanted to wake him. The Clipper was rapidly approaching the PSR. As usual, they had flown beyond the range of the San Francisco radio beam and wouldn't be picking up the Hawaii beam for some time. They were in solid overcast now and cruising at 8500 feet. There was no more time left—he had to wake Brewster.

He walked again to the rear of the plane. The tables had all been cleared and the galley secured for the night. The Pullman type berths had been made up and all of the passengers had gone to bed.

Alex opened the door to the crew rest compartment and said, "Captain Brewster, Captain Brewster, sir!"

He gently shook Neville Brewster's shoulder until he came awake with a start. "What! What's happening?"

"Captain Brewster, we are coming up on the PSR and I thought I should give you a run down on what's going on."

Brewster said, "Wait a minute…let me go to the head and get a cup of coffee. I'll come topside and you can brief me."

Alex was sitting at the navigation table when Brewster returned to the flight deck. He put one hand on the back of Alex's chair and the other on the table. He leaned over the navigation chart and flight plan and asked, "What's going on, Cannon?"

"Captain, when I got my last fix, we had a big ground speed bust. From the flight plan, we should have been doing 110kts right now. My last fix showed we were only doing 88 knots. Trouble is, that was over two hours ago; we've been in the soup ever since."

"88 knots…you must have screwed up boy! I've been flying out here since '36 and never had winds like that!"

"Well sir, at first I thought so too. I checked and double-checked everything but it came out the same. Joe and Roger shot the sun twice and came up with the same numbers. I have two chronometers and both read the same. I calibrated the octant in Frisco before departure; just to make sure there wasn't a gross instrument error we took a hack on sundown, just as the lower limb touched the horizon. Sundown confirmed the octant shots." Brewster looked at Alex with a blank terrified stare. It was then that Alex knew Neville Brewster had no idea what he was talking about.

"Here's the real dope, Captain: we're coming up on my estimate for the PSR…we're in the soup and don't have any bodies to shoot to get a fix. If we climb, there is no guarantee we will break out on top for celestial and the bets are we would get more headwind. From what we have seen so far there's no way we can rely on the forecast weather. Tom has been sending a CQ for any surface ship in this area to try to get an idea of the cloud height and wind down on the surface, but so far, no luck. Joe thinks that maybe we should start a cruise descent. Nine times out of ten, the wind gets less as we get lower and with a little luck we might break out a couple of thousand above the surface. I might be able to kill the drift and get a ground speed check dropping a flare…your decision Cap!"

"God damned you inexperienced kids!" Alex could feel the spittle on the side of his face and neck. "I leave you alone for a couple of hours sleep and you fuck everything up."

Alex turned to look up at Brewster. He was about to launch into a defense of their action when he noticed a look that could only be described as terror on the Brewster's face. He was alternating between wringing his hands and cracking his knuckles as he began pacing back and forth on the flight deck. On the other side of the Martin, Tom, the radio operator looked on but diplomatically showed no reaction to Brewster's outburst.

"Captain, it's not that bad. We have almost an hour before the ETP and we have some things we can do to try to fix our position before then."

Suddenly, Brewster closed the short distance between them and slammed him on shoulder with the palm of his hand. "Damn you…don't tell me about how bad it is…you don't have to make the decisions around here…I do!"

Alex rose out of his chair, grabbed the larger Brewster by his half-loosened tie and slammed him into the starboard cabin wall. For a second, he remembered all his Navy fitness reports, "Hothead," "Cannot control his temper," he remembered, but right now, they were just words in a report. He said, "You lay a hand on me again skipper and I'm going to deck you. That's not a threat…it's a promise!"

This time, Tom Paine swept his head set off and looked on with genuine alarm.

Alex continued, "I'll help you any way I can but I'm not going to put up with any that kind of crap! Now calm down and listen to me a minute, *Captain*!"

Alex backed away, shoved Brewster gently back and let go of his tie. There was a look of shock on Brewster's face. He turned and looked at the radio operator.

Brewster screeched, "Paine, did you see that! Did you see that?"

The radio operator paused a second for emphasis before speaking and said, "Yeah Skipper, *I saw absolutely everything that happened!*"

From his perch at the flight engineer's station, John Pettit said, "Yeah, skipper *I saw everything too!*"

Alex didn't think Brewster got the drift of Paine's and Pettit's messages. His baser instincts urged him to deck this dinosaur, but he knew that would serve no purpose other than to terminate his career. Already, he thought he had gone too far. One thing was certain...he wasn't going to let this idiot get them killed and he wasn't going to let him bully him again. After this trip, let the chips fall where they may—but no more of this lunacy in the middle of the Pacific Ocean!

"Captain, I gave you two good choices. For my two bits, I would go for the slow descent and I would do it right now, before the PSR, cause after that we can't legally go back. Chances are I can at least get a good ground speed and drift and update my DR. If we get lucky, I might even get a fix. Then, if we are still falling behind by the PSR, we could still safely turn around and head back to Frisco. With all the head wind we've had getting this far, just think how fast we'd go if we turned around and went back to San Fran!"

Brewster looked pathetic. He was cracking his knuckles again and wringing his hands in indecision.

"What's it going to be skipper? We have to do something now or resign ourselves to turning around!"

"OK, dammit! OK! Do something, anything...just get our position!"

Alex noticed Brewster was sweating profusely. He put his headset back on and called Mellon on interphone. "Hey Joe, John, Alex here...the skipper wants us to start a cruise descent. We're gonna try to tuck under the clouds and update our dead reckoning."

The taciturn flight engineer did not reply. Because he had observed everything, he had probably also heard the exchange above the engine noise. Immediately, the constant thrum of the engines changed indicating the laconic engineer had indeed heard. He had already begun reducing the manifold pressure and propeller revolutions for an economical cruise descent.

Alex checked his chronometer and glanced at their altitude. They had 14 minutes to go until the PSR. They were descending through 5200 feet. If they were still bucking the same wind he had calculated before, they would not have sufficient fuel reserves to continue. Alex made a quick calculation. At the new fuel flow, he figured if the head wind component came down below 45 knots and stayed that way, they could continue on to Pearl Harbor with reserves.

Passing through 4000 feet, the *Singapore Clipper* was still in the clouds. Brewster was sitting docilely in the off duty crew seat. They still had 12 minutes to go, but it wouldn't give Alex much time to fix on a wave with a drift flare in time to update their dead reckoning position. If the head winds were as bad as or worse than before, it was entirely possible they were already past the PNR! They needed that information as soon as possible.

At 1200 feet, the navigation light's reflection on the clouds became sporadic. They began to break out of the undercast. Alex couldn't see the water but hoped

to get an idea of the drift after dropping a magnesium parachute flare he had prepared for when they came out of the clouds. The total darkness below turned to
brilliant daylight as the first flare illuminated everything from the magnesium
fireball. Before the flare extinguished itself in the water, he was able to note the
spindrift, the state of the sea and snap two more drift bearings on the waves. He
quickly averaged the three, applied them to the master compass and determined
their drift and track over the ground. Not trusting his memory, Alex quickly
pulled out the ships copy of *Bowditch* and turned to the pictures of the sea corresponding to the nautical Beaufort scale. The waves he saw in the light of the flare
compared with the waves in the pictures suggested a "Force Eight" on the nautical scale or 39 to 46 knots. He split the difference and because of their altitude
rounded the wind velocity to 45 knots for his log. Since his last estimate, the
wind had dropped substantially and agreed with what he plotted.

Alex jotted the information in his navigation log and wished he were on the
last leg to Hong Kong rather than the first. His pragmatic side knew he had only
known Anna since last month, but because she was seldom from his thoughts, it
seemed oh so much longer.

CHAPTER 8

▼

ONE MONTH EARLIER

Pan Am seaplane base, Cavite
24 October, 1941

It was only by chance that Alex Cannon happened to be in Hong Kong the previous month. It started in Cavite, Pan Am's Manila base; it was there that he saw the openings for first officers. As much as he liked navigation, he liked flying the plane better. In Cavite, the captains were junior and of the new breed. He would be free of the "Sky God" captains found at the senior bases. Back then, before he met Anna, he did not apply for the bid because of Tracy. But, that was then.

An infected mosquito caused him to change his mind. Because of Tracy, he had not initially bid. That was the same day when the second officer scheduled for the Cavite, Macau and Hong Kong run came down with a returning bout of malaria. Alex was flying with a check navigator that trip who agreed to work the Manila, Singapore and Manila leg. Alex would make the Hong Kong run and rejoin the return flight back to San Francisco.

The crews called the *Hong Kong Clipper*, *Myrtle*. She was one of Pan Am's venerable Sikorsky S–42's. She was the type that began flying the first survey flights to the Orient in 1935. Now she was used on the last leg from San Francisco—from Cavite to Hong Kong.

That little leg seemed like a shuttle after the weeklong haul from San Francisco. Alex really liked the Martin and the Pacific crossings—long, but a hell of a challenge, he thought, especially when you had a "Sky God" skipper. It took you away from home a lot but it was the most unique commercial flying in the world.

The flight was routine. After splash down on Kowloon Harbor, the Clipper taxied to the Pan American flying boat base at Kai Tak and tied up to the dock. Alex made some last minute log entries and was the last one to leave the flight deck.

An official from Chinese Agriculture was in the cabin busy gassing all would-be illegal immigrant bugs. The two flight stewards were tidying up the galley and cabin. Alex was just about to step through the main cabin door onto the dock when a young woman wearing a Pan Am nametag stepped through the Sikorsky's door.

They both just stood there for a moment looking at one another. On reflection, Alex thought she was blushing, but then she didn't seem to be the kind of woman much given to that sort of thing. He was fastest to recover.

With one hand behind his back and his white uniform hat in the other, he swept the hat low before him in an exaggerated bow and said, "Your royal highness, it is with great pleasure that I have the honor…no the pleasure, to welcome royalty aboard my ship. I had no idea that Pan American Airways hired princesses as passenger service representatives!"

With a half-smile on her face the woman curtsied and said, "Well sir, it distresses me greatly that the company doesn't keep your colleagues better informed, for I really am a princess, and I am so glad that finally, someone in this wretched organization recognizes the fact and greets me appropriately. I would be happy to come aboard your ship!"

With that, she extended her hand in the way of royalty—Arm and hand straight out, with a slight bend at the wrist so supplicants could properly kiss the hand in the appropriate manner, which indeed, Alex did.

"My name is Anna Boreisha, and in real life I really am the Pan American traffic representative in Hong Kong. I came to collect a camera left by one of our passengers, a Mrs. Caitlin. I've really got to hurry…everyone is waiting for me in customs!"

In the order of important things in Alex's life, prolonging the search for Ms. Caitlin's camera suddenly went to the top of the list. Finding it quickly would be disastrous. For a moment, he considered suggesting they look on the flight deck first or maybe inside the wing tunnel. His tired brain came into full focus as he tried not to stare at this intriguing woman. For the first few seconds he didn't do very well on that point.

At first, he could only steal an occasional glance. Then he positioned himself so he could really get a good look at her as she searched under and around the passenger seats.

She wore a white dress with a long sleeved white shirt. White gloves and white shoes completed her uniform. The nametag over her breast pocket said, Anna Boreisha. She was tall—not quite as tall as Alex but close to six feet. She had an athletic figure and carried herself in a self-assured manner not consistent with her blushing during their introductions. Alex thought she was one of those rare women who would become more beautiful with age; she would never go to fat. The name and very slight accent suggested she might be Russian, but her English was so good that he could not be sure. For a moment, he wondered if there really was something to that princess line she just fed him. After resuming her composure, she affected that smile she had when she first came through the plane's door that suggested she had a secret for her amusement only. In time, Alex would think of that smile anytime her image came to mind.

To Alex's dismay, they found Ms. Caitlin's camera all too quickly. In a haze of insect spray, they walked back together through the plush main cabin of the Clipper. Alex walked through the door first and held Anna's hand as she stepped onto the boarding stairs to the main dock.

As he helped her onto the dock, he again took the opportunity to hold her hand. Even though she wore gloves, Alex would always remember the touch as electric. After the step up to the dock she turned and with a radiant smile said formally, "Goodbye Second officer Cannon, I do hope we meet again sometime!"

They did meet again and it changed Alex's life forever.

CHAPTER 9

▼

THE MISSION

Trans Artic Airlines flight 401
November, 1994

Stephen Cannon's 747 had about four hours to go before landing at Hong Kong and the momentous meeting with Charlie Fat's great-uncle that might finally shed light on his mother's disappearance. For the second time he calculated the fuel required on arrival due to the deteriorating weather at Kai Tak airport.

Shigao Matsumoto, Hong Kong
the same date

At the very time Stephen was busy with his computations, Shigao Matsumoto, stared out of his office window at the heavy downpour without realizing that it was raining. Then, as if returning from a daydream, he looked at the fax in his hand. If someone who knew him, a family member or one of his good friends from Kyoto saw him now, they would know that he had that look of tremendous resolve Shigao affected when he set his mind to an important task. He hadn't absorbed the details yet...only that once again, one of *those organizations* would try to sully his country's honor by suggesting his noble ancestors, his father, his uncles, all of his heroes, had been involved in committing war crimes.

This time it was that group in America...they were often worse than the Chinese and the Prisoner of War groups! How could they continue to persist in their lies, he wondered. This time some American was coming to Hong Kong to pick up one of those contrived stories the Chinese had fabricated about what happened in Nanking so many years ago. Some old man, somebody's great grandfather, had brought stories, more lies, from some woman's journals out of the PRC. It was so long ago…if it wasn't that they hated his country how could they care after all of this time? Why was it only organizations such as his that resisted these lies? Why did not all Japanese feel as he? It would be up to his dedicated group of patriots to make sure that everyone eventually would. This time the mission had fallen to him. It was up to him to stop the slander and the lies that brought disrespect on his ancestors. He could not believe that at last he had been chosen for this honorable duty. He would not fail!

Ever since Shigao could remember, he had been inspired by his father's stories of his noble exploits in the war. Shigao almost looked forward to the time that he decided to have his sake at home rather than at the bars. He was assured that when he drank at home, Mitsui Matsumoto and his friends would tell of their heroic exploits in the "Great War"—how they had triumphed over everyone for years, and how if it that wasn't for that accursed American bomb, they would have won eventual victory.

Matsui had been a major in the Japanese army—he had been stationed in Shanghai, just as he, Shigao, was now working in China for a Japanese office equipment company in Hong Kong. When the war was over, the Americans had repatriated his father and thousands of his comrades in arms back to Japan.

During drinking bouts with his fellow patriots, Matsui never failed to speak of Bushido, or the "Way of the Warrior." Shigao learned that everything they did was for the Emperor, and the way they did it was governed by observance of the ancient Bushido Code—the military code of behavior. Matsui taught that in every area of conflict since the Samurai, Japanese military behavior had been governed by this code. Japan's goal, he said, was to free Asia from the oppression of white rule and create an omniscient "Co-Prosperity Sphere" with Japan at its head. It was a glorious calling, and the secret organization he had belonged to since the war would one day once again bring this glory back to Japan.

As a drinking evening progressed, Matsui and his friends could always be counted on to return to the sword: the sword of the Samurai—the one he had used in the war. Many officers had their swords confiscated, usually by some lowly American soldier who no doubt wanted it merely for a souvenir rather than an aegis of honor. They allowed Mitsui to keep his, he said, because a good six inches were broken from the end that Mitsui claimed had been broken in combat.

The sword, they said, was the embodiment of Bushido—an expression of the new Samurai warrior during the war. Shigao was always assured of a demonstration: the various stances, postures, strokes and follow-through maneuvers with the battle-damaged sword. These were always accompanied by a narrative of how, if done properly, one could disarm and decapitate an enemy with one well-practiced maneuver. Shigao had always wondered why his father and his friends seldom demonstrated defensive maneuvers with the sword; nonetheless, Shigao never failed to be impressed by these sessions to the extent, as he grew to manhood, he too was accepted into their secret organization.

The fax had authorized up to twenty thousand U.S. dollars to purchase any information pertaining to Nanking from the American. Also, they were sending one of their professional *facilitators* from Japan to help persuade the American should he be reluctant to sell the information.

CHAPTER 10

▼

THE NAVIGATION NIGHTMARE

Clipper flight 801
20 November, 1941

Brewster leaned over the navigation table and asked, "What's going on?"

"Hang on Captain, let me plot this and see if it jibes with our last DR."

Alex spread his drawing compass to correspond to 45 knots. He put one end on the head of his airspeed and heading vector, swung an arc to cross the track line and noted the new information in his log.

Just as he plotted the new data, Tom Paine called on the interphone and said, "Hey Alex! I just got a ship on short range. He gave us a true wind from the west northwest...says the wind and seas are about "force eight."

Alex replied, "Thanks Tom. Let me finish plotting this and I'll be back with you in a minute."

From the plot, Alex was confident in the wind he had estimated. Everything was beginning to jibe! He looked at the wind at his last known position and the wind information he had just plotted. Then, he made his best guess at an average between the two, plotted that on his chart and came up with a new estimated position.

"Captain Brewster, here's my new dead reckoning position based on the estimated wind we just got from a nearby ship and what I just estimated from a single drift on the ocean. It's not a fix, but it's the best I've got for now. Based on this, the wind has diminished a lot. We only have a headwind component now of about 35 knots. That makes the new estimate for the PNR about five minutes from now.

The radio operator took his head set off and said, "Captain Brewster...you got a minute?"

Brewster responded, "Now what?"

"I just got a message from Pearl on long range. They say the Pearl long range DF just went down. They don't have an estimate yet on how long it will take to get it back in operation."

Alex thought, "Why me Lord, and why with Brewster?"

Brewster didn't respond but instead started wringing his hands and trying to crack knuckles that wouldn't crack anymore. He began pacing the back and forth in the confines of the small flight deck.

Alex asked, "What do you want to do, Skipper?"

Brewster continued to pace.

"Do you have a message for them Skipper," Tom asked?

The captain said, "No long range direction finder at Pearl?"

"That's what the message said, Captain."

"Damned, I already turned around last month because it was close at the PNR...what are they going to think if I do it again? What would you do?"

"You want my opinion," asked Alex?

"Yes!"

"OK, skipper, I'd go on. I'm basing that on three things: One: regardless of the time of the year, I've never seen it overcast all the way to Pearl; we're bound to get some stars somewhere down the road. Two: I have never seen the wind stay at gale force at this altitude for longer than a couple of hours at most. We're just at our minimum fuel now, with reserves. If we make flight plan ground speed or better for the rest of the way, we'll be fine. Three: those guys at Pearl are damned good. If it's a vacuum tube that burned out, they will have it back on line in no time. With the whole U.S. Navy next door, they shouldn't have any problem finding any other part they need even if the whole damned transmitter went on the fritz."

"Hey Alex...Mellon here. We're just a couple of minutes from PSR, has the skipper made a decision yet?"

"Hold on just a second, Joe...he's coming forward!"

"Captain...John just gave me the fuel figures. Based on my DR fix, we are right at minimum plus reserves to go on."

Neville Brewster finally spoke. "How about navigation without celestial and without Pearl's long range DF for a course line...can you handle it?"

Alex was silent for a moment. "Captain...without the DF or celestial, I'm stuck with night flares for drift and DR. We have five left. Unless Pearl's DF comes back on, or the clouds clear, we are stuck with dead reckoning until we get in range of some of the commercial broadcast stations transmitting from Hawaii."

For a moment, Brewster stared through the rain-spattered window into the blackness of the night sky. After a moment, he sighed and tried cracking his knuckles one more time and said, "OK...all right! We'll go on...I just hope you are right!"

Alex, said, "Captain Brewster...that's what they pay us the big bucks for!" Neville Brewster's ashen face stared stupidly at Alex. Without saying anything, he started forward. He didn't smile.

A few minutes after Brewster returned to cockpit, Joe Mellon came back for his break and paused at Alex's navigation station.

"Brewster been keeping you behind the eight ball back here, Alex?"

Before he could answer, the Martin began to be tossed about again as the gale force winds buffeted the airplane. His dividers and pencils began to bounce around on his table. Alex looked forward and saw nothing but heavy rain on the windshield. They were back in the clouds.

"I've had better crossings, Joe."

Joe Mellon shook his head and climbed down the flight deck ladder. He said, "See you later...I'm gonna catch some shuteye."

Just as Joe Mellon left the flight deck, Brewster called from the cockpit and asked, "What do you think we should do, stay here at 1200 feet, or climb back up?"

Alex said, "Skipper, I'm afraid if we climb, we might be climbing back into those hellacious head winds again. I think we should stay right here for another hour or so and give the weather a chance to break.

He turned to the radio operator and said, "Hey Tom, any thing more from Pearl?"

"No luck...even if they were calling, I don't think I could copy them with all of the precipitation static from this storm. Anyhow, they said they would give me an update on the estimated time the DF will come back on the air. Their next check in will be in about thirty minutes."

With no prompting John, the usually taciturn flight engineer said to no one in particular, "At least this rain storm will wash all the salt water off my airframe and engines!"

Two more hours went by before the rain let up enough to try another drift flare. The first flare was a dud and went out shortly after it was released. Alex was able to follow the second for about 10 seconds before it extinguished—just enough time to get a drift and a ground speed completely different from what he got at the PSR. In that he didn't have any idea just when the wind had shifted, he split the difference and updated his dead reckoning.

The new DR put the Clipper about 60 miles north of the great circle from San Francisco to Honolulu. It could be worse, Alex thought to himself.

He had no sooner plotted the new dead reckoning position than Tom called and said, "The DF is back on the line!" He turned the loop, got a null, and called off the relative bearing to Alex. He plotted the bearing and determined they were close to his DR position.

As if on cue, the Clipper broke out into the clear. It was a crystal clear night of the type that occurs after a strong frontal passage. There were stars everywhere!

Alex had already determined which stars would be visible and had selected the best choices for a three star fix. He yelled to the pilots to hold the airplane steady and climbed into position to shoot. Alex propped himself to see out of the Martin's viewing ports and methodically determined the altitude and the azimuth of all three stars he had pre-computed. He then took the readings and entered them on his work form and worked up three lines of position, or LOPs. With no wasted time, he took his dividers and plotter and drew the three LOPs on the chart. They formed a neat "cocked hat" on work form. The tightness of the small triangle gave him confidence in his work and he plotted it on the chart. The position fell about 30 miles ahead of their DR position confirming the wind had dropped off as he predicted. They were indeed north of track, but not so far as the DR had been. Alex let out a sigh of relief. Considering that it had been almost six hours since the last time he had been able to get a fix Alex felt very good about the navigation.

CHAPTER 11

▼

THE MARINES

Wake Island
26 November, 1941

Logbook entry: Flight 801
Slipped mooring at 17:30 GMT 06:30 LCL
Depart: Midway Island 17:40 GMT 06:40 LCL
Arrive: Wake Island 02:25 GMT 14:25 LCL
Enroute: 8:45
As Navigation Officer 8:45
Weather: 15 minutes
Radio Direction Finder Approach
Rain squalls—Circled 15 minutes waiting for it to clear
Number 3 engine began running rough at 01:15GMT. Ran Rough until splash down.

Just got into my room. Want to jot down these notes before I go back down to the float to give Pettit a hand with number three.

No time to write in the log at Honolulu. Too busy catching up on my sleep and sending a letter to Mom and Dad about Tracy and the move to Cavite. Probably get disowned after they read it. San Fran to Pearl dispelled any lingering doubts that my decision to transfer to the Cavite base was *right. Japanese shenanigans be damned! Not only will I be closer to Anna and have a shot at Captain in a year but also the chances of flying with an eight ball like Neville Brewster will be slim to none. Three more legs and with a little luck, I'll never see that sap again!*

Crossing the pond with Captain "Son of a Bitch" comes as close to hell on earth as I ever want to be! Normally, the only thing we have to contend with is simply one of the longest over water legs in the system and just barely enough fuel reserves carrying little more than the mail and a few passengers. Add to that a busted flight plan, lousy weather, no position for over six hours and the Pearl long range DF down, and then stir in 22 hours of Captain Neville S. Brewster in command and you know somewhere in your errant life you have invoked God's wrath. At least now, I know what Brewster's middle initial stands for. It gives credence to the cry of all us captains in waiting—"I would rather be an S.O.B. than fly with one!"

This hotel is more or less finished as it will ever be. It is island efficient and a carbon copy of the one on Midway—comfortable for overnight stops, good food, but certainly not luxurious. Probably a bit Spartan for the likes of Ms. Belinda, but at least it's as good as the one on Midway Island and it sure beats the competition out here. Pan Am's supply ships have brought in everything, as there is nothing on Wake except sand. Maybe they should import some of Midway's Gooney Birds; then, the islands would be identical! When you consider that the flight time is less than a week from San Francisco to Hong Kong, you really can't complain a lot.

On our way to the hotel from the dock, that Bonnie Belinda dame asked if I would be interested in going to the beach with her. I told her I had to help with some engine maintenance and got off the hook. She has been with us since San Francisco and is on her way to Hong Kong to "shake some guy out of her hair," so she says. She's supposed to be in the movie business in the U.S., but can't rightly say I remember her. I'll have to ask Anna—she's a movie buff. She gives off a strong signal of wanting to kick up her heels, but not for me—since Anna, I'm on the wagon.

There's is a small contingent of marines on the other side of the atoll. They are supposedly here to defend the island from Japanese attack. The last time through, they said they were expecting an air contingent of about a dozen Wildcat fighters. If we finish with the engine, I'm going to hitch a ride to the other side, and see what's going on.

After a quick shower, Alex changed into a Tee Shirt, shorts and sneakers. He journaled his thoughts and started for the dock. Just ahead of him, headed for the beach in swimwear, was Miss Belinda and the two new male passengers that had joined them in Honolulu. Alex held back a few minutes to avoid having to make excuses not to join them.

Approaching the Clipper dock, he stopped a few moments and took in the view. The sun was low on the horizon. As usual, there were midlevel, fair weather cumulus clouds over the atoll. With the American Flag in the foreground and the magnificent *Philippine Clipper* floating gracefully on the lagoon, he thought it quite the picture.

Only a few years earlier the takeoff and splash down area could only be navigated by small, shallow draft vessels. Now, Clippers could takeoff and land albeit with little room to spare. The Pan Am engineers had blasted enough coral heads out of the lagoon to make a landing area inside the reef but no more than necessary. After months of toil, they had created yet another stepping stone across the Pacific for the flying boats. Without these bases, transpacific flights would have been impossible. With them, mail and passenger service to the Orient had become a reality. Alex flushed with pride at being a part of this magnificent enterprise.

Pettit already had the jug off the engine and had the replacement cylinder head sitting on the dock. It was draped with a cloth to keep out any blowing sand.

Alex stepped onto the dock and yelled, "Hey Pettit! Need a hand?"

The flight engineer was squatting Indian style on the wing of the *Philippine Clipper*. Next to him was one of the Chamorro mechanics from Guam that Pan Am had hired to help build and run the station. The engine's fold out work platform had been swung into place, and Pettit had improvised a chain hoist that was temporarily bolted to the engine mount. He declared he had plenty of help from the Chamorro mechanics and declined Alex's offer for help with the Twin Wasp engine.

Alex hitched a ride to the marine base with one of the mechanics. He let him out at what was an island version of a guard gate that in reality was nothing more than a shelter half and a marine with a rifle.

Alex explained to the sentry that he was a pilot from the Clipper and just wanted to see what was going on. The marine took him to a tarpaper shack overlooking an improvised runway. He said it was the island's headquarters.

A sunburned corporal ushered Alex into the commanding officer's office. A middle-aged marine crossed the small room to greet him. "Hello, my name is Major James Devereux," he said. "I'm the C.O. in charge of turning this sand dune into a naval base and a Marine Air Station. What can I do for you?"

Alex's first impression of the C.O. was a "by the book," humorless marine. He noted that he did not offer to be called by his first name as most officers did on social introductions.

After introducing himself Alex said, "We just arrived from Midway this afternoon, and everything in the papers back on the mainland and Honolulu suggest the Japs might be up to something real soon like. What do you think?"

"I think the papers are right."

Alex said, "You know, it's strange...I was in Hong Kong just last month. The whole damned island is surrounded by Japs. They seem to have forgotten they have taken over a chunk of territory in China larger than France and they aren't very nice about the way they did it! Life goes on there as if they have forgotten the Japanese occupy most of coastal China and that Hong Kong is the only major strategic port left. They act as if they just go about their business they will be left alone."

"Well, we're taking it serious here...believe me. I think if they do something, they will do it here first. The brass says I've got until next spring to complete the defenses. In my opinion, I don't believe we have that much time. In any event, as of tomorrow, I won't be in charge. A Navy lieutenant commander is shipping in that will be in overall charge of getting the base and the defenses built. He will be taking over that part from me!"

Alex asked, "What do you think is going to happen out here, Major Devereux?"

"To me, it's not a matter of if...just when and where. I'm driving my troops and civilians like it could be at any time. I only arrived early this month and right now, we couldn't defend this sand heap for a week with all the work yet to be done. My marines are working like blazes trying to get some basic defenses in place; that will have to do until the Pan Am civilians the Navy hired can finish the rest of the battlements. Any time now, we are due to get a fighting squadron of marine F4F Wildcats, and right now, we don't even have revetments made for them yet."

Major Devereux showed Alex around the base. His description was accurate. He had about 450 officers and men and about 1200 Pan Am civilian construction workers under contract to the Navy to build the base. The runway was more or less complete, and a few machine gun emplacements were scattered around the strip. The Major was right. The defenses were pathetic. Alex thanked Devereux for the tour and invited him to breakfast at the Pan Am hotel the next day before they departed for Guam.

Alex jogged all the way back to the Pan Am hotel, showered, changed for dinner and went for a walk in the setting sun. He considered all he had seen and heard in the last couple of months and went to bed with a feeling of heavy foreboding.

His last waking thoughts before going to sleep were of Anna. Even though they had just met, he made up his mind to convince her to leave Hong Kong and join him in Manila, where it would be safe.

The next morning Major James Devereux joined him and the rest of the crew for breakfast. Alex introduced the Major to Captain Brewster, who said little and sat by himself. He looked strangely subdued. Alex introduced the Major to the rest of the crew who were as interested in the island's defenses as he.

Major Devereux said, "I don't suppose it hurts to tell you guys...I sure as hell won't be telling you anything that you and the Japs don't already know. This morning, we got a so-called flash message from Honolulu. It is what they called a "Warning of War," for whatever good it does us! I think it's a diplomatic way of saying 'We know these bastards are up to something...but we can't just come out and say it cause it will piss them off, so since we can't say what we know...watch out!"

Alex and the rest of the crew laughed. Brewster heard the remark but continued to stare at his coffee cup. Devereux stood up and said, "Gentlemen, thanks for the breakfast, but now I have to shove off and meet the new Wake Island C.O. He's coming in on the *U.S.S. Wright* today and it will be a full day explaining to him what has to be done and how little time we have to do it."

CHAPTER 12

▼

THE PENINSULA HOTEL

Kowloon
20 November, 1941

Anna's Journal
Home

I went to the Peninsula hotel today to help arrange transportation for two arriving CNAC passengers transiting to the outbound Clipper to San Francisco. As I was passing the barbershop on my way to the office, I saw the man who had visually stripped me on the flight from Chongqing to Hong Kong the other night. He was getting a shave in the hotel barbershop and was the only customer in the shop. His eyes were closed and he did not see me as I walked by. He was in animated conversation with the Japanese barber. DeRuffe was gesticulating with both arms as if trying to make a point; the barber was also speaking, but I couldn't hear the conversation. He just continued stroking lather from his face with a straight razor...I did not think about it much at the time as I had so many other things on my mind. On reflection, though, I think it strange for such interaction between strangers. I wonder what language they spoke?

When I returned to the office, I checked the passenger list and found a Mr. A. DeRuffe listed on the Clipper bound for San Francisco on the 30th. Nothing was noted regarding his return.

I do need to do some shopping. Alex is coming in a few days and I simply must find some eveningwear for the Bomber Ball on the seventh....

Early in the afternoon, Anna found the time to go shopping. She kept telling herself that she had needed a formal gown for a long time. The truth was, she admitted to herself, she wanted to look as good as possible when Alex arrived, and after all, there really was the ball to consider.

She turned the corner and literally bumped into Margaret Allen. Margaret had a garment bag in one hand and a hatbox in the other. After perfunctory greetings, she exclaimed, "Oh Anna, I've been shopping for something gay to wear for the Bomber Ball on the seventh, and I can't find anything that's right. You always look good in anything you wear; how do you do it?"

Before Anna could respond, she continued, "If you aren't in too much of a hurry, would you be a dear, and help me find something right?"

Margaret's husband was an army Major on General Maltby's staff. The general was commander of all forces in Hong Kong and as such was expected to speak at the ball.

Margaret was a twit of sorts, but Anna didn't want to offend her. Reluctantly, she consented to join her, if just for a little while. Margaret knew a place on Connaught Road, so they hailed a rickshaw and were off to Hong Kong's version of Bond Street and shopping.

As they bumped along the cobblestones, Margaret kept up an endless prattle of Hong Kong gossip. Anna only half heard what she said as she reflected a similar preoccupation with the meaningless by Shanghailanders just before the bombings began.

It was surreal! There was no palpable sense of crisis. Hong Kongers were imbued with an ostrich complex, she thought. Instead of sticking their heads in the sand though, they occupied their time with parties, polo and the races to insulate themselves from reality.

Collectively, they acted as if they ignored the events in Europe, Shanghai and Nanking, and if they ignored the fact that they were surrounded by a seasoned Japanese army, the reality of it all would simply go away. If only they could keep occupied with the busy work of the day the barbarians, lurking just beyond the city limits, would somehow not disrupt their lives.

CHAPTER 13

▼

KAI TAK SEAPLANE BASE

Kowloon
1941, 29 November

Anna's Journal
At the Pan Am Kowloon office

> No time for you today dairy! Alex arrives on flight 801 arrives today. It is
> so unlike me to feel this way! I am sure to be disappointed.

The Clipper was only going to be about one hour late which always seemed incredible to Anna considering that it took over a week for the journey from San Francisco.

She could hear the Clipper before she saw it. It was a relatively clear day and Anna held her hands to shield her eyes looking for the plane out over the harbor. Then she saw her. *Myrtle* was flying low paralleling the Victoria shoreline. No doubt, the captain was giving the passengers the grand tour before splash down. The venerable Sikorsky banked, turned gracefully into the wind and landed in a fine spray parallel to the Kai Tak shoreline.

Unmindful of her short hair being whipped by the brisk wind, Anna stood next to the dockmaster and watched him choreograph the Clipper's crosswind approach to the pier. The pilot stopped dead in the water some fifty feet out using differential thrust from his outboard engines to hold the ship's position in the wind. A crewmember in the nose of the ship cast a line to a dockhand who took a half turn on a mooring cleat. The tender then nudged the stern of the flying boat against the wind until she rested against the pier. Dockhands made the flying boat fast with bow, stern and spring lines as the crew cut all engines.

The Steward opened the door and to each passenger Anna said, "Welcome to Hong Kong." When the last stepped out of the aircraft, she followed them to the terminal casting a glance over her shoulder to see if the flight crew had yet begun to disembark.

Anna was still helping the passengers when she recognized Alex looking over the heads of the crew and passengers. When he saw her, his face beamed with delight, but in her official capacity the best she could allow was a big smile and a slight wave of a chest level hand. Alex cupped his hand to his face and mouthed, "I'll see you later at the Pen" across the customs terminal.

Alex checked in at the Peninsula, went to his room, tipped the porter, unpacked and went to the shower to wash off the fatigue and dirt of a long day in the air. Refreshed, he dressed in a white shirt that doubled as a uniform shirt and pulled on tan colored worsted trousers. As much as he hated the idea, the company and decorum of 1941 dictated he wear a coat and tie in a hotel like the Peninsula. In a little while, he knew he would once again meet the fascinating woman who seldom left his thoughts. With just enough time before their appointment, he went to the barbershop to get a haircut.

When he reached the lobby, he bought a newspaper and went to the sitting area to wait for Anna. Everything about "The Pen" suggested a timeless elegance—oriental architecture mixed with the modern. In the background, someone was playing a pleasant melody on the piano that he could not readily identify. Just as he unfolded his newspaper, he saw Bonnie Belinda step off the elevator. She was in conversation with some man and did not see him. To his left was a elderly gentleman in an all white linen suit sitting on one of the overstuffed leather chairs in *his* sitting area. He was looking at his newspaper with an intense concentration, only just glancing at Alex when he sat down. On the couch opposite him were two women sitting on a lobby sofa. They sat, hands in their laps, both trying to speak at once. They appeared in their early sixties, and they were dressed in afternoon attire with small hats and white gloves as if they were going to one of Hong Kong's many social events.

Alex opened his copy of the *South China Morning Post* looking for news of the war. Two articles stood out. Montgomery was counterattacking in North Africa and there were massive Japanese troop and naval movements in Indo China.

Most of the front page, however, was devoted to horseracing: the contenders, the favorites, the previous winners, and of course gossip about luminaries seen at the track. Complete coverage of the racing continued on the sports pages. Other front-page items spoke of the dignitaries expected to attend the British and Bomber Fund ball sponsored by the Chinese Women's Club. Alex noted the event would take place on the evening of December seventh.

Even though everyone knew the Japanese surrounded Hong Kong and the outlying Territories, there was little coverage of the threat on the front page.

As he turned the pages looking for any news on the war front, Anna walked in and filled the lobby with the light of her presence. The gentleman in the white suit who had hardly looked up when Alex sat down folded his paper and perused Anna with more than an appreciative glance.

Alex stood and before he could say anything but "Anna," she grabbed his hands, pulled him close to her and kissed him lightly on both cheeks. "Alex, it is so good to see you again. I received your telegram and have been looking forward to your visit."

Alex said nothing and wrapped his arms around her and said, "It is only a little over a month ago since we first met and it seems so much longer. I have been looking forward to getting back to you ever since I left."

For a moment, they both just stood there looking at one another. The man in the white suit looked over the tops of his glasses, first pursing his lip and then observing the scene with an expression of amusement on his face as if thinking, "I was there once." The two women interrupted their animated conversation and simply watched with the same knowing look of the man in white.

Alex broke the silence. "It's only the twenty-ninth and I don't go back until Monday, December the eighth; if you agree, I want to spend as much time as possible with you before going back to Manila to settle in…how about it? Do you think you could get some time off?"

She took a leather bag off of her shoulder that to Alex resembled a military map case. She withdrew a simple looking cloth bound book that served as her agenda.

"I have several CNAC planes to meet and disembark, but I have some time coming, and think I can coerce a friend of mine to cover for me for the next couple of days. After that, I will have to think of something."

She studied the agenda for a moment and said, "I also have two engagements I can't avoid. Maybe you would care to accompany me."

As she tucked the agenda under one arm Alex held both hands and said, "Darling, excuse me…ah maybe, darling, is too presumptuous."

"No...No Alexander...Alex...not at all. I like the sound of it. If anything, I think, Princess, presumptuous. Please call me darling if you like."

Alex continued, "Well, what I was going to say is...why don't we sit down? We have become a source of interest for that guy in the white suit. It's as if we are here solely for his personal entertainment."

Anna said, "He's not the only one. Look at those ladies just to your left. We seem to be the center of their attention, too. I cannot remember a time I have been in this lobby when those two were not here. They're as much a fixture in the Pen's lobby as the potted plants."

As Alex took Anna's hands in his, he felt the electric atmosphere between them must have permeated the atmosphere of their immediate surroundings.

Anna said, "I think they must think we are lovers!"

Alex looked into the deep pools of her brown eyes and said, "I think they just might be right. Maybe it is just we that haven't yet given it a name."

"Alexander, you are the only man in the world who has ever made me bloosh! You did it the first time I met your Clipper and now you are doing it again."

"Blush, darling...blush!"

"Right! Being embarrassed to the extent one turns red...right! You see...you have me doing it again! I think you are the only man who ever managed that with me." Anna momentarily thought of the first time she had seen Billy at the Far East Cabaret in Shanghai.

After they sat down the man in the white suit returned to his paper, and the two ladies returned to their conversation with occasional glances in their direction.

As they sat Alex said, "Princess...your engagements...you were about to tell me about your engagements with me as your escort."

Anna looked down at her almost forgotten agenda. "Oh yes...there are two. The first is a cocktail party given by my boss, Mr. Langhorne Bond. It takes place tomorrow night, 7 p.m. at his house. The second is Sunday next, December seventh. Both Pan Am and CNAC have contributed to the Chinese Woman's Club fund and I am committed to attending as their representative. The Woman's Club is sponsoring a gala ball to raise money for the British and Chinese Bomber Funds. It's right here at the Pen...at the Rose Room. In any event, if you aren't thoroughly tired of me by then I would like you to also be my escort for that occasion."

Alex agreed and after dinner saw Anna to her apartment. She had an early morning call to see the Eastbound Clipper off at 08:30 a.m. He was exhausted and wanted to sleep as late as the time zone differences would permit.

The next morning Arnaud DeRuffe arrived at the Kai Tak marine terminal with the rest of the passengers departing on the Eastbound Clipper. Anna thought her voyeur must have lost interest in her as this time he did not give her more than a passing glance. What she had no way of knowing was that the Peninsula hotel's barber was actually a Japanese agent and had given the Frenchman all the information he needed before he left for the United States. The barber had explained that not only was she the traffic representative for Pan Am and CNAC in Hong Kong, but that she was also a courier for Marine Colonel James McHugh, the commander of the Chongqing office of the United States Navy Office of Naval Intelligence. Both also knew that she had carried a package of great importance that Japanese Intelligence did not want to reach America. Both also knew that in a very short time she would be a valuable acquisition for the Kempeitai, the much feared Japanese Secret Police. What they didn't know was if she had been able to deliver the package in question to a Mr. William Cameron, the U.S. courier, and the intended recipient. What they had argued about was what they should do about it.

Pan American Second Officer Alex Cannon didn't know where he was. The slowly turning ceiling fan was his first visual cue as he returned to consciousness. It had been one of those very deep sleeps—the kind that imitates the sleep of the dead: no dreams, no nothing—the kind that leaves your body refreshed yelling *thank you*, as it gladly accepts a large deposit after far too many hours on the debit column of the sleep account.

The hypnotically turning fan brought a vignette of the beady eyed, jowly Sydney Greenstreet glowering at him in a sweat stained suit. Greenstreet? Returning to consciousness the image faded as the sticky sheets, oppressive humidity and a strong need to pee pushed the fat man into that shoebox of the mind reserved for almost forgotten dreams. At the same time, unmistakable sounds of China pushed its way in to his consciousness. He lazily rolled his head in the direction of the half-open window. The singsong yammering of too many Chinese, horns, barking dogs, car and truck engines and a steamship's whistle nudged him in to wakefulness. As he rubbed the sleep from his eyes, he was struck by the heavy ornate curtains shrouding the window casement. To the left was a beautiful wooden desk. A tightly woven sisal waste paper can sat by its side along with a brass vessel of some sort on the other—a spittoon? His gaze wandered farther right to beautifully carved dragons forming a border to an intricate ventilation lattice on the half open door of an enormous armoire where he had hung his clothes. Must have taken some underpaid artisan weeks to carve that door, he thought. The top went on the shoebox and the dream was forgotten. God it was hot! Manilla? Hong Kong? Of course, he was in Hong Kong—the Peninsula Hotel, the fat man…Greenstreet…The heavy from the new Bogart movie, *The Maltese Falcon*. He had taken Tracy Summers to see the Sam Spade thriller in San Francisco the night before this trip. It seemed months ago! Then the trip, Brewster, the navigation nightmare, Honolulu, Midway, Wake, the Warning of War, Guam, Manila, Macao and now Hong Kong and Anna. Yes, Anna! He was supposed to spend the day with her and attend a cocktail at her bosses' house this evening!

The couple arrived sociably on time at Langhorne Bond's residence. The host greeted Anna, and she introduced him to Alex. Bond welcomed Alex and explained that he had sent his wife and son to the States. He was sorry that he couldn't meet them, and began to introduce him to those of the station staff he did not already know.

Their host steered the couple to a long table where his houseboy was acting as bartender. Alex ordered a gin and tonic for himself and a lemon squash for Anna. As they waited for their drinks, they looked out over a panoramic view of Victoria Harbor. All looked peaceful and calm as the lanterns and lights of hundreds of sampans, junks and ships reflected off the water in the glittering splendor of a fine December evening. Even from their vantage point high above Hong Kong, there was no evidence of the circle of encroaching Japanese armies.

Their host introduced them to two other couples seated on facing couches overlooking the bay. One of the couples was Chinese: a Mr. and Mrs. Ching. The other was an English couple by the name of Smythe. Bond excused himself to tend to his other guests. As they sat down it was obvious that their interruption came just as the Englishman was trying to make his point regarding Hong Kong's invulnerability. After the introductions, Anna and Alex sat quietly and listened to Mr. Smythe.

"It would be foolhardy for the Japanese to invade Hong Kong," said Smythe. "They know that Britannia has ruled the seas for centuries and continues to do so. Even the slightest feint suggesting encroachment on a Crown Colony would be met with the overwhelming might of the British Fleet."

Anna noticed that Mrs. Smythe was paying no attention to the conversation. Uninterested, she twisted a little handkerchief in her hand and looked around the room as if searching for someone she might know. Anna supposed, like many wives, Mrs. Smythe had suffered her husband's views on the subject more than once and would no doubt focus on the conversation when someone else spoke.

Alex looked at Anna. He felt it would be futile to point out the tremendous commitment already being shouldered by the Royal Navy just trying to keep the

Atlantic sea-lanes open. He inched his hand toward Anna's and held it gently as the conversation continued.

Mr. Ching proffered the hypothesis that since only Hong Kong remained free along the entire coast of China it was just a matter of time until the Japanese could no longer resist cutting off this last port off entry. It would further tighten the stranglehold they already held on the mainland cutting them off from the rest of the world. They explained that with the exception of supplies reaching Western China by way of the Burma Road, and a trickle through Siberia and air from the West, China would be completely isolated.

The conversation turned to the ongoing struggle by Chiang's Kuomintang and the growing strength of the Communists forces. Everyone in the room knew that CNAC was in business only at the pleasure of Chiang's Kuomintang. Any transfer of power to the Communists would insure the ouster of all Western businesses and influence. Even now, they all agreed that the two parties would be at each other's throats if it were not for the greater evil of the Japanese occupation of China and a good part of Southeast Asia.

The conversation began to drift as to why this battle of ideologies had come to pass. The Chinese seemed to have a better grasp of the reasons than did the British couple.

Alex asked the Chings why they thought the Communists forces were gaining popularity among the masses. Mr. Ching stammered. He seemed to be reluctant to give his opinion just as Langhorne Bond rejoined the small group.

Mr. Ching said, "Mr. Bond, you returned just in time to save me. I was just asked by Mr. Cannon about what I thought the reasons were for the gaining popularity of the Communist in China. You are an old China hand…perhaps you would give us a Westerner's perspective. When you are finished, I will offer my own thoughts."

Bond said, "There is no doubt in my mind that the events transpiring in China today have been shaped by three main events. The first two are the Opium Wars that resulted in extraterritorial rights for foreigners and a major loss of sovereignty for the Chinese. I think that those two things were the root cause of the Boxer Rebellion and a further loss of sovereignty. The Japanese invasion of Manchuria was the third event that brings us to where we are today. The loss of sovereignty and exterritorial rights for foreigners has fostered the hatred of almost anything Western by the Communists. That hatred is trumped only by the greater threat and hatred of the Japanese."

Alex said, "I remember very little about the Opium wars, Mr. Bond. What started it all?"

Bond continued, "Correct me if I'm wrong, Mr. Ching. As I remember, it started with the British buying tea, silks, jade and all the good and beautiful things made and grown in China. Problem was, for exchange purposes the British needed a product the Chinese wanted and could afford...something that was profitable, easy to transport...something the Chinese would buy with the funds at their disposal. Until they had such a product, the English had a serious balance of payments problem. Lots of cash going out to buy tea and other things and very little coming back into the English coffers because they simply didn't have a product that was in demand and affordable."

Alex interjected, "That had to have been opium...right Mr. Bond?"

"Indeed, Mr. Cannon. To solve their balance of payments problem the British merchants found the ideal high profit, low cost commodity, and as Alex has properly said, that product was opium. The demand part of the business problem was solved with addiction. Over the years, not to put too fine a point on it, the British *acquired* India, Burma and other opium growing countries. Opium was cheap and required only native labor to grow and harvest the stuff. That cost them almost nothing. In addition, India and Burma were close to the end user...the Chinese. The sale of opium in China surpassed their wildest expectations."

Mr. Ching said, "Mr. Bond is right. The merchants trafficking in the stuff were making millions. That in turn gave the Chinese leadership severe social and economic problems. On the one hand, their citizens were rapidly becoming addicted to the drug; on the other, the Chinese now had their own balance of payments problem in that there was a net outflow of hard currency from the country to buy something they didn't want and couldn't afford. Sorry for the interruption, Mr. Bond, but the enormous profits is indeed the salient point."

Bond continued, "Around the middle of the eighteen hundreds, the Chinese Emperor ordered a crackdown on anyone trading in opium. By now, it wasn't only the Brits profiting from the trade. The Americans, Dutch and others jumped on the bandwagon. They saw the English merchants making enormous profits and they wanted some of the action for themselves. After a while, all of the traders were making a killing, not to mention the Chinese merchants trafficking in the stuff. None of them were about to stop because of some Emperor's decree."

"I can see what's coming," said Alex. "It would come down to who had the largest guns, wouldn't it?"

"Right again," said Bond. "The foreigners had larger and more guns on their trading ships and they didn't hesitate to use them all along the Chinese coast to enforce their interest. Well, it wasn't long until news of the armed intervention reached the Emperor in Peking. He was furious. Officials and many merchants along the coast were summarily executed. For a short time at least, the opium trade stopped."

"Is that what led to the Opium wars?" asked Alex.

"Right again. Back in England, the traders held a lot of weight in Parliament. They used their power to convince the government that it was in England's interest to use British forces and armed intervention in order that the trade might resume. They were successful, and an expeditionary force was sent to re-open trade. The overwhelming power of the British fleet was too much for the Emperor to oppose. The result was the Treaty of Nanking and exterritorial rights for the foreign powers. Added to that humility was the onerous imposition of reparations to be paid over the next forty years amounting to more than was held in the Chinese treasury. It was the same kind of reparations imposed at Versailles that helped give rise to Nazism in Europe, and it is the ignominy of extraterritorial rights and reparations that sowed the seeds of Communism in China."

Bond took a sip of his drink and continued, "Around the turn of the century, that loss of sovereignty gave rise to a semi-religious cult called the Boxers. They were intent on throwing all of the 'foreign devils', as we are called, out of China."

Mrs. Ching covered her mouth and suppressed a smile.

Bond continued, "They enlisted the support of the reigning Empress Dowager and although officially she rejected their cabal, behind the scenes she gave them her support. The Boxers were successful in surrounding the foreign enclaves in Peking until troops were summoned from their respective governments. When they arrived in Peking, they broke the siege; the Boxers were defeated, and guess what…more reparations and more loss of sovereignty for the Chinese.

It was humiliating! In Shanghai, for instance, a White Russian fleeing for his life from the Bolsheviks had a better chance, as bleak as that was, of making a decent living than your average coolie."

Everyone in the small gathering was quiet for a moment as they weighed what he had just said. Then, Bond looked at Anna and said, "Anna, you spent most of your life in Shanghai. You, better than anyone else, know what extraterritorial rights means to foreigners and what it did to Chinese sovereignty."

Anna stirred her squash and looked out of the window on the flickering lights of the harbor. She composed her thoughts before answering. With the exception of Mrs. Smythe, the other guests at the party looked on patiently.

Anna said, "Extraterritoriality is the reason my family, and thousands like us, were able to escape from the Bolsheviks and come to Shanghai with no passport.

We really didn't have the rights of other countries as officially we had no government. We fall under Chinese courts and Chinese law, but nonetheless, we were allowed to come. No other country would take us. It is the same for the Jews escaping from the Nazis. Very few countries will accept them. It is why any foreigner, with or without a passport, can come to any of the treaty ports in China.

Bond interjected, "Anna is right! Trality, as it became to be known, is the salvation for many people who suddenly found themselves without a country. Ah, but for foreigners doing business in China, extraterritoriality is the best of all worlds. It extended rights to them and their businesses unavailable in their own countries. Foreigners have their own courts, own laws, own police and in some cases their own armies. In all but a few cases, foreigners do not even answer to Chinese law."

Anna said, "I am not sure about the other treaty ports, but in Shanghai, only taxpayers can vote. You could be a taxpayer, for instance, by renting an apartment, such as my family did. The notion was, by renting, we indirectly paid taxes. Consequently, almost everyone pays and can vote. Foreigners who did not pay direct or indirect taxes could not vote, as they had no economic stake in what went on. Also, there are no income taxes.

"In my opinion, for the Chinese, extraterritoriality was, and still is, a double-edged sword. On one hand, it brought modernization to China that would have otherwise been a long time in coming. CNAC is a good case in point. Without extraterritoriality CNAC would probably not be here."

Bond said, "Your point is well taken, Ms. Boreisha. After the Boxers, English ministers were installed in Chinese cabinet positions. In most cases, they helped modernize those institutions that previously had been subject to corruption and graft by Chinese government officials. That action alone, however, brought about a tremendous amount of resentment as those positions were previously coveted and held by a governing class of Chinese that had now been disenfranchised.

"In my opinion trality is the deepest source of resentment for most Chinese. Many hate *all foreigners* for that, and they would embrace any *ism* to restore their sovereignty, and if possible, get rid of all of us regardless of any good we might bring the country."

Anna looked at Mr. Ching and said, "You know, since the turn of the century none of this went un-noticed by the intellectuals in China who watched the rise of the masses in Russia. Communism, and the success of the Bolshevik revolution, was not lost on the peasant class yearning for anything better in China. If it wasn't for the Japanese invasion going all the way back to Manchuria in '31, I have no doubt that war would be raging, right now, between the Kuomintang and the Communists."

The Chinese couple nodded in agreement. Mr. Ching said, "I think you both have summed up our feelings precisely. Sun Yat-Sen's vision for a united China will unfortunately not be realized now for a very long time."

Mrs. Smythe's attention was still on the couples dancing and not on the conversation. The rest of the small party was silent, each with their own thoughts. With the exception of the Smythes, each realized that in a very short time events would overtake them that would change China and their lives forever.

Mr. Smythe finally spoke and said, "Mr. Bond, you seem to have a very good grasp on what is going on here in China. If the Japanese ignored the British fleet, and foolishly attacked Hong Kong, how long do you estimate it would take for them to overrun the colony?"

Bond replied, "A few weeks at the most. Probably less than a month."

Smythe became agitated. "Mr. Bond! That just could not be so…we have been assured by Governor Young and General Maltby that Hong Kong could hold out for months. That would give the British Fleet and the Americans more than adequate time to come to Hong Kong's aid and teach those barbarians a lesson!"

"Yes, Mr. Smythe…I've heard that point of view. For various reasons, I simply do not believe they can do it. For one thing, the Japanese are some of the most tenacious warriors in the world. They are battle tested, well equipped and well motivated. In Shanghai and Nanking, Anna and I have seen the ruthlessness and speed with which they prosecute war. I have no doubt they can do the same thing here."

"Yes, yes, I understand Mr. Bond…but as of this date they have yet to come up against British troops and British steel! Wait until they test the professional mettle of the British Army!"

Bond said, "Anna…you have never spoken much about Nanking. Would you like to add something?"

Anna looked shocked as if she were unprepared for the question. "No…really, I don't want to talk about it. Let me just say that I thought it impossible for one group of human beings to be so barbaric…I didn't think it possible before Nanking. No offense, Mr. Smythe, but I hope the British put up a better show in Hong Kong than they did in France."

Smythe looked undeterred and said, "Well, Ms. Boreisha, they were up against the Nazi war machine. Surely the Japanese aren't half as effective as the Germans!"

"Mr. Smythe, I again defer to what has already happened in Shanghai, Nanking, Hankow and Peking. If they attack, we won't have a prayer."

Christmas music had been playing on the Victrola in the background. Someone had just put on Hoagy Carmichael's "Harbor Lights" and two of the couples began to dance. Alex looked at Anna; she assented "yes" with her eyes. "Miss Boreisha, would you give me the pleasure of this dance?"

"Why of course Mr. Cannon...I would be delighted!"

Their small discussion group looked at each other sheepishly as the young couple reminded them that this was, after all, a cocktail party at the beginning of the Christmas season.

Anna fell into Alex's arms as he began to guide her around the small space on the living room floor used for dancing. Alex looked into her dark brown eyes and said, "This is more like it...kind of a depressing conversation about China, huh, Princess!"

"Yes darling but Bond's right again...it's coming...it is only a matter of when...but just for the rest of this evening, let's forget about the Japanese. Starting tomorrow, we'll figure out what we can do about it.

Alex said, "I think it was Hannibal who said, 'We will either find a way, or make one.'"

CHAPTER 14

▼

THE LAST DAY

Hong Kong
7 December 1941

Alex found Anna's apartment again with little difficulty. He was carrying a wardrobe bag with his rented evening clothes.

The last time he was there, he had said good night at the courtyard door and returned to the Peninsula. This time he opened the garden gate and knocked on the ground floor entrance door.

Anna answered the door in a white silk dressing gown and a large towel tied in a turban around her head; she kissed Alex on both cheeks and asked him to come in saying, "Darling, I'm running late. A man came to the office just as I was leaving. He changed travel plans for his family to leave Hong Kong for San Francisco as soon as possible. He will be leaving with you on tomorrow's Clipper."

She motioned to a bar cabinet against the wall. "Please fix yourself a drink. I just need to change, put on my face and fix my hair. I should be ready in just a few minutes."

Anna went to a large wardrobe and held a long black gown clutched by its waist in front of her and said, "I picked this up the day before you came...what do you think?"

"I don't know much about these things, but I'll bet you'll be the belle of the ball."

Anna went behind the screen, placed the gown over the top, and began to dress.

Alex folded the wardrobe bag he was carrying over the back of a chair and looked around the apartment. It was comfortable but just shy of being Spartan. Even though there were only three rooms, it had the luxury of a private bath— rare for Hong Kong, and a separate bedroom. Along one wall was a simple wooden book cabinet. On closer inspection, he saw many were reference books: dictionaries, atlases and concise encyclopedias in several languages. There were several classics and contemporary novels including *Gone with the Wind*; that, he noticed, held a bookmark; all were in English. The only other pieces were the wardrobe, the bar where he was standing and a simple Chinese writing table. On the desk was a very narrow vase filled with flowers of a type Alex could not identify. A door to her bedroom was on the opposite wall. In that there was no separate dressing room, Anna employed a fold out silkscreen decorated in a beautiful Chinese floral motif with birds in the background. Anna had it folded out in front of the bathroom door as a divider and dressing area.

He turned to the bar and picked up a decanter about half filled with what looked like whiskey. He pulled off the stopper, sniffed and poured two fingers of scotch into an ordinary water glass. Nestled behind a bottle of Bombay gin were several bottles of squash. To his surprise, he found ice in a small wooden bucket with a lid. "Anna! could I fix you a squash...and where on earth did you find ice?"

"Oh yes, that would be grand, Alex. I knew you Americans like ice in your drinks, and picked up some just down the street, when I was coming back from work. I know the place; the ice there is pure and won't make you sick like the second officer who replaced you last week."

Anna threw the robe over the screen and said, "You have probably noticed from the papers and the conversations at Mr. Bond's cocktail party that the most important topic in Hong Kong is horse racing and these gala parties for one sort of benefit or the other. People speak of the war around them like it was a spell of bad weather or something."

Alex reflected on what she said, "I wonder if it was the same sort of attitude in Czechoslovakia, Poland and France in the days just before the Germans invaded? Do you think it's just a group defense mechanism to help people avoid having to think about the inevitable?"

He passed the squash and ice over the screen to her and went to the chair in front of the writing desk, turned it around and sat facing Anna's makeshift dressing room.

Anna took a sip of the drink and said, "You know, that probably explains it better than anything else I've have heard. No other explanation is rational. We know what the Japanese did in Shanghai, Nanking and the rest of China. How could any rational person reason they would do any different with Hong Kong? We heard some of those tired out diplomatic excuses at Mr. Bond's party: 'Free the Asiatic from the white man, Far East Co-prosperity nonsense' and so on. If they invaded, none of that would matter. I think it's safe to say that the Japanese know that the taking of Hong Kong would be an act of war. With that in mind, I think any overture they make here would probably be accompanied by a move somewhere else at the same time. They would know it would mean war, so why not take advantage of the surprise, and get as much as you could?"

She took the turban towel off and placed it over the screen, and for a few minutes there was a great rustling of taffeta. Then, over the screen, Alex could see that Anna was looking at a small mirror to one side of the bathroom door.

Alex said, "Darling, it is impossible to refute your logic. Everyone willing to accept the facts said as much at Bonds' place. This whole week, I've listened to the pros and cons. The only conclusion I can draw is it's going to happen as sure as we are speaking about it. The question still remains, will it be sooner or later? You know, with the monsoon about over I would vote for sooner. With less rain, it makes it easier for armies and air forces to maneuver. Anyhow—enough of that! Here I am in a room with a half-naked beautiful woman, separated only by a silk screen, and I'm talking about an invasion? I must be crazy!"

Anna came out from behind the screen, walked over to Alex, turned her back to him, and said, "I'm not half-naked any more darling, but I do need some help."

Alex stood and began to manipulate the tiny hooks into the eyes. When he was finished, she turned, made a mock pirouette and said, "So what do you think of thees poor leetle Rooskie Princess in exile?"

She was stunning. Alex stood up, the engineer in him wondering how those damned strapless things stayed up; he wrapped his arms around her waist, pulled her gently to him and kissed her on both cheeks—then fully on the mouth. He backed away and said, "Anna, you are absolutely spectacular!" Somewhat diffidently, she smiled and said, "I am glad you are pleased."

"Lets get a real cab and go to the Pen or I can't guarantee what will happen in the next five minutes."

"Nor could I darling, nor could I," she said.

Alex helped her with her night wrap and picked up his rented dinner clothes. He opened the door for Anna and they stepped into the street to hail a cab.

Even though unconventional for the times, Anna accompanied Alex to his room while he changed. She knew most of the employees at the Pen as she often met there with passengers to discuss their travel arrangements. In any event, she cared little for what others thought and conducted her life on a basis of doing what she considered right.

Alex would have been perfectly comfortable wearing his navy colored Pan Am uniform. In that there were no stripes or insignia, many times the double-breasted worsted uniforms performed duty where suits were required. Deferring to Anna's wishes, though, he had rented dinner clothes for the evening. The fit was perfect and she declared him handsome and suitable to be her escort.

Just before they left for the Rose room, where the ball was to be held, Alex answered a knock at the door. A shopkeeper's apprentice presented him with a box. Alex tipped the runner, opened the box and presented Anna with a lovely corsage of orchids. Anna beamed with delight as he pinned the small, beautifully crafted arrangement on her gown. She turned to admire the effect in the mirror, turned, put her arms around him and kissed him warmly on the mouth.

On the large double doors leading to the ballroom was a large poster board sign on an easel that read: Fancy Dress Victory Ball. A committee member collected their invitation and they were shown to their place at one of many banquet tables. Hand penned placement cards had been prepared for each guest.

Several waiters were circulating carrying drink trays of punch. Other assorted drinks were available at strategically located bar tables set up in the banquet hall. Alex ordered a squash for Anna and took a tonic for himself. He was flying early the next morning, had to be up at six and wanted to be sharp.

Anna pointed out Sir Mark Young, the governor of Hong Kong; he was surrounded by a group of prominent citizens and businessmen. As they passed by, they could hear that the subject of their discussion was the odds on favorites of the ongoing horse races.

Anna introduced Alex to Major and Margaret Allen, and they in turn introduced the young couple to General C.M. Maltby, commander of the Hong Kong garrison, his aide-de-camp and a young leftenant...Lionel something or rather whose names they both missed. General Maltby had been answering questions regarding the territory's defenses and had assured everyone that Hong Kong and the territories were safe.

Anna touched Alex on the arm and whispered, "This ball is like an extension of our conversations over the last week. With the exception of the General and a few others, it seems like the most important topic of the day was which damned race horse is going to win next week!"

"Alex, I can't help thinking it is Shanghai all over again. 'It just cannot happen here because we have other things to do'"!

"I'm afraid so darling…I'm afraid so. Look, tomorrow, before I leave, I will speak with Bond…we have to see about getting you out of here."

"But darling, my job is here…it is my home, now. I just cannot leave. I owe everything to Mr. Bond and CNAC, not to mention the fact that I am stateless and couldn't leave anyhow!"

The accomplished orchestra finished their intermission and began playing a waltz. Alex said, "Well, as Miss Scarlet said in that book you're reading, 'we'll worry about that tomorrow'…right now, let's dance!" He took her by the hand and led her to the dance floor followed soon by others who preferred dancing to social chitchat.

"You know, it's as if we had been doing this all of our lives," said Anna. "How do you explain it? We aren't even from the same side of the world."

"I think I'll just enjoy it and not question it. Have you ever had formal training?"

"You will probably laugh! The only formal training I've have ever had is from my father. Papa insisted learning a proper waltz was as important in a girl's training as anything. He probably forgot we wouldn't be waltzing in the court of the Tsar anytime soon."

"Did he teach you that swing we were dancing to the other night?"

"No: I learned that with friends in the Shanghai clubs."

"That should be a story worth hearing."

"Not really. It was just a phase. There are really more interesting things in my life now." Anna pulled him a little closer.

The music stopped and the players turned their sheet music in preparation for the next dance. Anna unconsciously reached for Alex's hand as she led him to their place at the table. They sat, saying nothing for the moment, savoring each other's company and watching others dance.

"You know Anna…in a short time I think we will be looking back on now as 'The good old days'."

He turned from the other dancers and said, "The only thing I know for sure is that I want my future to include you in it."

Still holding his hand, Anna turned her head and looked at him with an expression of relaxed contentment. "You know, we have only known each other for such a short time, but there is almost nothing you could have said that could have given me more joy."

The orchestra stopped, and the young couple picked at the banquet fare with little enthusiasm. As soon as obligatory attention was paid to speeches given by the Governor and the head of the Chinese Women's Club, they made their way to the roof to get some air and wait for the orchestra to resume playing after dinner.

They looked out over Hong Kong and heard the sound of an airplane on its approach to Kai Tak. Anna said, "That must be the last flight in from Indochina." They looked up and could not see anything because of the clouds.

Soon the orchestra began again. Perhaps in memory of what the ball was for, they played the melancholy English tune "A Nightingale Sang in Berkeley Square." The two held each other tightly, dancing to the music, both were lost in their own thoughts knowing that tomorrow they would part. Anna had her head on Alex's shoulder. "Oh Alex, I worry about my parents so much. They are trapped in Shanghai and there seems to be nothing I can do to help them. They are Russian, and as Russians they will be the last considered in any repatriation scheme."

As they continued dancing, he held her at arms length. He could see the distress in her face and said, "Darling, I know so little about the situation, I don't know what to say, but I promise you this…when I get back to Manila, I'll go to the American Embassy right away and see if there is anything that can be done. If there is, we will do it!"

Anna looked on the verge of tears. "I know there is not much that can be done darling, but it doesn't keep me from worrying about them."

They finished the dance and Alex suggested, "Come on Anna…let's get your wrap. I'll take you home. We both have to be up very early tomorrow to get the Clipper off to Manila. In the morning, we'll speak with Bond."

Anna glanced at her watch "Oh…yes, it's already eleven o'clock! I had lost track of the time. Just one more dance, Alex. I know it will only be a week until you are back, but I want one more dance to remember this wonderful week we have had together."

The two went to the coat checkroom, got Anna's wrap and took the elevator to the lobby. They walked to the Star Ferry and caught a covered rickshaw on the far side. Soon they were in front of Anna's apartment. Alex asked the rickshaw man to wait and walked her to the door. "I won't come in darling…not this time." Anna looked at him and said nothing. She put one arm over his shoulder and the other around his back and met his mouth with a prolonged kiss. As their mouths parted he said, "I've got to go before I can't!" Anna nodded, turned, unlocked her door and stepped inside.

Chapter 15

▼

The Longest Day

Hong Kong
8 December, 1941

Anna's journal
1941, 10 December; written in Chongqing China

Only the vestiges of night remained when the dawn of December 8 changed everyone's lives and mine forever. I had risen early to go to the seaplane base at Kai Tak and see Alex and the Clipper off. I was just about to begin writing in my diary when I heard the first explosions. This is the first chance I have had an opportunity to journal these thoughts since it all began.

I remember my first thought was it must have been another military drill out in the territories, and that they must be crazy to conduct exercises this early in the morning. After a late evening at the Peninsula, the outcry from the Taipans of the city would be louder than the shell bursts from the territories.

I set my pen down and went to the top of the building to see if I could see where the explosions were coming from. Dawn was only just beginning to break, and I still couldn't see the horizon from the top of my apartment building. I stood looking for a few more minutes when I saw orange blooms on the horizon. It must be starting, I thought! I wondered what Alex was thinking....

Anna knew Alex must be awake by now, busying himself with leaving the hotel for the 08:30 Clipper departure. On impulse, she dialed the Peninsula and anxiously held the telephone to her ear hoping to catch Alex before the crew departed for the Kai Tak. The instrument rang incessantly with no answer. Anna tried the operator. That too was unsuccessful.

It was still early, but she dressed quickly having made the decision to depart for the Clipper seaplane base when there was a knock at the front door. She opened the door on the chain and saw a rickshaw coolie standing in the vestibule with a note in his hand. He said "Masta give two melican dolla. He say give note missy here now. He say bring missy ferry chop chop and you sure thing gimmi two melican dolla more."

Anna took the note and read Alex's note.

> *Anna darling: it's beginning. Pack a bag with just essentials. Fred Ralph is taking the Clipper out of here no matter what! Take this rickshaw to the ferry and get yourself to Kai Tak ASAP. If it's a false alarm, you will only be a little early for work. See you soon! Hurry! I love you—Alex.*

Anna flushed on seeing the first written declaration of his love for her. She opened the door again, and in dialect asked the coolie to wait; she would be ready to go in about ten minutes.

Anna began to think methodically. She pulled a chair over to the armoire, stood on it, and took down her leather Gladstone valise from the top.

If it did turn out to be the real thing, she considered her options. She knew the Clipper would depart as soon as possible. She knew that Bond would try to save as many CNAC and Pan Am personnel as possible—just as he had done in Shanghai and Nanking. He would probably take them to Chongqing or interior China—for a seaplane, though, she could only guess where it would go—probably directly to Manila, where it was safe.

Anna opened the armoire, picked a pair of slip-on boots, gabardine slacks and a long-sleeved white uniform shirt with her nametag still attached. She began to dress. She had learned from Nanking that any mark of officialdom could be useful in the chaos that was sure to follow. She packed only sensible clothing: gabardine Jodhpurs, another silk long sleeved shirt, a light sweater and three changes of short stockings and underwear. On second thought, she packed her favorite silk dress with flowered prints and her comfortable dress shoes. It took almost no room in the Gladstone, she thought. She walked to the bathroom and packed only her essential toilet articles.

As a Russian, she had no valid passport. Assuming they made it out at all, she worried about what would happen should their destination be outside of China. Like Alex's mimic of Scarlet O'Hara last night, she continued packing and thought, "I'll just have to think about that tomorrow!"

She dropped all her journals into the Gladstone. She put the current journal into her map case. Then she crossed to the far side of the room and knelt down. From under a loose floorboard, she took out all of her cash and the sealed package given to her by Colonel McHugh. She had been unable to contact William Cameron, the American courier. The American Embassy said that he would be the next courier out on the Eastbound Clipper but so far, he had failed to show up. She only hoped he would be at Kai Tak or she would be stuck with the package.

Anna took one last look around the place that had become her first home of more than a couple of weeks since Shanghai. For a moment, she thought of her parents, Saul and her other friends trapped in China. Then, she slung her Leica over her shoulder with the map case, picked up the Gladstone, and left.

When Anna had gone to the roof and seen the explosions far out in the territories, the city seemed quiet. That had been only about thirty minutes ago. Now, as she stepped onto the street, there was the beginning of panic in the air. People were looking toward the North and the rumblings in the distance. There was a palpable sense of fear that this was something more than a drill by the British. Bicycles, carts, coolies with carry poles over their shoulders, individuals and whole families were beginning to move without direction. Some were going up the mountain as if height could somehow give them refuge from an invading army. Some were beginning to move down toward the harbor. From previous experience she knew, that in a short time, "The swarm" would take on a life all its own and start moving in one direction. *It always did!*

The rickshaw coolie was still waiting. He relaxed in an Asian squat, arms around his knees, a cigarette dangling from his mouth. Anna tossed the Gladstone up onto the rickshaw bench as he lifted the towing arms. She made no attempt to look feminine and jumped up on the bench in one flowing movement. The vignette of Nanking and the dress she had worn on that horrible day flashed through her mind; the slacks had been the right choice.

As they started down the hill toward the Star Ferry, the sounds of gunfire from the North became louder. She thought she heard the drone of aircraft overhead in the gathering light, but she couldn't be sure. More people were now in the streets, but the swarm still hadn't formed; no one seemed to have a plan or direction in mind. "*When in danger or in doubt*" flitted through her memory. She was sure it was the first time that many of these people had given thought to the problem of escape when in reality they should have been thinking about it for months. People ran in every direction at once. It was as if the very act of flight would somehow give them safety from the imminent invasion. "*When in danger or in doubt, run in circles, scream and shout.*" She thought of that horrible incident at the Cathay Hotel so many years ago in Shanghai.

With almost no effort the rickshaw coolie maneuvered in and out of the gathering crowds. Most of the short journey had been down hill. From her elevated perch on the rickshaw, Anna could see only a few civilians in the ferry queue for Kowloon. Most were soldiers. The coolie stopped and looked at her. She jumped down on the cobblestones and gave the man the two dollars promised by Alex and another of her own. Anna said in Mandarin, "You have done a good job. I wish the best of luck for you and your family."

He bowed and said, "Me no worry missy…Japanese soldier need rickshaw just same!"

Hardship had, and would be a part of his life for whatever remained of it, she thought. It seemed incomprehensible to him that anyone would even care to see him again much less how he or his family fared at the hands of the Japanese. The rickshaw man handed her the Gladstone and started looking for another fare. It was obvious that an imminent invasion would in no way stand in the way of his eking out an existence.

Anna pushed her way to the ferry kiosk and asked for a round trip ticket. The man in the cubby said, "Soldiers say no one go Kowloon side except with soldier pass."

Anna looked around for anyone in uniform and recognized a young leftenant who had been with General Maltby's aide at last night's Bomber Ball. He had given her an admiring glance and recognized her as she waved to him.

Anna went up to him and said, "Hello again Leftenant. Who would have thought last night that we would have met again like this in just a couple of hours?"

The leftenant smiled and said, "Yes…quite! Leftenant Lionel Adams at your service miss."

"My name is Anna Boreisha. I'm the Pan Am traffic representative at Kai Tak and I'm trying to get across to help with the Clipper's departure. What's the situation Leftenant Adams?"

"Please Miss Boreisha, call me Lionel. It seems that the Nips are attacking along our entire front in the territories. I'm trying to get to my unit. It is supposed to be forming up in Kowloon. All of these soldiers are doing the same."

Anna asked, "Would you be so kind as to be my escort to the other side, Lionel? The ticket people said that only those with a military pass could proceed."

"Why of course Ms. Boreisha. Just display such Pan Am Identification as you might have…I'll vouch for you, and I am sure we shan't have any problem at all."

By this time, other soldiers were lining up to board the ferry. She noticed that many were medium and high ranking officers whom she knew preferred living on the more socially active Hong Kong side. She was surprised that there were still so many trying to join up with their units in the territories.

Soon the ferry departed. The sun was up now. When they were about half way across the first bombs began to fall. Anna looked up and tried to locate the bombers. She couldn't see them, nor could she tell where they were falling. It looked like it might be in the direction of the Kai Tak airport. That made sense to her, but it was impossible to say for sure. She said a silent prayer for Alex and the other people at the field and the adjacent seaplane base.

The ferry dock was yet un-harmed when the second wave of highflying bombers released their deadly cargo. This time they were falling in Kowloon and she was able to hear the whoosh that always announced them just before they hit. The noise had become all too familiar to her in Shanghai, Nanking and Chongqing. The thought crossed her mind that it wasn't right to be so familiar with such a sound.

As soon as the soldiers disembarked from the Star ferry, they began looking for their units. All over the landing docks, the Army had cleared the area of civilians for unit formation. In ones and twos, the soldiers spotted a familiar face or their regimental colors and walked off to form up and depart for their designated forward areas.

Lionel Adams saw one of his colleagues and stopped to get the latest news and the disposition of his unit. In a minute, he returned to Anna and said, "General Maltby has ordered the bridges blown up at 8 a.m. It appears my unit is forming up just a block from here, just in front of our friends from Canada, there. I'll help you get a rickshaw and then I really have to get on."

A dollar bill held high helped find a free rickshaw. Anna said, "God speed and good luck Lionel. I hope to see you soon under better circumstances."

"God bless you miss! I hope to see you again soon too!"

Anna jumped to the rickshaw perch, Gladstone in hand, again thankful that she had worn pants rather than a dress. In moments, they were padding off to Kai Tak at a quick pace. Anna looked back over her shoulder and saw Leftenant Adams saluting another officer as he hurried off to join his unit. She wondered if she would ever see him again.

She shielded her eyes and looked skyward trying to see the Japanese bombers as the coolie jogged his way toward the seaplane base. At first, she couldn't hear them from the clack of the rickshaw's wheels on the cobblestones. There were high clouds, but then she could just make out the distinctive Vee formation she had come to know in Shanghai and Nanking. The formation seemed directly over the land airport when they released their bombs. It must have been their second raid. The bombs showed distinctly against the silvery morning clouds as the sunlight highlighted their path to the ground. They were exploding midfield as Anna's rickshaw approached the airport. The coolie slowed and then stopped as he saw the devastation ahead. Anna jumped down, grabbed the man's arm, and crouched behind a stone wall in case the bombs came their way. The Chinaman looked at Anna wondering why a white woman would care what happened to him.

In time, the attack passed and the two of them again padded off toward the marine terminal. As they approached, Anna could see *Myrtle* still floating unharmed at her mooring, away from the dock, where she stayed during overnight stays in port. Anna jumped down from the rickshaw, thanked the coolie for his help and tipped him double the normal amount. She grabbed her Gladstone and jogged toward the terminal building that so far appeared untouched by any of the attacks.

She ran through the small terminal building and out onto the dock looking for the crew. Almost at once, she saw Alex and the other Clipper crew looking out to where *Myrtle* was moored. She hurried out and yelled, "Alex…Alex, thank God you are still here. I didn't think I would be here in time."

The rest of the crew looked on as the two embraced, glad to have a pleasant distraction from their developing predicament.

Alex said, "You got my message? Did the rickshaw man wait for you? Did you have any trouble getting here?"

In her excitement at seeing Alex, explanations all ran together.

That nice Lieutenant Adams we met last night at the Pen escorted me to Kowloon, and I caught a rickshaw here."

Alex said, "Here's the situation darling. Captain Ralph first got word from Manila to stay put in Hong Kong. They were under attack. They thought they were the only ones. Then the bombing started here. Ralph called Bond and asked for his advice. He said we are sitting ducks and would surely lose the Clipper if we didn't get the hell out of here right away. He sent us a CNAC pilot who is going to guide us to a lake in the interior, not far from Kunming."

"Is he here yet?"

"Yes, he's just arrived. We're leaving just as soon as the launch can get everybody out to the mooring. No docking—we will leave from the mooring to save time. There are only a couple of passengers here now and Ralph says 'take everybody who wants to go.'"

Anna looked toward the terminal to see if William Cameron, the American courier, was in the group. He was nowhere in the small cluster of passengers.

Alex said, "Captain Ralph said we're going to save the Clipper and leave with whomever is here right now…no waiting or we'll lose her for sure. Anna, I want you to come with us!"

At that moment, they turned to the sound of the launch's engine.

Alex said, "I cleared your coming with us with the Skipper. He said, 'why not? You certainly are not going to be of any use to passenger service here anymore."

"Maybe not with the Clipper passengers, but there's still CNAC. If we have any planes left when this is over, I'm sure Bond will make an effort to evacuate CNAC to the interior. He will surely need me at least for the immediate future."

Everyone on the dock turned in unison to the crescendo of aircraft engines going into high pitch. The noise came from the east, directly in the glare of the rising sun. Alex was first to spot the fighters as they peeled off for their attack. The first was a flight of two in echelon formation. It wasn't apparent to everyone on the dock what the intended target was, but Alex didn't wait to find out. He grabbed Anna's hand and ran back with her to the insignificant cover of the terminal building. They crouched behind one of the counters just as they saw a stitch of bullets describing a staccato line directly toward the moored Clipper and beyond: straight towards the terminal building. Fred Ralph and several others dove into the water and took what little cover there was behind the dock's pilings. Alex threw himself over Anna trying to shield her body from the mayhem. All around them, pieces of roof fell, holes exploded in the walls and windows shattered as a fusillade of bullets struck the Clipper terminal. They huddled under the counter until they heard the fighters pass over and repair to the north.

The Japanese fighters turned back to the east repositioning themselves in the sun as two more fighters made another pass at the Clipper. From their vantage point, they could see *Myrtle* taking numerous hits, but she was still floating at her mooring. After several more attacks, the fuel-laden Clipper caught fire. Soon, the conflagration spread, and in a short time, the flying boat was engulfed in flames. Satisfied with their handiwork, the Japanese fighters turned to the North and disappeared over the hills.

The two came out from behind the counter and looked out at the Clipper. Alex let out a muted "damn" as surveyed the burning S-42.

"Princess…you can forget my invitation to go with us on a romantic flight to the West. Clipper service to inland China, Kunming and points beyond is cancelled indefinitely."

"Oh Alex, it makes you think about one of those Viking funeral, doesn't it?"

Fred Ralph and several other crewmembers and passengers climbed back on the dock, dripping wet from their plunge into the harbor. Everyone looked towards Myrtle, and watched her burn to the waterline as she began to sink.

Ralph said, "Well there she goes, people! Not much else we can do here."

He joined the rest of the crew and passengers, picked up the outbound mail sacks from the terminal building and said, "Let's go over to Kai Tak and see what's left of CNAC and the Brits."

The ragged band of aviators, mechanics, clerks and passengers walked the short distance from the Clipper terminal to the land airport. The runway was pock mocked with bomb craters. What they saw was heart breaking. Every one of the hangars had been shot up or destroyed. Sitting on the ramp, shot up beyond repair, were two DC–3s and a DC–2. Farther down the ramp were the remains of CNAC's cargo work horses—the antiquated Curtis Condors. Miraculously, two of the airline's newer DC–3s and an older DC–2 sustained only minor damage.

As they walked, everyone continued to scan the skies for planes. CNAC employees were beginning to come out of the hangars, a few at first, and then more, dazed at the destruction the fighters had wrought. As they came outside, they shaded their eyes from the sun and like the others squinted toward the skies for another attack. Some looked around for their colleagues as they began to emerge from their hiding places on the airport. Others seemed stunned, shell shocked, or lost in thoughts of their immediate future. Small groups gathered discussing the damage, their livelihood and their last hopes for getting out of Hong Kong.

Anna saw Captain Sharp organizing a work crew to push the undamaged aircraft off the tarmac before the next attack. Anna pointed him out to Alex and explained he was the captain who had invited her to observe the instrument approach into Hong Kong. She said, "Let's go over and see if we can give him a hand."

About a dozen employees were pushing against each wing. Just as soon as they were out on the tarmac and clear of the hangars, Charlie yelled for the ground help to grab as many pails and shovels as they could, and board the aircraft. He explained they would taxi all of them to the far end of the tarmac, push them off into the nearby fields and try to camouflage them as best they could before the next strike.

The work crews mounted the airplanes, as quickly as they could. Even before the last were aboard the pilots started the engines and began to taxi all of the airplanes, to the far end of the airfield, towards an area where the farmers surrounding Kai Tak had planted vegetable gardens. Alex and Anna jumped aboard and rode with the others.

When they stopped at the far end of the field, Charlie Sharp cut the engines, came out of the cockpit and began shouting instructions to the crew that had gathered to help save the airplanes. Most understood English but Charlie repeated the commands in Pidgin and Chinese for those that did not.

"Let's push these airplanes as far out into the gardens as we can," he said. "We have to make these airplanes invisible from the air before the Japs hit us again. Take dirt, vegetables and grass from the gardens and mix it with water in those buckets! Smear it all over the airplanes and push them as far as possible up under those trees."

Every major project in China was accomplished by using many hands. Sharp's camouflaging project was no different. The rest of the CNAC employees and all of the farmers from the area saw what Sharp was trying to do and ran over to help. Soon, hundreds of hands were mixing dirt, water and vegetables to make a rudimentary but very effective camouflage.

"Sharp has the right idea!" said Anna. "If we are going to save CNAC or have any chance of evacuating key personnel, it is going to be with these three remaining ships."

"Yeah, if this doesn't work we'll become indefinite guests of the Japanese in the next couple of days."

Anna said, "The Japanese fleet is surely just off shore, and there is no way they are going to let anyone come or go. All of the British planes were destroyed and you can bet the Japs aren't going to let any more land. The Clipper is sunk, the Condors are gone, and these ships are the only way out that's left."

The camouflage crew had just pushed the last of the ships under a tree when Bond came to check on their progress. He was walking with a noticeable limp. The crew gathered around and Anna said, "Glad to see you made it OK, boss! Why are you limping?"

The Operations Director looked exhausted. He answered with a grimace, "It's nothing, but I'm glad I ran into all of you. We just got news from the radio room. Pearl Harbor has been bombed!"

A group murmur mixed with many expletives went up from the crowd as Bond held up his hand and said, "There's more! They've also bombed Wake, Manila, Guam and Singapore...there's a lot of confusion...no reports on damage yet."

Bond looked at both of them and said, "We can't start any flight operations until tonight, and we can't do that unless we save these airplanes. As soon as Sharp doesn't need you any more, I want you both back at the Peninsula. I will save everything I can of what is left. I will start flying everything out tonight along with your crew, Ralph. Anna: I have made a list of all people the government will need to fight this war. I will use the Pen as the embarkation area after we collect everyone on that list for evacuation. Most speak English but many do not, and that's where I will need your help. Mr. Cannon: Captain Ralph and the rest of the crew have already gone to the hotel. The streets will be dangerous and I was hoping you will be Miss Boreisha's escort until you leave."

Without saying anything else, Langhorne Bond turned around and limped back toward the hangers. The small crowd broke up and everyone returned to the business of saving what was left of China's only viable air transportation system.

When they finished helping with the camouflage Alex took a drink from a canteen, looked at both of them, and began to laugh.

"Anna, if having mud and grass smeared on you will keep the Japs from finding something, then we are definitely safe...at least until we take a shower!"

Anna said, "I can't stand myself anymore! If there was any lingering doubt what these farmers use for fertilizer, there isn't anymore! Let's get back to the Pen and get cleaned up...we've got a lot to do."

The bombing continued sporadically as the two made their way back to the Peninsula. So far, meaningful air attacks were confined to military targets on the frontier and Kai Tak. The bombings around Hong Kong and Kowloon was indiscriminate and seemed to have little purpose other than to create terror and panic; just like in Nanking, they were successful.

The streets were jammed with people walking, pulling, pushing and riding in every known conveyance in China. Chinese non-combatants were streaming in from the territories, their carts laden with the detritus of shattered lives. "The swarm" was beginning to organize, but unlike Shanghai and Nanking, there was really no place for it to go except *away from the war*. Officials frantically tried to direct them to camps already filled to capacity with thousands of refugees that had already sought the perceived safety of Hong Kong. Anna wondered about Leftenant Adams and how he was faring.

CHAPTER 16

▼

THE PENINSULA HOTEL

Kowloon
8 December, 1941
10a.m.

The rickshaw pulled up in front of the Peninsula. The couple, both in their mud-covered clothing, jumped down from the bench and paid the rickshaw man. Alex's uniform was hardly recognizable as such. Anna too was still in the uniform shirt and the gabardines she had pulled on early that morning, but to an observer, it was impossible to tell what either wore, much less the color.

The doorman looked at the couple as they made their way up the steps of the elegant hotel. Not quite knowing what to do he backed away as far as possible and ushered them in. As they made their way to the desk the clerk and the hotel guests instinctively stepped back, overwhelmed by the stench from the young couple.

A queue of anxious people crowded around the clerk at the front desk pleading for rooms. Available accommodations had long since disappeared as more people arrived hoping for a way out of the colony.

Anna saw the American businessman she had helped only the evening before. He was one of the few who had recognized the mounting danger and re-booked to leave on today's doomed Clipper. Mr. Caruthers argued with the dispassionate clerk behind the desk for a non-existent room as his wife stood next to him, her arms around their teenaged daughter, trying her best not to look too concerned.

Bond had booked separate rooms for Anna and Alex. On seeing the plight of the family Anna turned to Alex and said, "Darling, give these people your room. You can come to my room to get cleaned up; these people have nowhere to go and you will only be here until this evening."

Alex began to protest when she said, "Don't be foolish! There's a dammed war on now and the reputation of one Russian girl is the last thing on anyone's mind right now."

Alex said, "Fine with me—anyhow, people would question my sanity if I declined that offer, now, wouldn't they?"

The Carutherses were effusive in their thanks as Alex went to the concierge desk for their key. While he was gone, Anna checked to see if William Cameron was registered. The clerk, keeping as far from her as possible, checked, and said he was. When she joined Alex, she told him the news.

"Thank God that courier Cameron is registered. He must have just come in. As soon as I'm presentable, I'll give him a call and get rid of this damned package I've been carrying for him all week."

"What's package is that?"

"It's some stuff from Chongqing I brought back for the Navy Department. I was asked to give the package to an American courier, a Mr. Cameron; he was to be on today's eastbound Clipper. So much for that...I'd say he isn't going anywhere for a while, but just the same, I want to get rid of the package as soon as possible. He might be leaving on one of tonight's CNAC flights."

"What's in the package?"

"It's stuff damning to the Japanese."

Anna looked around to see if anyone was listening, and said, "I'll tell you later, when we get to the room."

"If it is damning, seems to me it would have been a hell of a lot more important yesterday than it is today, don't you think Princess? C'mon: let's go get cleaned up before they throw us out of this joint."

The lobby was crowded with well-dressed people pushing, carrying and sitting on inordinate amounts of luggage; every chair and sofa was occupied.

"Hey Princess: look at all of these people! When I checked out a couple of hours ago the lobby was empty."

"Can you believe it? It's as if only now these people are beginning to realize there is no way out of here. The Japanese bombs have finally given them the energy to pull their heads out of their collective asses. Now, they expect to show up here, with all of that luggage, buy their tickets on CNAC, or Pan Am, and simply fly away from the war!"

As they stepped in the elevators, Alex saw Bonnie Belinda standing in a line that curved around the lobby to the Pan Am desk.

On the short ride to their floor, the guests and operator of the ornate elevator flattened themselves against the wall doing their best to stay away from the odiferous couple. When the doors opened to let them off everyone collectively exhaled. Then, as they made their way down the hall to their room, they nodded hello to small groups of hotel guests clustered in front of their rooms discussing their fates. As they approached, most retreated to their rooms and closed their doors. A floor attendant greeted them, kept his distance, took their key and let them into the room. Anna mercifully flipped a coin to him so he didn't have to get too close. He smiled his thanks and walked away.

As soon as they shut the door behind them, Anna started unbuttoning her shirt and said, "I don't know about you, but I can't wait a second longer to scrub this Chinese garden off of me. I feel as if I have been wallowing in a pigsty all morning."

"Yeah, I hope it was worth it," Alex said. "If they see those CNAC ships from the air, they're history and we would have turned ourselves into pigs for nothing!"

Dirty clothes began flying out of the half open door to the bathroom as Anna said, "Let's hope so. In any event, we have done what we can. I'll make it as fast as possible so you can get cleaned up."

"That will be swell, Princess…I can't even stand myself anymore!"

Alex took of his shirt and singlet and threw it on the collective pile. He paced the floor and said, "You know, Princess, everything we have been discussing over the past week is coming to pass, and it is as if no one saw it coming. I just don't see how any logical person could have thought it wouldn't or couldn't have happened, and yet it did, and all of the signs were there!"

Anna left the door ajar as she adjusted the water running into the tub.

"Alex: people have a way of convincing themselves of what they want to believe rather than what is logical. I saw it happen in Shanghai. I saw it in Nanking, and here we see it happening again—same sort of denial with Hitler in Europe. The evidence of what these tyrants would do was everywhere, and still people chose to ignore it.

Steam began to roll out of the bathroom door as she continued. "The whole world knew about 'Nanking', at least for a day or so; then, they collectively forgot. My god Alex, the estimate there is that over 300,000 were murdered! What does it take for the world to take an interest? It was in the papers; there were pictures and witnesses; the Chinese government even took it to the League of Nations. They did what they always do, though; they talked it to death and didn't do a damned thing about it! To the rest of the world the League condoned the Japanese aggression the same way it condoned Hitler's; they gave them legitimacy by their silence! You know, if the League won't condemn mass murder then, damn them, they are irrelevant! It wouldn't surprise me if the whole organization justifiably fades into history as just one more good idea where men didn't have the moral convictions to make it work!"

"Anna darling, that's quite a speech...how did you become so political?"

There was a slight pause with only the sound of gentle splashing and the filling tub in the background.

"Alex, my family...my life...my entire life is the result of politics that didn't work. Think about the Tsar. Tsarist politics looked out for only a few. His government was oblivious to the plight of the peasants...the common people. The ruling classes crushed any hope for change. My family was part of that class. The Tsar's indifference left Russia vulnerable to the promises of the Bolsheviks. They promised power to the people when in reality they were only replacing one form of tyranny with one even more ruthless. Things were so bad after the Great War, the people were ready to embrace anything that offered them an alternative. The only ones who fought the Reds were my father's peers who had everything to lose." In an exaggerated accent she said, "Enough of theese bool sheet! I'm going to soak in this tub until my mind and body are cleansed of this dirt and what is happening in theese feelthy world!"

Alex took a spare blanket out of the closet and spread it out over the bed.

"Jeez, Anna, I guess that means you are going to be in there a long time."

"The dirt should be the easy part, Alexander. Unfortunately, there is not enough water or time to cleanse the world of what is happening to it."

Soon, Alex heard nothing but the sound of light splashing in the tub. He took off his mud spattered uniform trousers and lay back on covered bed wearing only his boxer shorts. He listened to the far off artillery and mortar rounds exploding. He thought about their grave circumstances and of what Anna had just said. Everything was true. The reality of the moment was that they were simply two individuals caught up in a barbaric war. There was nothing they could do except become victims unless they got out of Hong Kong and out of China. He possessed skills few others in the world had. These skills would be needed now more than ever in the months and years to come. He was sure that the United States would now enter the war...probably on both fronts. He thought about what Bond had said,

"America entering the war would insure the annihilation and unconditional surrender of not only Germany and Italy, but Japan as well."

That man was right on the beam, he thought. For the present, however, his goals were much more immediate. Everything depended on the survival of those two DC–3s and that one DC–2 they had just camouflaged. Bond seemed to have a good plan, and he trusted him. He would employ those airplanes well. He knew he planned to evacuate the Clipper crew as soon as possible. He also said he needed Anna to help him with the task of evacuating key officials. So far, he had said nothing about when Anna would be leaving. He made up his mind right then that he would not leave without her regardless of orders to the contrary. His sole mission right now was getting himself and this woman he loved out of Hong Kong and preferably out of China. He was of no use to anyone if he ended up in a prison camp. With no passport, Anna's plight was even more dismal than most. He simply would not let it happen. She had alluded to some of what had happened to her when she was in Nanking and Shanghai. Every time either of those places were mentioned, her whole demeanor changed; it must have been a horrific experience. Someday, when she was ready, he felt that it would probably be cathartic for her to tell the entire story. That melancholy song they danced to last night...what was it?...Yeah, a Nightingale or something in Berkeley Square. It kept running through his head interspersed with the distant explosions and the gentle splashing from the bathroom. The last he remembered were thoughts on how to get them the hell out of here.

He was running through rice paddies in ankle-deep water holding Anna's hand when a kiss on the cheek and the fresh smell of soap and shampoo woke him. Anna was sitting on the side of the bed wrapped in a one of the Pen's enormous terrycloth towels. She had another wrapped around her head, like last night.

"Alex...I haven't been able to wash away the problems of the world, but my body is at least clean! The bathroom is free my darling. I even cleaned the ring around the tub. Phoo!"

Alex looked at his watch and said, "How long have I been asleep?"

"Only minutes...now go and wash that Chinese garden from your body and I will try to make myself presentable. I have brought very little in the way of clothing. You did say carry only the essentials, now; did you not? Unless I can get back to my apartment, the only thing I have is in that grip. Now go wash! I've really got to get dressed and find Mr. Cameron."

"Yeah...yeah, for sure...I'd better see if I can do anything about getting these uniform trousers cleaned. I have very little else to wear myself!"

Alex used the shower rather than the tub. After shaving and shampooing, he felt much better. He walked out of the bathroom using the last of the large towels around his mid-section. He thought of the other occasions he had been with a woman in similar circumstances—it inevitably led to love making. Not this time, he thought. This one is for keeps! I want it to be right when the time comes.

Anna had put on the only dress she had brought from her apartment. The only concession to anything professional was the nametag pinned to her silk dress. Much as a man might, she combed out her short hair after showering and was ready to go. He thought of Tracy back in California. She would be fooling with her hair and putting on makeup for the next hour. She was beautiful in her own way but vapid and without depth—nothing like this one. It had only been a couple of weeks since he had last seen her and already it seemed a memory from another life.

Alex threw his dirty trousers on the pile by the door and said. "Darling, if you still aren't too concerned about your reputation, would you call room service and see what they can do about getting these things cleaned? I'll get dressed and be out in a jiffy."

Alex opened his suitcase and pulled out a clean pair of khaki slacks and a uniform shirt. He grabbed some underwear and went back into the bathroom to change.

Rather than calling the hall porter with the hotel bell system, Anna bundled all their dirty clothes, crossed the room and opened the door to the hall to find the startled attendant who had opened their room listening at the door. The attendant stared at the floor with the sheepish look of one caught at something he wasn't supposed to be doing.

Anna asked, "What are you doing here?"

The attendant kept looking at the floor and for a moment said nothing. "Me maykee up room missy...me see you have clean towels!"

Anna looked at the porter suspiciously and then said in Chinese, "Take this laundry and have it done as soon as possible. Have everything back within the hour. I want the trousers, sponged steamed and pressed...understand? I need them back as soon as possible—plenty fast!"

The porter was shocked and at the same time relieved. He looked at the floor; he said in pidgin that he would have everything back in less than an hour.

Anna wondered if the porter was simply a voyeur interested in the lives of Westerners, or maybe, it was something more—robbery, or maybe something else! Anna closed the door, still thinking about the incident, when Alex came out of the bathroom.

"Alex, I think the hall porter has been eavesdropping. I opened the door to give him the clothes, and he was just there...listening."

"What do you suppose for? Do you think it had something to do with the package you are carrying?"

"Maybe...I hope not, but I can't think of anything else it could be."

"I think you better give me the whole scoop. Since this morning, it's a whole new ball game."

She took a long breath and began to tell Alex what had happened. "Shortly before you arrived from Manila, I flew to Chongqing on CNAC business. What I haven't told you is I have two jobs and two people to whom I answer. One, of course, is Langhorne Bond. The second is a marine: a Colonel James McHugh with the Office of Naval Intelligence. He's in Chongqing. I met him through Bond in the course of CNAC business. Because of my frequent travels there, they occasionally use me as a courier. I guess they reason a Russian woman trusted by Bond is less obvious than an American and certainly better than no courier at all."

She continued, "While I was in Chongqing, they gave me two assignments. One was for CNAC. I was to meet the next inbound Clipper in Hong Kong. It was to be a shipment of P–40 tires for Colonel Chennault's Flying Tigers. God knows what happened to the inbound Clipper with the tires! It was supposed to be in Wake Island today. The second job was to deliver this package I've been holding to William Cameron. He's an American courier I told you about. At least we know Cameron is registered at the hotel, but...how do you say...'I'm stuck with it' until I can give it to him."

Alex continued to listen attentively.

Anna continued, "Here's the other part: when I was in the departure terminal at Chongqing with Bond, I saw this guy taking more than a normal interest in me. On the flight back to Hong Kong, he did the same thing. He's easy to remember. He was one of those creeps that make a woman's skin crawl. Anyhow, when we arrived in Hong Kong, I asked a friend of mine who works in customs about him. He told me he was a French businessman. His passport showed he had been in China for some time. He works in aircraft sales and represents interest in several countries. His name is Arnaud DeRuffe and he left on last week's Clipper to the States."

Alex asked, "What does he have to do with the package?"

"Probably nothing, but here's what started making me think there might be some connection. The day before you arrived from Manila, I came to the Pen for work. When I first arrived, I first went to the ladies room, and on the way, I passed by the barbershop and saw DeRuffe...I think you say in 'animated conversation' with the barber. I thought that unusual. Men don't enter serious conversation with Japanese barbers using their hands for emphasis and the like...you know, they simply talk about the weather, make small talk or say nothing at all."

"What makes you an expert on barbershops?"

"The movies of course! Every time they show a barbershop scene, men don't have serious conversations, and they don't speak with the barber unless it's about sports, the weather...you know what I mean. On top of that, it occurred to me to have an animated conversation, they must have spoken in a common language...English, French, Japanese?"

"You know, you might be on to something! The first day I was here this time, before we met in the hotel lobby, I went down there to get a haircut. The place was busy. I had to wait for a while and was reading a magazine. I remember two British Officers, both getting shaves. They were speaking about Hong Kong defenses along something they called the 'Gin Drinker's line'...who could forget that? Anyhow, I couldn't help notice that the barber took particular interest in what was being said. He actually paused in the middle of a razor stoke...you know, as if he was making mental notes. I didn't think much about it at the time, but after what you said it begins to make sense."

Anna said, "The more you think about it, the more it makes sense. A barbershop is a perfect place to gather intelligence. Men are in a relaxed atmosphere. British staff, couriers and businessmen are constantly coming and going. There, they are under hot towels, getting a shave, making casual conversation with each other. Their guard is down, and a barber is in a perfect position to take it all in. Then there's our hall porter...maybe they work together! Maybe there's a whole ring working in the hotel!

"Probably all just a coincidence," Alex said, "It's beginning to sound too much like a Nancy Drew Mystery!"

"Who is Nancy Drew?" Anna said.

"Never mind, darling...this could be serious. The package for this Colonel McHugh...do you know what's in it that could be of so much interest to the Japanese?"

Anna hesitated, "I don't think keeping it secret matters so much now, so I'll tell you the part I know. In any event, if I can't get the package to Cameron you and your crew might be the only ones who have a chance of getting this information in the right hands back in the U.S. Here's what I know. McHugh's group, the ONI, has somehow acquired evidence that a Japanese organization called Unit 731, based not far from Harbin, in Manchuria, is performing medical experiments on human beings...mostly Chinese and Russian prisoners. They are using the experiments to gain knowledge in the manufacture of biological weapons"

"What do you mean by *biological weapons*?"

"You know, germs, plagues, diseases…kill thousands at a time and tie up manpower to care for the sick and dying. They want to use those weapons against their enemies, which now is just about everyone including the United States! There is a lot of evidence that they already tried them out murdering Chinese peasants. They used rats infected with fleas contaminated with Bubonic Plague."

"Jesus, Anna…that's beyond barbaric, it's inhuman!"

"No, Alex, unfortunately, it is very human. Animals could never do such a thing!"

"Yeah, I get your meaning."

"Besides the immediate military implications, the information was supposed to help persuade the Americans and the British to join the Chinese in their war against the Japanese."

Alex said, "Christ, Anna, that's powerful stuff!"

"There's more than just Unit 731…there's the report I wrote"

"What report is that?"

"When I was in Nanking, in '37, I was working with a Ms. Minnie Vautrin of the International Safety Committee. We were able to move more or less freely about the city. That work gave me the opportunity to observe and take a lot of pictures of what was really going on. Alex, it was horrible…it's really beyond my ability to describe. When I escaped, I had a whole package of information I wanted somehow to get to the West. I was sure if the world knew what really was going on they would unite to stop it…maybe it would have prevented what has happened since then—today, even. Well, when I fled Nanking, I lost it—film, my journals, some important personal stuff—I left it all. I got away on a sampan, on the Yangtze and I left it on the boat. I had everything in a map case my father had given me, the one he had used in the war—kind of like this English one I bought in Chongqing. I simply forgot it in the heat of the escape. I've always felt that was a great failure on my part. McHugh knows about what I saw and he asked me to write a report. I did, and it's in the same package. This time, I want to make sure it gets back, even if it is too late to do any good. The world needs to know the truth!"

Alex said, "You know, the Japs will still want to get this stuff, but probably for other reasons."

Anna asked, "Other reasons—what do you mean?"

"Unless they are psychopaths, these cowards are like any murderers. They don't like others to know what they have done. Maybe even at this early stage those responsible want to cover it up—just in case! Damned, Anna this stuff is hot—maybe we should just turn it over to the embassy people, here in Hong Kong."

Anna said, "No, I thought of that darling. They have less chance of getting the information out of here than you. In any event, I don't trust them with it. I just do not think they would attach as much importance to the information as others."

Alex asked, "Who is the courier going to give it to?"

"McHugh and the ONI want it to go to the Navy Department, in Washington. They think the Navy would be more inclined to make sure the information got to the President. They think the State Department would sit on it much as they did with what they already knew about the Nanking massacre. In any event, William Cameron was the only courier going on the Clipper, so the Navy was forced to use him. Unless Cameron gets out on CNAC tonight, it looks like you are the best bet for getting the information back to the States. You are an American, a naval reserve officer, and you have priority transport. I don't fit any of those categories."

"Cameron be damned…I want you to take it back to the states! If it is as important as they say, then it's important enough for you to get priority transport and take it back yourself. Add to that, you have first hand experience with what went on in Nanking!"

"No Alex…it is a wonderful idea but with no passport…how could I get permission to enter the United States?"

Even though Alex was looking in Anna's direction, he appeared to be looking through her. It was as if he was distracted and thinking of something else.

He changed the subject and said, "Look, we need to report the eavesdropping. With Hong Kong under attack, we can't take any chances. Let's go down, tell the people at the front desk what happened, and try to find Cameron. Maybe there's some more information about the war by now."

Anna shouldered the map case after dropping the package inside. She wanted to make sure the 731 package was with her at all times. Just before leaving, she opened her Gladstone and busied herself with its contents a moment, and then declared herself ready to go. They took one last look around and locked the door behind them.

Many of the guest's room doors were now open to the hallway. Radios could be heard in the background with the ominous monotones of newsmen reporting the latest war news. With no plan of action, everyone passed the time listening to the news and discussing it with their neighbors.

An Englishman spoke authoritatively to another guest—"I heard the British Fleet would be steaming into the harbor within twenty four hours!" Anna and Alex looked at one another as they remembered Mr. Smythe at Bond's cocktail party. That will show them who's in charge in this part of the world!"

The American family that had taken the room reserved for Alex was standing in the hall. Mr. Caruthers stood in shirtsleeves and suspenders leaning against the door to his room, smoking a cigarette, and listening to the hall gossip. His anxious wife and teenaged daughter hovered behind him with a deportment of anxiety. He stopped the couple and again thanked them for the room.

After glancing at the nametag on her shirt he said, "Ms. Boreisha: we didn't have the opportunity to thank you properly in the lobby. You might remember us: Mr. and Mrs. Eugene Caruthers, from Chicago. You helped me yesterday with our return reservations. This is our daughter, Valerie. We were booked on today's flight and heard the unfortunate news of the Clipper's sinking. Do you have any information yet on when the next may arrive so we can make plans for our departure?"

Anna spoke to him as if explaining something very simple to a child.

"Mr. Caruthers, World War II started this morning. There will be no more Clippers to Hong Kong until this war is over."

"But Ms. Boreisha, we simply cannot stay here…it isn't safe! What would you suggest we do?" The other hotel guests heard the exchange and gathered around to hear what she had to say.

"Mr. Caruthers, very soon we are all going to be captives of the Japanese. If I were you, I would take anything of value…jewelry, precious stones, U.S. dollars, anything portable and valuable…I would find sewing materials and sew it into your clothing because when you are taken prisoner, the Japanese will take everything they find. You will need those items to exchange for food, medicine and other essential items. I don't mean to alarm you, but those items will soon mean the difference between life and death to many of you assuming you survive to become prisoners. Now, if you will excuse me, we have many things to do just now. Good luck to all of you."

Without waiting for a reply, the two continued toward the elevators as the Carutherses and the other hotel guests looked after her, speechless. What this young woman was suggesting to them seemed an impossible invasion of their secure privileged world that up to now they had taken for granted. It was as if she were a prophet of doom from another world!

When they were on the elevator, Alex asked, "Do you think it will really be as bad as all that, Anna?"

"Oh yes…very much as bad as all of that, Alex. Unless there has been a total change in Japanese command authority over troop discipline, Mrs. Caruthers, her daughter, and all the women in this city…all will be rape victims within hours after the city falls. Western females will fare a little better than the Chinese, but not much. Those that survive will be imprisoned. Alex, on this point, I know what I of what I am speaking…I have seen it first hand in Nanking."

The doors to the elevators opened to what now seemed more of a mob than a gathering of people. The crowd had grown to the extent of filling the lobby since they first returned from the Kai Tak. It was further confirmation that everyone was using the Peninsula to find out about war news, and if possible, escape.

The two ladies who had become their not so secret voyeurs over the last week were in their usual place—still chatting away as if they were simply guests at another social gathering. The elderly gentleman was also in his usual chair; this time his attention was not on his newspaper but the conversations around him regarding the impending siege and everyone's speculation on their fate. The perennial lobby piano played in the background—its melodious notes almost lost in the cacophony of frantic conversations pervading the lobby.

Many still deluded themselves into believing their social status would somehow ensure their safety. With the exception of only the few high officials on Bond's list, Anna held no illusions about the fate of the everyone else. Soon, she thought, she would have to think about what she would do when Alex, his crew and the CNAC people were gone. At least it wouldn't be a new experience for her, she thought.

She forced the thought from her mind. Right now, she had to focus on a safe transfer of the Unit 731 information to a proper courier.

She turned to Alex and said, "I'm going to call Cameron and see what he wants to do about this package. I'll look for you with Captain Ralph and the crew. I'll see you when I've found Cameron and disposed of this damned package."

"O.K. darling, that will be swell…I have a little errand to run and I'll meet you there when I return." The two hugged and Alex joined the rest of the crew."

She waved to Ralph and the rest of the crew standing not too far from the lounge area and went across the lobby to the phone booths lined up near the hotel entrance. She picked up the instrument and said, "Mr. William Cameron's room please."

"One moment please."

Anna let the telephone ring for longer than she thought necessary. As it was ringing, she saw Alex walk hurriedly by her booth toward the hotel's outer door. She waved with her free hand, but he didn't see her. He disappeared in the swarm outside.

Anna had just seen him with the rest of the crew and wondered where he was going. There was no answer from Cameron. She reasoned he was either still in the hotel or maybe on consular business on the Hong Kong side. She went to the concierge and asked to have the courier paged in the hotel's public areas. Moments later the page marched off with the ubiquitous ornate chalkboard held high above his head that said, "Message for Mr. William Cameron." Above the clamor of hundreds of voices he shouted, "Mr. William Cameron!—Message for Mr. William Cameron!" Soon, he and his voice disappeared in the growing crowd.

When Anna returned to the lobby, the Pan Am crew was still in the same place they had staked out before—near the Reuters teletype, where they could read about any war news. Alex had not returned from wherever he had gone, and Bond had still not joined them to relay his latest instructions.

The hotel page was still canvassing the public areas, so Anna decided to look for Cameron in the opposite direction. She looked around the newsstand first and walked into each of the hotel shops. Then, thinking of their conversation about DeRuffe and the barber, she went to see if just maybe the courier was getting a haircut, or a shave.

As she turned into the corridor leading to the barbershop, she saw both of them through the shop's glass window. Their hall porter and the Japanese barber were in heated conversation in the otherwise empty shop. In an instant, the vision of the loathsome man in the pongee suit with that same barber came vividly to mind.

As she passed the striped barber pole at the shops entrance the porter looked up and recognized Anna as she stepped through the door. Without hesitation, he bolted for the curtains in the rear of the shop. The barber retreated behind a swivel chair and turned to face her as she stopped in front of the chair.

DeRuffe! The Barber! The Porter! In an instant her earlier suspicions about Cameron's disappearance moved from possible to probable. The barber stood stiffly without speaking. He eyed the map case and camera over Anna's shoulder and mumbled something guttural in Japanese she did not understand. There was no doubt as to its nuance, though; she had just been cursed.

As soon as he saw the tall, and oh so foreign looking woman, Lieutenant Commander Tashimura knew his cover as a barber had been compromised. She was nothing like the women of those British Officers, he thought. She was different. He had been told she was Russian, working for the Americans, but he hated her just the same. Even though they had fought like demons, their army had, after all, defeated the Russians in Manchuria. He knew his latest mission was a failure, but wait...maybe, just maybe it was not! Neither he nor the porter had found the package in this woman's or the courier's room. Perhaps the transfer had never been made! The Frenchman had mentioned the woman always carried a military looking shoulder bag with her, so maybe that was it...slung across her body. Perhaps the package was in that bag and he could still save face and complete his mission.

The barber glanced toward the vacant hallway. It was still empty. He began to circle from behind the chairs of his trade. In his right hand, concealed from view, he held a straight razor that he flicked open with the unseen movement of a practiced finger. As he came out from behind the chairs, the barber grunted again and crouched slightly in a classical martial arts fighting stance. At the same time he brought his left forearm in front of his chest parallel to the ground. It was then that Anna saw the razor. He held it low, in his right hand, almost out of sight.

She compared his stance with the fighting postures she knew. With no hesitation, Anna assumed the posture learned from long hours of practice under Master Cheng Tu. She cursed the fact she was again wearing a dress. With her right hand, she began to pull the hemline above her knees, freeing her legs for action. In a defensive crouch, she backed with deliberate steps toward the entrance of the shop. At the same time, she slung the map case and Leica around on her back, out of her way.

The barber was astonished at the woman's movement—she had training! Instinctively, he erred toward caution and circled as he advanced another step, and then another as Anna backed toward the door. Just as he was ready to attack both heard the pounding of boots and shouting in Chinese. His caution had cost him his chance! The barber glanced through the glass toward the corridor, glared at Anna, and retreated through the curtains in the back of the shop.

Just as the barber slammed the rear entrance door on the other side of the curtains two Hong Kong police officers, their revolvers drawn, burst into the shop. They saw Anna and asked in English, "Where is the barber?"

"The rear door officer...quickly, he just ran out!" One of the officers ran for the curtains. The other stopped, recognizing Anna as the Pan Am representative.

Anna shouted to the second policemen, "I think the barber and a hall porter might have something to do with the disappearance of an American courier. He might even be dead! Quickly, officer…come with me to the front desk! We'll get the manager to take us to Mr. Cameron's room."

While they were hurrying to the reception counter the policemen said, "You could very well be right, Miss Boreisha. The police and military authorities have been watching the barber for some time. With this morning's attack, we are rounding up all suspects for questioning."

The front desk attendant was busy fending off questions from the crowd for which he had no answers. He saw Anna and the policeman and moved down the counter to see what they wanted. The policeman explained to the attendant the Peninsula's barber was wanted for questioning and was suspected of espionage.

Anna interrupted and said, "I have reason to believe the barber might have something to do with the disappearance of one of your guests…a Mr. William Cameron. I also have reason to believe one of your hall porters might also be involved."

The clerk asked, "What can I do to help?"

"Open Mr. Cameron's room for us. He doesn't answer his telephone or page, and I have reason to believe we might find him there."

The clerk grabbed the master keys, summoned a bellman, and the four of them went to the elevators and the courier's room.

The manager tapped on the door insistently with the room key, the ever-present hall guests looking on. "Mr. Cameron, Mr. Cameron…are you all right?"

There was no answer. The manager gave the key to the bellman who opened the door. The manager called once more as they walked into the room. "Mr. Cameron…are you all right?"

They saw the blood on the floor before they saw Cameron's body. Regardless of how many times she had seen the dead, it never ceased to amaze her how much blood was in the human body. His body was lying at the obscene angle seemingly favored by victims of violent death. The courier's head was almost severed from his body. Without much thought Anna surmised it must have been a very sharp instrument—probably a sword or the barber's straight razor. The nightmare of Nanking came to mind as if it were yesterday.

Against the noise of artillery and mortar shells exploding in the distance Anna could not quite hear the exchange between the clerk and the porter. She looked around the room for the courier's brief case. Cameron and the other couriers always used the same type with its ubiquitous chain and handcuff clasped to their wrist. It was not in the room. She looked through the open grip on the room's low dresser. A cursory inspection revealed only the contents of one who lived out of a suitcase and nothing more. If there had been items a courier would protect, they were not there now.

She spoke rapidly in Mandarin to the clerk and the policeman and explained her suspicions regarding the barber and the hall porter. The clerk listened, and the policemen made notes. At her insistence, she persuaded both of them to come to her room on the next floor.

She thought of the hundreds of photographs she had lost on the Yangtze and before leaving, perhaps out of habit, she unslung her Leica and took a picture of William Cameron's contorted body.

Anna led the desk clerk and the policeman back to the room where she and Alex were staying. Many of the people they had seen earlier still congregated in the hall speculating on why she might be returning with a policeman and hotel staff.

When the porter, the policeman and Anna entered the room, everything looked as she and Alex had left it. Anna reiterated the story of the porter's eaves-dropping and searched the room for signs of entry since she and Alex had left. She went to her Gladstone and examined the contents. Before leaving the last time, she had carefully positioned several items so that any entry would be apparent. She remarked to no one in particular, "Someone has been through our things!"

The party made their way back through the onlookers and down the hall to the elevators. When they reached the ground floor, they had to push their way through the throng of curious guests in the lobby. She excused herself from the police when she saw that Alex had returned from whatever errand he had been on and had re-joined the Clipper crew by the Reuter's machine. Several of them were facing the elevators. Their waving caused Alex to turn and see Anna coming their way. When he saw her, his face lit up with happiness but changed to one of concern as he saw that she was with a policeman. Her normal demeanor and half-smile had been replaced by a look of grim determination he had yet to see on her. She motioned for Alex to come away from the rest of the crew.

Alex excused himself and went over to where she had stopped by a large column in the lobby. Anna looked to see if there was anyone within hearing distance. "Alex, Cameron is dead! His room has been ransacked, and there is no sign of the diplomatic briefcase he normally carries."

"Dead...How did he die?"

"His throats been cut...a sharp instrument...from what I have just experienced it was probably a straight razor. I am almost certain it was the hotel barber.

Besides that, I think our porter was involved, just like we spoke about. There are probably others!"

"What do you mean? What happened?"

Anna recapped everything that had happened since he left and finished with, "When they saw me, the porter got away through the back door. The barber had a razor in his hand and started after me. I think he wanted my shoulder case. If the police hadn't come along when they did, I think he would have tried to kill me."

Alex wrapped his arms around her and pulled Anna close to him. She continued, "The Police are also suspicious. They've been watching him. They want the barber and our hall porter for questioning. Besides, I am sure someone has been going through my suitcase and probably yours as well. It's my guess they were looking for the package I was going to give Cameron."

Just then, William Langhorne Bond walked into the lobby. He was still limping and looked more tired than when they saw him last, at Kai Tak.

Many of the prominent citizens of Hong Kong recognized Bond as the CNAC Operations Director. A throng of people gathered around him hoping for some news and any sort of favoritism for the only escape left. As he walked toward the gathered crew he held up his hands deferring their inquiries; he told them he would make an announcement when he knew something himself.

Anna and Alex saw Bond, and joined him with the rest. More than one looked up with amused expressions as the two approached their circle. Bond said, "Anna, Alex, glad you could join us. You all know about Pearl, Manila and Singapore. We still have no idea as to the extent of the damage. We have word now that our facilities on Wake and Guam were also attacked; both islands will almost certainly fall. If that were not enough, the Japs have completed their occupation of Shanghai and have taken over an American ship, the U.S.S. *Wake,* that was acting as a communications station. No word on how much damage in Pearl."

Someone said, "Sneaky bastards!"

Captain Ralph said, "What about our Clippers?"

"We don't have much information. There's no word yet on the *Singapore Clipper* outbound from Wake to Guam. We received a departure message that she had taken off from Wake and then turned around to go back just before the attack began. We don't know anything more at this time. If she's still operational, the crew is probably maintaining radio silence. From position reports, we know the *Hawaii Clipper* was inbound to Honolulu during the Pearl attack. I have reason to believe she diverted to Hilo. The *Pacific Clipper* was inbound to New Zealand. We assume they too are maintaining radio silence, as we have not heard anything from her yet either. Earlier, I was telling all of you about our plans to get you out of Hong Kong and back to the States. You will all leave tonight on a CNAC DC–3 for Chongqing. We'll figure out the rest after we get you there."

Ralph said, "What can we do to help?"

"Right now, just keep yourselves available. I have to get to my room and get cleaned up. I'll make some calls and be back just as soon as I know anything."

Before Bond left Anna motioned him aside and told him what had just happened with the barber and their suspicions of how the package was involved. The weary Bond said he was sure now more than ever that he wanted Alex as a full time escort for her.

Without saying anything else, Bond left the group and crossed the lobby still deflecting questions from the crowd. He stepped in the elevator and was gone.

CHAPTER 17

▼

THE PROBLEM

The Peninsula Hotel, Kowloon
8 December, 1941
at 2p.m.

Alex and Anna also left the group and walked to the lounge area of the lobby. In spite of the turmoil, their not so secret voyeurs smiled as the young couple stood not far from their usual gathering area.

Alex had already made up his mind to tell her what had been on his mind since early this morning.

"Anna, this is probably the worst possible time and set of circumstances to tell you what has been on my mind, but here's what I've been thinking. Ever since we first met on the Clipper, I knew that I wanted to spend the rest of my life with you."

Anna began to speak but Alex held up his hand and said, "Please let me finish. Before you stepped through that door on the Clipper I thought that love at first sight was the stuff of romantic nonsense…you changed all of that. The time we have spent together since then has just confirmed my judgment. The beginning of World War II is hardly the backdrop I had in mind for a proposal, but everything is getting pushed up on the priority scale right now. You also have to believe that I had better surroundings than the lobby of the Peninsula hotel in mind when I told you these things, but it is the odds-on favorite that I won't be in Hong Kong twelve hours from now and you may, or may not be with me; so, darling, as the saying goes, 'there's no time like the present'. I want you to marry me now. Not next trip, not after a period of time. I want you to marry me right now, just as soon as we can find someone who will perform the ceremony."

Anna again tried to speak. Alex held up his hand again signifying her to be patient. He reached into his pocket and at the same time turned his body to afford as much privacy as possible in a lobby teeming with frightened people. He produced the traditional dark blue velvet ring box, opened it, and slipped an art-deco engagement ring with a small diamond and baguettes on her finger and said, "It isn't much of a ring for a Princess, but it's the best I could do with the cash I borrowed from the guys. I think I about cleaned them all out, and after this morning, no one is about to give me credit. When we get home, I'll do better."

Alex remembered the uncharacteristic look he had seen on Anna's face the first time she walked through the door of the Clipper. She had it now. However this time, as much she tried, she was unable to keep tears from welling up in her eyes. For several seconds she said and did nothing except dab at the tears with the back of her hand. Then, still without saying anything she simply closed the short distance between them, wrapped her arms around Alex and gently pressed her cheek against his and held him tightly. Alex could feel her bosom heaving and for a moment thought she might be weeping.

Over her shoulder first one, and then everyone standing close to them, turned to look at the beacon of light the young lovers projected over the cloud of darkness that enveloped everyone in that lobby. The Clipper crew also turned and looked in their direction with quizzical amusement on their faces. Their voyeuristic elderly ladies and the gentleman in the white suit smiled with unrestrained joy at the two lovers perhaps remembering similar moments from long ago. Several of the crowd in the pressing throng began to realize what they were witnessing and began to applaud.

The couple stood that way for several moments without saying a word. Anna broke the embrace and said to Alex, "Excuse me for a moment."

She walked to the where the crew still gathered and said, "If Mr. Bond returns please ask him to give me a call in my room when he wants to brief me."

Someone said, "Sure thing Anna!"

Her demeanor did not invite further comment.

She walked back to Alex; without further comment, she took him by the hand and led him towards the elevators.

On the elevator, Alex began to say something and Anna said, "This is my moment Alex and I don't want you to say anything until we get to the room. Please just be patient a minute."

Alex didn't say anything.

The two got off the elevator and again went to Anna's room. Everyone in the hallway had left. She took the "Do not disturb" sign and hung it on the hall side of the door and closed it. She then turned to Alex and pushed the lapels of his uniform coat back over his shoulders and removed the jacket.

Again, Alex began to speak. Anna put her index finger to her lips, took off his tie, unbuttoned his shirt, and removed it. She then unbuckled his belt and slid his pants down over his hips until they fell to the floor. She did the same with his boxer shorts pausing for several seconds to take pleasure in his full erection.

Alex watched hardly able to catch his breath as Anna unbuttoned her dress and let it drop to the floor. In a quick motion, she kicked off her shoes and removed her bra and panties. This time there was not a hint of blushing. She was in complete control of herself and confident of exactly what she was doing. She pulled back the covers to the bed and gently guided Alex's head to the pillow. Then, just as casually as one would wash their face before going to bed Anna took Alex into her mouth simply because her passion insisted and that it seemed so right for the moment. After very little time she sensed his passion, rose on her knees to straddle him and take him inside her. She wished she could prolong the moment but knew instinctively that both of them would be obliged to their passions in a very short time.

Anna leaned over and hungrily sought his mouth with hers while continuing to thrust downward with her hips to take him deep inside her. Alex let out a guttural gasp while Anna made no attempt to restrain her own shriek of joy as they both convulsed in simultaneous orgasms.

With a leg on either side of him Anna collapsed on top of Alex's chest. He held her close to him luxuriating at the softness of her breasts against his chest and said, "Does this mean yes?"

She said, "Don't say anything now. Just hold me."

Both remained silent. The only sounds were the muffled explosions in the distance. After awhile, Anna thought her weight might be uncomfortable for him and she began to shift her position. He simply rolled her on her side and pulled her tightly against him as if he were afraid she would somehow go away.

The two stayed in that position, holding each other tightly, each with their own thoughts, listening to the ordinance exploding in the distance. Now, they could hear mortar and machine gun fire. They both had the impression that the noise of war was getting closer as the British garrison made their attempts to slow the attacking Japanese. Neither said anything, but both unconsciously tried to gauge how far they were from the encroaching violence.

After a short period, they made love again. This time, without the urgency of pent-up passion, they took the time to savor the wonders of each other's bodies in a complete capitulation of love and lust for each other.

Afterwards, without fanfare, Anna slipped the little ring off of her finger and laid it on the night table. "Alex, you have made me happier than at any other time in my life. I want you to know that under normal circumstances I would have accepted your wonderful proposal immediately. As it is, in good conscience, I simply cannot."

"What do you mean, you cannot?"

"No darling…let me finish! It's a lovely proposal and I love you very much for it…but we both know it is at least partially motivated by today's events. You are aware of my position. You know I have no passport. You know that no country with the exception of China is accepting stateless persons. I am totally convinced with the sincerity of the beautiful things you have told me, but if you looked at it from my point of view you would know that I would always wonder…wonder that if sometime in the future, when we inevitably had 'our bad day' together, the thought might come to mind that you were pressured into this marriage because of the immediate priority of getting me out of Hong Kong. No, I think it could forever taint our love with 'If it wasn't because of the war, maybe I wouldn't have married this woman!'"

Alex asked, "Answer me one question Anna; do you love me?"

"More than my life, darling! It's because I love you so much that I don't want your departure tonight in any way to pose a situation that might someday leave you in doubt."

"Anna, it's not a perfect world. Now you listen to me! I'm not going to leave your fate to what CNAC or the Japanese might do next because of your desire to have things *just right* or because of something that might happen later. It's simply out of the question. Listen you beautiful boneheaded Russian…even if we are captured it will be best if we are married. Damn it…this is the first time since I've known you that I have ever seen you think any way but logical. Now, let's get dressed and find Bond. I'll tell him we are getting married. We'll go to the consulate and get the necessary papers while there is still staff. I know your other motivation is you do not want to leave while your parents are still captive in Shanghai, but think about it: with American citizenship you might even be able to do something for them! With your present status there's not a damned thing you can do except get yourself raped, or killed, and that's not going to be an option! If you still feel strongly about some 'some possible future consequences' of your decision, you can divorce me in the United States. You will be safe, you will have a passport, and I will have the opportunity to woo you all over again."

Anna grinned at the thought. She started to say something, but instead, simply pulled him tightly against her again.

Alex said, "Not now! Darling, I would like nothing better than to spend the rest of the day like this, but in a few hours, the sun will be setting. The Japanese are getting closer, and we have to get going. We have the rest of our lives for each other, but now we have a lot to do and not much time to do it. Bond's getting us out of here tonight, and I have to let him know of our plans."

Anna started to say something but Alex said, "Save any more you have to say on *my later regrets* for the States. Right now, I simply want you to love me, and help get us both get the hell out of here so I can get back to flying and you can have a chance at a future, not only for us, but maybe even for your family. Let's face it, right now you are not even in a position to help yourself, much less anyone else!"

Anna went to the bathroom and washed. When she came out Alex was almost dressed. Anna said, "I have never had a close association with anyone except my parents who thought things through with my welfare in mind. All of what you are saying is true except for the divorce part. I will make sure that you never will want to get rid of this Russian girl. Now take that ring you went in hock for and slip it back on my finger!"

Anna slipped on her now clean jodhpurs and boots. She swapped her nametag from her dress to her white blouse and was still fastening the buttons when Alex came out of the bathroom.

"You look like you are ready for polo rather than running like hell from the Japs!"

Anna said, "At least with pants and sensible shoes I can have a fighting chance of running faster than they can."

"I'll bet you can, Anna! I'll just bet you can."

When they stepped into the lobby, they saw Bond had again joined the crew at their place near the Reuters machine. No one could help but notice the two had changed clothes and were holding hands as they walked toward them.

Captain Ralph said, "Hey Alex...Anna! Mr. Bond was just giving us an update."

Alex said, "Before you go any further, sir, I have an important announcement for all of you."

The entire crew looked at the two of them with amusement. They already knew what he was going to say. The money they had lent Alex made each of them heavily invested in what he was about to say.

"Anna and I are getting married. We wanted all of you to be the first to know."

The entire crew slapped Alex on the back, kissed his bride to be, shook hands and offered them congratulations.

Alex turned to Bond and said, "Sir, I know you have important duties for Anna to perform before she gets out with the rest of the Pan Am and CNAC employees. I would like to stay and help in any way I can until she is finished with whatever you have in mind. When she goes, I'll go, and not before."

Bond said, "That won't be any problem Alex. Like I said before, with that barber on the loose and the break down of order in the streets, who would make a better escort than her husband?"

Alex asked Bond about who could perform the ceremony and about the issue of a passport. Bond looked at his watch and said, "First let's deal with the formalities. I'll make a couple of phone calls and set things up. Wait here and I will be back in a minute."

Bond returned and said, "Get over to the consulate right away. They have the people there now and they said they would wait for you. I have phoned a cleric friend of mind. He's an Episcopal minister, but I assumed denomination wasn't the important thing right now. I asked him to meet you at the consulate. I called in a couple of favors and they will take care of the passport and visa business just as soon as the ceremony is over."

Alex said, "That's swell, Mr. Bond. I had no idea they were capable of working this fast. I don't know how to thank you."

Bond said, "No need for thanks! I've known this woman since '36 and I always wondered who might come along that would make a suitable match, and here you are! I can't imagine two people more suited to one another…just glad I can help! Now get going! I'll try to make it, but if I don't give me a call at the Pen when they are finished at the consulate and I'll let you know how things are shaping up."

Anna and Alex left the Peninsula and hurried to the banks of the harbor. By now, the ferries were out of the question for transportation. The British military had taken over the entire operation. Looking farther down the shore they found a sampan owner and after a lot of haggling and a promise of money from Anna's purse, they convinced him they were on important business. Both of them were certain that it was Alex's uniform and Anna's official looking nametag that persuaded him that there were dire consequences had he failed to take these *foreign devils* across. After negotiating the swarm on the other side, they met Bond's contact just as they arrived at the consulate.

CHAPTER 18

▼

THE CONSULATE

Hong Kong
8 December, 1941
3p.m.

Shortly after 3 p.m., Bond and the Episcopal minister hurried up the stairs to the consulate just as the clerk was finishing Anna's passport and visa. The ceremony was held in the same office and Bond gave the bride away in the presence of Captain Ralph, the co-pilot, the radio operator and Bond's friend from the consulate. With little fanfare, the minister read the simple words that made the young couple's union legal under the laws of man even though there was little anyone could have said that could have convinced either one of them that they were not already spiritually united.

There were no bouquets of flowers, no white dress, no bridesmaids or pews full of friends and family. There was no academy chapel filled with his classmates with crossed swords, no waiting limousine trailing cans full of pebbles to whisk them off to a honeymoon suite and yet the newlyweds couldn't have been happier. Dressed only in boots, jodhpurs and white shirt she was his perfect bride. Anna only had the movies to compare the occasion with and was still in a state of disbelief. Alex promised her that she would have a proper wedding just as soon as conditions permitted.

The clerk whom had helped with the formalities presented Anna her new passport and visa and said, "Congratulations Mrs. Cannon. Even though this passport and visa are your right as a citizen by marriage, please take it as a wedding present from the United States Consul in Hong Kong. You probably have the last documents that we will process for anyone for a very long time to come."

Anna took the simple little document that presaged a new country and a new life, opened it and looked at her picture clipped from old CNAC credentials pasted near the front, and ran her fingers over the official seal. She closed it, looked at the *United States of America* embossed on the front and tried to fight back the tears welling up in her eyes. Even though she tried to deny the passport was anything but ancillary to marrying Alex, she nevertheless realized how fortunate she was to have instantly become privy to the enormous largesse of a nation she only knew about from books, papers and movies. She wondered how many citizens of the United States had any idea how fortunate they were to be born Americans.

Alex said, "Darling: in years to come, I want you to look back on this day as the best decision you ever made." With the tears still in her eyes, her signature half-smile broadened lighting up the entire room. She threw her arms around her new husband still holding the small bouquet behind his back and held him tightly in a close embrace. She said, "Alexander Cannon, I will love you for the rest of my life. You complement my being and make me whole."

With the exception of the constant boom of artillery shells in the distance, the room was momentarily silent as the couple made a declaration of their love for one another. They stepped apart and continued to hold each other's hand as the crew patted them on the back and wished them luck.

The co-pilot produced a bottle of champagne, and the clerk offered some water glasses pouring a round of drinks for the small party. He then proceeded to propose a toast and said, "To the Cannons whose union will probably provide us with the only good news we're likely to hear this eighth day of December, 1941."

CHAPTER 19

▼

MRS. H.H. KUNG

Hong Kong
8 December, 1941
4 p.m.

Bond kissed Anna and congratulated Alex. He looked at his watch, reached into his coat pocket and took out a folded piece of paper. Bond said, "Anna, this is the address of Madame Kung. She is, of course, the wife of Mr. H.H. Kung, China's finance minister. Mrs. Kung is sister-in-law to Chiang Kai-shek and one of the most influential women in China. Her husband has called from Chongqing and instructed me to persuade her to leave Hong Kong immediately. Now, I want you to know I have previously spoken to her about how little time there is, and how important it is that she leave immediately. Unfortunately, I was unsuccessful in persuading her. Her husband has also spoken to her, but so far, she is totally intransigent in her notion that the Japanese are no threat. She persists in the belief that somehow the British forces will prevail. Anna, you have seen occupation first hand in Shanghai and then in Nanking. You also speak excellent Mandarin and Cantonese. I am counting on you to persuade Madame Kung that tonight is the last night she and her entourage can be assured air transportation to safety. Tomorrow night is by no means certain, but I do not want you to discuss that as an option. You must persuade her to leave tonight and to be at the airport no later than midnight."

Anna said, "I understand completely Mr. Bond. I'll do my best."

Bond and the crew saw them to the street and onto a hailed rickshaw. It wasn't until they turned to wave goodbye to the small wedding party that they heard the clatter of the tin can the first officer had tied behind the rickshaw.

Madamn H.H. Kung's residence sat near the top of the mountain with a splendid view of the island, the harbor and the ocean. Alex paid the coolie and asked him to wait with the promise of a large tip. The newlyweds went through the outer gate to the residence and knocked on the door. A servant answered and Anna presented their cards explaining in Mandarin the nature of their business.

The servant left them standing on the steps as he went to deliver their message and calling cards. They looked at one another and said nothing as they listened to the distant sounds of the battle raging in the far territories. From their vantage point at the Kung residence, they had an excellent view and saw smoke in the distance from exploding ordinance.

Presently, the door opened again. Without ceremony, the servant ushered them in. The furnishings were a mixture of old China and modern. He took Alex's hat and offered the couple two straight chairs, bowed, and announced that Madamn Kung would join them presently.

In a few minutes, a middle-aged woman in classic Chinese attire entered the room. Alex and Anna stood as the woman said in Mandarin, "I understand that your capable but worrisome Mr. Bond has sent you two to try to frighten me in to leaving Hong Kong."

"Madame Kung, my name is Anna Boreisha. I am Mr. Bond's traffic representative for Pan Am and the Chinese National Airline Corporation." With her characteristic smile she said, "This is my escort and husband of less than one hour—Mr. Alex Cannon. He is a stranded crewmember from the Pan American Clipper that was attacked and destroyed by Japanese aircraft this morning." Mimicking Anna, Alex bowed at the waist when Anna, speaking in Mandarin, spoke his name and gestured in his direction.

"Madamn, I assure you, Mr. Bond does not exaggerate. As a recent resident of Shanghai and Nanking, I can bear witness to the capabilities, ruthlessness and intent of the Japanese. If the true story of their infamy is told, they will go down in history as the equals of Genghis Khan. Perhaps more importantly, they consider Chinese as sub-human. They have treated them as such in the past and will do likewise after they occupy Hong Kong. Madamn Kung: you simply must leave this very night."

Ms. Kung said, "Young woman, surely you are exaggerating. After the world-wide attacks on American and British interests today, you can rest assured that in very little time one or both of their fleets will steam into Hong Kong harbor, and vanquish these horrid barbarians."

Anna said, "Madamn Kung: In Mr. Bond's judgment the British can hold the territories, Kowloon, and its airport for no more than three days, perhaps less. That means we will only have tonight for air operations. Mr. Bond has instructed me to inform you that after tonight, CNAC air operations from Hong Kong will cease. He is well aware of your position on this, Madamn Kung, but he asked me to implore you to reconsider. After tonight, air transportation on CNAC will not be available."

Madame Kung folded her hands into the large sleeves of her dressing gown and strolled to the window overlooking the territories to the North. It was obvious to both of them that Madame was not used to receiving news that did not agree with her view on a subject and then having to act on options not to her liking.

In a moment, she turned to the couple and said, "Please thank Mr. Bond for his interest in my safety. Also, please thank him for sending two such delightful emissaries, and accept my congratulations on your marriage. It gives me hope for the future to realize the world has young people such as you looking out for its interest. Tell Mr. Bond I will be in contact with him by seven o'clock. I will consider his counsel carefully and give him my answer at that time."

Anna knew that further argument would be considered impertinent. She had made her case for the seriousness of the situation and could do no more.

Madame Kung came forward, shook both of their hands, and clapped for her servant to show them to the door. Soon, their rickshaw was padding off down the mountain.

Anna suggested that since it was on the way to the ferry, she would like to stop by her apartment and pick up a few more things before they returned to the Pen. Alex unnecessarily helped her to the bench as she gave instructions to the rickshaw man and set off in the direction of her apartment.

All of the way down from the lofty heights of Hong Kong's plush residential area they watched the pyrotechnics of war in the surrounding hills of the territories. With the onshore winds, the sounds of war sounded closer than they remembered.

The swarm of humanity in the streets increased the farther down the mountain they went. Men and women were carried along with the crowd, their meager belongings hanging from both ends of the ubiquitous carry pole and balanced from a yoke over their shoulders. Holding hands with their siblings, obedient children clung to their parents so as not to be lost in the swarm.

The crocodile! It was Shanghai and Nanking all over again! She had come to think of the refugee swarms as a giant crocodile undulating back and forth trying to get anywhere other than where it was. It was hard to believe that the siege of Hong Kong would be any different, except they were trapped, and the crocodile had no place to go. She didn't try to explain it to Alex.

CHAPTER 20

▼

THE BARBER

Hong Kong
8 December, 1941
6 p.m.

With no brakes on the rickshaw, Alex wondered how the rack-thin sinew-hard coolie could handle their relatively heavy weight on such a steep hill. Down he went though, weaving in and out of the crowds, never faltering. As the steep road neared Anna's apartment, the rickshaw man shortened his steps so as not to be run over by his two Caucasian passengers. Alex paid the coolie what Anna had promised and persuaded him to wait until they finished.

The coolie was not even winded from the downhill jog with the heavy "foreign devils." The coolie, like his peers, were not xenophobic and they didn't discriminate. Soldier, sailor, merchant, missionary, male or female—he and his fellow workers referred to all white people as "foreign devils." He sat on his haunches, lit a cigarette, took measured pulls from the water bottle tied to the rear of his rented rickshaw, and waited.

Anna rummaged in the map case for her apartment key wondering if there had been any looting since she left. Although it seemed a lifetime, it had only been this morning since she left. She opened the gate to the courtyard and garden. The small courtyard was empty as the two walked across to her apartment. Just as she was about to insert the second key she noticed the door stood slightly ajar. She glanced at Alex as both of them considered the obvious.

Alex held his finger in front of his lips. If someone was still there, maybe they had not heard the outer door with the din from the swarm outside. He stepped in front of Anna and slowly pushed the door open. As he stepped into the room there was motion to his left. Alex dove, rolled on his shoulder and back onto his feet in a boxing stance. Just then a man's form slammed the door hard before Anna was completely inside. With his left hand Alex jabbed hard followed by a quick right hook. The jab was blocked, but the hook crashed firmly into what was taking shape as a man's head. His eyes tried, but they couldn't adjust fast enough to the shadows in the unlighted apartment.

In the second before Alex could connect with another left, he saw the glint of steel in the dim light as the blur became a man. In the millisecond Alex had for reaction, he grabbed the man's wrist with both hands, twisted sharply and stopped a slashing downward thrust directed at his face.

The momentum of the missed thrust brought them both crashing to the floor with them on one side and Anna on the other of the half open door. Anna didn't move. The man tried to yell something in a language Alex did not understand. It was as if he were gargling and trying to yell at the same time. It was then that Alex felt something warm and slippery spurting from the man that had fallen beneath him. He continued to hold his wrist as his assailant thrashed violently in the darkness of the apartment.

"Anna! Anna darling! Are you all right?" There was no reply. The man's thrashing beneath him became weaker. The wheezing and gargling sounds were hideous. He still couldn't see, but he knew the man beneath him was dying. Soon, there was no struggle at all.

Alex tried to stand, slipped, and fell on the body beneath him. It was almost impossible to get his footing in what was undoubtedly the blood of the man on the floor. He found a light switch by the door, threw it, but there was nothing. For a second, he wished he smoked—at least he would have a match. Most Asians did, he reasoned; from his language, Alex surmised the dying man was probably Japanese. He knelt over the shapeless hulk and fished through his pockets for a match or lighter. From one pocket he retrieved a Zippo lighter and flicked it open.

"Jesus Christ!" he said. There was blood everywhere!

He crawled back from the dying man now convulsing in the final seconds of his life. On hands and knees, he made his way over to Anna. She was lying on the floor and moaning faintly as she regained consciousness. "Alex, oh Alex—are you OK?"

He opened the door to get more light.

"Yes darling, that guy slammed the door on you just as I got in the room!"

Anna said, "It caught me right on the forehead! It must have knocked me out. Ohoo, my head hurts. What happened to the guy? My God, Alex, you're all covered with blood!"

"I think that guys burgled his last apartment, Princess. Seems when we fell, I twisted his razor hand, and somehow he cut his own damned throat with it. Jesus! What a mess!"

In the dim light of the flickering Zippo, Anna crawled the rest of the way around the door and sat with her back against the wall. Where most people would have reacted in horror, Anna just stiffened at the carnage and sight of the dead man.

For a brief second, Alex wondered why, but before he could give it much thought she said, "That's the Japanese barber from the Pen. He's the guy that connects DeRuffe, our hall porter, Cameron and the package! Alex, this whole thing has been about the package I am carrying. Cameron was killed for something he never had!"

"Yeah, I recognize him now from the barbershop…seems we guessed right."

Alex kneeled over the bloody corpse and went through the rest of his pockets. Other than a wallet with a little money, a watch and cigarettes, there was nothing.

"God help us Anna—I just hope that stuff you are carrying is worth it!"

Anna took the camera out of her map case, attached the flash and took several pictures of the dead barber. She put the camera back in the case and set it on the couch. She said, "Alex, give me your coat and shirt." She took the garments, put them on the shower floor and turned on the water. Alex helped, although on the verge of being sick. For Anna, the gristly task did not seem to her as much as he thought it should. She moved quickly through the room, threw a few more items of clothing in a pillowcase and said, "Let's get out of here. We need to get back to the Pen and let the police know what's happened."

The coolie stood from his squat and stared at Alex in wet clothes and blood soaked shirt. Usually, he gave very little thought to these "foreign devils," as he was convinced he would never understand any of them.

The ride down to the ferry terminal was a blur as they were swallowed up in the undulations of the crocodile and coughed out at the water's edge. By that time many of the ships, junks and sampans were not moving at all. Their captains were convinced that even as bad as the damage was along the shore it was safer than moving about in the harbor.

Finally, they found their captain from earlier in the day who now refused to go back across the harbor unless he was paid an additional ten dollars. Like the rest, he was fearful of being caught in the middle. Only after ten minutes of haggling and agreeing to pay ten dollars over the price negotiated earlier did the pirate agree to take them across.

The weary couple sat on the deck watching shells burst in the north as the war moved closer to the city. Anna said, "You know, it's as if an eclipse of the sun that began in the early thirties has finally succeeded in plunging the entire earth into darkness." They both sat in silence as their captain skulled the sampan back across Kowloon Bay near the end of the first day of World War II.

When they arrived back at the Pen, Anna and Alex went to the police to find that only one constable was still investigating Cameron's murder. The rest were busy supporting Army operations, rounding up Japanese nationals, and preparing for imminent invasion. While Alex went to find the crew, Anna told the policeman about the barber. Without much interest, the policeman perfunctorily jotted down what they said and returned to his interrogation of yet another hotel employee.

She left him and returned to the lobby to find her new husband. He was just hanging up the house phone.

Alex said, "What do you think the Japanese would do if during their occupation they found the body of one of their agents in Anna Boreisha's apartment.?"

"I can only guess. I've already seen what they do to people who didn't do anything!"

Alex said, "Yeah...I thought the same thing. Darling, I just got off house phone with Captain Ralph. Bond is back at the airport. He told him to get the crew together and get out to the field right away. They are loading the DC-2 with as much CNAC equipment as possible; just as soon as they are finished, he wants to send the airplane right away to Namyung. He wants to stage all of the ships there for return flights to Hong Kong. As soon as he gets as much as possible staged in Namyung, he will fly everything on to Chongqing."

"Alex: do you know where Namyung is?"

"No."

"It's almost due north of here, about 200 miles, right on the edge of Japanese occupied territory."

Alex said, "I guess he's weighed the risk. He will have to stage there if he wants to save the airline. He said the Japs are approaching even faster than he had originally thought, and he was beginning the evacuation right away. He wants the crew to be on the first shuttle out."

Moments later, Ralph stepped out of the elevator and elbowed his way through the throng of people to where Anna and Alex were standing. Every time they saw anyone in uniform, the crowd pushed in around them yelling questions to which there were only unacceptable answers. Some were belligerent, some with pleading faces and voices as if it would somehow make a difference. Ralph struggled to make his way toward where the couple was standing. It was then that Alex saw Bonnie Belinda at the edge of the crowd shouting for his attention.

With the throng still pressing in on him Ralph did his best to ignore them and said, "Well aren't you two the Cat's Meow? I thought you went to the Hong Kong side on a mission for Bond but from the looks of you, I'd say you just came from slaughtering a pig—in uniform yet!"

"Almost, but not quite—I'll tell you about it sometime."

Over the din Ralph put his hand to Alex's ear and shouted, "Just after you hung up, I got another call from Bond. I told him you two were back. He asked that you stay here at the Pen and keep away from the lobby and crowd. He wants you to wait for the Chinese lady you spoke with this afternoon…said you two must have done a good job."

"What do you mean, Captain?"

"After you left she called. He thinks she has finally made up her mind to leave. She'll be here with her entourage around midnight. He wants you two to fly out with her on the DC–3 at oh-dawn-thirty. Don't mention the destination to her or anyone else. Says he will tell her when it's necessary. He thinks there's a possibility some more of those Jap spies you guys dealt with this morning might still be around. If our destination got out, it could queer the whole operation. He says if everything goes as planned, you guys will be taking off about 3 a.m., got it?

"Yeah, Cap…we got it."

"O.K. you love birds…gotta go! The rest of the crew is waiting. Guess I'll see you when I see you. With the twenty-five percent interest I'm charging you on that ring loan, I plan to retire next time I see you, so take care of yourselves!"

Anna closed the gap between them and kissed Ralph on the cheek. "I'm proud to have had you at my wedding, Captain Ralph. I hope we can meet again under better circumstances."

Alex shook his hand and said, "Happy landings Skipper! It's been an honor to fly with you!"

The newlyweds watched Ralph as he and the rest of his crew disappeared through the main entrance of the Pen into the swarm outside. They made their way to the elevators for what seemed like the hundredth time today.

Throughout the evening and into the night, the intensity of the artillery and mortar fire increased. They sought solace in each other's arms and made love repeatedly until their thirst was temporarily sated.

Toward midnight, the two lovers wondered aloud if they were hearing machine gun and rifle fire suggesting the front was getting even closer than they first supposed. They agreed that it was improbable. It was probably the effect of nighttime on sound travel, they surmised. Events would prove them wrong.

Shortly after midnight, the front desk rang and announced the arrival of Madamn Kung. Anna and Alex had already dressed and went to the lobby to greet the great lady. Much of the crowd from earlier was still there. Many were asleep on the floor with their luggage. Madamn Kung's arrival was greeted with much commotion and obeisance by the hotel staff. Refreshments were offered and declined. Offers of a room to freshen up were also refused. From one only recently convinced that the Japanese would not prevail, Madamn Kung wanted to quit Hong Kong as soon as possible.

Transportation had long since been arranged by CNAC for the Kung party. The loading of the baggage took place quickly, and several of the hotel staff came to say goodbye to Anna. Many had worked with her on a daily basis, and as they said their farewells, Anna looked into her old friend's eyes knowing there was little chance they would ever meet again.

They were just about to step into the taxi when out of the shadows Bonnie Belinda pushed past an inattentive body guard and said, "Hey Captain…kinda late to be asking ya, but best I figure it you two got about the only tickets left out of this joint. Any chance you could help a gal get outta here?"

Alex said, "Ms. Belinda, believe me, I would help if I could, but I don't have any say-so about who goes or stays. The only reason we are going is they need us to help fight the war. I'm sorry, but I can't do a thing."

By this time the bodyguards had taken Bonnie Belinda by the arm and were roughly pushing her away from their charge. Alex yelled to them not be so rough and shouted, "I wish you the best of luck Ms. Belinda, but honest, there's nothing I can do for you!"

She shouted back, "OK, Capn', couldn't hurt a girl to ask. Guess I'll just go back in, start brushing up on my Japanese and help that guy at the piano sing *The Hong Kong Blues!*"

Alex looked out of the back window of the cab as they drove away. Already, the flashy blond had pushed herself through the revolving door and had disappeared into the crowd.

CHAPTER 21

▼

ESCAPE

Kai Tak airport
9 December, 1941

Their taxi slowed almost to a stop as their driver negotiated the cab through hundreds of coolies bent to the labor of repairing Kai Tak's bomb cratered airstrip. Both stared out of the window, each lost in their own thoughts, as the cab crept toward what was left of the CNAC hangers.

Alex touched her arm and pointed at the Chinese laboring to make the airstrip serviceable. He said, "Well darling, I guess the few on Bond's list and our own little party drew the only long straws left in Hong Kong. These poor people...the British, Indian, the Canadian troops on the front lines...everyone in Hong Kong and the territories...they don't have a Chinaman's chance, do they. Is that where that expression came from?"

"My father used almost the same expression in Russia except instead of *Chinaman*, substitute peasant. That's when members of the royal court were running from the Bolsheviks. Just like Madame Kung, they left with little thought for those left behind. It's those attitudes that guarantee the overthrow of governments who consider their citizens pawns to be used and discarded at their discretion. Remember Bond's cocktail party and what was said about the Communists? I'll bet if we are able to look back on this period we will find those predictions were right on the mark."

Anna continued, "From the peasant's view point if it's not the warlords or the Taipans, it's the fighting between the Communists and the Kuomintang. Now it's the Japanese! The result for them is just the same. If they had even a little hope for the basics most people look forward to, I don't think the Communists would have such an appeal."

"Yeah, Princess…It's definitely the *ism* of the have nothings! Is this kind of thing going on all over China?"

"Yes; China only has two plentiful war commodities, and you're looking at one of them: millions of peasants. The other is space that they can trade for time. Where the West uses machines to build a road, railroad or a runway, the Chinese use thousands of peasants, like here…it's all they have. On the mainland, with only a couple of exceptions, their army has been no match for the Japanese. Many don't even have rifles! Their only option is to feed thousands into the maw of the Japanese war machine and trade space for time. They did that at Taierchwang in '38 and won, but only with the loss of tens of thousands. In their defense, though, they have no other choice. The Communists and the Kuomintang both know it and have temporarily stopped killing one another to address this more immediate threat. In the long run though, the plight of the peasants will cost Chiang Kai-shek the nation."

The two of them couldn't help but notice the demeanor of coolies. Without pausing in their labors, they looked up at their entourage, not with envy, but more a look of fatalism. They knew that with the exception of these CNAC airplanes and a few British motor torpedo boats, there was no other means of escaping the onslaught. They knew they wouldn't be going anywhere. They were surrounded by land and sea. The stories of other captive Chinese cities and the fate of their inhabitants had circulated for years. They knew with certainty, that in a matter of days, they would be dead, in a prison camp, or slave laborers. They would be worked to death with starvation rations. Yet the enormity of what lay before them was only now beginning to sink in. The attitude of, *it can't happen here*, was rapidly being replaced by one of resignation—like the lamb at slaughter. Still, like Madame Kung, some still clung to the *hope gossip* that always accompanied impending disasters. "The British or the Americans would steam into Hong Kong harbor and vanquish the Japanese hordes! Chiang Kai-Shek's army would break through the cordon and liberate the city." Most of the laborers seemed to accept their fate and continued to repair the runways with the backbreaking work that they had known since birth. Unlike the Bonnie Belindas, the Carutherses, the English and so many like them that had a choice up until a yesterday, these people never did. It was all they knew. It had always been their destiny. Regardless, they worked on as if the labor itself would somehow insulate or at least distract them from their certain fate.

The taxi honked through the last of the laborers when they saw Langhorne Bond standing in front of a CNAC hanger speaking with a group beside a DC–3.

The Operations Director greeted Madame Kung and explained to her that they would first be flown to Namyung for refueling. In that there were no night landing facilities in Chongqing, her plane would be delayed only long enough to ensure there was enough daylight for their arrival in Chongqing. To make the flight in daylight would insure disaster and would not be contemplated under any circumstances.

Madame Kung was not used to having other people dictate her schedule. She insisted that they fly directly to Chongqing. Bond again explained their limitations, and told her that the Japanese occupied much of the territory between Namyung and Chongqing. Her daughter seemed to understand and persuaded her mother that everyone, including her father, was confident in Mr. Bond. He knew what he was doing, and she should put her complete trust in his judgment.

After a few moments, Madame Kung acquiesced in her demands and deferred to Bond's plan. In her typical fashion, the matter had been disposed of. After that, she made no further mention of it.

Bond beckoned to Anna and Alex. He motioned them to his side where he spoke to them privately. He explained that he had spent the last hours trying to keep the British forces from blowing up the runways. It was all he could do to convince them that Kai Tak offered the only hope of escape for anyone—they simply could not grasp the importance of delaying their destruction until the last minute. He explained that the rest of the Clipper crew had left on the first flight, and theirs was to be the second flight of the night.

"I want to thank you both for all that you have done to mollify Madame Kung. I have already explained to you that it was a direct request to me from Dr. Kung that I persuade Madame to leave. His support will be critical if we are to continue operation. Without you, I couldn't have done it. Now, then…I will be remaining here to coordinate as much as the evacuation as practical and trying to keep the Army from blowing up the runways. After I have done all that I can, I will come to Chongqing. I have arranged for you to stay at the Heavenly Palace hotel while you are there."

Bond handed Anna a letter for Colonel James McHugh. He said it explained their circumstances and that the two of them had priority transportation back to the United States. He told Anna that he explained about Cameron in the letter. He suggested she accompany the package back to the U.S.. Although he personally did not know what it contained, he felt that if it was important enough for the Japanese to kill a courier, and to try to kill Anna, it was important enough to have her safeguard it to the U.S. with her new husband as escort. He asked McHugh to use his offices to help expedite their return to the United States and get the package in the right hands. Bond handed them a second letter for the station manager at Chongqing regarding operations.

Anna said, "Mr. Bond, I am afraid you will stay here too long. CNAC is more important to China now than at any time. If you are lost, the airline will be lost too…so don't stay any longer than absolutely necessary."

Bond assured her he would not. He explained his wife and boy would never forgive him if he did.

Bond said, "Anna, you have been in China since this thing started. You have seen what these barbarians are capable of. I have not seen the documentation you are carrying but I am sure it will be helpful in showing what we are up against; so get it in the right hands."

The Chinese CNAC pilot began to board Madame Kung's party. Anna and Alex boarded last. The entire aircraft was crammed with Madame's luggage, CNAC business records, spare parts and tools. Alex was sure that weight and balance calculations consisted of putting things on the airplane until it was full and keeping the heavy stuff over the wings. The captain's careful eye was the only scale. He depended on his experience to determine when the aircrafts *real* limit was reached. Alex looked around and although he had never flown a DC–3, he figured they were damned close to that limit.

Even before they sat down the starter whined, the engine caught, started, and with all lights off, they taxied to the takeoff position guided only by shielded flashlights from ground personnel. Without the usual line up, the pilot advanced both engines to full power and the overloaded Douglas trundled down the just-repaired runway and staggered into the air.

Immediately after lift off, the pilot banked out over the bay to gain altitude and avoid flying over Japanese held territory until they reached the safety of the clouds. If there were any lights left on in Hong Kong or Kowloon, they were blacked out or overwhelmed by the brilliance of exploding ordinance.

Alex held Anna tightly around the waist, and they both pressed their faces against the small rectangular window to get their last view of the city and the embattled armies. From their seats on the left side of the airplane, they had a good view of silent explosions and tracer fire. The pyrotechnics were spread out in a large semicircle around the territories and Kowloon. In the darkness, it was impossible to tell if the Japanese fleet blocked escape by sea, but they were certain it was there. Alex said a silent prayer for everyone left behind and made a vow that he would work with all the intelligence and skills God gave him to avenge everything that had happened to his country and his company. He also vowed that if ever put in a position of command, military or otherwise, he would never let anyone who trusted him for their safety become as vulnerable as the people of Hong Kong.

Most of the flight was flown in the safety of the clouds. The few times they broke in the clear, they saw nothing but a few lights and fires from peasant homes on the ground. For the rest of the flight there was only the blackness of the night and the inside of a cloud.

Namyung was almost due north of Hong Kong, some 200 miles away. They landed with the minimum of lighting, as CNAC's secret landing field was just on the edge of Japanese occupied territory. They had been using the field for a contingency airport with no way of knowing how long it would be before its presence was discovered. The base was not much more than a flat spot among the rice paddies. Fifty-gallon drums of fuel had been pre-positioned and camouflaged for re-fueling by Bond to avoid daylight detection by air patrols.

Not long after landing, their party was served a meal of hot rice and pork. Alex surmised a hot meal at this Spartan base was only because of the importance of their passengers. After eating, he helped with the refueling that had to be hand pumped from the fifty-gallon drums. Anna stretched her legs and returned to be available for Madame Kung.

Soon, they were in the air and again had the safety of clouds for the rest of the flight to Chongqing. The newlyweds slept fitfully in short naps as the DC–3 bounced through safety of China's nighttime skies. Anna was sleeping with her head against the window when Alex woke from one of the catnaps he had become so expert at in his years of long distance flying. He looked out to see the first rays of sunlight touching the face of this beautiful woman who had only yesterday become his wife. As he regarded her, a feeling of great love and responsibility came over him as he tried to imagine what would become of them in the coming months. As if she felt his concentration, Anna opened her eyes and saw Alex regarding her. Even in her sleepy state, she seemed to sense what had been going through his mind. He leaned over, put his cheek against hers, and pulled her close to him. He said "Good morning Mrs. Cannon! I just wanted to make sure that I was the first one to say that to you on the first whole day of our new life together."

In spite of herself, and in spite of her sleep-filled face, Anna blushed, not unlike the first time she met Alex on the Clipper dock at Hong Kong. The two held hands and contemplated the gathering daylight of day two of the Second

World War. The pitch of the propellers changed and the airplane began its cautious descent into Chongqing.

Their plane broke out of the undercast in the gathering daylight revealing a panorama of farmland that characterized most of central China. The Chinese pilot stayed in and around the clouds as much as possible. With daylight breaking, the clouds were their only cover from Japanese fighter patrols. The Douglas let down low and began to parallel the Yangtze River as the pilot prepared for landing. Anna explained that the wartime landing strip was in the Yangtze gorge at the edge of the river. As they descended into the gorge, she pointed out the numerous caves dug into the cliffs on both sides of the river. She explained they had been dug as air raid shelters against the daily bombings.

Just then, something flicked by just at the edge of Alex's periphery. It was just as they were beginning their final approach to the airport. He leaned over Anna and pointed at two mustard colored fixed gear fighters, in a high G steep bank turn. They were maneuvering to attack the Douglas at its most vulnerable time and configuration—wheels and flaps down, slowing for landing!

Just before the red "meat balls" disappeared in their six o'clock position, they both spotted two drab colored fighters with distinctive shark's mouths painted on their nose. Their high G turns caused vapor to stream from their wing tips as the two Tomahawks set up for a deflection shot inside the arc of the Japanese fighters now passing out of the couple's sight behind their DC–3.

Alex pulled his new wife's body over his shielding her from the imminent crash of machine gun bullets as the now unseen number one P–40 arched tracers into the lead Japanese fighter. Alex looked out the other window just in time to see the enemy fighter cartwheel in flames into the cliffs overlooking the river. Seconds later, the number two fighter disappeared over the tops of the cliffs trailing smoke and fire. The AVG wingman was right on his tail pouring machine gun fire into the doomed fighter until both disappeared from view. Seconds later the Tomahawk zoomed up over the ridge in a steep climbing victory roll and fell in trail behind their DC–3 for landing.

Anna shot a glance toward the front of the plane where Madame Kung's party was seated. Most were asleep, but not Madame. She was in club seating, facing aft. She had observed everything and sat transfixed as she realized that they had just been delivered from sure destruction by American mercenaries.

Alex was sure the CNAC pilots were totally unaware of the attack as their flight path changed not in the least. Seconds later the tires of the DC–3 barked their arrival; they rolled to the end and turned off the runway.

The aircraft came to a stop in front of a makeshift building that appeared to have been bombed repeatedly in the preceding months. Even as they disembarked, the two Flying Tiger Tomahawks that saved them from certain destruction touched down and taxied toward their DC–3. Two more flights of P–40's made a low pass over the field and zoomed back up to their covering position above the Chongqing airport.

Even before the Flying Tiger pilots shut down their engines, Chinese ground crews pulled fuel bowsers from revetments and began to re-fuel the fighters.

CHAPTER 22

▼

THE TIGERS

Chongqing
9 December, 1941

The DC–3 crew, now fully aware of their near escape, walked over to the Flying Tiger pilots to thank them for delivering them from sure destruction. Mrs. Kung approached Anna and asked that she be introduced to the AVG pilots. The three walked over to where the group was standing.

Anna introduced herself and Alex and said, "This is Madamn H.H. Kung. She is the Generalissimo's sister-in-law and wife of the government's Minister of Finance. We are just arriving from Hong Kong. You guys just, how do you say it Alex?...'Saved our Bacon!' Madamn Kung has asked that we make introductions so that she might properly thank you."

One of the pilots said in an almost unintelligible Southern drawl, "How do you do Ma'am! My name is Marlin Olds, and this here is my wingman, Sonny Springman. We've been flying CAP to see if we couldn't help to discourage some of the bombing attacks on your fair city when those two Japs burning up there on them cliffs pounced on you people in the landing pattern. We just stopped to take on some fuel; we need to get back to work right away."

Alex asked, "How did you guys just happen to be here?"

Olds replied, "Colonel Chennault has set up an early warning system. It's really kind of simple. There are Chinese spotters, mostly farmers, who live at intervals radiating out from likely Jap targets, this being one of the most likely. They hear or spot aircraft, pick up the telephone or a wireless and call intercept control. Control plots their position and the direction of flight, note what kind, and how many aircraft; they call fighter control, and if we have the planes and pilots, we make the intercept before they arrive. Kind of like the Brits have been doing in England, except they have radar that looks out over the channel and all. We're hoping to get some sets soon, but so far, no luck."

Anna said, "Speaking of planes, how are the spares holding out for your P–40's? I was supposed to be accompanying a delivery of tires for your planes due to arrive on this weeks Clipper. As you know, chances of that happening now are about zero unless something comes from the West."

"Yeah," said Olds "Fat chance now of getting anything from the east! Did you guys hear the Japs are attacking Wake Island? Started this morning their time! Best we can hear on our wireless is the marines are giving them a hell of a fight. Speaking of marines, we heard the Japs captured the last of the North China Marines and hauled them off to a prison camp somewhere. They also captured our communications ship, The *Wake*, in Shanghai. They have sunk the Brits only boat there. I think it was called the HMS *Petrel*, or something like that."

"Yeah, we heard about the *Wake* back in Hong Kong."

The Tiger pilot continued, "Come over here and I'll show you what we are dealing with on spares."

Anna excused herself from Madamn Kung's party. She and Alex followed Olds and Springman over towards the two P–40's that were being refueled. Two coolies were hand cranking aviation gasoline from the bowser and cleaning the windshield.

"Take a look at those tires, Ms. Cannon. That's why Chennault was using a Clipper to get them here."

Anna looked down inexpertly at the fighter's tires. There was no tread and they were worn through at least two reinforcing plies. They looked totally worn out to her but Charlie explained these tires were among the good ones left.

Alex, let out a whistle, "Damn, Olds, in commercial operations these would have been tossed twenty or thirty landings ago! And these are the good ones?"

"That's right. When a tail wheel tire goes we just stuff it with newspaper, bind it up best we can, and try to make it stiff enough for takeoff and landing. Every time there's an accident, if we can get to it, we cannibalize just about everything serviceable on the ship. The tires are the first thing we get. Colonel Chennault has been sending out messages for weeks trying to get re-supply, but with the Japs occupying just about every major port now, the only way it is going to happen is by air, over the hump, or the Burma Road. It's not just tires, though. As good as the Chinese are at making substitutes, there are some things they just can't make due to lack of raw materials. Rubber is one—gas another, to mention only two. For something like an airplane though, just about everything has to be imported."

Alex said, "What else are you really short of?"

"Motor oil!…we go about triple the time required between changes on these Allisons. We spend a lot of time at combat power with these ships and it really beats up the oil. Without good lubrication, they eat themselves up in a hurry. Best we can do is strain it through cloth and try to catch the big chunks…then put it back in the engine and keep on going. It's amazing we haven't blown more engines than we have!"

Alex said, "Anna and I are just on our way to hook up with the rest of a Clipper crew who arrived a little while ago. The dope is that Pan Am, the brass, and powers to be, want to get us back to the States as soon as possible. We have some messages for Washington from Hong Kong and here. They were supposed to go to Washington via Clipper so we're taking them back the long way around. If you have anything you want to put in writing, give it to us and we will do our best to see it gets to the right people. Maybe it will help to get your supply people on the ball."

Sonny laughed, "Boy oh boy…you've been away from the military a long time haven't you, Alex boy? We've got to forward anything we want to say through the chain of command and that means Colonel Chennault! Now Chennault is busting his butt to try to get us what we need but so far no tires or much of anything else. If it was bad up to now, it's bound to get worse since yesterday."

Alex laughed, "Sonny, why do you think I left the Navy. Really, though, if we happen to see someone with the right horsepower to make a change over here…well, I'm just going to open my mouth and tell them what I've seen and heard…that's all! They might not listen, but at least I would have made your case!"

"Yeah, it couldn't do any harm to let them know that you and Madamn what's-her-face had your asses saved by a Tiger pilot who won't be in the air a week from now because there's no rubber left on his ship to takeoff and land on!"

"We'll do what we can, Marlin. Looks like Madamn Kung and her party are being taken care of by their people so we will be on our way into the city to see what they are going to do with us. Good meeting you two. Good luck and good shooting! Only hope I can in some way help!"

Marlin Olds gave them a kind of a salute and jumped up on the wing of the Tomahawk. The Cannons waved goodbye and walked across the field to their waiting CNAC driver.

On the way into the city, Alex began to get an idea of what a city looked like after Japanese *total war* had been perpetrated on a civilian population.

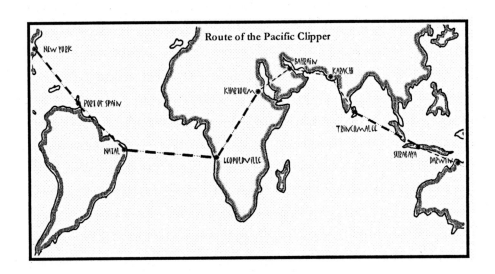

Route of the Pacific Clipper

CHAPTER 23

▼

LI SHIH

Chongqing
9 December, 1941

Everything not buried underground, or in a cave, seemed to have been bombed at one time or another. In spite of the devastation, Alex sensed a dogged determination in most everyone he saw. They went about their work with the same *work as usual* resigned attitude of the runway workers they left behind in Hong Kong. It was as if they all understood they were simply one little cog in a giant wheel that had to keep turning. If their cog broke there were thousands more to replace it. Alex wondered at the differences in them and those in his world where the feeling of *self* was seldom subordinated to that of a greater cause. He wondered if December seventh had changed all that back home.

The two hadn't given much thought to where they would stay in Chongqing. When the CNAC driver pulled to a stop in front of the more or less in tact structure he said, "Welcome to the Heavenly Palace!"

Alex let out a long whistle and declared, "This ain't no Peninsula Hotel!"

Over the months bomb damage had rendered the hotel barely habitable. Still it was one of the best Chongqing had to offer.

Anna said, "You Americans are spoiled. There're no doubt a lot of people standing in line for any sort of shelter and here we are accommodated before them simply because you, ah...we are Americans and of course there's Bond's intervention."

"You're right of course. I would guess if I had been through some of the things you've witnessed, I wouldn't even question it. But as an American, I reserve my right to complain! Come on Mrs. Cannon; let's see what our temporary home is going to be like."

The entire lobby was full of people. Most appeared to be Chinese businessmen—others foreigners. Many were in uniform. There were some American and British officers standing in line waiting to get to the front desk. Businessmen stood in groups in conversation. Everyone was discussing the alarming advances of the Japanese.

Li Shih looked like most other Chinese businessmen in the lobby. Although he preferred the traditional tunic when he was conducting his *business*, he found it prudent to blend in. He had even given thought to shaving his traditional mustache that tapered to a point at both ends but considered that too much of a break from tradition. Today he wore a three-piece grey suit that he thought served his purpose splendidly. He was concluding a transaction with another Chinese businessman regarding a shipment of black-market goods on the Burma Road when he noticed the tall man in dark uniform come through the hotel entrance. The young man was obviously American, dressed in what he first took to be a rumpled United States naval uniform. Naval officers were rare in Chongqing, and he wondered what his mission was in China.

While continuing to converse with his acquaintance, he noticed the insignia was somewhat different from the few American naval Officers he had seen before; there was no gold braid on the sleeves. In addition, he was escorting a woman whom Li Shih could not see, as the tall officer was between her and himself.

Before he could discern what type of uniform and insignia the tall man was wearing, the woman stepped in front of the American. He immediately recognized her as the beautiful Russian girl he had seen in the company of Sergei Hovans, at the Far East Cabaret, in Shanghai.

If one were observing Li Shih at that moment, it would have been impossible to discern anything other than his rapt attention to his companion's conversation. This was only partially true. Li Shih found it profitable to be an excellent listener. After all, his real business was selling information to the highest bidder, and that presently was the Japanese. At the same time however, his mind was racing with the dozens of possible explanations as to why this beautiful Russian was with this…what kind of American officer was he?

When…when was the last time? It must have been three or four years ago at least! By my ancestors, it was in '36 or '37…before the occupation! This one foreign devil was even more beautiful than he had remembered! He continued to make small talk with his business acquaintance while at the same time surreptitiously observing the American and the Russian woman.

He was just about to relegate the chance observation as nothing more than another morsel of information to be filed away in his formidable memory when Marine First Lieutenant Joseph Hadley walked through the hotel entrance. As usual, the lieutenant was in civilian clothes although Li Shih knew him to be an assistant to Colonel James McHugh, the Chief of Naval Intelligence in China.

Li Shih's heart jumped as he struggled to continue his focus on his companion's conversation while at the same time waiting to see what would happen next. He made a bet with himself that Hadley would precede directly to the officer and the Russian. Yes, yes…he did! Hadley removed his civilian hat and greeted the woman warmly. The Russian introduced Hadley to the tall young officer and joined them in the queue as they inched toward the busy desk. In Li Shih's mind, he at least confirmed the tall American was actually a naval officer, but then, after introductory pleasantries, Hadley began speaking exclusively to the woman and not her companion. It was as if he had been expecting her arrival and not the tall American.

Li Shih was fascinated by the possibilities. Sergei Hovans, her frequent companion of only a couple of years past in Shanghai, was now not only an employee of the Japanese but highly regarded as such. Li Shih toyed with the various ways he could exploit this information for profit. He made up his mind to invest a little capital and find out more about the reappearance of this woman and her companion.

First Lieutenant Hadley looked furtively around the room trying to insure they were not being observed by the usual Chongqing spies. As discreetly as possible Hadley said, "Ms. Boreisha…ah…rather, Mrs. Cannon, Colonel McHugh was so glad to hear you were on the latest CNAC transport from Hong Kong. As you know, the situation there is chaotic and he was very concerned with your safety especially in view of our…our recent business together with regard to the ill-fated outbound Clipper. We still have no idea if the package in your possession is still safe or not."

Anna looked at him and said only, "It is safe."

Lieutenant Hadley said, "Boy, that's a relief! We were afraid it would fall into Japanese hands. You know Hong Kong will fall, don't you?"

They both nodded yes.

"Colonel McHugh says he needs to see you at your earliest convenience. He's been exceptionally busy since the eighth. Give me a buzz when you're ready and I'll have transportation sent around." Hadley left them his number.

When they got to the front desk, they were asked for their passports. Until now, Anna had forgotten that she was now officially traveling on a U.S. Passport. It was the first time in her life she was able to produce anything other than an émigré's identity documents.

The clerk took the couples' passports and retreated a short distance to enter their information into the register. Alex was drumming his fingers on the counter and happened to be watching when the clerk asked her for the documents. An expression came over her face that was unfamiliar to him. He asked, "What's wrong?"

Anna blinked and returned from her reverie. She was trying hard to hold back tears. "Nothing…nothing at all!"

The clerk was still recording the information in the register. She touched him on the arm and said quietly, "Alex, I have never had travel documents that allowed me outside of China before. It's difficult to explain if you have never experienced it. You…you've had that privilege as a birthright and never had to live with the fact you could not travel freely in the world without special intervention by some nation on your behalf. This is the first time I have had this kind of freedom."

For the next week, all CNAC aircraft were busy with the evacuation of first Hong Kong and then flying out the equipment staged in Namyung. Anna had one meeting with Colonel McHugh. He was very busy but agreed that they would no doubt be the first ones able to get the package back to the United States and locked the Unit 731 package in his safe until they continued on their journey.

Anna continued to work with the station people setting up Chongqing as the new CNAC operations center. The evacuation was successful in getting most of the CNAC records, spare parts and tools evacuated before Kowloon was overrun. More importantly, they were able to save many people from certain death or imprisonment and salvage what was left of China's only remaining civilian air transportation system.

Bond arrived in Chongqing on one of the last flights. He was completely exhausted after 72 hours of non-stop operations to save key people and the airline. He was trying to arrange transportation for them, and as soon as he had something definite, he would notify them.

Li Shih had not been idle during this time. His agents found out that the man he thought was a naval officer was indeed the beautiful Russian's new husband and one of the Pan American pilots that had fled Hong Kong. Li Shih filed this information away and continued to look for *a hook* that he could use to persuade the Russian to work for his masters.

The next day Bond called and told the couple to get their things and get out to the airport for an immediate departure. Bond was in operations when their taxi arrived from the hotel. He greeted them in his office and said, "I spoke with Colonel McHugh and we both agreed it best to get you out on the first available flight. We're in luck! Remember we were wondering what happened to the *Pacific Clipper?* Well, she's on her way to Trincomalee in Ceylon, by way of Sumatra. There's an RAF Dakota fitted with long-range fuel tanks leaving here within the hour for Ceylon, and Colonel McHugh has arranged for you to be on it. It will be tight getting you there before she leaves, but if all goes well you'll just make it."

Anna asked, "Where is it going?"

"The final destination is still a highly held secret but I can tell you: it's New York."

The two looked at each other and at Bond with surprise. Alex said, "Isn't all of that desert between the Arabian Peninsula and the Atlantic Ocean going to be a problem for a flying boat?"

"I'm sure you guys will figure it all out."

A CNAC clerk in Li Shih's employ overheard William Bond's instructions to the young American couple, and as soon as he was alone, he dutifully relayed the information to his master.

Li Shih's first reaction was that he had missed his opportunity. He was sure there was some way he could use the unique Russian for profit, but they were leaving before he could assemble all of the nuggets of information he needed to develop a suitable plan. Curses on their ancestors! She would have been the perfect instrument to gather Allied intelligence. Then, he thought of Arnaud DeRuffe!

CHAPTER 24

▼

FLIGHT

Kunming, Yunnan
18 December, 1941

Anna's journal
In flight and in Kunming, Yunnan Province
1941, December 18

Just before we left, we all gathered around the CNAC shortwave and listened to the war news. Almost all of it was bad. First, there was the ongoing news of Hong Kong. All of General Maltby's remaining forces have
now retreated to the Island. Kowloon and Kai Tak are under Japanese control. I can only imagine the horrors my old colleagues are going through as
captives and what will surely ensue when they take Victoria, as they surely
will. I know only too well what will happen to the Caruthers025, my friends
and that poor Ms. Belinda.

The next bad news was that the battleships Repulse and the Prince of
Wales were sunk by Japanese planes not far from Malaya. Alex says the
debate that has raged in admiralties around the world for the last twenty
years should now be settled for the last time. Last year it was the German
battleship Bismarck, then all those battleships at Pearl and now this—all
sunk by airplanes that in terms of national treasure cost less than one of
those ships guns! And to think, these were the ships that so many in Hong

Kong had staked their safety! Alex says that the day of the battleship is now gone forever.

Back on the 11th, it was official! Germany declared war on the United States. Alex said the same thing as Bond: it was probably the biggest mistake Hitler ever made. It will take time, but with America now in the war, because of the men and machines at her disposal, Germany, Japan and Italy will be defeated at the cost of unthinkable lives and treasure.

In Manila and the Philippines, all of the news is bad. The Japanese are advancing on all fronts. Alex's base at Cavite has been obliterated. The outcome seems to be very bleak indeed for the allies. I can't help but wonder how Billy is faring.

The only good news came from Wake Island. Alex had spoken with their Commanding Officer on his flight out from San Francisco; at that time, they hadn't even received their combat aircraft. From the news, however, it looks like they got them. The question remains though, how many did they get, and how many are left? Amazingly, with only a handful of marines and some Pan Am construction workers they have so far managed to repel a sea attack. From what we could gather in Chongqing, the free world news media is making the best of it, as it is the only good news from the war.

Chongqing has changed a lot since the Kuomintang and the Communists, although separately, are actually working together to defeat the Japanese. There seems to be a grim optimism among everyone that now that the United States is in the war it will only be a matter of time until these barbarians are defeated.

Neither of us had been to Kunming before—way out here in Yunnan province. On the approach to the airport, we crossed a beautiful lake and were told by the pilots that much of their time off duty is spent there fishing and swimming when the weather permits. We did not have the opportunity to go into town, as there was only time to eat and to refuel before continuing on to Trincomalee via Lashio and Rangoon in Burma.

We ate at the CNAC crew hostel during our stopover. The facility was better than I would have expected, and the food was excellent. There were several AVG pilots there and they were speaking about the possibility that the Burma Road would be cut if the Japanese were not stopped in southern Burma. The good news is that today the Tigers intercepted a formation on their way to Kunming and shot down nine of the ten bombers. They also confirmed the bad news we heard in Chongqing about the lack of spare parts. They said they were still able to conduct operations, but just!

I wonder how my parent's are faring under the Japanese. Even though I am not as religious as Mama and Papa would have liked, I pray for them daily.

Anna's journal
Kunming—Lashio
1941, 19 December

It was cold in Kunming. With the last of his money, Alex bought me a traditional Chinese quilted coat from a cart merchant outside of our hostel. It is probably a good thing, as Alex said the winters in New York and Washington can be brutal in January. It's bound be better than just the army blanket over my shoulders that I have been using so far. I thought it a real thoughtful thing to do, and I love him even more for it.

On departure, we had a wonderful view of the Burma Road. For as far as you could see it was crowded with trucks carrying the stuff of war. As we climbed to cross the southern part of "The Hump," we could see it winding its way to west like a giant snake. It made us both think of 'The Crocodile' as those poor refugees tried to find safety in Hong Kong. Alex said this southern route was nothing compared to the dangers of the northern route to Assam. Everyone is talking about it as an alternate way to get supplies into China from India should Burma be occupied and the Burma Road cut.

Alex is a horrible passenger. He has a hard time just sitting there and looking out of the window. Even now, he has spelled the captain and is sitting up front as I pen these words. The pilot gladly accepted his offer for help as they have been flying continuously since the war began.

More bad news for battleships! The radio operator tuned in the BBC and heard the RAF just attacked two German battle cruisers in France. He didn't get the German ship's names very well but he thought one was the Scarnhorst and the other sounded like Geesenhow? Not a good time for ships these days!

The British are holding their own the in North African desert. Rommel, the vaunted German Commander, is retreating to a place called Tobruk. When we are settled, I must get another atlas and find out where these places are!

The other good news is that my countrymen are giving the German Army hell for being in mother Russia. They have stopped their advances and have succeeded in driving them out of someplace called Klin....

Anna's journal
Lashio—Rangoon
1941, 19 December

On landing in Lashio, we flew into a beehive of activity. Everyone was busy repairing bomb craters on the landing strip or improving the make-shift airport. After dropping dispatches and a Chinese liaison officer, we were off again to Rangoon and our last fuel stop on the way to Ceylon.

Anna's journal
Rangoon, Burma
1941, 20 December

It was supposed to be a quick fuel stop but that was not to be. A few hours delay turned into three days! It seems our Dakota was requisitioned to fly ammunition from this major lend-lease supply depot to the British fighter base called Highland Queen. Seems they encountered engine problems there and did not get back to Rangoon until the afternoon of the 23rd just after a major bombing attack on that city.

It was during this time that we got a measure of the hatred for anything British in this part of the world. When the Japanese bombers arrived over-head, many just ordinary citizens ran into the streets cheering on the Japanese and yelling things like, "Strike them hard boys, give it to them" only to be killed by their falling bombs moments later.

Alex and I watched the whole air battle from a trench just outside of the RAF Officers Club. They came on and on in their traditional Vee-formation as RAF and AVG fighters rose to shoot them down. And shoot them down they did! Fighters and bombers from both sides were falling like fowl at a hunting shoot. We saw at least eight airplanes fall from the sky but from our vantage point in the trench, it was impossible to say who was getting the better measure.

When we left that evening, our Dakota pilot told Alex that more than a thousand civilians were killed that day. Already they were calling it the battle of Rangoon. No one expects the city to hold out for very long against the expected air and land invasion. There seems to be little heart to fight in the indigenous troops and even less in the civilians.

It is supposed to be hot where we are going, so before I left, I managed to buy part of a small Indian soldier's kit consisting of shorts, a belt, one OD tee shirt, a singlet and his regulation field blouse complete with epaulettes and large patch pockets. Just as soon as I make alterations, I should have something to wear in the warmer climates of Ceylon, India and Africa. The quilted coat Alex bought me won't be of much use again until we get to New York. Alterations—then sleep!....

Li Shih knew that all out going wireless messages from Chongqing were being monitored by Tai-Li's Kuomintang intelligence organization. If Chiang Kai-shek wasn't already suspicious of everyone he was doubly so after Pearl Harbor. He only knew that the first leg of the message would be by civilian cable to a manufacturer in California. It would appear as a normal business communication explaining that because of the war the usual shipments of Wolfram (or Tungsten as the Americans call it) that had previously gone by way of Hong Kong would now be considerably delayed.

In reality, the message was in code. In California, before passing the communication on to the receiving department of his import company, Strategic Resources Inc., the clerk, as always, copied the message by hand, and when he returned to his home after work that evening, he methodically decoded the message and complied with the decrypted instructions. This he dutifully did for his masters in China and Japan. Then, as usual, he re-encoded the message and sent it on to its final addressee, again by Western Union. The intended recipient this time was a Mr. Henri Piccard, in Washington, D.C.—a name that appeared more frequently in the decoded messages since the beginning of the war.

CHAPTER 25

▼

TRINCOMALEE

Rangoon—Trincomalee
24 December, 1941

RAF Dakota

Alex was being chased through rice paddies by faceless men in uniform. It was the recurring dream of the last days since Hong Kong. He was being shaken from side to side when a cockney voice said, "Sorry to disturb you suh! We have started our descent into Trinco suh! You and the misses are going to have to return to your benches and fasten up your seat belts; you see!"

"Uh yes! Thank you Corporal." He looked up to see the Royal Air Force flight mechanic.

Alex rubbed the sleep from his eyes remembering now where he was. He looked at his watch and calculated that they had been en route now for almost ten hours.

"Beggin your pardon suh, but if it's all the same to you, I'll leave it to you to wake the missus…we have about ten minutes before we land."

Anna was still blissfully asleep on a pallet she had made of blankets and her quilted coat. He shook her gently and said, "Wake up Princess; we're about to land in Trincomalee where hopefully, our magic carpet is still waiting to take us to your new home in America."

Still half-asleep, she sat up from the pallet she had made for herself, stretched, and crawled on her knees to look out of the Dakota's small window. She had no sooner peered through the window when she said, "Oh Alex...look! There it is now. There's the Clipper down on the water."

Alex squatted, pressed his face to the window with her, and caught a glimpse of the graceful flying boat almost lost in the reflected sunlight shimmering off of the waters of the Trincomalee naval base.

"Pretty sight, huh Princess? As much as I see them, I never get tired of the sight...simply beautiful!"

"I hope you say the same thing about me after I've been around about ten years!"

Alex put his arms around her and massaged her shoulders gently. "Come on darling...let's sit down and fasten in before the corporal throws us off of Her Majesty's royal airplane."

They both sat down on the long bench leading up the side of the utilitarian Dakota; what the British called a C–47, the military version of the DC–3. As they fastened their seat belts, the Corporal said, "Begging your pardon sir...the radio operator says you're to be met as soon as we land and be taken straight away to the Pan American seaplane what's down floating on Trinco bay."

Alex thanked the Corporal just as the engine's hypnotic drone of the last ten hours changed to the unsynchronized thrum of descent. The gear and flaps were lowered and in minutes they we were on the ground.

The aerodrome officer in charge met the couple and explained that the Clipper captain was in a great hurry. On their arrival, they had spotted a Japanese submarine not far from the base. He went on to explain they had taken off that morning but had to return due to an engine problem; the whole base was on alert. No one knew for sure when a Japanese attack might come. The officer had a Royal Navy staff car and driver waiting. After they said their goodbyes to the Dakota crew, they were off to join the Clipper.

Everywhere they looked soldiers and sailors were stacking sand bags and improving defensive positions. The naval staff car whisked them quickly through the naval base and took them to a waiting launch. Soon, they were speeding across the bay to the Clipper moored in the lee of land just at the mouth of the harbor.

Anna had seen the Boeing 314 only a few times before it was replaced by the venerable Sikorsky, now at the bottom of Kowloon bay. Months before the war began, Pan Am had taken the Boeing off of the Hong Kong run and used its greater range in their expanding South Pacific service.

When they flew over the flying boat, they had noticed the normal bright aluminum finish had been painted over with a flat grey paint. Up close, it was even more noticeable. The barely discernable American flag on the nose, the registry, everything had been painted out.

The crew had positioned a marine float under the right wing. It was tethered between the end of the wing and the huge sea wing, or sponsons, at the inboard end. As the launch prepared to dock against the sea wing, Alex explained the sponsons not only gave the seaplane stability on the water but also provided storage for a good portion of the Clipper's fuel.

Two men in Pan Am coveralls turned to look at the approaching launch. They were standing on the engine's built in work platforms that had been swung out directly from the engine. Alex wondered what the problem was that caused them to return as the launch crew coiled lines preparing to make fast to the sea wing.

Alex recognized First Officer John Henry Mack standing on the sponson. He remembered he had met Mack in San Francisco in one of the company's many pilot training courses. The Royal Navy crew throttled back the launch's engine and tied up to the sponson.

After so long away from home any woman's presence on their home of the last three weeks would have been reason enough to interrupt their work routines, but standing there, on the gentle breezes of the bay, in her bush shirt and modified army shorts, Anna brought their labors to a complete standstill.

A seaman helped her out of the launch as Mack let out a low whistle in appreciation of their visitors. As Anna stepped onto the sea wing Mack said, "Alex, what in the name of Sam Hill are you doing in Ceylon, and who is your beautiful companion?"

"Hey Mack…long time no see! This is my wife Anna of only two weeks; we came here hoping to hitch a ride to the states. We just got married in Hong Kong to celebrate the start of World War II."

Anna said, "Pleased to meet you John Henry Mack. We were afraid you might have already left."

"Charmed, Anna…simply charmed. You two birds are lucky! Just after we returned this morning, we received a 'high priority signal,' as the Brits call it. It was so high priority it sat in somebody's in basket until we had already taken off! It said we had two uppity-up passengers en route to Trinco from China. It told us to wait even though we had already left! If we hadn't lost number three, you two would have *missed the boat*, no pun intended…must be your lucky day!"

"Missed the boat?…come on Mack, cut me some slack. The Brit Officer over at the field said you were in a hurry but guess that's not the case if that engine is still on the fritz?"

Mack motioned in the direction of the two engineers up on the wing and said, "Yeah, no hurry now except for them. Number three blew on takeoff out of here."

Mack continued, "You're really full of surprises, aren't you? Last I heard you were transferring to Cavite and now you show up here with this beautiful creature on your arm."

"Johnny Mack: since I've known Alex he has always called me 'Princess', and now, after knowing you less than a minute, I have been relegated to creature. Besides, if you knew the things about Alex that I knew, you wouldn't be surprised at all."

"I'm sure I wouldn't want to know Alex that well, Mrs. Cannon...ah 'Princess'! Seriously, though, what gives you guys the horsepower to hold the Clipper and join us in Ceylon?"

"It's kind of a long story, John. Anna is a CNAC employee...used to work out of Hong Kong. Because of some personal knowledge she gained over the years, and some other circumstances we can't talk about, she has been elected a de-facto courier. Some stuff has come her way that some people in the States felt important enough to get her back as soon as possible. She needs to be along to explain some of its content. Besides, it's the only way we could figure to finagle a free honeymoon trip out of Pan Am."

Mack laughed and said, "Alex, you're as full of it as ever."

"Man, are we glad we caught up with you! We knew it would be tight especially after the delay in Rangoon. Introduce me to the rest of the crew and I'll fill everybody in on how we ended up on your doorstep."

"You might not think you are so lucky when you hear what we're up to! The skipper is busy now with Rod Brown...Brown's the nav. We're planning to go westbound to the States. Both the skipper and New York figure it's probably the best way to avoid both the Japs and the Krauts and get the ship home safely. In spite of the lack of suitable landing places for a seaplane, it's the best we can come up with, but won't know for sure until we get there. Come on topside and we'll get the straight dope from the skipper and Brown."

"Sounds like old home week! Mack...who's the captain, anyhow?"

"Bob Ford...he's topside, now."

"Bob Ford? I hear he's the best. After flying across the Pacific with Neville Brewster, I'd say I'm first in line for a break!"

"Brewster! You poor S.O.B.! I'd say you're due for a change in luck. Come on aboard, you two. I'll introduce you to the skipper. Ford will give you the straight scoop on what we're planning."

The three stepped into the fuselage and were surprised to see two partially built up engines chocked on pallets and chained in place. There were boxes of spares and parts everyplace they looked. File boxes of company records were stacked and strapped down where passenger seats would have normally been.

Somewhere in the airplane, they could hear the soft purring of an auxiliary power generator. Mack saw his guests' expression and said, "The parts were evacuated from Noumea, New Caledonia, along with all of the Pan Am people there. We dropped most of their station people in Australia, but Ralph Hitchcock and Bud Washer are going with us as far as Bahrain to set up a new station there. Going the long way around with no Pan Am maintenance or any spares, we thought we could use all the parts and help we could get."

As they walked forward in the Clipper Anna said, "Where are all of the beautiful furnishings you always see on the posters and in the advertisements?"

Mack responded over his shoulder, "It's not the Clipper of your honeymoon dreams, is it…just kidding. No…really, we needed to take off as much weight as possible in order to load enough gasoline to make some of the long legs. Ford will fill you in when we get to the flight deck."

Almost all the plush furnishings had been removed. With the exception of the galley and a few seats for the crew, the luxurious first-class accommodations were all but gone.

The threesome climbed the steps to the bridge. As large as the Boeing's flight deck was it, was crammed with busy crewmembers. Captain Bob Ford was leaning over the navigation table with Rod Brown. All of the crew had shed their Pan Am navy blue uniforms normally rigidly required by company regulations. Most had traded them for shorts and open neck shirts of various descriptions.

Rod Brown was laying out a course line on a chart with a parallel rule and picking off distances with his dividers. A radio operator Alex did not recognize was seated as his station, a headset clamped to his ears. He ignored the crowd, listening to radio traffic and making notes in a logbook. His, and every other head in the cockpit turned as Anna, followed by Alex and Mack, climbed the last step to the flight deck.

"Captain Ford, this is Second Officer Alex Cannon from the late *Hong Kong Clipper*, and this is his wife Anna. They were getting tired of the war in China and decided to join us for a honeymoon trip to the states."

Alex broke in, "He's only partially right Captain Ford. I was with Fred Ralph on December eighth. We were trying bug out of Hong Kong with the Clipper when the Japs attacked. They sank her in Kowloon Bay, right in front of our eyes!"

Ford asked, "What happened to the rest of the crew?"

Alex continued, "William Bond, the CNAC operations director managed to get most of the CNAC people and some major Chinese officials to the interior and then on to Chongqing. Bond got in contact with New York and they gave us our marching orders. They sent the rest of Ralph's crew to Calcutta. Somehow, they have arranged to get them home from there. They told us to rendezvous with your ship as they thought you would get back first."

"How did you two manage to get here?"

"We hitch hiked with the Brits on a Dakota from Chongqing to Kunming, and stayed with them through Lashio, Rangoon and on in to here. Rangoon is really taking a pasting. As for the honeymoon suite, Anna and I will take anything you care to offer."

Ford smiled and said, "Now that's a story that will rival our own!" He smiled and extended his hand to Alex and Anna and said, "Welcome aboard. How much do you two weigh?"

Anna was taken a little aback, but Alex understood immediately and said, "Together with the little stuff we have, I would say both of us are just a little over 300 pounds, Captain."

"What the heck...as much over grossed we have been during this sojourn, what's a few pounds more? We must have left at least that much weight behind in busted engine parts...we've had bad luck finding aviation gas along the way and have been eating exhaust pork chops like candy. Anna, a pork chop is a metal plate used to hold the exhaust stacks in place. Anyhow, in a lot of places, best we've been able to pick up is car gas...they advertise 78 Octane, but I would be surprised if it is even as much as that. With the exception of military bases, it's about as good as it gets in this part of the world."

Ford went on, "You might have seen Swede Rothe and Jocko Parish out on the wing when you came alongside in the launch. They are changing a jug on the number three engine. It blew about thirty minutes after takeoff...damned car gas...causes pre-ignition, and the detonation just lifted the cylinder, studs and all, right off the engine. It has really been testing how well the Wright people put these engines together. With all the detonation going on at high power, I'm surprised any of them have held together this long."

"What's the gas prospect for the rest of the trip?"

"Brown and I just got back from British military headquarters in Colombo. We picked up some intelligence on the military situation...got some charts, dinner, some sleep and little else. We had a gracious invitation to dine with General Wavell, the CO. As it turned out, General Wavell was away on military business so we only embarrassed ourselves in front of his wife and other guests by falling asleep at the table. Mrs. Wavell was a real lady though…acted like it never happened."

Brown said, "Yeah, Cap…just wait until you get the letter from Trippe!"

Everyone laughed.

"We got some good poop about our route, but not much information on the availability of aviation gasoline. As you might expect, the military is keeping the good stuff for their fighters. You couldn't expect them to get in a mix up with the Japs using car gas, now could you? About the only good news is that if number three hadn't blown, and we hadn't come back, you and your new wife would have missed us."

"Johnny Mack said we would have missed the boat," Anna said.

"Please, Anna…don't encourage him."

Ford continued, "Just as soon as they have the engine buttoned up, we're out of here for Karachi. Maybe you don't know…on our way in we were flying low, below the clouds, and saw a Japanese sub…could be just a patrol, or could be part of an invasion fleet…no one knows for sure, so we're leaving ASAP."

As if on cue Swede Rothe and Jocko Parish, the two flight engineers, dropped down into the bridge through the overhead hatch leading to the top of the Boeing's wing.

"Swede…Jocko: maybe you two know Alex Cannon; this is his new wife as of the day World War II started."

"Sure we know Mr. Cannon from our Martin days! We saw you two come aboard and I damned near dropped my socket wrench in the water when we saw the misses…congratulations you two!"

"Ms. Cannon this is Swede Rothe and Jocko Parish. Without them and the assistance they got from Mr. White and Mr. Washer, this lash-up wouldn't have gotten this far much less the rest of the way round the world."

Anna extended her hand regardless of the fact the two flight engineers were covered with grease. She said, "Glad you didn't drop your tool on account of me!"

"Glad to make your acquaintance Ms. Cannon…that husband of yours never got us lost so lets hope he steers a good course for the both of you!"

"How's the engine coming, Swede?"

"We need to have Poindexter call the launch. We've got to get to shore and scrounge some stuff to get the studs out. Shouldn't be too hard with all the machine shops they have for working on ships."

Rothe tapped Poindexter on the shoulder who was still busily copying messages into his logbook. He pulled off his headset and looked around the bridge as if it were the first time he were aware there were others there. With his headset in his hand, he turned to the gathered group.

"It's confirmed! I just got word from Pearl. The Japs have taken Wake! No one knows what's happened to the marines and the Pan Am people there that didn't get away with the Clipper. Word from Pearl is...they did themselves proud. They got five ships...sunk em, they did. A cruiser, two destroyers, a gunboat and a submarine...all that with a measly five inch and a three and a half inch gun! Air did O.K. too! Shot down a whole slew of Japs with what they could cobble together from what was left of their fighters after the first attack."

Alex said, "On my last outbound trip to Hong Kong I met their CO. An old time marine...the guy's name was Devereux. A Major. God bless them...must have fought like demons with what they had!"

Ford asked, "Any word on the Clipper that was at Wake when they first attacked?"

"Nothing more than we already know. Somehow they managed to get out...took a lot of the Pan Am people with them, but that's all we know right now."

"I'll bet when we finally find out what happened that will be some story, people."

Mack said, "That makes four Clippers that fell into harm's way on the first day of the war. Do you think any other airline could make that claim?"

"Just CNAC," Anna said. "You know we lost everything at Hong Kong with the exception of two DC–3s, one DC–2 and what we could fly out."

"Yeah...some claim," somebody said. The crew nodded grimly and returned to their task of getting their Boeing the rest of the way around the world, on the edge of a war, with almost no support.

In a short time, the navy launch arrived with the two stewards, a Naval Lieutenant and two other Pan Am employees: Verne White and Bud Washer. They had been ashore trying to find critical tools to effect the repair on the blown cylinder head.

The lieutenant was shown to the bridge where he reported to Captain Ford. With the customary double stomp and vibratory crisp salute he said, "Suh! Wing Commander Harris sends his compliments Suh. Suh, the Wing Commander requests the pleasure of your company at his quarters for a 'little Christmas celebration'. Your entire crew and passengers are invited. If that meets with your approval, he will have his barge sent around at five o'clock to take you all to his quarters, Suh."

Bob Ford looked at his watch. "There is no way we will finish replacing that jug and be ready before dark so we'll just plan on leaving in the morning. Tell your base commander that we would be delighted to share Christmas with his family and guests."

Swede, Jocko and the lieutenant left in the launch to look for the tools they needed.

Ford turned back to Alex and Anna and said, "As scarce as air transport is these days, you two must have had someone high up the totem pole trying to get you home."

Alex replied, "It's really Anna, skipper. She has some information that she tried to get out on the last eastbound Clipper to the states. The air authorizations for transport to here came through the ONI chief in Chongqing. The Pan Am authorizations came from New York."

"What about you, Alex?"

"Pan Am wants all their straggler pilots in Dinner Key. They said get to Miami, as soon as possible. Pearl left pilots strewn all over the Pacific. In that we were both going the same way, it made sense for Bond to have me escort Anna back to the States. Kind of kills two birds with one stone. Sorry if it's an imposition, but that's what we have been told to do."

Bob Ford paused a moment as he thoughtfully regarded Anna. "Mr. and Mrs. Cannon, nothing gives me more pleasure than to help you two get back home. You must really have something awfully important that will contribute to winning this damned war."

"Thanks Captain. Anna and I will do everything we can to help carry our weight...no pun intended!"

"And to think I thought Mack's puns were bad! Don't worry Alex; we'll make good use of you two. Right now, you can go below with Mack and stow your stuff. Find yourself a comfortable spot in the rear. Barney Sawicki or Verne Edwards will give you a hand. When you've stowed your things, how about coming back to the bridge and get together with Brown, Henrikson and Steers to familiarize yourself with what we're planning."

Johnny Mack led them below to the rear of the airplane. They found a place near the tail where several empty mailbags were stowed in a small aft cabin in the Boeing. Barney Sawicki helped them with blankets and two Pullman mattresses they had not left behind. The doors and bulkheads between the cabin's had been removed to save weight and make room for the cargo. Being the only female aboard, Anna took one of the blankets and hung it from the cabin's ceiling for privacy. The small space they had staked out for themselves for the rest of the journey would offer the only privacy they were to have.

Alex returned to the bridge to give Brown a hand. Anna went to the rear lavatory and took off her shorts and army shirt to give herself a sponge bath from the sink. What a Christmas Eve, she thought! Instead of a romantic honeymoon she had always dreamed about—the kind they had always had in the movies, here she was, with a new husband, running for their lives in this overloaded seaplane, without the right kind of fuel to keep its motors from coming apart. A lot better off than those left behind in Hong Kong, Shanghai or Nanking, she thought. She wondered how their voyeurs from the Pen's lobby, the Caruthers family and Bonnie Belinda were fairing.

As she did every day, Anna thought about her parents. The last time she had seen them was '37—just before the Japanese invaded. The memory of leaving Billy at the Shanghai docks, his reluctance to give her the money he owed, that pig Rabin gloating over Tanya's murder and then running away when her parents were left to cope for themselves—it was a recurring scene; a recording she played over and over in her mind—she had run for her life, and left them alone. Since then, every time she thought about it, she felt tremendous guilt. She simply must do something to get word to them—to see if they were well—to do something to get them free from the Japanese! Maybe now, as a citizen of the world, she could at last do something. Right now, though, she had not the slightest idea what that might be.

Through the portal of the lavatory, Anna saw the launch returning from shore. It was the two flight engineers: Jocko and Swede. The launch went to the bow of the Clipper, hooked on, and after casting off from their mooring began towing them towards the inner harbor. She finished dressing and went forward to find the two flight engineers had only spent a little time looking for the required parts and tools when they were invited by the Royal Navy to have the Clipper towed to a ship maintenance dock for their repairs. There, they had access to machine tools, compressors and calm water to work on the blown cylinder head.

CHAPTER 26

▼

CHRISTMAS EVE

Trincomalee
24 December, 1941

At five o'clock a bus, rather than a barge, pulled up to the Clipper that was now tied to the ship repair dock. Alex, Anna and the entire crew boarded for the short trip to the Wing Commander's home.

Anna wore the only dress she had. It was the flowered silk one she had packed as an afterthought just after the attack on Hong Kong begun. Captain Ford and the rest of the crew were dressed as best as they could for the occasion in the few remaining pieces of uniform that weren't ruined or relegated to a laundry bag. Anna thought Alex quite the handsome young husband, thankful for the camouflaging effect his navy uniform jacket had on dried blood from the Japanese barber.

Christmas Eve notwithstanding, the base was still a pother of activity. Lookouts were standing at their posts scanning the skies for enemy aircraft. Everywhere, sailors and laborers were stacking sandbags preparing defensive positions. All of their actions belied the holiday; the sense of imminent invasion permeated everyone's activities.

When the bus arrived at the wing commander's quarters, an aide was waiting to show them inside. A manservant and houseboy took their drink orders as they entered the house. When they stepped into the foyer, Wing Commander Harris and his wife greeted the Clipper crew with genuine warmth and hospitality. The extent of the preparations the Harrises had made were evident everywhere. Considering the limited resources in the sub-tropical climate, the decorations were extraordinary. Someone had woven ribbons together with bougainvillea creating a chain of color for a long table set up as a makeshift bar. In place of traditional wreathes, woven palm fronds interlaced with indigenous flowers served as substitutes. The Harrises' improvised decorations reminded everyone of the season even though all of the guests were thousands of miles from home.

As Anna walked into the living room one of the guest said, "My word, there's living proof; there really is a God!"

Hors d'oeuvres were passed around to the guests. Everyone in the crew was careful to limit their drinks as they had an early departure and wanted to be at peak performance.

As she tasted the foie gras, Anna remarked, "Leave it to you British! Regardless of the circumstances you will always manage to turn up good spirits and hors d'oeuvres."

Introductions were made and the officers in the group immediately engaged the crew with questions regarding their escape from the South Pacific, but before the story was told, a series of toasts began—first to the King George, then to Franklin Roosevelt, and to their guests, the Pan American crew, their passengers and the war effort.

Captain Ford stood, and although generally a taciturn man he toasted the King, Winston Churchill and their host.

A few of the officers gathered around the piano and sang the "Whiffenpoof Song." The Americans gave their best rendition of "Silent Night," and all soon joined in for a good try at "Auld Lang Syne." Anna held Alex loosely around the waist and she hummed along with the rest of the guests to their foreign, melancholy Christmas music. Helped along with the generous supply of spirits and the American crew, the British tried their own rendition of "Home on the Range."

Soon, many of the curious guests gravitated to where Captain Ford was standing. They asked how they began the round the world odyssey that had brought them to Ceylon.

Ford was generally a laconic man, comfortable with command, but not given to long speeches, or story telling. Nevertheless, he felt he owed his gracious host and their guests his best try.

He began, "We were on the fourth leg of our flight from San Francisco to New Zealand. About two hours out of Auckland, Gene Leach, our relief radio operator, was on duty. He came bursting into the cockpit waving this message in his hand saying, 'Pearl Harbor is being bombed!'"

Well, as you all know, tensions had been running high in the Pacific for some time; so back in New York, our boss, Juan Trippe, had his operations people draw up contingency plans for all of our crews. I dug ours out of the ship's safe and began to try to comply with the directives. We have some pretty smart eggs in New York, and it looked to me like they had given these plans a lot of thought."

One of the RAF officers said, "At least your blokes took the Japs seriously and had a plan! Can you give us an idea of what they said?"

"Sure...nothing to hide at this stage. Most of the stuff was just common sense.

"We darkened the aircraft, ceased to transmit on the ship's radio, posted a lookout, and proceeded to the safest port within our range, which was our destination, Auckland. I even broke out the ship's pistol as indicated in the orders and checked the chambers to see that it was in working condition. I sent for Barney, our steward, and asked him to check the passengers for anyone who looked like he might be a potential threat. I told him to be discreet so as not to give away what was happening.

"Now there was good reason for that last one. In '38, we lost the *Hong Kong Clipper*...absolutely no word from her before she disappeared. A lot of people at our headquarters in New York still are not entirely convinced that ship wasn't hi-jacked by the Japanese because of a courier onboard carrying a lot of money to Chiang Kai-shek. In addition, there was reason to believe the Japanese wanted to copy the airplane's design.

"After we arrived in Auckland, we spent the next couple of days trying to get direction from New York. Information was kind of hard to come by since Pearl. The military, embassy, and even Pan Am were coding all of their messages by then, and of course, they all had to be decoded at the Auckland end. All of that took a lot of time and really backed up the messages coming out of the Embassy.

"In the meantime, we heard the Japanese had bombed Wake, Midway, Hong Kong and the Philippines. Everyone reasoned there were better than even odds the Japanese would bomb and probably invade the Hawaiian Islands at any time. We figured that the company would not want us to go back the way we came as that possibility was, and still is, just too great. So, while we waited, we started getting ready to come this way—the long way home, if you will.

"We gathered up all the charts for this part of the world: Sumatra, Java, India, the Arab countries, Africa...everything we could get our hands on. Onboard, we only had charts as far as Australia where we normally turn around...after that, we didn't have anything going this way. We ended up going to the public library to get the geographical coordinates of the primary stops and waypoints along our route. Other than Atlases and some sailing directions from the Navy, there just wasn't much available. Rod...Tell us what you did with all those coordinates."

Rod Brown shyly said, "Well, basically, we figured we could make our own crude charts using just the lat/long coordinates for prominent land marks, our departure point and our destinations. I took the coordinates of the waypoints we collected, scaled them off on graph paper and drew a course line. Then I sketched in the lat/long of any prominent landmarks we might be able to see visually along the way. You know...big mountains, capes and the like. Since we were using celestial as the primary navigation, all we were interested in was lat/long positions of those landmarks. From that we could figure what our celestial shots should look like at that point and use the information for course corrections and to update our flight plan."

Most of the flight officers present looked perplexed. Few, if any, had any training in aerial celestial navigation.

One of the naval officers present said, "Jolly good show...and all without charts, what? Brilliant...corresponding the prominent land marks with the expected altitudes and azimuths of your celestial shots, what?"

"Yes sir, that's about it...so far, it has worked O.K."

Ford continued, "It's good we did all that preparation because when the message did come through, they wanted us to do just that: Fly home westbound. First, though, they wanted us to go back to Noumea, New Caledonia, pick up all of our Pan Am station people and get them out of harm's way. Some are with us now on their way to man new stations we are setting up in the Middle East because of the war. From what we hear, the war department has contracted with Pan Am to start regular routes from the States, Eastbound: all the way out to India, Burma and China...what you chaps are now calling the CBI.

"While we were in Noumea, we loaded a spare engine that was there. We figured with no support there was a good chance we might need it. You sure don't find many GR 2600's in this part of the world, and we have already used a lot of those parts.

"Also, we tankered as much aviation gas from Noumea as the Clipper would hold. We knew it would be tough talking military commanders out of aviation gas when it was needed for their fighters. I can just hear it now, 'Sorry about the 78 octane petrol, Reginald...we just gave it to the yanks! They need it so they can safely fly off to New York, you know. If the Japs get on your tail, you'll just have to use gravity to out run them, what?"

Everyone laughed as Ford continued.

"Next we flew back to Gladstone, Australia, and off-loaded our Noumea station people. Many were planning to make their way back to the United States by ship. It was there that I had the brilliant idea to camouflage the Clipper. That almost turned out to be our un-doing. We painted out the whole seaplane...even painted out the American flag on the nose of the ship. Except for a sharp-eyed Dutch naval pilot, painting over that flag almost got us shot down! I'll get to that in a minute."

"What route did you take to get here Captain Ford?" The question came from one of the naval officers.

"After Gladstone, we considered taking the long way around Australia by the coast. The idea was we could effect a water landing in an emergency. Landing in the desert is not the approved way to scrape barnacles off of the ships hull!"

There was more laughter from the crowd.

"Anyhow, we decided on the direct route. Gladstone didn't have aviation gasoline and we figured we had just enough aboard from Noumea to make it if we flew directly to Port Darwin. That we did. Since we had no charts, we relied on the skills of Rod Brown and Jim Henrikson. They simply plotted a direct course to Darwin's lat/long and away we went. It was almost all dead reckoning checking our DR with sun lines."

Ford stopped and took a sip from the glass of water he had been nursing since the end of the toast. He continued, "Darwin was truly Darwinian! Everybody there had his or her own war rumor. 'The Jap fleet was heading their way; they would attack at dawn'...any rumor you cared to believe was there for your picking. On top of that, it seemed that almost everyone in the city was doing their best to drink all of the alcohol before the Japs arrived. Anyhow, we got on with our work, notified the Navy of our next intended stop in Surabaya and received the proper procedures and signals for the approach and landing at the naval base there. After a night of intense electrical storms, we got away the next morning at dawn again loaded down with as much good gas as we could take.

It was only about an eight hour flight to Surabaya, but gentlemen, were we in for a surprise. Now I know this never happens in the Royal Air Force or Navy, but believe it or not the Dutch didn't get the word that a U.S. registered flying boat was coming their way!"

Again, there was laughter from the crowd of mixed officers.

"Working from the information we received from the Navy at Darwin, we flew over the prescribed authentication check point on the right heading and at the right altitude. Nevertheless, we were intercepted by a flight of Dutch Brewster Buffaloes who had me pretty well convinced they were intent on shooting us down. Here we were, this big lumbering flying boat in this makeshift camou-flaged paint job flying toward their base where the Japs were expected to attack at any time. They hadn't got the message we were coming their way…what would you have thought? Jap bomber…shoot them down…right? Well luckily they didn't. We weren't able to speak with them as they had different frequencies than we did. One of their sharp eyed pilots saw the American flag through the bad paint job, put two and two together, and escorted us the rest of the way to the base."

"We thought we were out of the woods when we landed, but oh no…not yet! After we splashed down, a patrol boat came toward us but stopped some distance away. The boat's crew was waving this flag at us like mad men trying to get us to follow them toward a buoy. At the time, we didn't know what they wanted, but later we found out; seems like we had managed to land in the middle of a mine-field. The only thing that saved our bacon was our dumb luck and our shallow draft. We landed in the shallow water…where the mines weren't."

A murmur went through the crowd of guests as they made their personal rejoinders.

Someone from the crowd said, "Captain Ford, someone said you saw a Japa-nese sub not far from here."

"Yes we did…and I'll get to that in a moment, sir. I just want to say that once the Dutch found out who we were, they couldn't have been more hospitable. They fed us, they housed us, gave us shots for tropical diseases and charts; but they wouldn't turn loose of any avgas. With regret, we had to leave these fine people and get on our way here to Trinco. A note about the engines…In that the best we could get in Surabaya was 78 octane car gas, we had to figure out a way to get here without destroying our engines. This we almost succeeded in doing…almost!

"Our two flight engineers, who even as I speak are down at the docks working on the Clipper's number three, devised a way to use the little 100 octane fuel we had left just for takeoff and climb. They figured, correctly so, that our high com-pression engines would need the good fuel mostly at the high power settings required for the initial stages of the flight, when we were heavy. They were right! Everything worked beautifully for takeoff and climb. When we leveled off and switched to the tanks with the car gas, all hell broke loose! Those twenty-six-hun-dreds sounded like they were coming apart: backfiring, popping, flames shooting out of the exhaust stacks; if they kept that up, they were coming unglued for sure…only question was, when? Well, the flight engineers reduced power as much as they dared, played with the mixtures, advance, and revolutions to find the best settings; they kept on doing this for about the first four hours. After that, we had burned enough fuel to where our weight required less power; then the engines settled down. All we had to do for the next 17 hours was hope that the first four hours hadn't done enough damage to cause one or more of the engines to fail. If that had happened, the increased power on the others to maintain flight with the lousy gas might have meant even another failure. That of course would have meant an open sea landing, at night, with no rescue possible, except maybe from the Japanese, who these days own the seas in this part of the world. Everyone did their part in keeping the engines together, but it was mainly our flight engineers. If it wasn't for them and the mechanics we have with us, believe me, we wouldn't be here.

"Because of the cloud cover, Brown and Henrikson weren't able to do their star magic with the octant during the night. At dawn, we decided to descend below the clouds so we could get a visual landfall on Ceylon. We set up a shallow descent, and just as we broke out of the clouds we saw Ceylon dead on our bows. Just as I was spreading the word to the rest of the crew on interphone, Johnny Mack here yelled, 'Japanese submarine straight ahead!' Sure enough, there it was, rising sun on the side and all. The crew were out on the deck, getting some sun and fresh air, and oh what they must have thought when they see this giant airplane barreling down on them!"

More laughter from the small crowd.

"As you might expect, they ran straight for their deck gun but before they could bring it to bear we pulled back up into the clouds! We were perfectly lined up! If we had a couple of bombs we couldn't have missed...could have marked up one Jap sub to the *Pacific Clipper*.

"Anyhow, that's our story...or at least half of it. After all, we still have half the world to cross before we get back home."

Once again, there was the murmur of soft laughter around the room.

Alex had his arm around Anna and whispered, "I had no idea what they went through to get this far! Damned...wouldn't it have been great if they had been carrying bombs?"

"Darling, don't be too impatient. This will be a very long war and I have no doubt you will have many opportunities to place yourself in harm's way. Please don't do so any sooner than you must."

As she looked at his beaming face, Anna had no doubt that her comments fell on deaf ears. He was young, impatient and in his own mind still indestructible. He did not yet know the horror of war, she thought.

Ford tapped on his water glass with a stir-stick and said, "Ah, ladies and gentlemen—while I have the floor, I want to thank all of you...thank you for my entire crew, for the great service and exemplary hospitality you have shown us. Regardless of what's looming over the horizon out there, on behalf of Pan Am, our crew and our nation, I want to wish you all the happiest of Christmases and a New Year that will certainly see the tide of this war turn against the Japs. Without your help, there is no way we could have even made the next leg of this trip."

Wing Commander Harris joined Ford and addressed the group. "I know Captain Ford and his people have an early departure in the morning so just one more toast, sir, and I'll give you your leave...I promise!"

Harris held one hand behind him and held his drink glass at waist level.

"These yanks have accomplished a feat that only a few in the world are capable of. The distances, obstacles, technical and navigational difficulties you have encountered and overcome bring great credit on your crew, your nation and your company. May I wish you, and the *Pacific Clipper* 'God Speed' and a safe passage to New York."

The group responded with a loud, "here...here," and emptied their glasses.

Captain Ford and the rest of the crew shook hands with the gathered officers and their wives, once again wished them luck and said their Farewells one more time.

They were about to depart when Wing Commander Harris approached Ford and said, "I have just one more favor to ask of you sir."

"Sure, anything I can do."

"General Wavell is at the Officer's Club, Captain. He sincerely regrets not having met you at his home. He sends his compliments, and ask if it is not too much of an imposition, would you and your navigation officer drop by the club for a few minutes so that he might pay his respects?"

"Of course, I'd be glad to. We met Mrs. Wavell the first night we were here but didn't have the pleasure of meeting the General."

Minutes later, Ford and Brown were at the club. They were met promptly by the General's Aide de Camp who ushered them into the bar. No one was there with the exception of Ford, Brown and Wing Commander Harris. Presently, the General came into the bar. The Aide dismissed himself leaving the General with the three aviators.

The general was leaning against the bar. He again offered his regrets at having to excuse himself from the dinner engagement. After an exchange of pleasantries and again recounting the highlights of their journey, the General pulled a ten-shilling note from his billfold and used it to write a personal note to Captain

Ford. Ford did the same on a dollar bill for General Wavell. In the tradition of military airmen, they all downed a short round of sherry, bid their goodbyes, and went their separate ways.

CHAPTER 27

▼

FIRST LEG

Pacific Clipper
December, 1941

Anna's journal
Trincomalee—Karachi India   *1520 miles*
1941, 26 December

What a difference an airplane makes! The last time I flew on a seaplane was that Loening, in the winter of '38. If it weren't for Moon Chin risking his life with a landing on the river that night, who knows what would have happened to Chung Si and me? I have never been so cold in my life!

So far, this flight has been wonderful. I have been taking catnaps, catching up with my journal and reading "Gone with the Wind." Mrs. Harris kindly gave me her copy when I told her my copy was left during our hurried escape from Hong Kong. I feel only a little guilty as Alex has been up front (I think they say spelling) the co-pilot for about the last three hours. So far, we have experienced none of the engine problems the crew had on previous legs.

The sky is mostly clear this morning as I look down on India. The sun is rising, leaving an almost purple morning mist over the verdant green tropical forest. The forests are just now beginning to give way to plains that stretch before us as far as the eye can see.

Out of the right hand side of the Clipper, I saw what appeared to be a large city. I will have to ask Alex what place it was when he returns from his turn at the wheel.

His ears must have been burning! He just came back, and sat down in front of me. I will continue this later....

Later

Alex is sleeping. If I ever thought for a minute any eyes but mine would see these words I would never commit what I am about to say to journal. In years to come, however, I want to be able to relive these moments as time has its effect on memory, and these wonderful experiences will fade slowly from consciousness.

Alex was finally relieved by another crewmember. When he returned he sat down on the mailbags in front of me and told me he had announced to the rest of the crew "that he would spend a little time with his new wife." As usual, he told me they chided him as men seem compelled to do, and, asked they respect the "do not disturb sign" on the blanket we hung back here. He said they all laughed and said they would.

My mailbag was positioned a little higher than Alex's was so I wrapped my legs around him so my feet were in his lap. I massaged his shoulders to help relieve the fatigue of sitting in one spot for all of those hours at the wheel. He took the hint and gently began to massage my feet and calves. He made small talk telling me about the surrounding geography. He told me things that were probably interesting at any other time, but not now. I felt the fatigue begin to drain away from both of us after the tension and almost constant travel since leaving Kunming. Alex turned and gently pushed me back on the mailbags. He caressed my face and hair and said my name in that wonderful way I had come to know in the short time we had known one another. I felt that warm liquid thrilling sensation in my belly that I had come recently to identify with his presence.

He unbuttoned my army shirt and slid it back over my shoulders. I pulled my arms free and started unfastening the buttons on his shirt as he worked the army shorts I was wearing down over my hips. He alternated his kisses between my lips and breasts that excited me in such a way that is difficult to describe. When his mouth was free, he kept saying my name, over and over, in a low guttural voice I had come to know that he reserved only for lovemaking.

I worked his trousers down over his hips experiencing that wonderful drive and passion that has assured mankind's survival since time began.

I was appreciative of Alex's patience, something that was wanting in my only other lover. We continued to caress and kiss as we lay on our sides.

He entered me just a little. I think he was actually teasing me! I could hardly stand it. He rolled me on my back and lowered his chest against my bosom. I spontaneously arched my back and spread my legs inviting his entrance as if we had been lovers all of our lives. All the time he continued kissing my lips and breast as he slowly began a controlled thrusting that I met with hips and pelvis to his rhythm. When we climaxed I thought I could not breathe and thanked God for the roaring of the engines to cover my uncontrolled cries of joy. If ever a baby were to be made, this was certainly the time....

Mr. Henri Piccard, Washington, DC
26 December, 1941

Henri Piccard answered the door in his Georgetown apartment, tipped the Western Union clerk fifty cents and wished him a Happy New Year. When he saw the sender's name, he nervously looked up and down the street looking for anyone that looked out of place. Recognizing the recipients name, he shut the door, went to his library and began to decode the message.

Anna's journal
Karachi to Bahrain—1026 miles
1941, 28 December

Karachi was a blur and a nightmare. I slept until splash down—I wonder why? Alex went forward to observe the landing as it was the first time any of the crew had been there; it was more or less a survey flight, Alex explained, where all crewmembers were supposed to comment on every stop of a new route with regard to their own disciplines.

Verne White left us here to be Karachi's first station manager. They unloaded one of the two engines aboard as a spare for the expected future flights through here.

Some astonishing information for everyone! Unknown to any of us, everyone on the crew has more or less been drafted into the United States armed services. Effectively, Alex and the rest of the crew are soldiers! At the same time, Pan Am has sold one of the Boeing 314Clippers to the armed services, and they, in turn, leased it right back to Pan Am to operate for them.

More news! Captain Harold Grey, of Pan Am, New York, just came through Karachi Eastbound on the Atlantic Clipper. The news answered the question of how the Flying Tigers would continue to operate—they are on their way to Calcutta with a load of P-40 tires and parts for the AVG. They will also pick up Ralph and the rest of his crew. No doubt CNAC will take the parts the rest of the way to China.

The British have been very helpful. They provided us with a berth and helped Verne White get the engine off with their heavy lifting equipment. More importantly, they furnished us with aviation gasoline trucked in from the land field. Since we took the engine off, we were able to take a full load of aviation gas. That should really help should we not be able to get 100-octane fuel at Bahrain.

We were hoping to be able to have a restful stay, but the Carleton hotel was horrid—bad food, questionable water, plumbing that didn't work and a filthy city. Everyone was happy to leave.

Anna's journal
1941, 29 December
Bahrain to Khartoum—1434 miles

More farewells as Ralph Hitchcock and Bud Washer left us in Bahrain. They will set up a Pan Am station there. Everyone thanked them for the great help they offered in keeping the engines together. They will be missed!

No aviation gas here. Worse, we were told that we could not fly directly to Khartoum as permission to fly over the kingdom of Saudi Arabia has been refused. We told them that we would fly all the way around the Arabian Peninsula, but there was no way Captain Ford was going to add all of those extra miles to an already long journey. As soon as we were airborne and out of sight, we set a course over Saudi Arabia, direct to Khartoum. For the first few hours it was undercast, and we could avoid detection. Then the clouds began to clear, and it was not long until I heard the Clipper begin to climb. As soon as power was applied for the climb, I thought the engines would come apart. They began back firing and shaking the entire airplane. Alex said we had lost yet another exhaust stack, and even though it was still daylight, I could see flames shooting from the engine. I heard later that our route took us directly over Mecca. Everyone aboard *was worrying about the possibility of interceptor aircraft or anti aircraft batteries.*

Anna's journal
Khartoum to Leopoldville—1900 miles
1942, 1 January

It is New Year's day, 1942! The R.O. just briefed us all on the BBC war news. The only good news for the last week is that the British have occupied Benghazi. Nothing else offers any hope. It seems the Nazi's and the Japanese are unstoppable. I think the whole free world is fearful of what the New Year will bring. The Axis seems to be winning on all fronts. The only good thing this New Year's Day is that we are heading for the States. Of all the people caught up in this war, we are probably the only ones heading away from, rather towards it. I only wish Mama and Papa could be with us. I worry about them so!

There was a delay here yesterday for three VIPS who had priority transportation to the States. They were supposed to be flying down from Cairo to meet us on a British Overseas Airways amphibian. Captain Ford did not want to accommodate them, but the British Commander insisted and would not release the Clipper until Bob agreed to carry them. As it turned out, they never materialized.

Swede and Jocko were able to use the delay for good use. They were up the whole night repairing what components they could from the limited spares we have left. With the gas that's available, these poor old engines are taking more abuse than they were ever designed for. The repairs were to no avail. During our takeoff on the Nile, I literally came off of my seat as yet another one blew, but on we flew. There was no turning back.

There was a long discussion yesterday on the best route for us to take across Africa. Pan Am is in the process of building a base at Fisherman's lake, Monrovia, in Liberia, on the west coast of Africa. It is to be part of the Trans Africa air route to the CBI (China, Burma, India Theater of operations). If we went there, it would take about 1000 miles off of our next leg over the South Atlantic, to Natal, in South America. Trouble is—it is only about 600 miles south of Senegal where the British say the Germans have a fighter squadron of Messerschmitts. After weighing the pros and cons, Captain Ford decided to take the longer route to Leopoldville, on the Congo River. It must have been a difficult decision for him. Besides adding *many miles to our journey, Captain Ford says there are serious operational considerations especially with regard to the River.*

Continued

Right now, Henriksen is flying and Alex is topside, as they say, helping Rod Brown with the navigation. I heard Alex and Rod discussing the navigational aids, or lack of them. In a word, there are none! If that wasn't enough, there are very few distinguishing landmarks along our route. Our charts and maps consist mostly of pages torn from school atlases we pirated along the way. They said they would have to fly the entire route using dead reckoning, and that, I think, is holding a heading and speed for a certain time and hoping you end up where you wanted to be! Alex explained they would use sun shots to "update our dead reckoning," there being so few opportunities to fix our position over the known landmarks.

CHAPTER 28

▼

ARNAUD DERUFFE

Georgetown, Washington D.C.
1 January, 1942

A rented room

About the same time the Clipper was making its approach into Leopoldville, Arnaud DeRuffe was just waking up in a small apartment in Georgetown, just outside of Washington. D.C. He looked at the woman lying next to him but decided to let her sleep a moment until he gathered his thoughts. It was Henri Piccard…that nervous little clerk from the French Embassy that had changed his plans. He had contacted him the night before with instructions from his control in China to get to New York as soon as possible and intercept Anna Boreisha, now Mrs. Alex Cannon. It was that same Russian girl he had asked the Japanese barber about in Hong Kong. Somehow, she managed to get on a Clipper flying westbound to New York. He wondered briefly if the barber had been able to keep his cover until his colleagues took over the city.

So—he was to see her again! The thought intrigued him, but he had to be discreet. She was going to be in New York in just a few days, now with a husband!

"Get the package if he could, but concentrate on the girl," they said.

The value of the package was probably ancient history now, and he probably wouldn't be able to get to it in time in any event. Li Shih's plans were much more insidious…clever even. He had to hand it to him; sometimes his plans were good, and this time very good, though it was up to him to do the tough part…*get her to turn*! He wondered what hook he would use to do that…the parents, certainly them, but he had to find a hook that would sink deep, and stay.

He also wondered what would happen now that his masters had shaken these damned Americans from their sleep. Did they have any idea at all about the available manpower and their manufacturing capability? Merde! They had stirred up a hornet's nest and would soon find out what they had unleashed.

All of that ground work he had laid before the war…finding out what Chinese bases the Americans were planning to use for long range bombing attacks on Japan…all of that intelligence was now worthless. If Tojo and his impatient generals could have only waited a little while longer, he would have given the diplomats the evidence they needed to expose American and Chinese plans. Now, all of that work was for naught. Fools! Pearl Harbor gave Roosevelt the excuse he needed to bring America into the war and they would be bombing everything they could reach! Short of a declaration of unconditional surrender, nothing any diplomat could say would be of any use. Those barbaric fools had decided to do it! Stupid, he thought. Anyhow, what the hell did he care as long as he wasn't caught by the Americans and kept producing for the Japanese…he was being handsomely paid and would profit regardless of who won. DeRuffe rolled over and realized the prostitute beside him was still asleep. He shook her roughly and told her to leave. He had to get to New York. He must devise a plan that would persuade that beauty to do his bidding.

CHAPTER 29

▼

THE GREAT CHALLENGE

Leopoldville, Belgian Congo
January, 1942

Anna's journal
In flight
1942, January 1

> *I must have been sleeping. The engines just changed their pitch for the first time in hours...my ears are popping...we must be letting down....*

The Congo River appeared first as a slit in the jungle and then as a undulating snake the color of coffee with two extra creams. He eased the four throttles back and began descending to his survey altitude. He looked at Johnny Mack in the right seat and with a grin spoke into the intercom and said, "Rod, you are really going to have to tighten up that navigation a bit. You missed your ETA for the river by a minute and a half."

Before Rod could answer, Alex answered, "It's my fault, Skipper...If Rod had been doing the navigation he would have been right on. It's just the pick up help you get these days that knocks your whole operation off the beam."

The rest of the crew offered their usual disparaging remarks on Rod's remarkable feat of navigation.

As they leveled off at 1000 feet to survey the landing area, Johnny Mack said, "It doesn't look as bad as they said, skipper. Looks like three to four miles available for takeoff from where the river straightens out until the rapids…should be plenty for the takeoff run."

"Yeah, that part looks OK, but it's the current we will have to worry about. Unless there is a very strong wind from up river, we will have no choice except to takeoff down river and down current. That would mean no aborted takeoff in the last mile or so. Depending on the current, it would sweep us right into the rapids."

Even though they were still in the air, the oppressive heat and humidity began to creep into the non air-conditioned seaplane. Ford started a captain's preferred left bank to enter a downwind leg for landing on the Congo River.

The final checks were completed and Ford gauged his base leg to land just as the river straightened out on its last straight run before Leopoldville.

The Clipper touched down going with the current towards the city and the rapids. Even though Alex wasn't flying, his sailor's eye saw that because of the current sweeping them down river, Ford would have to start turning the large seaplane long before they were abeam the Pan Am dock. He anticipated the turn, but even so, the Clipper was swept a long way down river before the turn was completed.

As Ford taxied dead up current to hold the bow of the seaplane into the current, Henriksen stood in the open nose hatch, picked up the mooring line with a boat hook and made it fast to the Sampson post on the bow of the seaplane.

Several lighters came along side the sea wing and took the crew to the main dock. On opening the door, the oppressive heat and humidity fell on the tired crew like a wet blanket. The only breeze came from the forward motion of the lighter on their short journey to the dock. Already, everyone aboard was soaked to the skin with perspiration.

No sooner had they stepped on the dock than Dick Dixon, the new station chief, greeted them with a tub of iced beer. After introductions and before anyone started on their second beer, Bob Ford said, "Listen up people! Before we all get too loose, I want to go over the game plan. As you all know, we only have one critical leg left before we get to the States…and that's the next one."

The aviators stopped their socializing with the ground crew and gathered around Ford on the dock.

"One…for those of you who don't know…that city on the other side of the river is Brazzaville. It's in the hands of the Vichy French. I'm sure our landing was observed by just about anybody who cared to watch and heard by everybody else. By now I would guess they have reported our arrival to their masters in Vichy, so no telling what kind of mischief they might be cooking up for us! Point is…I want to get the hell out of here just as soon as possible.

"Two…If you haven't noticed, it's hot! On top of that, there isn't a whiff of a breeze, and Dick Dickson tells me there isn't likely to be one this time of the year. Now all of you junior birdmen know what that means…high-density altitude and poor engine and airplane performance on takeoff!

"Three…The leg to Natal in South America is about 3100 nautical miles. In a word, it's going to take every drop of gasoline we can get on this bird just to get there, and I don't even want to think about how over grossed the airplane will be for takeoff.

"Four…We have about a three and a half to four mile run on the river that normally would be plenty. Trouble is…the current will be with us! Dick tells me it runs about six knots. The good news is that helps our airspeed on takeoff. The bad news is that it effectively shortens our takeoff run and the "go-no-go" point considerably. You all got a preview of what will happen when I turned up river to pick up the mooring. If it's impossible to get her on the step, or we abort for any other reason, we have to do it in time to water loop the bird before we come to the rapids. If I do it too late, or too fast, I could dip a wing and really damage the bird, but we have no other choice. The only good news is we at least don't have to worry about a flock of Messerschmitts intercepting us!

"In what little time we have left today, I want to start refueling and keep at it until there isn't enough light to work. At first light tomorrow, we'll pick up where we left off and finish the job. As you can see, they aren't fully set up here yet, and we will have to lighter the fuel out to the Clipper in five-gallon jerry cans. That's a lot of round trips by boat! We need to take on about 4000 gallons so the arithmetic says almost 800 cans of gas have to be run out and loaded before we can even think about leaving. The good news is it is 100-octane aviation gas and with that in our tanks maybe we won't blow another jug or eat up the last of Swede's exhaust stack spares on takeoff.

"Lastly, Dick had the company work up the best long-range weather forecast possible. For the immediate future, it looks like we might even have favorable winds for the flight to Natal. As you navigators know, the South Atlantic is fickle this time of the year and usually not so kind as now…so, I want to get going while the going is good!

"I hate to do this to you after that long leg, people, but I think getting out of here in as little time as possible is the right thing to do…any questions?"

No one said anything. Most had thought about one or more of the problems, but hearing Ford summarizing the hurdles made each of them realize just how many obstacles they had to overcome on tomorrow's critical leg.

"One last thing! All of you know what *get home-itis* is. It's a killer, and we are just as susceptible as any other crew. Just because we are getting close to home, we can't give in to it. Do your duties just as if it were the first leg leaving San Francisco! Enough said...I know you will all do your best."

Dick Dickson had mobilized enough lighters and labor to fill the jerry cans and get them out to the Clipper. The engineers were going over the performance numbers with Mack and Ford. Rod Brown was preparing a howgozit, navigation charts and celestial tables for the next day. Anna and Alex were helping pour the gasoline into the sea wing tanks on the Clipper.

Alex saw two of the local laborers looking furtively in Anna's direction. She was straddling a funnel with one of the five-gallon jerry cans—leg and arm muscles rippling and dripping with sweat in the oppressive heat and humidity. He couldn't blame them for staring. She still wore the cut down army shorts she had picked up in Burma, but had shed the regulation shirt with its large patch pockets. Now she wore only the regulation olive drab army singlet that was completely soaked through with perspiration displaying her beautiful breasts and nipples as if she were wearing nothing.

Alex whispered, "Anna!"

At first, she didn't hear with the clanking of the jerry cans.

"Anna!"

She looked up quizzically from her just emptied jerry can with her hallmark Mona Lisa smile he had come to love. He pinched his own tee shirt in the center of his chest, pulled it away from his chest and looked where he grabbed. For a second she hesitated, looked down, at the same time looking at the two laborers who immediately averted their gaze.

Anna stood up, shook her head and stepped into the sea wing door of the Clipper. Before she disappeared inside to change, Alex smiled and said, "The sun is about gone, darling...grab what you need and we'll go with Dick to the hotel, get cleaned up, and get something to eat."

Alex finished emptying one more jerry can of gasoline in the sea wing. In a few minutes, his wife returned with a small bag of essentials. Now, she wore the army shirt with the large patch pockets. The two of them boarded the next lighter to the dock and joined the rest of the crew at the hotel.

When the hired jitney pulled up in front of the hotel Dick Dixon said, "Ladies and Gentlemen—your palace for the evening!"

Alex looked at the squalid one story building and said, "Well, it ain't the Peninsula, Heavenly Palace or the Waldorf, darling but it can't be any worse than what we've had in the Middle East. A couple of more legs and I'll make it up to you...I promise!"

"I'm sure it beats anything in Hong Kong these days, and as long as it has a shower, I don't care! I don't think I've ever been so hot and sweaty in my life. Shanghai was steamy in the summer, but this is like living in a Turkish bath!"

The hotel had prepared a large table for the crew in the only dining room. With the exception of the two flight engineers, the rest of the tired aviators gathered for dinner as soon as they had showered and cleaned up.

Anna changed into the same dress she brought from China, and lit up the entire dining room when she entered. Her short pageboy haircut saved her again. Much as a man, she had simply toweled it dry, parted it and combed it straight back. She wore no makeup, and even though she wore the same dress that everyone had seen before, no one cared. Everyone had been away from home for so long; a beautiful woman at the table brightened all of their spirits.

After dinner, the whole crew retired. Everyone wanted to be at the docks at first light to finish with fueling and preflight.

Alex jerked awake at the sound of the hall porter knocking on each crewmember's door. He smiled as he looked down at his new wife of some three weeks waking up in his arms. In spite of the oppressive heat, Anna had still curled up to him as close as possible. After a quick breakfast, the crew assembled on the docks just as the sun made its first appearance on the fourth new day of 1942.

CHAPTER 30

▼

THE CONGO RIVER

Leopoldville, Belgian Congo
January, 1942

Alex's logbook

Dropped the mooring at 12 noon, local time.

Everyone knew today would demand the utmost of our professional abilities. In spite of the oppressive weather, the atmosphere tingled with anticipation. So far as we knew, there was no interference from the Vichy sympathizers on the other side of the river. Dick Dickson's laborers were already pushing off with the first lighter load of five-gallon jerry cans. The engineers had stayed on the Clipper all night, not only to keep watch, but to repair what they could of the broken exhaust stacks.

Everyone did their part. While the regular crew was busy with pre-flight duties, we hitch hikers resumed the back breaking work of pouring gas into the airplane, one jerry can at a time. This morning, in spite of the heat, Anna wore the army shirt with the large patch pockets!

About noon, we had finished topping every tank. I hope we never have to gas a Clipper by hand again as long as I live.

Just as we were finishing an Army major from the attaché's office in Brazzaville showed up with a document in a long tube. I heard him tell Captain Ford that they needed to get the document to the War Department in

Washington just as soon as possible. Captain Ford agreed to take the package and had Rod Brown lock it in the navigator's locker. We could only speculate on what was in the package.

All was ready for the departure. We said our goodbyes, boarded the flying boat and took our duty positions. The whole crew was on headset and interphone. Anna wanted to hear what was going on so I fixed her up with head set of her own....

The *Pacific Clipper* was still tethered to the mooring when Bob Ford called for the pre-start checklist. When the last challenge and response was complete, he ordered—"Turn number three!"

Still tied to the mooring in the almost six knots of current, the rest of the engines were started in sequence. It was easier that way. Gradually, Bob advanced the inboard engines. As the strain came off of the mooring line, Henriksen cast off and the airplane became an ungainly water vessel in a rapidly running river.

As the Clipper eased out into the river to taxi upstream, everyone with a window took one last look at the white water rushing past the rapids just downriver from the dock.

Bob Ford wanted to have as much water as possible for the take-off run so he headed upstream to the bend in the river they had spotted during yesterday's survey. While taxing up river Captain Ford gave his take-off briefing.

"OK guys, this is the big one. On this takeoff, we are going to exceed every airframe and engine limit this bird was designed for.

As I said yesterday...it's hot, we're severely over weight, we've got a six knot current behind us and there are rapids just below the city. When we get airborne, we're gonna be down below the rim of that canyon you all saw when we landed. We will probably have to fly 'S' turns in the canyon to get enough airspeed to fly out. So here's the drill: during the takeoff run and in the climb I want all the normal call outs so that I can check our actual performance against what we should be doing. Keep in mind though, I'll just use them as cues. I'll have to ignore them if we are going to get this bird off the water.

John, as you know, the Clipper is stiff enough on the controls at heavy gross weights when things are normal. I'm guessing it will be even more so now...so stand by to give me some help with the ailerons in those 'S' turns we'll have to negotiate just after takeoff.

There's a little wave action on the river so it might help us get her on the step. We might have to porpoise her a bit to get her up on it so we'll just do what we have to. If we don't get her on the step, we aren't going to fly…so don't be surprised if we are rocking her more than usual."

Everyone listened as Ford continued sailing up the coffee colored river.

Ford continued, "Swede, you know as well as I that all the temps are going to be in the red even before we break water. Sorry, but we don't have any choice. We will have to keep max power on the bird until we're well into the climb…make the over temp and time calls for max power, but just keep in mind I'll probably ignore them. As over grossed as we are, and as hot it is, it's the only chance we have of turning this boat into an airplane!"

Swede said, "OK, Skip! I'm gonna keep the cowl flaps full open until we can make the first power reduction. It will give us a bit more drag, but we don't have any other choice if we want to keep the cylinder heads anywhere near the red line. It's either that or pre-ignition, and a chance of the engine coming unglued."

"OK Swede…do what you have to do to keep em running. One final thing! If I decide to abort the takeoff and water loop, or turn back into the current, it might be far into the takeoff run. If that's the case, it's probable we'll dip a wing and maybe do some damage…so make sure you are all strapped in tight.

If there are any questions, ask them now. We are almost at the up-river turn around spot and I don't want to use any more gas than I have too on the water."

With the exception of the engines and the water splashing past the hull, the Clipper was quiet.

Just as Ford began his turn down river, someone yelled, "Take us to New York, Skipper!"

Even before the bow was pointed down river, Ford called for maximum power. Swede Roth rapidly eased all of the throttles forward on the four Wright Double Cyclones to give Ford all of the power available for the dangerous takeoff.

Acceleration was slow. The heavy Clipper plowed through the brown water trying to change from a displacement, to a planeing vessel. If the hull didn't plane, they wouldn't fly.

After the first mile of plowing through the water, the two pilots began working in unison—rocking the ship by pumping the yoke. They had to break the suction on the hull to get the Clipper on the step.

Johnny Mack called out, "*thirty seconds!*" This was the point the Clipper would have normally become airborne, but like a great whale, they were still plowing through the water.

"*Sixty seconds, Skipper!*" The Clipper was still not on the step and they had used over half of the distance to the rapids.

"*Decision point!*" Rod Brown called out the go-no-go point they had decided on earlier. The flying boat still wasn't on the step.

Johnny Mack called out, "*70 knots!*"

The pilots continued rocking the plane. There was one skip, and then two and then everyone could feel they were no longer plowing through the water. The little waves of the river slapped the hull with increasing frequency. The Clipper was planeing now and accelerating much faster with less than a mile left until the rapids.

At that moment Ford made a mental calculation that he still had room left to abort, but in the process of stopping and turning around before hitting the rapids it was probable that he would dip a wing and do some major damage. Instead, he continued towards the white water and eased back on the yoke trying to coax the heavy airplane to fly.

With almost no distance left until disaster, the ship made the third transition from planeing vessel to airplane.

The Clipper became airborne, but only just! They didn't have enough airspeed to maneuver or climb. As he skimmed across the first of the boulders in the river only inches from tearing out the bottom, Bob Ford eased the backpressure on the yoke and began a slight descent following the rapids down into the canyon. He needed to trade that little altitude he had above the bottom of the gorge into the airspeed the Boeing needed to maneuver and climb out of the canyon into unrestricted air.

As they skimmed across the rapids in the descending river, the pilots eased the flaps up in increments that decreased the drag on the airplane but also the lift. It was a good trade. The slight descent gave them the extra few knots they needed to begin an ever so gradual climb.

With urgency in his voice, Swede Rothe said, "Skip…all the cylinder head temps are in the red!"

Bob Ford said, "Sorry Swede…I've gotta keep max power for a little while longer!"

Swede said nothing and continued to look at the instruments for the first signs of detonation and power loss.

Bob Ford eased back on the yoke leveling the Clipper off just above the rushing waters of the canyon floor. He willed the airspeed to inch up to the point he begin a climb. Just ahead, the two pilots could see the first of the "S" turn they would have to negotiate as they climbed to an altitude that would put them over the rim of the canyon.

Bob said, "First turn coming up, John—work with me on this!"

"I'm with you Skipper!"

Bob eased in pressure on the aileron and rudder to negotiate the first turn. The ailerons wouldn't budge!

"John! Give me some help on the aileron!"

"I'm on it, Skipper…it won't move!"

The whole crew listened in horror to the two pilots speaking on interphone.

"Jocko…The ailerons are frozen! She won't turn!"

Jocko tore off his headset and dove into the wing tunnel where cables ran from the pilot's flight controls to the ailerons on each wing.

The two pilots realized that even if it was possible, they didn't have time for an in flight repair.

"We'll have to skid her through the turn using rudder, John…work with me on this! We can't give away any power using differential throttle!"

At first, the two pilots used moderate left rudder pressure and found the rate of turn was not fast enough. The *Pacific Clipper* rushed toward the first turn.

The nose began skidding around—too slowly at first.

"More rudder, John…more rudder!"

Both pilots stood on the left rudder pedal and then the rate of turn was too great! The right wing was developing too much lift in the skidding turn!

"Back the other way, John! Back the other way! OK, hold what we got…ease off a little!"

With the opposite rudder, the airplane leveled off and began an ungainly turn to the right…not so abrupt this time, as the pilots learned how much rudder was enough to coax the Clipper through the non-conventional skidding turns.

"*Ninety knots*, Skipper!"

Bob Ford heard John's speed call-out. It was the normal cue that the ship had enough speed to climb.

Bob eased the control column back and the ship began a gradual climb out of the canyon floor.

After the first "S" turn, the two were beginning to master the un-conventional turns and were able to anticipate the right amount of rudder.

Jocko Parish appeared breathlessly between the two pilots.

"Skipper, I can't see anything wrong in the wing tunnel. It's my guess that we are so over grossed that the wings are deflected more than the design limit and one of the aileron cables became so slack it has jumped a pulley."

Bob said, "We can't do anything other than what we are doing right now, Jocko. Once we get out of this hole, we'll have more time to figure out what's going on."

Over the intercom the pilots heard Swede's anxious voice, "Skip, everything on my panel is in the red! Recommend a power reduction if we can live with it."

"OK, Swede! We're just coming level with the canyon rim…ease off about an inch of manifold pressure and we'll see how she responds."

Everyone listened for the first sound of trouble as the flight engineer retarded the engines from max takeoff power.

"How's it feel, skipper?"

"I think I can live with it! We're out of the gorge now…try coming back to METO power."

METO power, or maximum except takeoff, was the maximum power the manufacturer would guarantee the engines for continuous operation. Characteristically, the engines thrummed out of synchronization as Swede changed the manifold pressure and revolutions to the less abusive power setting for the initial climb.

As they topped the rim of the gorge, the entire crew felt an immediate change in temperature. The *Pacific Clipper* had freed herself from the heat and humidity of the trapped air of the Congo River.

Except for the pilots and the flight engineer, no one had said a word since the takeoff run had begun. It seemed an eternity, but in reality, it was fewer than ten minutes since they had turned around in the river and began their epic voyage.

Everyone looked at everyone else to see their reaction—some had looks of relief, others just a smile. All were lost in their own thoughts, and all were sweating profusely. Most said nothing. Some made perfunctory comments to cover their immense relief.

Rod Brown called out the initial heading, and Ford and Mack skidded the airplane's nose around in the direction of Natal.

CHAPTER 31

▼

THE SOUTH ATLANTIC

Leopoldville to Natal
January, 1942

Alex's logbook
Leopoldville to Natal   3100 miles
2 January, 1941

---

*I don't think I have ever been through a takeoff quite like that the last one
I wrote about in this journal.*

*Right now, the regular crew is on duty, and I'll catch up with my logbook
and journal before someone needs to sleep. After all the backbreaking
work at Leo, it won't be long till someone gets tired and wants a break.
Anna's asleep and I have just spent the last couple of minutes just looking
at her. When she sleeps, it seems her features change into those of a little
girl in a grown woman's body.*

*After the first hour, the ailerons began responding correctly—thank God!
The guys are speculating about cable stretch in the extreme heat or maybe
distorted wings from our overweight condition. At least it's gone. I think
it's probably the former. In my opinion, the Boeing people will probably
have to put some sort of compensator in the system to keep this from happening again.*

The two stewards are whipping up a gourmet meal from what is left of the galley supplies—how they keep coming up with these goodies considering the slop available in the shops is beyond me. Truth is, what we eat in flight is better than what's available on the ground.

Just got my call to duty—thought it would be longer! I'll finish when I come back. I'll let the Princess continue to sleep.

Later—Co-pilot's seat—finishing my entries.

Just passed the ETP and finished my second trick at the wheel. A little while ago one of the flight engineers called up to the cockpit and said, "Hey Alex! We half way there yet?" I looked at the flight plan and yelled, "Yeah Swede! Just a little over half way."

"That's good...cause we just used half the gas!"

Everyone laughed at his simplicity. He really netted it out. Of course, he knew that everything else being the same, long-range flights used more than half of the fuel in the first half of the flight. The airplane is heavier and requires more power and consequently more fuel. As fuel is burned, the weight is less and less power is required to maintain the most efficient speed in the last part of a flight. Nevertheless, Swede's quip made a very important point—a good grip on the basics. Many times crews got so wrapped up in the minutiae, they lose sight of the big picture.

Uh Oh! Princess just came forward and let me know my presence is required back in the Cannon honeymoon quarters. I wonder what she could possibly want?

Alex's logbook

Natal—Trinidad—New York

January 5, 1941

We no sooner landed in Natal than we were ordered off of the aircraft so government people could spray. Luckily, Anna, as always, carried her map case and her Leica with her. When we returned, we found that the document given to us for safekeeping in Leopoldville was missing!

We cannot help but wonder if it was mistakenly taken thinking it to be part of Anna's package for Washington.

A short rest and then on to Trinidad.

Alex's logbook

Trinidad

Showers, sleep and rest! Everyone thinks of nothing but getting home....

▼

CHAPTER 32

THE CHILD OF RUSSIA AND CHINA

New York
January, 1942

Anna's journal
Port of Spain—New York
1942, 5–6 January

It seems an eternity since fleeing Hong Kong; yet, when I look at the date in my Journal I see that it is just a little less than a month!

Alex came back a moment and pointed out a string of lights that keep appearing off of the side of the aircraft. He says it is the coast of New Jersey. The winds have been more favorable than we predicted, and the Pacific Clipper has been going around in circles now for some time. Captain Ford is waiting for sunup to make a visual approach into New York.

I still can't believe it. After years of Papa's tutoring, American movies, and reading newspaper articles about this country, those lights are my first glimpse of this strange and wonderful country.

Alex is furious! He says he cannot believe that lights are still allowed at night along the shoreline. He says it silhouettes coastal shipping against the coastline making them sitting ducks for Nazi submarines. "We are sure to sustain heavy shipping loses until such madness is no longer tolerated," he said.

I heard the engines change power and felt the Clipper start the descent into New York. Alex returned again to point out the Statue of Liberty, the Chrysler and Empire State buildings and the city, all crammed onto the island of Manhattan. He was excited as a young boy at Christmas. Soon, Captain Ford made a perfect landing on icy Bowery Bay. After some difficulty maneuvering to the dock on the low tide, I, Anna Boreisha, now Cannon, child of Russia and China, have come home to my new country: The United States of America!....

Sailing toward the Pan Am dock, Alex reached over and put his arms around Anna in a warm embrace. Pulling her toward him he said, "Welcome home darling."

"Are the winters always so cold here Alex? There is ice and snow on the banks. It looks like my parent's pictures from Russia in the wintertime." She reached down for her Chinese quilted coat jammed between the handles of her Gladstone and pulled it on.

Two dockworkers in Pan Am coveralls and parkas made the Boeing fast to the dock in the gathering daylight. The Steward opened the door to the sponson and a blast of winter air rushed in to meet them. One of the ground crew shouted, "Where in God's name did you people come from?"

Barney shouted back, "We are the *Pacific Clipper* inbound from New Zealand!"

The ground crewman yelled back "Yeah and my names Babe Ruth, and I'm doing this cause I like to hang around airplanes in the winter time!"

Minutes later the flight crew began to come down from the flight deck, hugging themselves and flapping their arms, trying to keep warm. Captain Ford approached Anna and Alex and said, "Well Alex, we made it...welcome to your new home Mrs. Cannon."

Anna said, "Captain Ford, with the priorities of this war, I don't think any of us can guess what will happen to us in the coming days...or even if we will ever meet again. I just want all of you to know I will never forget you and what you have all done to get us safely here."

She went to each of the crewmembers, gave her personal thanks and kissed each of them on both cheeks in the Russian manner. Alex followed and said his good byes. They all shook hands promising to keep in touch, but knowing that as soon as they stepped off of the airplane events would take over their lives, and only chance would bring them together again.

The Pacific crew stepped out on the dock with nothing more than their tropical uniforms for protection against the winter winds off Bowery Bay. Because of their self-imposed silence, the news media missed their arrival. They had just completed the first circumnavigation of the globe by a commercial aircraft, and nobody was there to meet them. Even the Pan Am officials did not expect them for a few more days. Soon, John Leslie, the Atlantic Division manager, and Captain Harold Grey who had himself only arrived back in New York on the *Atlantic Clipper* with Captain Ralph's crew, got the word and arrived with the public relations manager. With no one to meet them, and no offices at headquarters yet open, Grey and Leslie treated the whole crew to breakfast at the La Guardia terminal.

The young couple sat with Captain Grey during breakfast. He knew of the newlyweds plans to continue on to Washington and deliver their package. They were told that after they completed their Washington mission Alex would be given two weeks leave and then assigned temporarily as a navigator instructor at Dinner Key. In the meantime, operations would decide where he would be permanently based.

It was then that the rest of the crew was told that they were to be transferred from Treasure Island to the Atlantic Division, in New York. The crew was devastated. They all had homes and families on the West Coast. Since the war began, they had no choice in the matter. Just like everyone else in the airline, they had been drafted and would have to answer to the needs of the service.

Captain Ford found that he too would be traveling to Washington, but on a separate mission. Even though it wasn't planned as such he and Grey had just flown the first survey flights from the CBI, and the War Department wanted to be briefed on the epic flights. The Army was planning massive airlift operations to Africa and beyond and needed all the operational information they could get on the routes.

Their first order of business was to swing by payroll, recover the month's travel expenses, and take an advance to pay the crew the money he owed them before everyone went their separate ways. Then, he wired his father for some more funds until he could get in contact with his bank in San Francisco. Just before they left, a payroll clerk came to the front desk and said, "Mr. Trippe has asked that you stop by his office with Mrs. Cannon as soon as you are finished here."

The two were shown to Juan Trippe's office. The secretary announced their arrival and ushered them in. Juan Trippe greeted them at the door. He ordered refreshments and asked for a verbal report on their ordeal in Hong Kong, how they escaped and how Langhorne Bond was faring.

The couple described the ordeal as Trippe listened. When they finished Trippe said, "Mrs. Cannon, I remember you from 1936. You might remember. You translated for us during the inaugural celebrations and my tour of CNAC's operations."

"I had no idea you would remember that, Mr. Trippe, but I will never forget it. Many things in my life changed that day"

Alex looked quizzically at his new wife.

Trippe said, "Langhorne Bond assures me that you have some valuable information regarding certain events going on in China and that you already know we have set up priority transportation for you to Washington. Mr. Cannon, I have had my secretary call the Waldorf-Astoria and secure accommodations for you and Anna. As you have probably guessed, the hotels have been swamped with all of the activity since Pearl. I explained the situation and called in a couple of markers they owe me from the past, so don't worry, you're covered. Don't worry about payment. It has been taken care of. Just put everything on a tab...they know all about you, so let this be my wedding gift and my way of thanking both of you for your service to Pan Am."

Alex was still dressed in his stained navy blue uniform; Anna was still in her jodhpurs, boots, and blue quilted coat. Regardless of the cold weather, they decided to walk to the Waldorf. They wanted to stretch their legs and see what they could of the city. When they walked into the lobby, they stamped their feet and swung their arms trying to warm up. Then, chilled to the bone, they joined the long queue to the check-in desk.

As she looked around, she was conscious that she looked quite different from the other women in the lobby. Most wore smart costumes complete with hats, gloves and in some cases, veils. How different from China, she thought.

"Alex...everyone is dressed so elegantly and I feel like a peasant...I think you say a ragamuffin or bum!"

"Honey, you could be standing stark naked and you would look better than anyone in this lobby...don't worry about it."

Suddenly Alex felt a sudden squeeze on his arm. "Alex...that man in the camel overcoat...just leaving the front desk...He was staring at me and turned away when I looked his way. I'm certain it was that Frenchman, DeRuffe...you know, the one mixed up with the barber, the porter, Cameron's murder!"

Alex turned to look, but the man was gone.

"We're a long way from Hong Kong, Princess."

"Alex! I'm certain that was the guy!"

"Maybe it's just someone who looked like him. With a little luck it's probably the last time we will ever see the guy. Try to forget him and have a good time."

The weary travelers finally got to the front desk. A red-faced businessman was espousing his importance to the reception clerk explaining why he should be given preference for a room over everyone else. The indomitable clerk explained in that manner affected by reception clerks the world over that *there were no rooms*!

The clerk finally tired of telling the businessman that no rooms were available, turned to Alex and asked, "How can I help you sir?"

"My name is Alex Cannon. I have been assured that there would be accommodations for my wife and me under Cannon. Mr. Juan Trippe's office, at Pan Am, would have made the reservations for us."

The clerk shuffled through the card file and replied, "Why yes Mr. Cannon...you will be in one of our bridal suites...your reservation is confirmed...just a moment sir!" He rang for the bellman.

The businessman looked dumbfounded at Alex's rumpled uniform and the beautiful woman in the little blue peasant's coat. He was about to open his mouth when Alex said, "Don't even ask, mister...it's too long a story to tell right now."

The bellman arrived, took the keys from the reception clerk and said, "Ah yes...the bridal suite! And where is your luggage sir?" Alex handed him Anna's Gladstone and his suitcase. The bellman looked as if he was about to say something—thought better of it and said, "Welcome to the Waldorf, Mr. and Mrs. Cannon. Please follow me!"

The bellman opened the bridal suite door. Alex picked up his bride, and before stepping into the room said, "I think this will be the closest thing to a real honeymoon suite since we've been married, so here goes!"

After he set her down inside the room she said, "You Americans and your traditions—I think it will take the rest of my life to understand you!"

The suite was luxurious. To the relief of the bellman, the tip was much larger than he had any right to expect for only two traveling cases. He left shutting the door behind him. Anna went straight to the bathroom, stripping away her clothing as she went. She pranced out naked to the sitting room, gave Alex a coquettish look, took the do not disturb sign from the handle of the front door and hung it on the bathroom doorknob.

"Sir, I will be indisposed for the indefinite future. When I am finished, perhaps I will not smell of engine oil, gasoline and mail bags!"

Alex picked up the telephone and made reservations for 8 p.m. in the dining room. He then rang Western Union and asked if they had a cash transfer for a Mr. Alex Cannon. Assured that the transfer had been made, he called the concierge and explained they had just arrived from abroad with very little to wear. He asked if there was a woman's clothing shop in the hotel. The concierge suggested he speak with Bonwit Teller, an exclusive women's store nearby. Alex took the number, called the store and again explained the situation. He gave the customer representative a description of Anna, her approximate sizes and asked that she use her own discretion as to style, taste and accessories to see her through the afternoon and evening. Alex suggested he would pay cash on delivery and asked that the items be sent to their room within the next thirty minutes with the understanding that they had the right to exchange everything when they returned to Bonwit's later in the afternoon. The customer representative on the other end said she understood and was glad to be of assistance.

DeRuffe seldom forgot a face, especially one as unique as the Russian's. He reflected on the scene at the reception desk. He was certain it was the same beauty he had seen on the flight from Chongqing, although this time, she wasn't dressed so elegantly. Something was different, though. In the brief instant he had to observe her, she seemed somehow more self-assured, less melancholy. He wondered what it could be. In any event, Li Shih's intelligence had been correct. Getting here this soon required priority transportation, so he was certain she must have the package even though now that was less important than before. He would have to be very careful not to be recognized. Besides being beautiful, this one looked intelligent and just might be more perceptive than most. Never underestimate your quarry, he thought.

After almost forty-five minutes, the door to the bathroom opened. Anna emerged in a cloud of steam sporting towels around her head and torso. "Ta Da! A few more days of this, and I might be clean!"

She saw the new coat, dress and accessories laid out carefully on the bed. A look of astonishment came over her face. "Alex, what...where did these...how did you get these things so quickly? Her eyes sparkled like a child's at Christmas as the thought of new clothes sank in. Whomever Alex had spoken to at the store had thought of everything: a smart woolen suit, overcoat, a simple necklace, gloves—even a scarf and underwear.

Alex smiled at her reaction. "I wouldn't presume trying to shop for a Russian Princess. I just had to get you out of that blue coat and those things you've been wearing since Hong Kong. You can exchange these for anything you want when we return these to the Bonwit's."

"Bonwit's?"

Alex explained.

Anna immediately dropped the towel and tried on the women's travel suit sent by the store. She threw her arms around Alex and gave him a warm kiss. "Darling, you really are so thoughtful! You knew how much I hated to be seen in my old clothes in such an elegant place."

She tried on the clothes with exaggerated fanfare; she knew Alex enjoyed the fashion show. She turned first one way and then the other looking at herself in the mirror. She had definite opinions on what she liked and what she didn't, but this Bonwit clerk hadn't done too badly, she thought.

"Alex, you are a dear! Now, I won't feel so much the hobo the next time we go through the lobby. I want so much to look good for you"

"I still say you look best with nothing on at all! But, if you must wear clothes, these don't look bad for a start."

"Now, if you have not used all of the hot water in the hotel, it's time for me to wash some of the trail dust off."

"Trail dust?"

"I'll explain later, darling."

When Alex came out, the clothes were folded neatly over the couch in the sitting area. His wife of one month was lying sound asleep on one side of the bed.

Alex finished toweling off, gently lifted the covers and nuzzled up to Anna's backside in the spoon position. With his free hand he gently reached under Anna's arm, and cupped her breast—she responded with only a small purr. In seconds, he too was asleep.

Later, she awoke with a start and let out a muffled cry. She felt Alex's hand on her breast and heard the rhythmic breathing of his slumber. It immediately calmed her as she realized where she was.

She had been dreaming of the man she had seen in the lobby. Just before she woke, the leering face from that flight to Hong Kong flashed through her memory. It seemed so long ago. Was it possible she could be mistaken? No, she thought not. Even though she had only seen him for seconds, she knew it was the same man. Why the thought made her think of the Japanese rapist in Nanking, she could not say, but she thought of the Frenchman in that way. How could it be that she had not the slightest bit of remorse for those soldiers? Was it that she had a character flaw? Was she incapable of compassion for fellow humans? Anna felt her new husband's wonderful closeness to her and thought not.

Still not moving, she listened to the thumping of the hotels steam radiators and reflected on how fortunate she was. She was married to a wonderful man who loved her as much as she loved him; they had escaped the horrors of the Japanese occupation. She could only imagine what was happening to all of her CNAC family still there, the Carutherses, that Belinda woman what would have happened to them had they not been able to escape? They had been so fortunate! If only her parents and Saul could be safe with her. She said a short prayer for their well-being and wondered what they could do to help them get out.

Alex was still asleep. With her free arm, she reached across to the nightstand, glanced at Alex's wristwatch and saw that they had been asleep for about an hour. She gradually lifted his hand from her breast, turned slowly over and began to kiss him on one cheek and then the other. She exaggerated her almost non-existent Russian accent and said, "Eheet ees time to wake up darling! Wake up and take care of your poor Rooski wife. She needs love! She needs food! She needs clothing, but first she needs love!"

Even though his eyes were still closed, his mouth betrayed a grin as she straddled him and began to indulge her pleadings.

It was getting late in the day when the Cannons stepped off of the elevator into the lobby. This time, though, she couldn't help noticing other women looking her over in that unique way peculiar to women when they compared themselves to others of their sex. After her luxurious bath, short nap, lovemaking and her new ensemble, she felt wonderful and equal to any of them. She sat down in one of the lobby chairs and waited while Alex put her *package of stuff* for Washington in the hotel safe.

The couple picked up the money transfer at Western Union and walked to Bonwit's to finish her purchases. Next, Alex bought a suit and some accessories. They spent the balance of the afternoon just window shopping, enjoying the sights of New York and each other's company.

For the first time since Anna could remember, she was having an ordinary day without a feeling of foreboding. She was in America, and with the exception of World War II raging over the entire globe, she, for the moment at least, felt secure. Only one little thing kept creeping into her consciousness. The Frenchman—DeRuffe, it was him—she was sure it was—what was he doing here? It couldn't have been a coincidence; it must have something to do with her.

That evening, the couple had dinner at the Waldorf and went to bed early. Tomorrow was a big day—the train, Washington, the Navy, and meeting Alex's parents.

Early the next morning the newlyweds checked out early and caught a cab for the short ride to Penn Station.

Even before they left, DeRuffe had made it his business to know when the couple checked out and executed one of his many ruses to find out their destination and forwarding address. He then checked at the front desk for any new cables from his paymasters in China.

CHAPTER 33

▼

THE TRAIN

New York to Washington
January, 1942

Anna's journal
Penn Station
1942, 8 January

We are running every minute! Will journal when time permits.

The world travelers arrived at Penn Station, found the huge marquee displaying their train and track number, and waded into the crowd. The station was a sea of men. Some in uniform, many still in civilian clothing on their way to military training facilities. Anna thought of *the crocodile*, or the swarm of refugees in China escaping from slaughter and slave labor. Instead of escaping, though, these men were on their way to bring war to their enemies.

It was less than a month since Anna and Alex heard President Roosevelt's "Day of Infamy" speech over the shortwave in Hong Kong. This sea of men confirmed the Japanese attack on Pearl Harbor had amalgamated disparate Americans like no other event. In the short time, since she had been here it seemed everyone in the country was of a single purpose.

The Cannons mounted the steps still carrying the same bags they'ed had with them since Hong Kong. Their only addition was a small cardboard grip for the purchases they had made in New York. Nevertheless, Anna still clung to her map case with its contents and her precious Leica, never letting them leave her person.

Without a priority ticket from the War Department, it was obvious they would not have gotten a seat. G.I.'s were everywhere. Some were standing in the isles, some sat on the floor playing cards, some were down on their on their knees shooting dice.

Anna was one of the few women on the train and attracted almost non-stop wolf whistles. For Alex, it was expected. For Anna, though, it was different and took getting used to. No one in China, except maybe American marines and sailors, whistled like these guys.

Just as they took their seats, the train lurched out of the station in a cloud of steam, cinders and smoke. It remained in the city for what Anna thought a very long time and then broke into an area of heavy industry on both sides of the train.

Alex saw the pensive look on her face and said, "Not very pretty, is it? But it's this heavy industry that will make the stuff all of these guys will need to crush the Axis. Why don't you just close the window shades and try to catch a nap until we get out into the countryside?"

"No, darling, I know from the movies that not all of America is like this…but I want to see it all! Anyhow, I'm waiting to see a cowboy."

"Patience, Princess, Patience! Tom Mix might ride by any minute. Why don't you lay back and shut your eyes for a while. I'll wake you when we come to the country."

She ignored him for a while and sat staring out the window. After a while, she took Alex's hand and asked, "Do you really think I just imagined seeing that Frenchman…or could it be that it's just a coincidence?"

In the short time Alex had known her he had learned not to shrug off her concerns. After watching the outside scenery begin to give way to countryside awhile, he said, "Tell you what, darling: when we get to Washington, we'll tell that ONI officer, Bergantz, that we might have seen DeRuffe in New York. Tell him everything we know about him: what happened in Hong Kong and the fact that the last you saw him, he was on his way to the States. Who knows, maybe he already has something on him."

Not long after lunch, the train pulled into Washington's terminal. The scene was the same as Penn Station—thousands of young men and women were making their way to places all over the country that would mate them with the weapons of war coming from the heavy industry they had just seen. The armed services would train them how to use the stuff, and create the most formidable army in history.

Pan Am had made reservations for the newlyweds at the Willard, but it was no easy job getting there. With the tempo of war preparations moving into full swing transportation of any kind was difficult, and they ended up sharing a cab with two Air Corps officers who dropped them at 14th and Pennsylvania.

CHAPTER 34

▼

THE BRIEFING

Washington, D.C.
7 January, 1942

The mob scene at the Willard was a repeat of the Waldorf in New York and the Heavenly Palace in Chongqing. War seemed good for the hotel business and it appeared the necessary commodities to get a room were connections, military rank and large tips. Without Pan Am's intervention it was evident they never would have gotten a place to stay.

As soon as they got to their rooms, Alex called the number Colonel McHugh had given him in Chongqing. A no-nonsense female voice answered and explained to him Captain Bergantz was in a meeting. She took their telephone and room information, and she promised she would give the message to the captain as soon as he came out of the meeting.

They were still unpacking their few belongings when the telephone rang. Captain Bergantz said he had been expecting them and before Alex could speak, Bergantz suggested he not mention names or anything else on the telephone, and asked that he and his wife both come to his office at 3 p.m. that afternoon.

They were greeted by a young wave. She told them that they would be visiting a secure area, and in that both of them were civilians with no security clearances, it would be necessary for Anna to leave her camera with her. When asked about the map case Anna assured the wave that the items in the bag were intended for Captain Bergantz.

The wave had just taken the camera when a when a short, rather book-ish-looking naval officer, came through one of the closed doors and introduced himself as Captain Bergantz. He thanked them for coming so promptly and ush-ered them back through the same door. The outer office led to a large conference room; Bergantz told the wave to hold all of his calls, and that they were not to be disturbed.

A marine colonel, a navy commander and a wave stenographer were seated at a conference table. On one wall was a large map South East Asia. On the table was a device that they later found out was a voice recording machine.

Captain Bergantz began by saying, "You know: you two are among the first people to get here from the CBI since Pearl Harbor. Could we please start by you telling us about your escape and journey back to the U.S.?"

Anna placed her map case on the conference table. She and Alex comple-mented one another with their summary of their days since December 8—one would speak, and the other filled in the gaps.

When they finished with their summary Bergantz said, "We received word that besides the package from McHugh, you had some photographs and verbal recollections of Japanese war crimes and other intelligence that might be of inter-est in our war effort."

Anna told them of her experience in Nanking and of the pictures that were lost after her escape early in 1938. She explained that the only pictures that remained of the some ten or twelve rolls she had taken were those that were in her camera at the time of her escape. She took the contents out of her map case and put them on the table. The officers were examining the 1937 black and white photos as she continued to speak. Most were of murdered and raped Chinese vic-tims that she had photographed just before her escape. The three officers' expres-sions confirmed their collective disgust. As much as they were horrified, however, it was clear for them that these revelations paled in importance since Pearl Har-bor. Everyone's emphasis had shifted to prosecuting the war effort. Justice, they suggested, would have to wait for war crime trials after the war was won.

More important to the gathered officers was the information Anna had brought with regard to the secret Japanese research unit recently uncovered in Manchuria.

Anna explained to the group that the information on Unit 731 had been delivered to Colonel McHugh by a network of Chinese agents working out of Harbin, in Manchuria. As Anna continued to speak, she didn't think it necessary to mention her suspicions that one of the agents was Irina Federenko, a Russian childhood friend whom she had grown up with in Shanghai.

The officers looked at the photographic evidence and read the Harbin agent's report on what she had observed as Anna continued to speak. She said, "They had taken the evidence from an area where the Japanese unit had conducted their experiments. The scientist in Unit 731 had infected fleas with bubonic plague and then infested thousands of rats with those fleas. They then turned the rats loose on the peasant population and killed thousands to prove the effectiveness of biological warfare."

Everyone in the group was dumbfounded. All knew of the effects of chemical warfare as practiced by both sides in World War I but none thought that any country could sink to the barbarity of the Russian woman's revelations. Deliberate experiments on humans with disease, vivisections, gunshot wounds and chemical agents—the hideous list gave evidence of an inhumanity that made wild beasts noble by comparison.

The gathered officers asked the same questions in many different ways, but Anna could offer little for substantiation as the report was not hers. It was obvious they wanted to insure the veracity of her story and at the same time get an accurate description of this Unit 731's activities, but she could not help them.

What was more important to all of the officers was how Anna was able to come by the information. They were intrigued with the extent of her Chinese contacts—not only with CNAC but also in Shanghai, Nanking, Hankow, Harbin and Chongqing. Not only did her informants have contacts but also an amateurish, but effective network by which they communicated.

After describing the little she knew of Unit 731 the officers switched the inquiry to what she knew of individuals in China. They asked how well she knew Sergei Hovans, Akimora, Ostafii Rabin and other enemy collaborators in Shanghai. They asked how much she knew of the Kempeitai's activities.

When she had finished, Anna also told them of her suspected sighting of Arnaud DeRuffe in New York. Captain Bergantz, too, thought it more than coincidence and made a note to look into the Frenchman's activities.

Both saw where the inquiry was leading. Not only did Anna have superb language skills and the ability to move in the circles of this ruthless enemy, she also had knowledge for the foundation of a very good intelligence network.

Bergantz finally asked the question. "Mr. and Mrs. Cannon, as you have probably guessed, the United States has only a rudimentary intelligence gathering capability in South East Asia in general, and China in particular. Most of what we learn comes through whatever Chiang Kai-shek and the Communists are willing to share with us. Anything we receive is highly suspect, as anything they give us has been distilled by both of them for political as well as military advantage.

What would you say to going back into China and utilizing your extensive con-tacts and formidable language skills to set up an intelligence network for the United States? Of course there would be extensive training in the skills necessary to prepare you."

Alex was first to speak. "Captain Bergantz: Anna and I were only married on December the eighth!"

Anna reached for Alex's arm to stop him and said, "No, Alex, this is not your decision alone. Let me respond to these gentlemen."

"But Anna, we just got back!"

"Alex, please, just listen a moment! Captain Bergantz, as you probably know, I have parents still living in Shanghai. I would do anything to insure they could leave China or at least insure their safety and well-being. If there were no extenu-ating circumstances, I would return to China to do anything I could to see them to safety."

"Mrs. Cannon, you could count on all the resources the United State's gov-ernment could bring to bear should you make the decision to return. You wouldn't be alone, you know. We would help you bring your parents out any way we could."

Anna continued. "Captain, that's not all. All the time I was growing up, I had great respect for the Japanese. They are a cultured and intelligent people. Much as the Nazis have seduced their nation, the Japanese have allowed themselves to be seduced by a militarism condoned by their Emperor that is more ruthlessness and more heinous than the barbarians of the Middle Ages. Even though I am now safe in America, I would return to fight them in any way I could for what they have done. Don't forget, I witnessed first hand what my photographs show."

Bergantz turned to Alex and said, "Surely, Mr. Cannon, you could support your wife. Why, with your affiliation with Pan American and the Chinese airline, both of you returning would be a perfect cover."

"Yeah, listening to you two, I couldn't help but think of that. It would be a good cover."

Anna said, "Another thing: long before I met Alex, I came to love your...I should now say, our country. I know your history. I know what America stands for. For all its flaws, it's a lot better than whoever might be in second place. I would do this for my new country as well as China."

Bergantz said, "Then you both agree?"

Alex said, "Now wait a minute, Captain!"

Anna interrupted, "No Captain Bergantz, Alex...I won't do it...I can't!"

Anna looked at them with her characteristic half smile and said, "I had wanted to say this in private, but you gentleman have kind of forced the issue. Alex, gentlemen...I am almost sure I am pregnant, and regardless of my feelings about my parents, the Japanese, or the war, my first duty now is to our baby."

Bergantz and Alex's faces assumed the surprised, almost stupid expression affected by men since the beginning of time when presented with such news. True to form, they looked at her as if she were the first woman ever make such a proclamation.

Alex threw his arms around her in a tight embrace. "Anna, darling...why didn't you tell me?"

"I wasn't sure and to be perfectly honest—I'm still not, but all the signs are there. Until I prove otherwise, the answer is definitely no, but I will still be available to tell you anything I can that would help you set up operations in China."

Bergantz stammered, "Ahem...well congratulations, Mrs. Cannon!" He shot her a glance that questioned the veracity of her announcement.

Alex left Captain Bergantz the contact information for his parents in Maryland. He explained that he had orders to proceed to Pan Am's Dinner Key seaplane base by Monday, the nineteenth, giving him very little time to acquaint his new wife with his parents and her new home. He explained that if he remained in Dinner Key, he would have Anna join him there. If he were transferred, it could be she might have to remain in Maryland.

With the meeting concluded, they stood and said their goodbyes with the promise that the captain would be in touch should he need further information from either of them.

After they arrived back at the Willard, Alex telephoned his father. They would meet tonight for dinner. Tomorrow, they would return with them to their home in Maryland.

CHAPTER 35

▼

HOME

Maryland
9 January, 1942

Anna's journal
The Cannon home in Maryland
1942, 9 January

Alex is still asleep. My first impulse on awaking this morning was to put my thoughts to journal while I still have time. So much has happened in the last days it is difficult to find a suitable starting place. Perhaps the best place is at the beginning.

Landing in icy Bowery Bay, then wonderful New York, shopping, dining, and a train ride through the industrial might of New Jersey and then the beautiful countryside of this fantastic country, the nation's capital, are akin to this child of Russia and China landing on another planet.

In case my entries are ever compromised, I must be discreet in what I write. Yesterday is a case in point. Let it suffice to say Alex and I concluded our business with the government and spent some delightful time alone. I hope that the information we supplied will help in their efforts and not be forgotten in the furor of war. I spoke to them about my parent's situation. They grieve along with me at not being able to find a solution for Mama and Papa's plight.

After our business, I was successful in persuading Alex to give me a tour of Washington. It was short to be sure, but Alex hired a horse and carriage for the outing. Papa's insistence of studying this country's history prepared me to know what some of the monuments and statues we saw stood for. It is a wonderful city and after we are settled, I hope to be able to explore it at length. Best of all, there are no bombs!

Zachary and Clara Cannon's greeting was more gracious than I had reason to expect. Alex told me long ago that his parents had hopes of him marrying the daughter of a personal and political friend. From the outset, they have treated me cordially but with reserve—I think that is the appropriate term. It is not what they had hoped for; so what more can I expect? If they had any doubts about "that Russian" their son was bringing back from China, though, they were very clever at hiding it.

Instead of cocktails, Alex ordered champagne for everyone. When everyone's glass was full he made a little speech telling his parents, "Not only were they gaining a daughter but they he was also bringing them a Princess that wanted to give them a Grand Prince or Princess! They both affected restrained delight when Alex told of our first meeting in Hong Kong and how the name had stuck. Zachary Cannon proposed a wonderful toast sounding more like a politician than a grandfather-to-be. Not to be outdone, Clara made a little speech to the effect that she had always told Alex to "never put off until tomorrow what could be done today," and to get right to the problem at hand! I too proposed a toast expressing my delight at meeting my surrogate parents. I proposed a toast in Russian wishing them and my real parents the best of good health and good luck and wished that in the near future they could meet my Mama and Papa.

It was after the toast that Alex explained to his parents that he would be going to Dinner Key, at Key Biscayne, near Miami, in Florida. Pan Am had given him a temporary billet training Air Corps and Navy navigators aerial celestial navigation for the war effort. After that it would be, "back on the line," as he called it—probably.

Alex and I spent the night at the Willard. His parents stayed at his father's Washington apartment. They picked us up the next morning and before we all set off for the family home in Maryland, Zachary showed us more of Washington with the promise of "A grand tour" of the Capital, and the White House within the next few weeks. Alex has to leave for Florida and duty in little over a week; I will be staying on with them until we know something definite.

The drive to my temporary home in Mr. Cannon's automobile took us through the outskirts of Washington and the beautiful countryside of Maryland. We were there in less than two hours.

The Cannon house is out of the American dream. It sits on a promontory overlooking the Chesapeake Bay. Unlike China, the house is made almost entirely of wood with horizontal overlapping boards. The roof is made of a composition of tar that Zachary told me is common in the United States. There is a large garage with room for two automobiles and another building that Alex told me was a workshop where they worked on their sail boats.

The front of the house is surrounded by a screened porch extending from one side of the house to the other. Sitting there, one has a wonderful view of the Chesapeake. The living room is warm, comfortable and like the rest of the house, not as pretentious as one might expect for a member of the United States government. There are four bedrooms, two bathrooms and many closets. Every window in the living room looks out over the Chesapeake. The rest of the areas downstairs consist of the dining room, kitchen and Mr. Cannon's library.

As we drove up, two large dogs ran to the car to greet us. Zachary said they were Labradors. One's name is Gurty and the other Toby. I could not help thinking that if this were China, even in good times, someone would be chasing them with a cleaver rather than petting them. Here, they are treated as members of the family. The other member of the household is Shelly Ann. She is the hired housekeeper and the daughter of a nearby farmer.

Zachary has promised to tell me all about the good times he and Alex enjoyed sailing together on the Chesapeake. When the weather permits, he has promised to take me sailing.

I am now sitting at an old writing desk upstairs in what the parents call "our bedroom." It was Alex's room when he grew up....

Trans Artic Airlines flight 401
Anchorage to Hong Kong

In flight
November, 1994

The regular captain assigned to the flight had relieved Stephen and was now on duty. Stephen had retreated to the crew rest area and tried to sleep, but it didn't work. He still couldn't get his mind off of the China Diaries.

From his mother's journal entry, read only last night in Anchorage, he tried to imagine her sitting at his father's writing desk, knowing she was pregnant, that his father would be leaving for Florida, and probably returning to the war in the near future. Her entries suggested she felt more accepted by his grandparents as time went on. Nonetheless, it must have been difficult for her to realize that now, safe in the United States, she was still powerless to help her parents escape from Shanghai and the Japanese. Still, he could not imagine whatever possessed her to return to China. He thought of her graphic description of the sex she had with his father and wondered if that was the extent of her desires. Maybe he was just prudish, but what other reason could be so compelling that she would abandon him right after birth with no explanation. Even though the missing journals had to have been written before 1943, when she disappeared, he still hoped they would shed some light onto why she might have left.

CHAPTER 36

▼

THE NEW ASSIGNMENT

Washington-Miami
Winter, 1942

Alex's logbook
Washington to Miami and Dinner Key

Tried bringing this journal up to date on the train but found it next to impossible. Every mode of transportation is filled to capacity with men of every size and background.

Can't believe I'm going to be a father. Miss the Princess so much I ache!

There's a crap game going on in the aisle and a poker game across from me. The car is a haze of cigarette smoke and there is no respite for the only non-smoker left in the world. I'm off to somewhere to try to find some air....

Alex caught a cab from the Miami train station to Dinner Key. He was worn out from his all night train ride from Washington and had no idea how long he would be at Dinner Key. He decided that if he had any time at all, he either would have to sell his Ford or have someone in San Francisco drive it to Miami for him. He knew with the training, he would not have time.

Dinner Key was the main Pan American base for the Caribbean and South America. Already it was becoming the most important embarkation point for anything going to Africa and the CBI. It was also Pan Am's largest training base and rapidly becoming a training facility for all of the services aerial navigators and flight engineers.

Alex paid the cab driver and was just jogging up the steps of the main administration building when Roger Kent came walking out of the front door. "Roger, how in the hell are you doing? Long time no see!"

Roger took Alex's extended hand and said, "How's it going Alex! Last time we flew together was with that eight ball Neville Brewster. You were being transferred to Cavite."

"Jeepers Roger…that seems like a whole lifetime ago! You know, after I left you guys in Manila, I went on to Hong Kong. I was there a week before the Japs hit. I was supposed to go back to Cavite with Fred Ralph but in the mean time World War II broke out."

"Yeah, I heard *Myrtle* was sunk, but I had no idea who was on the crew except 'Captain Fred Ralph and crew' as it was phrased on the bulletin board."

Alex asked, "What brings you here, Roger? How was that return trip with "Smoothie Brewster?"

"Brewster's history! When we got back to Frisco, Pettit turned his ass in, and the chief pilot dumped him. That caper of keeping Pettit from entering that sprung plate in the maintenance logbook did him in. Last I heard the Navy had him flying PBYs."

"I'll ask you the same question everyone else seems to be asking these days. Where were you when they bombed Pearl?"

Roger said, "Since Pearl, it seems like all the stories are long ones and mine's no exception. I was third on the *Philippine Clipper* on December eighth."

Alex let out a long whistle and said, "Yeah, we heard in Hong Kong she was caught in Wake, but I had no idea you were on it! Getting news in China was nearly impossible. We were spending most of our time just trying to figure out how to get out of there. Look, I have all day to check in; got time to tell me about it?"

"You bet! Let's go sit in the shade, and I'll bring you up to speed."

There were a couple of tables and chairs near the Pan Am terminal building. Sightseers, knowledgeable of Clipper schedules, were waiting to watch the graceful flying boats takeoff and land on Biscayne Bay. Alex walked over to the refreshment stand, slapped down a dime and bought two Cokes. The two pilots sat down and Alex said, "So, what happened to you guys, Roger?"

"Well, we got off on schedule from Wake O.K. and were on the way to Guam. We had just leveled off when we got a call from Wake. Get this! They told us to return immediately! As you know, that never happens. You can imagine how surprised we were. Why…we were so close we were still receiving them on low frequency. We recognized the voice…it was John Cooke, the station manager. We all just looked at one another. Well Ham…Ham Hamilton was the skipper; he asked Wake; 'Why the turn back?' Cooke came back and said, 'Just turn back and land as soon as possible,' he said we would get the full scoop after we landed."

Roger continued, "Well it didn't take a brain surgeon to figure out it must be something other than someone had left their passport. With the news of the last months, the warning of war that everybody in the Pacific was getting…we knew it had to be the Japs; the question was, what had happened, and where? Anyhow, we did a one eighty, dumped a lot of fuel to get down to max landing weight and splashed down as soon as we were finished."

Roger paused to take a sip of his Coke. "We were still sailing up to the dock and saw Cooke waving like a mad man on the dock. Just as soon as we shut the engines down Cooke came aboard and told us that Pearl Harbor had been under air attack most of the morning, and Wake, and all the other islands, were on wartime alert. After getting that turn around message, we were expecting to hear the Japs had attacked somewhere…maybe Manila, or Indochina. Hells bells…the last place in the world anybody expected was Pearl!"

"What did you guys do then?"

"Well, the engineers got busy re-fueling and the rest of us went up to the radio room to see if there was any more information coming in. We had no sooner gone through the front door than we heard the radio operator from Guam saying they were under air attack. The speaker was on, and we could actually hear Jap airplane engines, guns and the bombs dropping! The guy was describing the action like he was an announcer at a football game. Then he said, 'That last one was too damned close, I'm getting out of here. This is Guam KVX5, out!'"

Roger lit a cigarette and went on, "Ham, like the rest of us, didn't know what to expect, so he carried the mission briefcase ashore to see what the company guidelines were. He pulled out the sealed instructions, and he read them to Cooke and the others that had come to the shack. Basically, the orders said: save the passengers, crew and aircraft, in that order; burn the mail, and get the hell out of there.

"The orders were in enough detail to put you to sleep if it wasn't for the fact that they were the only thing we had to go on. At least a contingency plan."

Alex said, "Yeah, that's what Ford's crew said coming the long way home. What did you do about the plans?"

"Cooke and Hamilton had already decided we were going to try to make a run for the Hawaiian Islands. Of course, no one knew what the Japs were up to there. For all we knew they would invade the Islands before we arrived! In any event, Ham told us to fuel for Midway with the idea that if the Japs had occupied Hawaii, we would try to skirt the 'big island' and land at Hilo. The idea was, we could re-fuel there and make a run for Frisco.

"Just as we were getting geared up to go to Midway and Hilo, Cooke got a call from the naval commander—a guy named Cunningham, on the other side of the island. He and that marine major, you know, Devereux, the guy we had breakfast with the day they got that 'war warning' back in November...well, he said they wanted a meeting with Cooke and Hamilton about what was going on. They sent a car, and the two of them took off to the other side to see what they wanted.

"While they were gone, the rest of us got ready to high tail it for Midway. The only passenger we had aboard was an AVG lieutenant named Ajax Baumler...hard name to forget. He was riding herd on a shipment of P–40 tires and parts bound for China."

"Small world," Alex said, "My wife, Anna, would have met that shipment in Hong Kong had the war not started."

"Wife...when did you have time to get married?"

"Go ahead and finish, and I will tell you all about it."

"Yeah—should be some story! Anyhow, you probably guessed what came next. While Ham and the station manager were gone, here come the Japs. They were hitting the navy and marine squadron with everything they had. The attack was so bad we figured Ham and Cooke must have gotten the schnitzel on the other side. Then it was our turn. When they finished with the marines, they strafed and bombed the hell out of all the Pan Am facilities: hotel, dock, fuel dump, Adcock direction finder...the whole shebang. Hell, we couldn't even see the Clipper with all the smoke and water being thrown up in the air. We thought she was a goner.

"Well, just as the Japs finished giving us a pasting, here comes the car, all shot full of holes, back with the skipper and Cooke. Seems they had to dive in a ditch on the way back when the Japs strafed their car. They told us that Commander Cunningham and Devereux wanted us to escort their F4F Wildcats on combat patrol and search for the Jap fleet for Christ's sake. The fighters were pretty basic. They didn't even have a bird dog aboard; so Devereux and Putnam, the fighter squadron Commander, were afraid that once out of sight of land there was a good chance they couldn't find their way back to the island. Anyhow, the skipper and Cooke agreed and were on their way back when the Japs hit us. Of course, the attack put the kibosh on the whole escort and search plan idea. All they wanted to do then was save what, and whom they could, and get out of Dodge.

Well, the good news was the Clipper survived the attack. Cooke and Ham organized work parties, dumped the P–40 tires, tore all the seats and furniture out and burned all the mail. Then we took on all the station people we could, and got out of there.

"Even after removing the cargo, mail and furniture, we were still overloaded big time! When we left the dock, we wallowed through the water like an over-stuffed whale.

"It took us three tries to get her off the water; you know how short the lagoon is at Wake."

Alex nodded.

"First time, Ham just couldn't get her on the step...too heavy. The Clipper just plowed through the water like the overloaded ship she was and never did start to plane. We taxied back for another try. This time Ham had us throw absolutely everything overboard that wasn't needed...hatches, what was left of the furniture, suitcases, Martin parts, tools...you name it.

"Second time we got her on the step, but there wasn't enough lagoon left to get her off, so back we went again for another try. This time, while we were taxing back, Hamilton had us move about ten people to the back of the airplane for better trim, and this time we made it, but just!

"You know where that flag marks the end of the dredged part of the lagoon?"

Alex said, "Yeah."

Roger went on. "Well, we went well past that and we were still on the water. It's a good thing we were on the step and not plowing or we would have torn the bottom out and ended up scuttled on the beach. During the takeoff, Cooke was yelling like crazy, 'we're only two feet over the coral heads! Get her off! Get her off!' Well, Ham eased her off, touched again, bounced and skimmed just over the beach and headed right for the burning hotel. It must have been a sight for those left on the ground. When the ship felt right, Ham zoomed at the last minute, and everyone aboard smelled the smoke and felt the plane buffet as we just cleared what was left of the hotel roof."

Alex said, "Sounds like the takeoff we made at Leopoldville on the *Pacific Clipper*, but we'll save that story for another time...go on, Roger!"

"Well, we held it on the deck until nightfall for two reasons: one, we were so damned heavy we couldn't climb anyhow, and two, we were harder to spot flying just above the ocean. After nightfall, we climbed and finally cooled the ship down."

Alex asked, "Did the Japs get Wake's Adcock?"

"Yeah, they got it all right. Without Wake's direction finder, we had nothing to steer out on...no nav aid outbound to Midway. John Hurtsky was the navigator. He really had his job cut out for him cause most of the time it was daylight...nothing but the sun to shoot. We had no idea if Midway had been attacked, and the sixty-four dollar questions were: one, would Midway's direction finder be working, and two, would there be anything left to help us make a night landing when we got there?

"Well, Hurtsky and the skipper finessed the navigation. After the sun went down, he had the stars, so that helped. When we got in range, suspicions confirmed...no direction finder! What we did have though was a bright light on the horizon...small at first and then larger and larger. It was Midway on fire! The Japs managed to provide us with one humongous homing beacon!

"Anyway, there was so much light from the fires there was no problem at all landing in the dark. After landing, and after seeing all those fires, we wondered if the Japs had gotten the fuel dumps. Boy was that a relief when we found they were O.K. We tanked up, put on some more Pan Am people and high tailed it out of there for the Hawaiian Islands. With the extra Pan Am people, we weighed even more than we did leaving Wake, but we had a lot more room for takeoff on Midway's larger lagoon. With no Adcock, it was still the same drill all the way to the islands. Until we got the lead in islands, it was celestial all the way.

"Figuring there would be a lot of trigger-happy troops wanting some pay back after the seventh, the captain decided to break radio silence and have the radio operator give Pearl a call on voice. We were all relieved to hear that they knew we were coming, and they told us to go ahead and land at the Pan Am facility at Pearl Harbor. Somehow, it had escaped the entire attack unscathed...must have been low on the priority list with all those juicy battleships around."

Alex said, "From the pictures I've seen, Pearl must have been a real mess."

"And how! When we descended for the approach, we could see the damage. Alex, those bastards really did a number on us. A lot of the ships on battleship row were still burning. You could see the smoke a hundred miles out. With the exception of the carriers and the subs, they got just about everything: battleships, harbor facilities—caught army and navy air with their pants down...really a bad day for us.

"Alex, it was enough to make you cry, and some of the guys did. With all the stuff on the radio and in the papers, it was hard to believe we were so totally unprepared. How could this have happened?"

"Yeah, Roger...I know exactly what you mean. It was the same thing in Hong Kong. The island and all of the territories have been surrounded by the Japs for God knows how long...right? And, right up until December eighth, it was the eighth over there...everyone just turned a blind eye. Ignore them, and they would just go away. Well, they didn't, and except for the CNAC planes that they missed, Anna, I, the crew...we would all be in a prison camp with that blond, Bonnie Belinda, you and I carried out there on our last trip."

"Yeah, I remember her...movie star or something."

"My new wife is a Russian. She is an émigré. Escaped from the Bolshe-viks...lived in Shanghai most of her life. She's seen the Japanese in action since the beginning way back in '37. They've killed God knows how many Chinese since then! She can't even talk about what she saw in Nanking, and she's about as strong a woman as you will ever meet. It must have been awful! Worse, her parents are still there."

"Yeah Alex, I remember a couple of years back...guess it was '38...they showed a piece in a newsreel about a lot of people getting killed...but that was about the last you heard of it."

"Yeah...there was a lot more to it than on those newsreels. There was the world press and then there was Anna. She shot a lot of pictures of what happened. When she left, though, the pictures were lost and she still feels guilty about that. She wanted so much to get those pictures out of there and show the world just what was really going on over there."

"Well finish the story—how did you finally get back to the States," Alex asked.

Roger took the last swig of his Coke and went on. "After we splashed down and sailed to the Pearl float, the station manager greeted everyone coming up the ramp with a shot of whiskey. Guess he figured we needed it after being in the air over 30 hours.

We slept like the dead; we gassed up, and with only the crew, flew the Clipper back to San Francisco the next day."

The two young aviators paused to watch a double column of Army Air Corps officers marching off to a Pan American classroom.

Alex motioned over his shoulder to the column and said, "For now, that's what New York tells me I'll be doing...training Air Corps and Navy navigators! Guess they figured if we're going to get bombers and transports to Europe and the CBI, we're going to need a lot of them, and guess what? Other than a handful in the service, we're about the only ones in the world that knows how to do it right now."

Roger said, "Guess you heard the government requisitioned our entire fleet of flying boats. The Brits got one of the Boeings and we will be flying the rest...at least for the immediate future. Seems we are the only ones in the free world with a long range over water passenger and cargo aircraft. I'm supposed to train as a first on the Boeing 307, but that's still up in the air."

The two continued to talk about their immediate future. He explained to Roger that the P–40 parts made it to China with Harold Grey, going the other way in *Atlantic Clipper* in yet another Boeing 314, and that he had picked up the rest of *Myrtle's* crew in Calcutta. Roger thought that Alex would only be in navigation training long enough to train the initial cadre of the Air Corp's instructors and then they would be doing their own training.

Both wondered if the powers to be considered them more valuable in their present position with Pan Am, or as fighter pilots, the position they both held in the Navy before coming to the airline. Both agreed the skills they had developed with Pan Am would probably serve the war effort better, at least for the present, until the military could handle what they were doing.

Alex told Roger about his new wife, and that if they kept him at Dinner Key long enough, she would join him there and he would somehow get his car from San Francisco.

CHAPTER 37

▼

THE VISIT

Maryland
fall 1942

Alex trained only one class of Army and Navy navigators when a telegram came from New York asking if he were still interested in flying as captain for CNAC back in China. He reasoned if he were there, he might at least be able to get some word about what had happened to Anna's parents. Anna agreed with his decision. She would stay in Maryland and have the baby as long as he promised to come back to her. He accepted the assignment, and as soon as he was route checked by CNAC, he started flying the hump as captain on the DC–3.

Winter and summer gave way to fall. Anna stayed busy helping Clara Cannon and Shelly Ann with household chores, and trying to make herself useful. Occasionally she visited Washington with Zachary and Clara for shopping and sightseeing. On two such trips, she was asked to visit Captain Bergantz to answer questions regarding China.

As the months went by and she got larger with the baby, those wonderful trips became less frequent, and she contented herself with long walks to the town, writing letters to Alex, and reading from Zachary's extensive library.

By August, Anna had relegated herself to staying almost exclusively at home.

On a particularly oppressive day, she was sitting in a rocker on the porch reading. Shelly Ann, the housekeeper, had the day off. Through the screened door, Anna could hear the clatter of pots and pans as Clara worked in the kitchen. There was scarcely a breath of air as Anna waved a paper fan with one hand and read from a book in the other. She heard the crunch of tires in the gravel and looked up to see a large car turn into the circular driveway. It was just after noon when the black Buick stopped with its passenger side facing the front of the house.

Anna could not see the driver. She could only see that he wore a white suit and was in the process of putting on a white Panama hat. She stopped fanning herself and sat up rigidly in her chair as she recalled her night flight from Chongqing almost a year ago. She was galvanized with fear as the man approached the porch stairs.

He took off his hat, began to dab his forehead with a sweat-stained handkerchief and said, "Ms. Anna Boreisha, or rather Mrs. Cannon?"

He had a heavy French accent.

"At last, I am in a position to introduce myself. Ah! I see you are with child," the man said in mock surprise.

Anna wondered if Clara had heard the approaching car.

"My name is Arnaud DeRuffe, and I bring you word of your parents, in China."

Anna couldn't speak.

He continued dabbing his forehead and said, "They are still living in Shanghai, you know. We have mutual acquaintances there who have located them, and as of this moment they are seeing to their well being."

He put on his hat again, and stuffed the dirty handkerchief in his breast pocket. He reached into his side pocket and withdrew an envelope and handed it to Anna.

Anna rose; with one hand she held her unborn child; with the other she took the envelope. She could hear Clara walking on the hardwood floors toward the front of the house.

"Follow the instructions in the envelope and you can be assured of the continued good health and happiness for you and your loved ones."

Anna said breathlessly, "How can I contact you?"

"You must follow the instructions in the envelope exactly, Madamn Cannon. I will make the necessary allowances for your present condition, but nothing in these instructions can be altered. Again, you must follow the instructions exactly. If you do not, I cannot guarantee the safety of your parents, these lovely people you are staying with, or for that matter, your new baby."

Clara opened the screen door from the living room as DeRuffe walked down the front porch steps.

Clara Cannon asked, "Anna, who was that gentleman?"

"He was lost, mother. I just gave him directions back to the town."

Anna felt a sharp pain below her stomach that almost took her breath away. She clasped both hands around her abdomen, sat back down in the rocker and said to Clara, "Mother, I think it's time!"

BOOK II

CHAPTER 38

▼

THE PENINSULA HOTEL

Hong Kong
November, 1994

Stephen awoke from a fitful sleep after the long flight from Anchorage. He remembered he was in the Peninsula Hotel. Today was the day he would meet Charlie Fat's grandfather. The Pen reeked with history and had a special significance for Stephen. His mother and father had met here. A faint smile crossed his face. From his mother's diary, he had good reason to suspect he might have been conceived in one of these rooms.

Modern conveniences aside, the room still suggested the distinct elegance of the orient. There was television complete with CNN, a telephone with modem connection and a mini bar stashed with everything from Bombay gin to Coca Cola. The ornate teak and glass desk, brocade drapes, cabinetry and scenes of Hong Kong's harbor in lacquered frames—all of this suggested a permanence of Chinese opulence. He wondered how much difference there was between the Pen now and his parent's day.

Stephen swung his legs over the side of the bed, stood, and pulled a towel from the copious supply in the bathroom. He spread the towel on the floor by the bed, sat down, hooked his feet under the lip of the bed and did his 50 obligatory sit-ups. Push-ups and lunges completed his daily routine.

He went to the bathroom and stood in front of the mirror. "Not bad for an old guy, he thought." He was 52 years old, right at six feet and still had the 34 inch waist he had in his thirties. There was no flab and still good definition in his chest, stomach and arm muscles, and he still had the legs of a long distance runner. His grandparents had said he had his mother's hair. Even now, there were but a few grey streaks making their appearance in his once raven black hair. Women had told him it looked "dashing," but he saw it differently. He looked in the mirror and was acutely aware he was single, had no family and unable to enter into lasting relationships; he was unfulfilled, uneasy, and didn't know where he fit in the world; worse, he didn't know what to do about it. He felt no sense of permanence. He was lonely with no prospect of intimacy except for his on again off again non-relationships—dalliances, really. He shrugged off the feelings as he had so many times in the past. Stephen showered, shaved and dressed in his standard layover uniform when he was working—khaki tropical gabardine trousers and a dark blue golf shirt.

Stephen considered Charlie Fat's relatives. The grand parents must at least be in their eighties and probably were somewhat intimidated meeting a Westerner. After a lifetime in a society where any ostentation was considered bourgeois, and simplicity a virtue, a meeting and luncheon in the opulence of the Peninsula was no doubt a formal occasion for them. The least he could do was wear a sports coat. He walked to the closet and pulled the Travel-Smith wrinkle free blazer from the hanger and threw it on the bed. He slipped on his black Rockport dress loafers that doubled as his uniform shoes, threw the blazer over his shoulder, and left the room.

Stephen took the elevator to the main lobby and bought a Herald Tribune at the newsstand. Walking as he read, he began skimming the headlines as he made his way toward the coffee shop.

One of his favorite things to do in Hong Kong was to read the newspaper in the Lobby Restaurant, and have eggs florentine, a specialty of the Pen.

"Mr. Cannon? Excuse me sir…my name is Shigao Matsumoto." Stephen stopped and looked up from his paper to see a middle-aged Japanese man proffering a business card. He glanced at the card and saw the Hong Kong address of an office equipment firm written in English, Chinese and Japanese. Before he could gather his defenses, the man continued.

"Mr. Cannon, I have reason to believe I might have a proposition that could be very important to you. Could I have a moment of your time?"

By this time, Stephen had snapped out of the reverie of his newspaper headlines and the anticipation of a quite breakfast. He was not good at this, but he suspected the man must be in his mid forties—maybe a little older. At home, he hated intrusions on his privacy. Abominable salesmen—telemarketers, they drove him to distraction. Christ—not even a public lobby in Hong Kong was sacred!

Unconsciously, he rolled his newspaper into a tight roll. Holding the paper in both hands he said, "What is it that you want...was it Matsumoto?"

"Yes! Matsumoto! Could we please sit down a minute? I shan't take more than a moment of your time."

"Mr. Matsumoto, I was just on my way to breakfast. I have an important meeting in a little while. How is it that you know my name?"

"Please, Mr. Cannon. Just sit down with me a moment and I will explain everything."

Stephen slapped the rolled newspaper gently against his leg. Reluctantly, he gestured toward two of the lobby's large overstuffed chairs and motioned for Matsumoto to take the chair next to him.

As the two sat Stephen said, "What is it Mr. Matsumoto?"

"Thank you for your time, Mr. Cannon. I will be brief. I belong to an international group interested in insuring the history of the Japanese people is not...how do you say, sullied by those who would have it in their interest to do so. At present, several organizations in the world are attempting to do just that. Some discredit us for political reasons...others ideological. Some have old hatreds of the Japanese because of what they perceived was an injustice put upon them, or someone they knew in the war."

"What does that have to do with me?"

"My organization has reason to believe that you have been contacted by one of the groups I have mentioned. We believe it is possible you are being coerced into believing some of the lies that have been perpetrated regarding Japanese activities during the war in China. We also believe you came to Hong Kong in order to receive such information, and perhaps, unknowingly, help them disseminate this misinformation. Mr. Cannon, my organization has authorized me, on its behalf, to pay you twenty thousand U.S. dollars to buy that information from you to insure more defamatory lies are not made public."

Stephen felt the blood rising in his face. He paused before speaking and regarded the man before him. He made a deliberate effort to take a deep breath and calm himself before he spoke.

The man was handsome, Stephen thought...he seemed to have one of those faces that evoked character and yet it was better than even odds he was somehow tied up with the bastards who had burglarized his home.

"Mr. Matsumoto, what makes you believe that I have been contacted by such an organization, or that I might be privy to such information as you suggest?"

The Japanese looked Stephen squarely in the eye and said, "I have no idea how my organization connected you with this information, Mr. Cannon. I simply received a fax regarding your arrival and where you would stay in Hong Kong. They have asked me to contact you and present you with this proposition. I hope that in no way I have appeared discourteous or have in any way offended you."

"Mr. Matsumoto, not that it's any of your business, but my mother disappeared in China in 1943. No one has seen her since! I have recently found out that she was in the city of Nanking in late 1937 and early 1938. I have come to Hong Kong to hear an account of what happened to her while she was running for her life from the Japanese...when they laid siege to that city. I have also come to claim some of her personal items and maybe find out the circumstances of her disappearance. That's all!"

"Mr. Cannon, please..."

"No you wait, damn it and hear me well! My home in Maryland was burglarized a couple of weeks ago. One of the items stolen was a letter written to the gentleman who is going to tell me what he knows about my mother. In that you knew I was coming to Hong Kong at this particular time, I can only surmise that it must have been someone from your organization who was involved with the burglary and contacted you with that information...and that, sir, really pisses me off!"

The Japanese's complexion became visibly red as he weighed what Stephen said.

"Mr. Cannon, ah, I...I had no idea, no knowledge...please believe me, I simply received a fax from the United States saying that you would be at the Peninsula today. I have no knowledge of how that information was obtained."

Visibly shaken, Shigao Matsumoto put his hands together and contemplated the carpet. There was an audible hiss as he sucked air between his clenched teeth.

"Mr. Cannon, please forgive me. I too lost someone in China. My father was an officer in the imperial army as was my uncle. My father came back, but my uncle did not. My father felt a great loss not only for himself, but for Japan."

He continued, "My grandmother was a casualty of the American fire bombings, in Kyoto."

"A lot of people died in the war, Mr. Matsumoto."

"Mr. Cannon, my father was a war hero in China. His name was Major Matsui Matsumoto, and he fought with a special unit in Shanghai. His brother was also a war hero, but as I have told you, he died in the war. Both of them fought honorably for the Emperor. They lived by the Bushido Code, the code of the warrior. When my father returned from the war he joined an organization whose purpose was to help Japan remember the glory of those who fought and died in the war and to help suppress the lies of those who might diminish that glory."

"Mr. Matsumoto, has it ever occurred to you or others in your organization, that maybe there is some truth in what is being said about the Japanese atrocities in the war?"

"No, that is impossible! It is not only my organization, Mr. Cannon, everyone in Japan knows about the exaggerations. There is nothing in our schoolbooks to suggest we were doing anything other than defending Japanese interest and trying to promote prosperity! They are lies…all lies! I think, though, that some of my colleagues are over zealous in their pursuits."

"If it's any consolation, Mr. Matsumoto, there is almost nothing in our history books about the war or those atrocities either. However, there are plenty of books, personal accounts of soldiers and prisoners, and plenty of photographs that describe what happened."

Stephen continued, "Please listen to me well Mr. Matsumoto! I am here to find out the truth of my mother's disappearance…nothing more. I have no interest in promulgating a lie, or for that matter, finding out the truth about what the Japanese may or may not have done in the war. As far as I am concerned, it's over…it's an unfortunate history, but it's done with. Personally, I just want to get on with my life, and part of getting on with it requires me to try to find some closure on what happened to my mother…do you understand?"

Shigao sucked some more air between his teeth.

"Mr. Cannon, I am sorry about your mother and hope you find out what happened to her. You have my card. Please understand my only interest is in seeing that no more lies are spread about my ancestors…nothing else! I only want respect for their memory. If there is anything I can do to help you, please do not hesitate to contact me.

The handsome man bowed, both hands at his side. He did not extend his hand and neither did Stephen.

Disconcerted, Stephen went to the café and had his breakfast. Instead of collecting his thoughts and focusing on the meeting with Cheng, he kept thinking of what Shigao said. Could it really be that they had so little knowledge of their complicity in the war? He wondered if they had ever heard of the Armenian slaughter by the Turks. Probably not…the Turks still deny that ever happened as well.

After checking at the main desk, Stephen went to the concierge. He gave the clerk a copy of Cheng Fat's telephone number given to him by Charlie. He explained the situation to the concierge and asked he suggest to Charlie's family that they meet here, at the Peninsula, for lunch or dinner, whatever was more convenient for them. He explained it would be an honor for him to meet his mother's old acquaintance, and that he would arrange for a car to pick them up and return them to their home.

The concierge was able to reach them on the telephone without difficulty. Stephen assumed old people stayed in their apartment most of the time, probably watching television much as retired people did in the United States. Cheng agreed. They did not want to be out late, and lunch at the Peninsula met with their satisfaction.

Stephen then called his airline's handling agent at Kai Tak airport and asked if they had been able to arrange for a translator for the meeting. They said they had. They had arranged for a woman from the American Consulate. Her name was Karen Hardesty, and she had called only moments before suggesting she were free this morning should he desire to meet her first. Stephen asked the concierge to call her back and ask if she might be able to join him for brunch at the Peninsula so they might talk over this evening's meeting. He said he would wait for her reply in the lobby.

Stephen went to the sitting area not far from the concierge's station, sat down, and began to read his newspaper. Almost immediately, he lost the thread of the article as passages from his mother's journal entries came to mind regarding the day the war broke out. The overstuffed chairs, the couches, the man in the white suit, the old ladies—all trapped and unable to escape the juggernaut pointed at Hong Kong. It might not have been the same furniture, carpets or the light fixtures, but it was here that the Clipper crew made their plans to escape. It was here that his father proposed to his mother. It was here that so many people lived with the realization they would soon be dead, rape victims, prisoners or slave laborers. After having just re-read the China Diaries, the place had an almost mystical attraction for him.

"Telephone call for Mr. Stephen Cannon."

The bellman's mantra snapped Stephen from his reverie. He folded his newspaper, tucked it under his arm and walked to the concierge's desk.

"Hello, this is Stephen Cannon."

"Mr. Cannon? My name is Karen Hardesty. I am the translator from the American Consulate. The story you told in your letter regarding your mother and Mr. Fat is fascinating, and I would be more than happy to help you with your meeting."

Stephen said, "You are most kind, Ms. Hardesty. The message you left suggested you might be free to discuss this evenings meeting."

Karen said that something had come up; she couldn't make it this morning, and she would see him at this afternoon's meeting with Cheng Fat.

Stephen made sure he arrived early to check the preparations. He had arranged for a private alcove so they would not be disturbed by other guests. He asked that the maitre d' let him know when his guests arrived so that he might greet them personally. As Stephen was speaking to the Maitre d' about his requirements, a female voice asked, "Mr. Stephen Cannon?"

Stephen turned and found himself looking at a Paula Zahn look alike.

"Paula Zahn! So glad to meet you!"

"Not quite…but I get that all the time"

"Yes, I'm sure you do! Just thought I would get that out of the way right up front. Please call me Stephen."

"Karen Hardesty, Stephen." She offered her hand, arm straight out, hand angled slightly down in the manner affected by so many professional women. She had a slight accent that Stephen couldn't place.

Stephen said, "Please have a seat Ms. Hardesty. I was just discussing privacy issues for our meeting with the Maitre d'. He's reserved this alcove for us so we won't be disturbed."

Karen Hardesty was in western professional mufti, not as severe as some Wall Street "yuppies," but yet professional and understated. Her hair was cut like the real Zahn and Stephen wondered if she tried to promote the resemblance.

Stephen said, "You know quite a bit about me and what's going on here today, Karen…how about telling me a little about yourself?"

"Sure…as you know I work for the American Consulate. I speak Mandarin and several dialects as well as French and German. Coincidently, my primary work involves me with cases much as yours: re-uniting relatives from Hong Kong or the PRC and someone with American ties. I've been here almost five years and for nonofficial cases, such as yours, I charge one hundred dollars for everyday I do something for you."

"That sounds fine, Ms. Hardesty. You sound like just the person I need. It's hard to describe what this meeting means to me. I want to get as much information from Mr. Fat and his wife as possible…yet, at the same time I want to make sure I observe Chinese customs, and in no way seem to pressure, or in any way show disrespect for these people.

"Yes, I understand, Stephen."

"Ms. Hardesty, I…I gave a lot of background information in the letter you received from my agents in Hong Kong. It's…ah, this meeting is much more than just retrieving some of my mother's journals and possessions for me. You see, I never knew her, or my father either. She returned to China shortly after I was born…I guess to be with my father who was a commercial pilot flying for the

Chinese. I was raised by my grandparents who knew little else. There was almost no correspondence from them before they disappeared. I…I guess it's something I have been trying to come to grips with all my life; I need to find out why she left. I'm hoping this meeting will somehow bring some closure."

Karen sat erect, hands in her lap, and leaned forward in silent concentration. Her demeanor suggested a good listener…that she was absorbing everything Stephen said. As he finished, she didn't say anything for a moment and simply waited for his revelation to sink in. Then she said, "Yes, I think I understand, Stephen…I am sure I can be of some help."

Stephen motioned for the waiter and asked if she would like anything to drink. She asked for mineral water and Stephen ordered the same. As the waiter departed they looked up to see the Maitre d' greeting a very old Cheng Fat at his station in the front of the restaurant. Both joined their guests. Karen made the formal introductions and ushered the old gentleman to their table. Cheng took Stephen's hand in both of his and continued shaking it as the introductions were made. He had that look of wisdom that seemed to grace the faces of only a few his age. It radiated a knowledge of one who had lived and survived China's warlords, the Western Taipans, the onslaught of the Japanese, the horror of World War II, the clashing of the Communists and the Nationalist, the excesses of both, and indeed the paranoia of the Cultural Revolution.

As soon as the introductions were complete, Cheng Fat held out the ancient leather map case to Stephen. He presented it at arms length almost as one would with a formal offering. Smiling broadly with betel nut stained teeth, Cheng looked much like the child who simply couldn't wait to give a parent his surprise present.

Stephen was slow to accept the bag as Cheng Fat stood, nodding his head in affirmation still proffering the map case with outstretched arms. The smiles of the introduction faded from Stephen's face. He looked at the bag as if acceptance might somehow reveal something he really didn't want to know. After an awkward pause, Stephen accepted the bag and held it as if someone had handed him stolen treasure.

CHAPTER 39

▼

THE MISSING JOURNALS

Kowloon, The Peninsula Hotel
November, 1994

With the help of the waiter and Karen, Stephen ordered a grand dinner. Stephen and Karen ate little but instead listened to Cheng's fascinating recollections of his mother, his family and their escape together on the Yangtze. As expected, Cheng pleaded fatigue and gladly took the car back to his brother's apartment after the elegant luncheon. Stephen pleaded jet lag and dropped Karen Hardesty at her apartment building after declining an offer for coffee. His mind was racing with emotions he thought long forgotten. He wanted to get to his hotel, clean up and perhaps get up the courage to peruse the missing China Diaries.

At the Pen Stephen picked up his key, asked for any messages, and went to his room. He thought he would have a feeling of great anticipation at the thought of finally seeing the contents of the bag. Instead, it was more a feeling of dread. After all of this time, he was going to confront at least some of his mother's past. By the time he entered his room, he was choking with emotion.

Stephen could not explain his feelings. By the time he opened his door it was all he could do to keep from sobbing out loud. He slammed the door, flung the map case on the coffee table, threw his jacket on bed and went directly to the bathroom to wash his face and try and regain his composure.

He suspected that his worst fears might be realized after reading the diaries: that his mother had returned to China for a reason more important than being his mother. Worse, he might find he had misjudged her all of these years. When he dried his face and returned to the living room, all he did for a few minutes was stand, arms akimbo, and stare at the map case lying on the coffee table. After some time, he sat on the couch and un-fastened the ancient buckles that secured the flap, reached in, and placed the contents on the table.

Stephen looked at the contents. There were two packages. One contained the journals—he could tell by the shape. The other, was a rectangular tin. Both were wrapped in a kind of checkered oilcloth, sticky with age. The other items were what looked like a home made military medal and two taped 35mm film canisters. He picked the medal up and read the inscription on the ribbon bar. It read, "Soochow Creek, 1932." He wondered what the hell that was for and why his mother would have it.

Fat said he had only recently opened the package containing the journals. After he came to live in Hong Kong, he wanted to see if the journals gave some clue as to where she or some relative lived. He had seen entries regarding her family in Shanghai but had been unable to locate or find any record of the Boreisha family. Cheng Fat said he was certain that they were the same journals he had seen Anna writing in shortly before she and her companion left them on the Yangtze, early in 1938.

There were three journals. All looked as if they had come from the same source. The covers were made of leather, and all were cracked—but only a little. Each had acquired mildew, as leather is apt to do over time. They were bound together with a piece of ancient string, of a type he had never seen in the West.

With a sort of reverence, Stephen untied the bundle and picked up the one on top. He recognized the hand writing as his mothers and wondered if there might be more journals before these began, or, after those already in his possession. The first entry was 1936, the last two, 1937 through early 1938. He knew his mother was born in 1918. That would have made her only 18 years old when these began.

The second package was also wrapped in oilcloth. It too was tied with string of the same type as the first. From what Cheng Fat said, no one had touched the contents of the tin since their chance meeting on his sampan in 1937. Since he said it had remained unopened, Stephen wondered if some 57 years ago, it was his mother that had tied that simple knot. He removed the string and the protective covering. It was a rectangular tin of the type good English short bread came in. Besides the string, it was sealed with a kind of tape. It seemed to be made of cloth with one sticky surface. He determined the easiest way to open the tin would be to cut the tape where the overlapping lip met the sides. He stood up from the couch and rummaged around in his flight briefcase for his Swiss Army knife, opened one of the smaller blades, knelt beside the coffee table, and cut the tape at the seam. There was not as much rust as he had suspected and the lid came off with little difficulty.

Inside the tin were more than a dozen 35mm film canisters. Each canister was sealed with the same tape that waterproofed the cake tin. Still kneeling, Stephen picked up one of the canisters and turned it slowly in the light. It was marked with a date in the Eastern, or European date format. The one he was looking at read SH 37/7/5. Another read N 37/11/11. The markings appeared to have been made with a brush stoke using black paint or maybe ink. All but two of the canisters were marked in a similar manner.

Stephen stood up, picked up the journals, turned on the floor light, sat down on the occasional chair and began to read.

CHAPTER 40

▼

PETER AND LILIA

From Anna' missing journals
After the revolution

After the Russian revolution, Prince Peter and Lilia Boreisha were not so different from other Russian Émigrés in Shanghai. An accident of birth had brought them into a world of privilege. It was no accident, however, that caused them to lose that privilege. It was caused by an aristocracy that looked out mainly for itself, as the rest of society was left to receive the crumbs that fell from their bountiful tables. As in every such case in history, where disparity between the haves and the have-nots was too great, their society was doomed to revolution.

The Boreisha family, and others who had so much to lose, thought their position in the scheme of things a birthright. Worse, many didn't think about it at all. Like so many others of their class, Peter joined ranks with his classmates to defend that right for themselves and their heirs. Many of Peter's peers attended military school in Sebastopol. Almost all of his fellow cadets were from similar circumstances as their's, and as such, were staunch supporters of the Tsar. When revolution broke out, much of the regular military supported the Bolsheviks, and Peter and his comrades found themselves at war with the same army they had trained with. The lines were drawn, and the two armies clashed in an inglorious battle for control of Mother Russia.

The pro-Tsarist forces were called the White Russians. It was with the "Whites" that Peter cast the lot of the Boreisha family. From the diaries, many of the details were vague, but some of the salient facts were quite clear. Anna's mother, Lilia, was the more pragmatic of the two. She wanted them to salvage what they could and leave Russia while it was still possible. From what Stephen could elicit from the diaries, though, she had little to say about the decision. Even if she had been consulted, Stephen felt sure her desires would have been subordinated to her fathers.

Early in the conflict, the Whites were made up of three armies. Each army tried to free Moscow and Petrograd from the Bolsheviks, and initially, they were victorious and made rapid progress. It was about 1918 that the tide of war began to turn for the Bolsheviks and against the Whites. Anna was born in the same year.

Leon Trotsky, one of the leading Bolsheviks, was successful in organizing the Reds into a well-trained force. Before his leadership, they were nothing more than a disparate group of revolutionaries willing to die for anything better than a life under the Tsar. Die they did, as life under the Communists did little to free most of the common folk from an existence of abject depravation. After Russia became fully engaged in senseless slaughter with the Kaiser's troops the window of opportunity for escape gradually but surely shut. In any event, Trotsky was able to lead the Bolsheviks to victory over the Whites, and the pro-Tsarists supporters who remained were caught up in a reign of indescribable terror. At the last moment, at great risk, and with tremendous difficulty the Boreisha family chose, as many did, to flee east on the Trans Siberian Railroad. Peter took his family first to Harbin, in Manchuria. Later, they went to Shanghai. The remainder of the officer corps that didn't flee, or waited to long, were captured and executed. There were few if any exceptions.

Russians had no status in Chinese society, but it was their only option. They were stateless persons with no passports. If it were not for the extraterritoriality laws imposed on the Chinese as a result of onerous treaties, they would have had no place at all to go once the Western borders were closed.

Employment opportunities for women were limited. They had no passports, and Chinese considered them chattel. It did not take young Russian girls long to realize that if they were to change their circumstances it was necessary for them to obtain a passport by *any means*. They worked in the nightclubs, performed on stage, anything to get closer too, and with luck, marry someone with a passport. American and English men were their primary targets. Fat, thin, stupid, belligerent—it made no difference. Most would do *anything* to get that document that gave them the freedom to leave China if they chose.

For young Russian men, prospects were even worse. Like women, they had no social standing. Their pedigrees from Tsarist Russia meant nothing. Most had escaped with only their lives. They left behind the trappings of their status and brought with them only their character, their titles and memories of a life lost. Many spent their lives sotted with alcohol, living in the past, boasting how they and their comrades would one day return to Mother Russia and resume their rightful place in the old Russian aristocracy. They had no money, no job and no future. Among Russian women they were the last choice for a marriage partner. Other than a meaningless title, they had nothing to offer.

On the expatriate social scale, Russians were lower than the Chinese. As such, they were a source of ongoing embarrassment to the expatriates of other countries living in China. Sadly, a majority of the foreigners in this group thought themselves superior to the Chinese because of their race.

In China, as in Tsarist Russia, there had always been a tremendous gulf between the ruling class and the peasants. First, it was between the Mandarins, War Lords and the peasants. Then came the foreigners, the Opium Wars, one onerous treaty after another and of course, extraterritoriality. For the peasant, foreigners only represented another class at the top. Their own plight changed not a wit.

As Anna grew to a young woman in Shanghai, her father was well aware of the limited opportunities that awaited his daughter. He knew in this new world his Russian title meant nothing. He also knew that her best opportunity would lie in finding a *suitable arrangement*, and that meant marriage, or being kept by a foreign gentleman of means. In Peter's mind, only the former was an acceptable alternative, and that being the case, and regardless of his families modest means, he made it his life's mission to make sure that she was prepared.

The first part of preparing her was a gift. Anna was beautiful, and growing more so by the day. He thanked God daily that he did not have the almost impossible task of preparing a *plain* daughter for this mission.

Secondly, Peter Boreisha had to face the fact that he did not have the means to pay for a girl's formal finishing school, and even if he did, he had little confidence in the final product. Therefore, he devised a course of study for his daughter he thought would produce the best result considering his limited resources.

CHAPTER 41

▼

THE JOB

Shanghai
September, 1936

Anna's journal
I must find work
1936, 9 September

This is the first day my journal entries will be entirely in English. Papa has insisted! Up until today, when I had difficulty, I would write in Russian, or whatever Papa's language of the week. It seems so strange, but I really must practice the writing as much as possible to improve, no? I also need to speak and write more in French, but Papa feels it is more important to improve speaking and writing English. From what I read in the paper today, I think it is time for the Chinese to start learning Japanese.

It is amazing to me that the few times I encounter English people they immediately recognize me as a Russian, and rather than speaking to me in English, they speak to me in Pidgin, as if I were an un-educated Chinese! Even though many have lived here for years, few have taken the time to learn the language and seem surprised when I speak English. Although I have never had the opportunity to speak to an American, I understand they use many slang words. Every time I hear a new one, I add it to my notebook. I have learned most from the movies, and oh how I love the *movies! It takes most of the money I earn and is just one more reason I simply must find regular work.*

A Chinese man stopped me the other day and asked if I would like to work as a dancer at his club. I forgot the name of his establishment, but he said it was on Rue Chu Pao San. Papa said I was never to go there. He said that the area was called Blood Alley, and only soldiers, sailors, and low class people frequent that area.

For Papa's lesson today, I read of a wonderful aeroplane that lands on the water called the China Clipper. It is operated by the Pan American airline company and has actually flown all the way from San Francisco, in the United States, to Manila in the Philippines and on to Singapore. Soon, they will be flying to Macao and Hong Kong to connect with CNAC, the Chinese National Aviation Corporation. What a marvelous thing if I could find work with an aviation company and associate with those interesting people who travel! Papa says that it is amazing what the Americans are doing with aeroplanes and how far they have come since the simple flying machines that Papa's Whites flew against the Bolsheviks around the time I was born.

There are only a few aeroplanes here in Shanghai. Some are small sea-planes that operate on the river next to Lunghwa airport. The rest are land planes. Almost all are owned by CNAC. Saul doesn't think I have a chance of getting a job with them, or any other aviation company for that matter, as all the jobs there are filled with men. Regardless of what he says, I'm going to try! Perhaps I could get a job selling tickets or maybe cleaning aeroplanes....

Saul Abrahamson knocked on the door of the modest Boreisha apartment. Since Saul was just coming from work at the Goldman's electrical repair shop, he still wore his suit of black woolen trousers, a matching coat, white shirt and black tie. The suit was about two sizes too small for him. The trousers revealed most of his black socks over well worn, but polished, if not dusty, high topped shoes.

His family had arrived in Shanghai much the same way as Anna's: via the Trans Siberian Railroad, Harbin and Shanghai. His father had been a civil servant in the Weimer Republic until the Nazis came to power. After that, he and other Jews in government service were summarily dismissed. Saul's father was more prescient than most and quit Germany before it was too late. He took his wife and only son and joined his brother in his baking business in Shanghai.

Saul held a small wooden cylinder wrapped with copper wire in his hands. He had large hands and feet, and when Saul wore his suit it reminded Anna of a large black puppy who had not yet grown to fit his paws. He kicked at some pebbles in the dusty street and absentmindedly turned the coil over in his hands as he waited impatiently for Anna. The large hands and powerful wrist jutting from the jacket sleeves served to demonstrate just how small the suit was and how fast Saul was growing. His mane of black wavy hair was combed at least once today, but was now matted and almost flat from the hat he had stuffed in his hip pocket.

Saul continued to fidget with the coil. "Anna! Would you hurry up? The movie starts in forty minutes, and I don't want to miss the beginning!"

"Just a minute, Saul!"

He stared at his feet, and kicked another stone down the dusty street. A Chinese cart merchant pushed his wares past the house not even looking up at the gangly white boy wasting his time kicking rocks. He kept an even pace behind his cart. Hard working men didn't have time to observe the foolishness of *foreign devils.*

The door opened and Anna danced out. Saul felt a lightness of being just at the sight of her. It was not yet cold, but since it was her best outfit, she wore her long woolen skirt, woolen sweater and sensible walking shoes. Today she wore no hat and no gloves. Regardless of how she dressed, Saul thought she was the most beautiful girl in the world—even more so than the Hollywood "bombshells" he looked forward to seeing at the cinema.

Today, her usual half smile was even more radiant than usual in anticipation of going to the movies with her friends. Anna saw the look on Saul's face. She knew he was in love with her, and enjoyed the knowledge thoroughly. He and Wan Ting, from Master Cheng Tu's boxing school were her only male friends. Her only real girl friends were Irina and Tanya Federenko.

Anna kissed Saul perfunctorily on the cheek and said, "Hi Saul! Irina, Wan Ting and Tanya are going to meet us at the theater. I saw Tanya yesterday. She had to work late and said she would sleep in this morning and would meet us there."

Irina was four years younger than Anna, and when they were not studying, or doing odd jobs to make a little money, the two were inseparable. Anna was her idol. Tanya, Irina's sister was eighteen, the same as Anna, but these days had little time for *their little group.* Like so many Russian girls her age, she was a nightclub hostess. She worked at the Far East Cabaret, and unlike Irina, Anna and Saul, she didn't like books, studying, or their stupid Taijiquan classes taught by that foul-mouthed Cheng Tu. She liked the "good life" and about the only thing she had left in common with them was their love for American movies.

Tanya Federenko never missed any opportunity to show off her new clothes and makeup in front of her sister or Anna. Seldom would she let a meeting pass where she failed to mention handsome foreigners she had dinner with, or, the presence of some famous celebrity at the cabaret.

Even though Anna always greeted Saul with a kiss on the cheek, he still had trouble maintaining his composure, and almost never failed to reward her by turning a bright crimson. Every time this happened, Anna pretended she didn't notice, but had no illusions of the effect she had on men and on Saul in particular. She enjoyed it throughly. She was beautiful, knew it and was pleased with the power it gave her.

Anna thought Saul very handsome and getting more so by the day. For her, though, there was nothing more to it than that. Saul was just a boy. She had fantasies of meeting someone strong, handsome, and powerful—someone who would "sweep her off her feet" as so often happened in the movies.

Anna asked, "Saul...how is your English coming along?"

"Good...or should I say Oke Doke? That's what they say a lot of times in the movies."

Anna said, "Yes...I've heard that many times, and it sounds right, but maybe the right word would simply be, O.K."

"Yeah, the movies help a lot but it comes a lot faster when I have someone to speak with who already knows it good—like you Anna!"

"Knows it well," she corrected.

Anna smiled to herself. She didn't mind at all for now. She liked Saul and liked teaching him what she knew. He was a particularly good sparing partner, but she knew she was better than either he, Irina or Wan Ting. If she got a job, though, teaching English to Saul, Cheng Tu's long-range boxing lessons, and going to the movies was going to be a lot more difficult. Something would have to give.

"Saul, I'm going to get a job! Not a job like Tanya's, though—a real job, doing real work and meeting important people—something in aviation!"

"Anna, are you nuts?"

Saul loved that expression. It was just one he had picked in the movies.

"Only men have jobs in aviation. Think about it! If you're going to be in the aviation business, you have to be a pilot, radio operator, a navigator or a mechanic. Kripes, girl...all of those jobs are filled by men!"

"Oh yeah?"

Anna too tried to imitate their slang whenever possible.

"What about Amelia Earhart? What about Anne Lindbergh? Those women fly all over the world! The Lindberghs were just here in their Lockheed Sirius a couple of years ago. Anyhow, who's to say that a woman couldn't fill some of those jobs?"

They continued walking north on Tibet road. As they continued to talk, they watched the Chinese jockeys working out the thoroughbred horses for the cities' gentry on the Shanghai Race Club track. They crossed Foochow road, totally absorbed in their conversation and oblivious to the traffic and chaos of Chinese commerce going on around them.

"Yeah Anna, but those women are not just pilots; there're American pilots! Over there, man or women…doesn't matter…Americans can do just about anything! Remember, we're in China—you're a Russian woman, and I'm a Jew!"

Anna ignored him and said, "Just remember, *dufus*…they were women before they were pilots. Then, there's always clerical staff."

Still turning the coil over in his hands, Saul didn't say anything as they continued to walk to toward Nanking Road and the movie theater.

"Yeah, I guess you could try to get into that. Who're you gonna try for?"

Anna said, "Last week I drove out to the Lunghwa airport with Papa. He was driving an English client who booked a flight on CNAC. He was flying to Hankow on one of their nifty Loening amphibians."

"Say, maybe I could get a job there too! They use radio operators on the ground and in the air; anything would be better than working in the bakery with Papa and Mama. I hate it there…that's why I got the job at Goldman's electrical repair.

"You know, this coil is for a new radio set I'm building from spare parts Mr. Goldman gave me. I'm learning Morse too, you know. Maybe if I learned it well enough, and got a license, maybe I could get a job there too! Wouldn't that be swell? Just think…we could work together for an airline!"

Anna looked at Saul's beaming face and said, "Yes Saul…that would be swell!"

Wan Ting, Tanya and Irina met them in front of the theater as promised. Tanya was a pretty girl but not beautiful. Like so many of the cabaret hostesses she wore too much makeup and dressed much as she would have at work—really out of place in the middle of the afternoon on Nanking Road. She really looked like a taxi girl, the Shanghailanders' term for a streetwalker. Irina was always ashamed to be seen with her when she dressed like this, but her comments had little effect on her older sister. She would not listen to either her or Anna on the subject.

Wan Ting's family was perhaps the most affluent of their group. His father owned a fleet of rickshaws that he rented to hundreds of coolies who earned their livelihood pulling customers all over Shanghai.

As always, Anna greeted them all with a kiss to both cheeks immediately causing looks of consternation from movie patrons standing around her. A white skinned woman kissing a yellow man! Anna took devilish delight at being the cause of their anxiety. Caucasians immediately gave a look of distaste as if they had just witnessed a repulsive gaffe. The Chinese responded by pretending they didn't see.

China Seas was playing today with Clark Gable, Jean Harlow, Wallace Beery and Rosalind Russell. Anna especially liked Clark Gable. He was handsome, debonair, an adventurer—she was certain it was this kind of man who would someday sweep her off of her feet.

For the present, though, her immediate task was to find employment. She needed money to help her family and to make her own way. She wanted a job where she could at least meet people who traveled, maybe just a little bit like Clark Gable. She reasoned that her father would approve of her efforts; she knew he wanted her to marry a proper Englishman, or American.

After the movies, Saul walked with Anna to the post office, where she looked up the telephone number of the Chinese National Aviation Corporation. She gave the number to the operator and was connected to their booking office. She explained that she was applying for a job, and they in turn, connected her with their main office in the Robert Dollar building on the Bund. They suggested any application for employment should be turned in there.

CHAPTER 42

▼

SERGEI HOVANS

Shanghai
September, 1936

Anna's journal

> Today was a day of conflicting expectations. I left home on my bicycle this morning for the Robert Dollar building where I was to be interviewed for a position by a Mr. L. Bond, Operations Manager for the Chinese National Aviation Corporation.
>
> I had my hair styled at Madame Faunaux's. It cost more than it should have, especially as my hair is so short, but I feel it was worth it. I put on my best day clothes, the plaid woolen skirt and the brown jacket. I wanted to look as professional as possible. I was riding my bicycle to the Robert Dollar building, on the Bund, when it happened. Looking back, I should have been paying more attention to traffic, rather than thinking of what I would say at the interview, but I didn't. It happened in an instant. I heard a loud automobile horn and found myself lying in the street looking up at a large black limousine.
>
> Before I could get up, two men stepped out of the car and started speaking to me in Russian. Rather than thinking of my well being, my first thought was do I really look so Russian that the first men to hit me in a car would start speaking to me in my native tongue?

While I was still lying on the ground, I noticed I had slightly skinned one knee and worse, I had scuffed my best-polished shoes that I hoped would make a good impression at the interview....

Anna pedaled steadily as she kept going over in her mind what she would say to Mr. L. Bond at the Robert Dollar building. Her greatest asset was her appearance, but she couldn't depend on that. She of course spoke Russian that she felt was of little use to an airline. She also spoke Mandarin, Wu, Min dialects and English almost equally well. She had a working knowledge of French and Japanese but not so well as Mandarin and English. She also had a good knowledge of geography, history and current events in the world. Maybe that would be enough, she thought.

The sound of a powerful automobile from behind her snapped her from her musings. Before she could do anything, a black and chrome object came into her periphery and stuck her bicycle sending her tumbling out of control. The front wheel struck the curb, bent the rim, twisted the fork and sent Anna sprawling in the cobblestone street. As she skidded to a stop, she caught one leg between the bike and the street, pulling her skirt up around her waist. As she pushed the bicycle away, she could see that the cobblestones had skinned one leg superficially, but other than being dazed, she felt all right.

Anna was aware of someone stepping from the driver's door of the large automobile.

"Young woman: are you all right?"

Anna looked up towards the voice addressing her. The man was incredibly ugly!

He had Eastern European countenance, piggy eyes, barrel chest and a powerful looking body. He wore a long black leather coat, black trousers and out of place white shoes. As Anna pulled her skirt down over her knees, he regarded her with a leer.

"Are you all right?" Another man spoke to her in Russian as he stepped from the rear of the large car. He wore a black cape with a red lining, black skullcap and a black suit as well. The ugly man stood back in deference and said, "Stand up girl! Stand up...see if you can walk! We can't wait here all day!"

The other man with the cape regarded Anna as she began to get up. He seemed to be weighing something in his mind and said, "Not so fast Ostafii...the young lady has had quite a crash. Look at her poor bicycle!" His voice was educated Russian—not a commoner like the other. He reached for Anna's hand to help her stand.

"Of course Mr. Hovans…it's only…"

The man in the cape held up his hand, silenced the driver and said, "No Ostafii. Never be in a hurry when a beautiful woman needs help!" The man referred to as Mr. Hovans leaned over and extended a hand to help Anna to her feet. As he did so, his open suit jacket revealed a pearl handled revolver in a black leather shoulder harness.

"My dear lady: My name is Sergei Hovans. This is my associate Mr. Ostafii Rabin. Please accept my humblest apologies for striking your bicycle, and please allow me to pay for any damage I may have caused."

Hovans reached into his coat pocket and withdrew a glove leather wallet. He began to thumb out several bills and a business card.

"Young woman: my card."

Anna glanced at the card and saw, "Sergei Hovans, proprietor, Far East Cabaret." She immediately thought of her friend Tanya.

"Please accept this money for repair of your bicycle and any trouble I may have caused, and be so kind as to call on me at my little cabaret on Bubbling Well Road, and be my guest for dinner."

"That's very kind of you Mr. Hovans. My name is Anastasia Boreisha, but my friends call me Anna. I have an appointment at ten o'clock, at the Robert Dollar building. Without my bicycle, I fear that I will be late. Would it be too much of an imposition to ask you gentlemen drop me? That is, if it on your way. If not, I will leave my bike and catch a rickshaw."

The man called Rabin began to speak but again Hovans held up his hand and said, "There is no such thing as an imposition when a favor is asked for by a beautiful woman, Miss Boreisha…ah may I call you Anna?"

Before she could answer Hovans said, "We will be glad to drop you at the Robert Dollar building…won't we Ostafii."

Ostafii Rabin said, "Of course Mr. Hovans" He opened the trunk of the Bentley and wedged the bicycle under into the bonnet. He picked up a neatly coiled piece of cordage in the trunk and cinched the lid closed over the protruding bicycle. Rabin went to the driver's side, slid in behind the steering wheel and started the car.

Sergei Hovans opened the door for Anna, held her hand as he ushered her in, closed the door, and stepped into the car from the other side.

Anna considered Mr. Hovans more carefully. He was not handsome but at the same time not repulsive. He seemed a character right out of the movies. The skullcap was the type worn by pirates while the cape seemed appropriate for a villain or the opera. The shirt he wore, like everything else, was black and buttoned at the neck with no tie. Black patent leather shoes completed his ensemble. The effect was wholly theatrical, bordering on the bizarre.

As the large automobile turned into the teeming traffic of the Bund, Hovans asked, "Anna, what is it that you do?"

"I am presently unemployed, Mr. Hovans. I have an appointment at the Robert Dollar building for an interview. I am applying for a position with the Chinese National Aviation Company."

"Oh, I am well aware of CNAC, Miss Boreisha. My business takes me frequently to Hankow, Chongqing and Hong Kong. I find the airline to be of great assistance in bringing China into the twentieth century. If you do not find anything that suits you there, please give me a call. I am sure we could find something suitable for you at my little cabaret."

The elegant limousine presently came to a stop in front of the Robert Dollar building. This time Sergei Hovans opened the door for her and said, "Anna Boreisha, it has been a pleasure meeting you even under these most dreadful circumstances. Please do not forget my invitation. I would be delighted to escort you to dinner and introduce you to some intimate friends. It is the least I could do to apologize for your discomfort and inconvenience."

Anna was taken aback. This man was different! He spoke strangely, and although he looked Mongolian, he was definitely Russian. Besides Papa and his friends, she had never had a real gentleman speak to her like she was a woman—especially since she was only eighteen. The thought thrilled Anna. He spoke just like the heroes did in her movies—when they spoke to their leading ladies!

"I have the number on your business card Mr. Hovans. If possible, I will be glad to accept your invitation."

Hovans clicked his heels in the aristocratic manner, gave a half bow at the waist, kissed Anna's hand and said, "I will await your call Anastasia Boreisha." Anna visibly beamed.

CHAPTER 43

▼

MASTER CHEN TU

Shanghai's Chapei district
September, 1936

Anna's journal

They turned me down at CNAC today! They said their director of operations wasn't there. Worse, they said they only had openings for flight and
mechanical staff. There was nothing for me. Maybe Saul was right—in
China, you have to be a man to get a job in the aviation business.

Papa and Mama say that I will be different from the other Russian girls in
Shanghai. They both insist I will not work in the "male entertainment business," as Mama calls it. Papa has told me about the "professional women"
of Shanghai. They generally are located in the Rue Chu Pao San section
and I am never to go there. He says that he will not allow me to ever fall
into any of those "Russian girl traps" as he calls them. He said those
women have no dignity, and they will sell themselves, not for love, but for
money, or advantage. I know he thinks he is doing this all in my best interest but sometimes he drives me crazy.

Mother says practical education is the only hope I have for surviving in
China. Without an education, there is simply no prospect for a Russian girl
except marrying another Russian who has no future. Papa says I will be
educated—his way! It takes most of every day. He has a whole course of
study mapped out for me and he is the headmaster. Even though he works

very hard chauffeuring his Packard, I know he cannot afford to send me to the posh McTyeire School on Yunnan Road or any of the other western girl's schools for that matter....

Anna Boreisha willed the disappointment of the CNAC interview from her mind. She feinted at Saul Abrahamson. He weaved, dropped into a low crouch and pivoted on the balls of his feet. Just as he reached the bottom, he continued with his pivot, rose to full height, extended his leg and reached full velocity at the completion of his turn. At the time his outstretched foot should have made contact, he felt nothing but air.

Anna rolled on her shoulder and landed in a defensive crouch. She shifted her weight and squatted even lower just as Saul's outstretched foot grazed the top of her head. Her instincts knew he would use the momentum of the missed kick to carry him into position for his next attack. Anna uncoiled from her crouch with an airborne double kick of her own and connected with Saul's cheek just as he was recovering from his last attack. Saul swayed back to absorb the force of her blow. Before he could recover though, Anna landed and in a rapid graceful movement, pivoted on her hands and swept Saul off of his feet with her legs. As he attempted to stand for another attack, she countered with yet another foot sweep again knocking him on his back. Before he could recover, she grabbed his arm by the wrist, twisted his hand down and at the same time planted her foot in his chest.

Cheng Tu clapped twice indicating the exercise was over. Anna and Saul stood, attempted their best solemn face and bowed to their Taijiquan master. Irina Federenko and Wan Ting sat cross-legged trying to look somber, but in reality, they were doing everything possible to keep from giggling. They had already demonstrated today's lessons to the master and were now learning by observation.

Anna tried in vain to suppress her own giggle, but her failed attempt was not unnoticed by the Taijiquan master. He gave her a reproachful stare, but for the moment, maintained his dignified silence. Anna and Saul went to their respective positions on the mat, bowed, sat down, crossed their legs and awaited Cheng Tu's critique.

In a quiet voice, he began his critique in Mandarin. "Mr. Abrahamson...regardless of which way you face, you must always know where your opponents are. Indeed, you must know where they are in order to target your next move or blow...you must anticipate!"

"Anna! Taijiquan requires concentration! You must always focus. This ancient style of Wu fighting requires discipline and will not tolerate childish thoughts such as those now floating through your otherwise empty head!"

He walked close to Anna, looked at Irina and Wan Ting and said, "Especially, there is no time for giggling children!"

She knew it was coming, but until he opened his mouth with its betel nut stained teeth, she had almost forgotten how bad his breath was. She winced from the smell but did not move. Saul, Irina and Wan did their best to contain themselves as they had all experienced Cheng Tu's "dog breath," as they called it. It happened every time he came close to emphasize a point.

"Miss Anna—you are only eighteen. Your progress is good, but you must concentrate and focus totally on your opponent and the situation around you. You cannot let anything distract your thoughts. When you are not in my classes, you must use every free moment to visualize the postures and movements you have learned here. This is of singular importance when you encounter stressful situations…it will calm your mind and help you to focus."

She thought, "If you breathe on me again, the only thing I can focus on is leaving the room as fast as possible!"

"You come again on Thursday! Miss Anna, you concentrate…focus! Mr. Abrahamson…you anticipate. All of you visualize the postures you have learned. Now you go! I am tired and will now rest."

CHAPTER 44

▼

MADAMN LUDMILLA

Shanghai
September, 1936

Anna's journal

> *I had a very successful match today against Saul. It makes him furious when I am able to beat him just because I am a girl. The Master said I was improving but that I must be more serious and concentrate if I were ever to master Taijiquan. He has been very kind to me and says that Irina and I are the only Russian girls he has ever taught his Wu style boxing. If it were not for Saul and Wan acting as intermediaries, I don't think the master would have ever accepted us for training. I am still disappointed not to have obtained the position with CNAC. The Operations Director, Mr. W.L. Bond, was called away to business. They said they could not offer any encouragement for employment without Mr. Bond's recommendation.*
>
> *Papa was disappointed, but encouraged me to keep studying and to keep trying.*
>
> *For now, I will forget that and go to the movies by myself. Today, Mutiny on the Bounty is playing with Clark Gable!*

Peter Boreisha banged on the horn rim of his 1935 Packard. As usual, the rickshaws on Bubbling Well Road ignored the big American car as it inched its way through the traffic. He glanced at his watch for the third time in as many minutes. Ludmilla was always impatient with him when he was late.

He recalled the last time she had derided him—"Petrich dear, perhaps you are spending more time with your aristocratic wife and no longer have time for poor little Ludmilla!"

Wan Chang, Ludmilla's manservant, met Peter with his usual inscrutable smile as he got out of the Packard.

"Good Afternoon Mr. Boreisha! Madame Ludmilla say you sit and wait."

Peter said nothing to the man. Wan Chang, bowed, turned and shuffled out of the room.

No one could deny that Peter Boreisha was anything but a handsome man. He wore an expensive suit. He justified the expenses as being necessary to chauffer his well-heeled clients. After paying for his apartment and his family's expenses, he had little left for anything extra.

Even though many of his fellow White Russian émigrés affected mustaches and other facial hair, he preferred to be clean-shaven. He combed his hair straight back, with no part, using only a little mousse to hold it in place.

When standing still, as in conversation, he held his hands clasped behind his back if not otherwise occupied. He was taught that way as a cadet in Sebastopol and still observed the discipline. Characteristically, he stood with one knee slightly bent presenting an air of casual confidence to others.

After what she considered a suitable delay, Ludmilla Petrova stopped at the top of the stairs and looked over the railing at the waiting Peter Boreisha and said, "Petrich, dear...I'm so sorry to keep you waiting!" With a cigarette holder in one hand and a small handkerchief in the other, Ludmilla began her glide down the stairs to the entrance hall of her very expensive brothel. What a delight it was to have these aristocrats wait on her, she thought. When she lived in Russia, it was she who waited for them.

A few days ago, she had just turned thirty years old. As a thirtieth birthday was a major milestone in her profession, she looked at her reflection in the stairwell mirror, and gave herself an honest appraisal. She was still one of the most beautiful whores in Shanghai. Not just an ordinary whore any more, as she was now a businesswoman and partner in her own brothel. The petals of her youthful bloom had not quite dropped from the flower, but when they did, she would at least be prepared.

She rather liked the tight curls Wang Chu had styled on her naturally blond hair. She knew her ample breasts, blue eyes and rounded figure were still her best assets. At least they were the objects most of her clients doted on assuming they were still sober enough to notice. Thank God Petrich didn't drink himself into a stupor like most of these asses. In fact, he was a good lover and one of her favorite clients. Unfortunately, he was also one of the poorest and could not afford the expensive gifts to which she had become accustomed.

The cash cows in her business were the English and the Americans. With the exception of an occasional rich Chinaman seeking variety, it was these men who grew her business year after year.

Yes, it was her time now. With seven Russian girls working for her it was she that could afford servants and luxuries. It was she who had power over these displaced royals and not the other way around.

Ludmilla considered herself an expert at exploiting the psychological depravations suffered by these displaced Whites. The poor fools would never quit living in the past, and she knew exactly how to play that to her advantage. Profit motive aside, Ludmilla Petrova thoroughly enjoyed the power she held over them.

She thought about Peter's family as she continued her descent down the ornamented staircase. She had seen the wife of this one on several occasions. No longer did Madamn Peter Boreisha live in a beautiful Dacha. No longer was she waited on hand and foot by servants. And yes, she no longer had the wardrobe or jewelry of a nobleman's wife. She could see it in their demeanor. It affected everything about these women. They no longer acted so superior. Better, their new circumstances negatively affected their relationships with their men and drove them right into her arms.

Then, there was Peter's daughter, Anna. She had seen her only once, but oh what a beauty! If only she could bring her under her wing. With a proper wardrobe, a makeover and her supervision, Ludmilla was sure she could profit immensely from this rare find. If only someone else didn't snare her first!

Ludmilla's spiked heel shoe came off of the last stair. She noticed her delay had the desired effect. He was smoking and pacing back and forth like a caged panther. Peter Boreisha was agitated as she entered his embrace. Yes, it was good to make them wait a little. She greeted Peter with kisses to both cheeks and made her usual comments regarding his standing within the community of old Whites. Her greetings and small talk of his friends from the court of the Tsar had its usual effect—if even only for a moment, she brought Peter back to the past. At least for the time, he was in the company of a paid enabler; she helped him remember a time that in his more lucid moments, knew would never be again.

Ludmilla locked her arm in Peter's and led him up the stairs. For the time that his money bought, the lavish surroundings of her boudoir, and her attention to his needs, Peter would forget the present and gladly slipped back into the past with her.

As usual, the time with her passed far more quickly than he would have liked. He was finishing a vodka and smoking a cigarette when Peter noticed Ludmilla looking at her diamond-studded watch. He quickly returned to reality and realized he was overstaying the time his wallet allowed.

After the perfunctory pleasantries of departure, Peter withdrew his European style wallet and took out her payment in U.S. dollars. Just as he was discreetly pressing the bills into her hand, the depression and guilt that usually accompanied his departure began to return.

Knowing that waiting customers were drinking her vodka in the downstairs waiting room, Ludmilla held Peter's hand and exchanged perfunctory good byes as she nudged him toward the street entrance of her brothel.

It was one of those moments that inevitably beset everyone engaged in a dalliance outside of marriage. At the very moment Ludmilla was seeing Peter to the door of her establishment, Anna Boreisha was returning from the movies. First, she noticed her Papa's distinctive Packard parked outside the building; then, she saw her father in a part of town that she herself was forbidden to frequent.

CHAPTER 45

▼

DISCOVERED

Shanghai
September, 1936

Anna's journal

I was returning from the cinema today and spotted Papa's Packard. It was in the section of the city that I was never to visit, but it saved a lot of time getting home. At first, I assumed he was with a client, and then I saw a woman come out of the building beside him. She gave him a long embrace—the kind you see in the movies. He had his arms around her and kissed her on the lips. It was nothing like the kisses he gives Mama!

When I saw Papa giving the woman money, I was sure she must have been a whore—a woman in the "male entertainment profession" as Mama likes to call it! The woman was definitely Russian. That—after all the lectures he has given me on Russian girls entering that profession!

Poor mother. I wonder if she knows? There are numerous "houses of assignation," nightclubs and cabarets on that part of Bubbling Well Road; it is also very close to Mr. Hovan's Far East Cabaret!

I'll show him! I'll call Sergei Hovans first thing tomorrow! He invited me to his cabaret anytime. He even said he would introduce me to his "intimate friends." I won't even bother with Tanya; she too works at the Far East Cabaret, but I know the owner! Won't she be envious when she sees I am the owner's companion my very first time there? If that commoner Tanya can wear nice clothes and make a living, I'm sure I can also. I have no doubt I could fit right in as a hostess, and I wouldn't have to consider being a prostitute like that Russian with Papa!

How hard could it be? I already know how to dance. I'm pretty! What more could be required? From what Tanya says, it's mostly a matter of being a companion and persuading them to spend their money on champagne. She says you don't have to leave the club with the gentlemen if you don't want to, but she didn't speak very much about that part.

All I really need to go to work for Mr. Hovans is a Chi-Pao; one of those long dresses with slits up the side that the taxi girls wear. Better, I could buy an American flapper dress, the ones like they wear in the movies.

Tanya says that most of the clubs will lend you the money you need to buy the clothes and you can pay them back out of your compensation. She also says if I were a club hostess I would have to start using makeup. She says men really like a lot of makeup. I asked her why. She said she didn't know why; she just knew they did. Maybe she knows I hate a lot of makeup—maybe that's why she said it. She knows Papa won't even allow me to think about being a hostess, so I guess she didn't care what she said.

The good part is I will start making money almost immediately. Besides paying my own way, I could also start helping Papa pay some of the bills and maybe even save a little. I'd be furious if he spent what I brought home on that Russian whore.

At least I will be meeting some foreigners—maybe some gentlemen like you see in the movies. I can practice my languages, enjoy the cabaret, dance, and maybe have fun while I am doing it. I will call Sergei Hovans the first thing tomorrow!

CHAPTER 46

▼

THE FAR EAST CABARET

Shanghai
the next day

After confiding her thoughts to her diary, Anna went to sleep. Much later, she heard her father's car pull up in front of the house with the familiar sound of its powerful engine. She pulled the covers up over her head and tried not to think of him in the arms of that Russian woman. Eventually, she went to sleep.

The next day Anna called the number on Sergei Hovan's business card. At least she didn't have to address the problem of telling her father as he had left to pick up a client before she woke up.

She finished the newspapers and wondered what her topic would be for this evening's research and recitation when Papa returned. Early in the afternoon, she kissed her mother on the cheek, and said she would was going to the public library to study foreign newspapers. She said she would be late, and not to worry.

After awhile at the library she tired of perusing the *New York Times* and the *Chicago Tribune*. She screwed up her courage, hailed a rickshaw, and directed the coolie to the address on the card. The Far East Cabaret was located in an area of many fine looking restaurants and nightclubs, and from the outside, all looked more refined than she had imagined.

She went up the stairs to the entrance, opened the door and stepped into the foyer of the building. Off to one side, double doors opened into a bar where she could hear a piano playing. Straight ahead was an entrance to what appeared to be the cabaret. On the other side was a coat checkroom, rest rooms and three closed doors. In the foyer were several chairs and occasional tables. On the walls were mostly European paintings and two large ornate mirrors, one facing the other, on opposite sides of a paneled entrance wall.

After several minutes, a gentleman in dinner clothes, without a coat, came out of the bar, greeted her, and asked if he could be of assistance. She told him that Mr. Hovans was expecting her. He ushered her to one of the chairs in the foyer and then hurried off through the doors to the cabaret.

Anna had worn her best woolen skirt and sweater and still wore her overcoat when the doorman returned. He said, "Ms. Boreisha, Mr. Hovans sends his compliments; he is engaged at the moment, and will join you shortly. He asked if you would care to have refreshment while you waited."

Anna declined and contemplated the hundreds of images of herself in the two opposing mirrors. With the exception of the woolen overcoat, that she thought made her look like a peasant; she was pleased with what she saw. Only a few days ago Madamn Faunaux had styled her hair for her disappointing interview with CNAC. She had combed it out but thought it still looked good.

Before she finished her thoughts, two Japanese gentlemen, both wearing business suits, came out of the cabaret followed by Sergei Hovans. Anna stayed seated. Hovans shook their hands. Everyone said goodbyes in English. The two Japanese regarded Anna as they opened the front door to leave. Hovans came to her directly, kissed her hand, and said, "Mademoiselle Boreisha, so nice of you to come. I am so glad you took me up on my invitation, my dear."

"I couldn't pass up such a gracious offer Mr. Hovans. I am looking forward to seeing your cabaret."

"And indeed you shall my dear. You have already seen the entrance hall. My guests meet here or in the bar before going to the cabaret. Please let me show you my theater that most of my clients call the cabaret. When we are finished with the tour, maybe I can persuade you to join me for dinner and the show this evening."

"Oh, Mr. Hovans…It's so kind of you to ask, but I am expected at home, and as you can see, I am not dressed for dinner." Hovans appraised Anna and did not reply. He took her coat and hung it on a peg behind the check desk. He then ushered Anna through the double doors into a large room. Arcing around the room in a semicircle were several rows of booths and banquettes separating descending levels of dining and viewing areas for the audience. The tables were set for dinner with highly starched white tablecloths, china, silver, crystal and a candlelight lamp at each table. Besides booth seating, each level had tables and chairs that were two steps lower and closer to the stage than the booths and banquets. The orchestra pit and the stage were situated on the lowest level. The two walls of the cabaret, terminating at doors on each side of the stage, were festooned with art-work having a modern, almost art deco theme. The artwork along the two walls were lighted by sconces at regular intervals, while the remaining wall, at the rear, was covered with heavy dark green drapes. Anna thought the paintings to be a dramatic departure from the type she had seen in the entranceway.

Anna's host led her through the levels to the door by the corner of the stage. "Lets take you back stage and introduce you to some of my employees and friends,"

"I would be delighted Mr. Hovans."

Hovans guided Anna through a hallway traversing the rear of the stage. He exchanged perfunctory acknowledgements with several employees in the hall and led Anna to a large room populated entirely by young women in various stages of dress.

As they came through the door, the buzz of multiple conversations stopped as if cut off by a switch. All heads turned towards Hovans and Anna. Her immediate impression was hard to describe—fear—envy? Before she could give it much thought Hovans said, "Ladies, may I introduce Anna Boreisha. I am trying to persuade Ms. Boreisha to be my dinner companion for the evening." There was no response.

Most of the women appeared to be Russian or Eastern European extraction. Their appearance ranged from attractive to plain. She considered none beautiful. To Anna's taste, most appeared garish—affecting skimpy, if not downright cheap looking evening wear, much as her friend Tanya preferred. A few wore the Chi-Pao. On the right type of woman these garments were smashing, she thought, but not on any of these girls. Others wore everything from the twenties flapper attire to conventional eveningwear.

Hovans said, "Ms. Boreisha did not bring evening attire with her. Nadja, Anna is about your size. Why don't you look through your wardrobe and see if you can't find something appropriate for her. I'm sure with the proper clothes and some accessories, we could persuade Anastasia to join us this evening."

The girl Hovans called Nadja blanched with fear. She said in heavily accented English, "Right away Mr. Hovans. I...I'm sure I can find something for your friend."

"Nadja, thank you so much for the offer but I simply cannot accept! Mr. Hovans, it would be too much to ask, and I had not really planned on staying for dinner."

"Nonsense, my dear! Nadja doesn't mind...do you Nadja?"

Nadja said, "Of course not Mr. Hovans."

"There…it's settled! After dinner, I will have Mr. Rabin run you home. Now, I'll leave you in Nadja's capable hands. I have some business to attend to and will be back in just a little while."

Before Anna could object, Hovans was gone.

The frightened girl took Anna by the hand, switched to Russian and said, "Let's get you something to wear before Sergei gets back!"

Just as soon as the door closed behind their employer, the women returned to furtive conversations casting occasional glances toward Anna and Nadja. The looks she received were not the kind the *new girl* received on the first day in school. Rather, it was a knowing look of foreboding, as if they had knowledge of an outcome, and Anna did not.

Nadja led Anna into a small room that served as a large wardrobe for all of the women. She went to section that had Nadja chalked on a shelf above a clothes rack. She pointed to several garments on hangers.

"Pick what you want; it's all the same to me. Just make sure you have on something that shows you off to his friends…if you know what I mean."

She turned to ask what she meant and found herself alone in a room full of club attire. Anna had never worn such clothes and could only rely on her usually good sense for a choice.

As she tried on first one dress, and then another, she realized she was committing the most grievous of offenses in the eyes of her parents. It will serve him right, she thought, she would look no different than *that Russian woman* she had seen him with! She would worry about the consequences tomorrow.

She found a sheath dress a little more tasteful and modest than the rest. A quick inspection showed her everyday bra revealed straps and protruded from the low cut dress, so she quickly removed it and placed it with the rest of her street clothes. She had no shear stockings and was thankful she had shaved her legs only this morning.

She looked in the mirror and was pleased with her reflection. The low cut sequined sheath dress showed off her athletic figure to good effect and made the short dress look far more expensive than it actually was. She ran a comb through her hair, renewed her lipstick and walked back into the other room with a new-found confidence she had not felt before.

This time, the looks of foreboding were replaced with those of envy. One of the girls brought over a headband studded with rhinestones popular with night-club set. The others continued to speak with each other in guarded conversation. None spoke with Anna.

In a little while, Hovans returned. When he saw Anna in her short evening sheath, he opened his arms in an expression of admiration and said, "My dear Miss Boreisha—you are simply breathtaking."

The other women looked on vapidly at their boss and the new girl and continued their preparations for the evening.

Sergei Hovans guided Anna back through the theater to the bar. In the cabaret, Chinese waiters were busy finishing the table settings for dinner. The curtain was up, and stagehands were busy preparing props for the nights entertainment.

The two went through the rear entrance door, made their way along the sides of the cabaret and through the foyer to the bar that already had begun to fill with guests. Anna sat on a bar stool facing Hovans, legs crossed, her back to the bar. Hovans stood facing the entrance. The first thing people saw on coming into the bar was a beautiful girl in a sparkling sheath dress and the imposing figure of Hovans in evening clothes. Men were drawn to Anna like a moth to the flame. Paying their compliments to Hovans gave them the excuse to study his latest acquisition at closer range. Women too welcomed this opportunity for the reasons women have always wanted to scrutinize other women.

After several introductions, Anna had the definite feeling that her escort was showing off an object that he had just acquired rather than introducing her as a person. After the perfunctory introductions and handshakes, Hovans returned to be his public persona of being perpetually on stage.

"What can I offer you to drink, my dear?" Anna did not like alcohol and had prepared herself for the question.

"Could I please have gin and tonic with no gin and a twist of lemon?" She had seen a movie character deflect the *what to drink question* in this manner. Hovans ordered the drink and went back on stage for his gathering guests.

Anna tuned one level of her consciousness to the conversation at hand while at the same time she continued to peruse the club's other guest. To the guest Hovan's was speaking to at the moment, her demeanor suggested nothing but rapt attention to what they and their host were saying. In reality, though, Anna was absorbing almost every detail about the club and the other arrivals.

The bar, where their group was now gathered, was of a beautifully polished wood, probably native to China or South East Asia. Unlike the entrance hall, the cabaret's wood paneling was adorned with European hunt scenes as the prevalent décor. It suggested a European mens' saloon, she thought. Windows on the street side of the bar were completely covered with heavy velvet drapes sheltering the guests from anything so distracting as the real world of Shanghai streets just on the other side.

An American Negro in black tie was playing the piano and singing something about Christopher Columbus steering the world without a compass. The gifted musician played at just the right volume to complement the pleasant ambiance and not be a distraction to conversation. There was a small dance floor, but as of yet, no one was dancing.

She continued to sip her drink and surreptitiously observe the arriving guests. In the corner farthest from the bar and the piano were two Western gentlemen, probably English, engrossed in conversation. Next to them, facing the entrance, was the Japanese gentleman she had seen Hovans with when she first came in. He sat by himself at a table for four. Sitting just next to him was another Western couple. They were holding hands across the table and simply listening to the piano and the amusing exploits of Mr. Columbus.

Anna was still absorbing the atmosphere of the cabaret when a Chinese man, perhaps in his fifties, approached Hovans, shook hands and began to speak. He wore a three-piece grey suit and the traditional drooping mustache that tapered to a point at both ends. He was accompanied by a younger, unwholesome looking man with a poor complexion, who undressed Anna with his eyes while Hovans and the older man spoke in muted conversation. She thought it odd that he wore a white pongee suit at this time of the year. Sergei Hovans did not introduce them to her, and after a short time, he gestured in the direction of the Japanese man sitting alone at the table. Hovans turned to Anna, excused himself and ushered them to the Japanese gentleman's table. After introductions, Hovans returned to his on stage persona and resumed his vigil.

It was the contrast of clothing that brought Anna's attention to the foursome in her periphery. Normal instincts made her want to turn and see what it was that was different, but her intrinsic discretion kept her attention and half smile towards her immediate companions as if hanging on to every word of their less than scintillating conversation.

Hovans had positioned himself so that Anna and the present conversationalist were kept in sight, while more importantly, he could observe who was coming into the bar. That part of his persona was consistent with his position, she thought. It was, after all, his cabaret, and he should be interested in the guests coming through the door. It was his expression, however, that told her someone of significance had just come into his cabaret.

While still paying rapt attention to the conversation at hand, Anna watched her small group shift their gaze to follow the new arrivals until her attention was no longer heeded by them.

Passing directly in front of her were two United States Marines accompanied by two stunning Chinese women. The marines wore splendid navy blue uniforms enhanced by shiny brass buttons, insignia, medals and perfect tailoring.

Both of the marines were taller than any other guest in the cabaret. They looked superbly fit, an appearance enhanced by their impeccable uniforms. Their companions both wore the elegant Chi-Pao—one with a flowered motif, the other a gown of uniform raw silk with an almost golden cast. One marine could rival any of her movie star idols. The other guests in the saloon turned to watch the passing group, and so did Anna, as subterfuge was no longer necessary. As they passed, she wore her perpetual half smile as if everything in the saloon was there for her personal amusement. She was so disposed when the marine caught Anna's eye. It was as if for that instant he saw no one else in the saloon except her. In that split second, before she could divert her attention she felt a pleasing sensation in the pit of her stomach. It was as if an electric shock had passed between them. Something significant had just happened.

Hovans animal quick instincts caught the exchange and he turned to the object at his side. He wasn't fast enough, however, to gauge Anna's reaction. She flashed her usual smile at him but said nothing. For the last five minutes, she thought, that is probably the first time he was even aware I was here!

Hovans made small talk about the marines and something about their continued relevance within the International Settlement when the small group's attention was drawn to yet another couple coming into the bar.

Anna turned to order another tonic. In the enormous mirror behind the bar, she caught a glimpse of the marines as they pulled chairs for their companions. They sat at a table next to the Japanese gentleman and the two men who had just joined him. The foreign but pleasurable feeling returned and again she averted her gaze just before the marine looked at her in the mirror.

She felt foolish and began to think she was making more of the exchange than was warranted. She chanced one more glance at the marines and their companions in the mirror and noted the Japanese man sitting next to them writing in a small notebook.

She swung her seat around in time to see the gentleman who had first greeted her announce, "Ladies and gentlemen: The Far East Cabaret and theater is now seating for tonight's dinner and performance. Dinner can now be ordered. Please bring your refreshments with you if you like. First curtain will be at nine p.m."

Hovans guided Anna by the elbow to his private table in the theater. It was situated to provide a good view of the stage and all levels of the cabaret. The other guests began to arrive from the bar and were shown to a banquette or a table by the maitre d'.

A waiter appeared almost immediately, took drink orders, and left menus for Hovans and Anna. With no warning, they were joined by Ostafii Rabin and one of the hostesses Anna had seen, but not met, in the dressing room. As if an annoyance, Hovans introduced the girl.

"Anna, this is Irena. Perhaps you saw her back stage when you changed."

Anna nodded as the girl nervously fished for a cigarette from her sequined clutch purse. Hovans motioned to her escort and said, "You remember Mr. Rabin…he was with me during our unfortunate accident the other day."

With a charming smile Anna said, "Yes, it was an occasion that would be hard to forget."

Rabin said nothing and did not smile.

Several guests paid their compliments when passing by. Most simply went to their tables in anticipation of the evening's entertainment.

The Japanese gentleman from the bar stopped by their table, leaned over and whispered something into Hovan's ear. He pressed something into his hand. The elderly Chinese and the man in the pongee suit were not with him. Without further discussion, he turned to Anna and said, "Anna my dear, this is Mr. Akimoto. He is a very important envoy from the Japanese government and is alone tonight on his country's business. I was wondering if you might be so kind as to join him for dinner and the performance. I am sure he would be so ever grateful for the companionship, and it would be a personal favor to me that I would not soon forget."

Anna was not naive. She knew that Hovans wanted her as a hostess and had not invited her here simply as his companion. She did not, however, think her apprenticeship would begin with no warning or guidelines on what was expected of her. Moreover, Hovans had mentioned nothing regarding remuneration or payment for sitting with this guy.

She regarded the Japanese gentleman. He looked educated and refined. She estimated his age to be late forties or early fifties. Without further hesitation, she replied directly to him in good, but not fluent Japanese, "Mr. Akimoto, My name is Anna Boreisha. Mr. Hovans has explained you are in Shanghai on behalf of your government, and that you have no dinner companion for tonight's entertainment. On behalf of Mr. Hovans and his cabaret, I would be delighted to have you as my escort for the evening."

Hovans, Rabin, Irena and Akimoto looked at Anna in astonishment. None had the slightest idea that she spoke Japanese. Fluent in many languages, Hovans understood enough of her reply to understand she had a much greater working knowledge of the difficult language than he.

The Japanese diplomat reacted with a bow. Anna did not stand, not sure how she should respond in such circumstances. She understood most cultures considered females inferior but had no idea of the correct protocol for this situation. Unsure, she simply bowed her head slightly as if acknowledging his understanding. She characterized his reaction as surprise that any foreigner understood his language. This pleased her immensely.

Hovans recovered his theatrical composure and declared, "My Dear Anna, you are full of surprises. I had no idea you spoke Japanese, and I won't forget your kindness to my guests. I will have your drink sent over to you." He motioned for a waiter to see the two to their new table.

As they departed, Hovans and Rabin stood and paid their respects. The diplomat took Anna by the arm, himself unsure of the correct protocol to follow with a Caucasian woman. The waiter guided them down to the next level to a table close to the stage. As a waiter pulled Anna's chair she could not help noticing the two marines and their companions were seated only one table behind them.

The Japanese ordered scotch whiskey for himself. Anna ordered a club soda with a twist. The waiter seemed surprised. She suspected it was because most of the other hostesses were instructed to order the more expensive champagne.

Presently, the orchestra began, and a black female singer Anna had not seen before began crooning, "So you met someone who set you back on your heels...Goody goody!"

Her escort had no interest in, nor understood the nonsensical American song, and began to study the dinner menu. The waiter returned with their drinks as the vocalist began the refrain again, "Goody goody for you...

The diplomat said little and ordered several more drinks as they waited for dinner. The stage show began and dinner came; to fill the voids in the entertainment and in their conversation, Anna asked about simple things in Japan. With each successive drink, her companion became more loquacious, speaking to her amiably in formal Japanese.

Akimoto ate very little and continued to drink. After declining desert, the china and silver were cleared and it wasn't long until it became apparent the diplomat had little interest in the floorshow. Instead, Akimoto made clumsy attempts to hold Anna's hand. His cumbersome advances were embarrassing to Anna who had yet to engage in anything more than a teasing kiss with Saul. She had no experience in coping with drunken suitors. Other than occasional whistles from concession soldiers on the streets, there was nothing that had prepared her for such a public display.

During his first attempts to grope her she simply suggested that he watch the show. When this didn't work, she moved her chair away to the extent she was now facing the rear of the cabaret. When she looked up, she found herself looking directly into the face of the handsome marine at the table behind her.

The new distance between Anna and her companion did nothing to assuage his ardor. In his stupor he was probably unaware he was causing a scene. By this time, many of the guests were looking at their table. Not discouraged, Akimoto scooted his chair right after her and again tried to put his arm around her, trying to kiss her on the face and bosom. The marine looked somewhat amused and pointed to himself with a facial gesture and body language that asked, "You want some help lady?"

In response, Anna diverted her eyes and continued to parry the drunk's advances. When she looked up again, she saw the figure of the tall marine in his splendid uniform towering above their table.

"Hey Buster, can't you see the lady isn't buying what you are selling? Why don't you take your paws off her and enjoy the floorshow. You're bothering me and everybody else around us, so either can the Romeo stuff, or shove off!"

The diplomat stood on wobbly legs and faced the tall marine; the top of Akimoto's head was just below his shoulder level. The few words Anna was able to understand concerned barbarian, and something to the effect that, "You would soon learn proper respect for the Japanese."

To avoid further embarrassment, Anna left the table without saying a word and made her way towards the rear of the cabaret. She returned to the dressing room, took off the headband and slipped out of the sheath dress. Ostafii Rabin came into the room as she stood half-naked putting on her street clothes. She turned her back towards him and continued to slip on her bra, shirt, skirt and sweater.

Speaking in heavily accented English Rabin said, "Don't change your clothes! Mr. Hovans spoke to the Jap. He take you his hotel. You meet him in the foyer now!"

Anna continued to pull on her woolen skirt. She couldn't believe what she was hearing. She grabbed her purse and started past Rabin. She was almost to the dressing room door when the big Russian slapped her on the face so hard she almost fell to the floor. Before Rabin even recovered from the follow through of his blow, Anna countered with two short rapid punches to his groin. His natural reaction was to double up in pain. Just as his head reached waist level Anna brought her knee into the fat man's face and at the same time slammed the open palms of both hands against his ears. With one hand clutching his crotch and the other his bloody nose, Rabin crumpled to the floor howling in pain. Anna stepped over him, opened the door, and left.

The cabaret was still dark except for the spotlights that were now on a male comedian with a hat and cane. In the darkness, she was able to make her way to the front of the cabaret without being seen. When she reached the foyer, Akimoto had retrieved his overcoat, scarf and hat and was obviously waiting for her to appear.

Without asking the coat check girl, Anna went behind the counter, found her overcoat, put it on and started toward the door. The diplomat attempted to grab Anna by the arm and she simply placed her hand in the center of his chest, gave a slight push and sent him plopping into a one of the foyer's ornate chairs.

As she hailed a ubiquitous rickshaw, a blast of cool November air cleared her senses. She told the coolie her address, pulled her arms around her overcoat for warmth, and began reflecting on everything that had happened that day.

CHAPTER 47

▼

THE DAY AFTER

Shanghai

Anna's journal
Facing Papa and Mama

It was almost midnight when I got home. I should have known better than to think Papa and Mama would be asleep. Both of them were sitting in front of our living room stove.

Mama was first to speak. She wanted to know where I had been. Papa said nothing, that was just fine with me. I was afraid if he started to lecture me on my behavior, I would have exposed his own indiscretions.

I told them everything that happened. From first meeting Sergei Hovans, his invitation, the cabaret, Akimoto, the marine, Rabin—everything! I told them that I understood why they opposed me working in such a place, and how after tonight I saw that they were right. I also told them that I was 18 years old, was a burden, and wanted so much to have a job of my own to help out.

When I told of my confrontation with that brut, Rabin, his slapping me and how for the first time I had a practical use of Master Cheng Tu's training, a strange thing happened. Mama just looked at me, astonished; she had always been against such nonsense. Until then, Papa had been strangely quiet. He still said nothing, but just came across the room and wrapped his arms around me in a tight embrace. He said over and over,

"My little Anushka, My Anna, I am so proud of you. You have done the right thing by telling us. I promise—things will be different for you. You will not have to live like those other girls. I promise I will do everything to help you find something better than that!"

As Papa held me, I could see Mama standing in her nightclothes. Her hands were clasped together twisting her simple gold wedding band—the only piece of jewelry left after selling everything to buy Papa's Packard. It was as if she were happy, miserable and jealous at the same time. For the first time, watching her then, I knew she lived with the knowledge of Papa's other life and had never said anything about it....

C H A P T E R 48

▼

MASTER CHENG TU

Shanghai's Chapei district

It was easier for Anna to stop by Saul's apartment in the French Concession as it was on the way to Master Cheng Tu's classical Taijiquan boxing school in Hongkew. Saul was standing in the street waiting for Anna when she arrived.

After her perfunctory kiss to Saul's cheeks, she told him everything that happened at the Far East Cabaret the previous night emphasizing her rescue by the handsome marine. She dramatized every facet of her story knowing full well that Saul would not only be jealous, but green with envy in hearing of her adventure. She knew she was twisting the dagger in the poor boy's heart, but she couldn't resist telling him that everyone treated her not as a girl but as a woman of the world.

Saul said, "Anna, maybe that wasn't such a good thing. Maybe it would have been better if everyone treated you simply as a lady rather than a *woman of the world*. Things might have gone better for you. Hell, Anna, sounds to me like they were treating you just like those pros in 'Blood Alley'…only difference between you and them was the quality of the joint you were in!"

Anna blanched; she was about to defend her position but knew Saul was right. She bumped him with her shoulder and threw one arm around his neck and said, "Let me see if I understand you Saul. You're saying that the only difference between a one dolla ho and a fifty dolla ho is how much she makee…right?"

Saul blushed. "Yeah, that's about it. If it were you though, Anna, and I had the money, I'd pay a hundred dollars for you anytime."

Anna stopped, stood arms akimbo, looked at Saul and began to laugh. Saul laughed too when Anna said, "Saul, I think my days of working as a lady of the evening are over. I must say that it was intriguing, though…seeing those people all dressed up—the music, the cabaret, the swell surroundings. Looks like if I'm ever to go back, I'll have to wait for some knight in shining armor. Fat chance of that! I can't even find a job so I can get enough money to go to the movies! At least you have your job at Goldman's!"

When they arrived at Cheng Tu's Wu School of classical Chinese boxing, they promptly changed their clothes and waited for the master to come. Before he had a chance to compose himself Anna lapsed easily into Mandarin and told the Master what had happened the night before.

Cheng Tu listened patiently until she was finished and said, "As in any situation where combat becomes necessary one should always try to avoid confrontation unless absolutely necessary. In almost every situation, flight is better than fight. However, when combat became necessary, only enough force should be used as the situation dictated. The decision on how much force was appropriate took wise consideration and sometimes had to be decided on immediately least an assailant be given more opportunity than prudent for the circumstances."

Anna demonstrated what she had done when Rabin accosted her using Saul as prop. Cheng Tu suggested she was correct in leaving her assailant when she did. He took Saul by the arm and demonstrated how a half twist to his arm and wrist held the assailant's in the proper position for a foot chop to the larynx. Cheng Tu then made the two demonstrate the necessary postures and maneuvers to him until they were performed to his satisfaction.

As happened with many youngsters, Cheng Tu could see that they were beginning to tire of the practice and told them to rest. He then handed them two wooden mock-ups of Chinese broad swords. After he had their attention, Cheng Tu began to lecture his charges on the history and utility of his family's Wu style of broadsword fighting. After his introduction to the discipline, Cheng Tu dismissed them until their next session.

Anna and Saul changed clothes and began to make their way towards the French Concession. Saul had to get to work at Goldman's, and Anna had to make up lessons after last night's episode.

Walking backwards, so he could face her, Saul said, "You know Anna, I'm eighteen now, and I know Morse code probably better than anyone else my age in Shanghai. Remember when we were talking about me working for CNAC as a radio operator? I was half kidding at the time, but then, I began thinking about how swell it would be, and you know what?…I'm gonna do it! I'm going to go out to Lunghwa airport tomorrow and just see what might be available. You never know...maybe I'll get lucky!"

"Oh Saul, that would be grand! Say...how about me coming along? I'll go with you tomorrow and try again. Maybe I'll have better luck there than at the Robert Dollar building!"

CHAPTER 49

▼

LUNGHWA

Shanghai

Anna ate little that night. Moreover, she said little to her parents, and they to her, except that tomorrow she was going to try to find work again.

The next day the two of them met early. They packed a lunch and rode the streetcar out to Lunghwa airport. When they arrived, they saw one of CNAC's new Douglas DC–2s being readied for a flight. Down on the river they could just make out a Loening and a Douglas Dolphin bobbing at the docks. For a while, they just stood there, dreaming of flying to far off places and meeting new and exciting people.

Saul took Anna by the hand and said, "Come on, let's go!"

They went to the building where Anna's fathers always delivered his passengers, opened the door and found themselves in a small ticket office and combination waiting room. On the walls were several CNAC advertising posters, a route map and a schedule of the airline's arrivals and departures. Several passengers had already arrived for departure on the DC–2 they had seen on the ramp outside.

There were no passengers at the ticket counter, and Anna approached the Chinese clerk and said in English, "My name is Anna Boreisha, and this is Mr. Saul Abrahamson. We are both looking for employment and were wondering if you would be so kind as to direct us to the proper place to make our inquiries?"

The clerk looked at them and asked impatiently, "What services could you two provide the airline?"

Anna said, "I think it would be better if we explained our qualifications to the manager in charge of determining the airline's needs...are you that person?"

The clerk glared at them and said, "Go away, I have work to do!"

Anna and Saul were just leaving when a gentleman and his manservant came through the door. The man went to the clerk and began to speak to him in French. In a moment, it became obvious that the clerk had no idea what he was speaking about.

Anna heard the exchange and said to the clerk, "He said his name is Monsieur Didier. He has just received a last minute telegram from his office, and he wants to purchase a ticket on this morning's flight to Peking."

The clerk told Anna the information Mr. Didier needed. She translated for the clerk and helped them complete their transaction. Anna asked his manservant to fetch his bags from the car when it became apparent that he too spoke no Mandarin or pidgin. The French gentleman was so grateful he tipped Anna two dollars for her service.

The two youngsters were just about to leave again, when the clerk said, "Wait a minute, you two!"

He said a few words to another clerk behind the counter and said, "You two come with me! Maybe there is something for you."

He led them to the large hangar and up a flight of stairs to an office with a sign over the door that said, Operations Director.

The clerk explained to the secretary that the two youngsters were looking for employment, wished them luck, and left. The secretary asked them to have a seat as the MD was in a meeting with the Operations Manager, and she had no idea how long it would be.

The secretary returned to her typing and both sat down, still in their over-coats, and began waiting for whoever the MD and the Operations Manager were. Anna picked up an American magazine and began to read. Saul pulled out his Morse practice key and added to the office cacophony with the clacking of code practice. Distracted, the secretary looked over the top of her typewriter at the young people but said nothing.

Anna was reading, and Saul was intently tapping away at his practice key when a Chinese employee in an airline uniform came through the office door and dropped a piece of correspondence on the secretaries desk.

As he turned to leave he paused a moment, turned to Saul and said, "If that's Anna sitting next to you I'll bet she doesn't know Morse! If she did, she would know how beautiful you thought she was and exactly how many ways you were going to show her how much you loved her, and five will get you ten she wouldn't be sitting there quietly reading that magazine!"

Saul stopped tapping the key and turned a bright crimson. At first, Anna just looked surprised and then said, "Oh I know Saul loves me, but I *would* like to know just how he is going to show it!"

She stood and introduced herself. Still beet red, Saul stood, not looking at Anna and did the same.

The employee introduced himself as Roger Chang and told them he was a flight crew radio operator. Anna said, "He must know code pretty well or you wouldn't have understood. Any chance he could get a job around here?"

Chang said, "I know Ronnie Peterson needs some help. If Mr. Bond went for it, I'll bet you could be hired as an apprentice."

The amused secretary heard the conversation and said, "Mr. Bond is in a meeting with the MD right now. They were waiting to see him when he gets out."

Chang said, "Well you tell Mr. Bond that I just heard this kid tap out, well, I won't say what he tapped out…just tell him Chang says he's well over 40 words a minute. Tell him he has a good fist, and if he has any questions, I'm down in the ready room."

Chang continued, "What about you Anna? You obviously don't know code and I think it's safe to say you aren't his sister! So what's your story?"

Anna said, "Since I am neither a pilot nor a radio operator, I thought I might do something that could make use of my language skills…maybe a job that put me in contact with your customers. I think they call it public relations."

As they were speaking, two distinguished looking gentleman came out of the MD's office. Both wore business suits. One was Chinese, the other American. Both were middle-aged and had a presence of command about them. The Chinese gentleman shook the American's hand and hurried out of the office.

The American looked at the gathered group, smiled, and said, "Mr. Chang, good to see you! What brings you up here, and who are your friends?"

"Oh…hi Mr. Bond. I was just here to drop off the new equipment requisition list and ran into these young people. They are both looking for work with CNAC. This is Miss Anna Boreisha, and this young man is Mr. Saul Abraham-son. This is our Director of Operations, Mr. Langhorne Bond; the gentleman who just left is our MD, or managing director of the company."

Bond said, "Glad to meet you."

He stepped forward and shook their hand.

Chang went on, "Ms. Boreisha speaks languages…ah…how many languages did you say Anna?"

"Seven, Mr. Chang."

"She is looking for something in public relations.

"Young Mr. Abrahamson here is a Morse operator; I got a sample of his proficiency when I came through the door. He was tapping Morse on that practice key he's carrying. I won't tell you what he was sending, but he's got a good fist, and you know how much Ronnie needs help in the radio room. Maybe he could be his apprentice."

Bond said with a smile, "What is this, Chang; you get an employment fee from these young people?"

Chang laughed, "No sir, but I've always had a good feel for people, and I'll bet these kids could be a real asset to CNAC."

Bond said, "Miss Boreisha, didn't you leave your curriculum vitae at the Robert Dollar Building just the other day?"

"Yes Sir, they said the Director of Operations was out of town and wouldn't be back for a couple of days."

"Persistent, aren't you."

"Why yes sir…when I set my mind to something there has to be a good reason for me to change it."

Bond looked at his watch and said, "We are on a pretty tight budget around here. Let me talk to a few people. I won't be able to pay you much until we see what you can do and it will probably only be part time to begin with…would that be satisfactory with you?"

The two looked at Bond as if he had given them the keys to the kingdom.

Bond said, "Mr. Abrahamson, as Mr. Chang said, Ronnie, our station radio operator does need an apprentice. Could you start next Monday?"

"I could start right now sir, but Monday will be fine."

"Good, be here at six o'clock. Our first flights leave early and we have to be in continuous contact with every ship. Ms. Boreisha, I would like you to start Monday too, but I won't need you here until eight o'clock."

"Oh! Thank you so much Mr. Bond. I'm sure you will not be disappointed!"

"Leave your names and how you can be contacted with Mrs. Woo; I'll see what I can do."

Anna and Saul thanked Bond for his time and left the building hardly able to restrain their joy.

CHAPTER 50

▼

CNAC

Shanghai

Anna's journal
1936, 22 September

Last night I announced to Mama and Papa that I had secured employment at the Chinese National Airline Corporation as a public relations trainee. They were delighted that Saul and I had both found employment at the same company and that we could look out after each other. Papa did not seem to mind that the starting pay would not be very much. They both agreed it would help me grow as a person and be ever so helpful in furthering my studies.

They couldn't believe the good luck that Saul had in becoming an apprentice radio operator. They both agreed that aviation and radio were the coming thing. CNAC was an affiliate of Pan American; I couldn't have been more fortunate.

Papa said that since I was going to work for this CNAC and Pan Am that my assignment for today would be to find out, and write in my journal, everything I could about their history and plans for the future.

Saul and I have had to re-schedule our sessions with Master Cheng Tu. Our daytime jobs make it necessary to practice our disciplines at night. Now, half of our sessions are spent in broadsword practice that I find somewhat comical. No one even uses swords any more except in ceremonies. In any event, Dog Breath says practice with the sword will instill discipline in us and further help our concentration in anything we attempt to do.

Now that I have a little money to go to the movies, I don't have the time! I miss all of my heroes saving heroines! About the closest I will ever come to being saved is when that gorgeous marine tried to keep me from the clutches of that awful Mr. Akimoto at the Far East Cabaret. Silly, but I think of him often. I can't get over the feeling I had when I first saw him. I wonder if I will ever see him again.

CHAPTER 51

▼

BILLY

Shanghai
October, 1936

Anna's new woolen suit was her only barrier against the October wind whipping across Shanghai's Whangpoo River and the Bund. The suit, complemented by high heels and new white gloves were her latest purchases. She was delighted with the tipping of hats and the "good days" of passing gentlemen.

Mr. Bond had explained that she would be expected to dress as a professional and had given her an advance on her pay to purchase essentials. In spite of the pleasure she derived from her new image, she suffered in her new heels as she approached the entrance to the Park hotel. It was then she saw Rabin. He was sitting alone in Hovan's Bentley. Smoke curled from the cigarette he held between his index finger and thumb, in the Eastern style—not like the guys held them in American movies. The window was half way down for ventilation. Anna flushed in anger when she saw him and without thinking said in Russian, "Is your master letting you out today without a leash, Ostafii?" He watched her with baleful malevolence as she passed. It was only afterwards she thought of the huge pistol she had seen under his coat, and it was then she thought of Cheng Tu's admonition, "When possible, walk away from conflict!"

Anna walked into the hotel's revolving doors without looking back. The Chinese doorman tipped his hat and said, "Good afternoon miss."

Why temp the devil, she thought, "And good afternoon to you too," she said in Mandarin.

The Park was a magnificent hotel but nothing like the Cathay just up the street. It was just a little over an hour before she had to meet the Trippe party. She still had time. Glancing at the Elgin watch her parents gave her for her sixteenth birthday she made a quick decision, went to the hotel's newsstand and bought a copy of the *North China Morning Post*. She would use the time she had and go through the ritual of picking out what Papa would consider the most thought provoking columns of today's Op Ed section. She could at least decide on the subject matter, she thought. As she sat down, she began to scan the newspaper for a subject that would pass scrutiny and require little or no research to satisfy her father.

She held the newspaper open at eye level. As she read, she was aware of the hotel's string ensemble's disharmonious cords as musicians tuned their instruments for the afternoon tea dance. The pleasant disharmony came from the dance floor on the river side of the lobby. So engrossed was she in an article about Amelia Earhart's planned trip around the world next year that she didn't notice the towering figure in khaki standing over her. She looked up, and realized the figure was speaking to her.

"Excuse me miss; we haven't formally met, but wasn't it you I interrupted the other night at the Far East Cabaret?

Anna lowered the newspaper to her lap and at once recognized the handsome marine from Hovan's cabaret. He was standing very close to her, so close, that she couldn't immediately stand. From her seated position, he seemed very tall and powerfully built.

He was wearing a tailored uniform but different from the one in the cabaret. This one was khaki, with a Sam Brown belt. His cap was tucked between his side and his left arm. He had sandy hair, cut very short and parted on the right side; his complexion was of one used to the out of doors.

She extended her gloved hand as naturally as if she had been a lady in the court of the Tsar. The marine dutifully took it, and helped her to her feet; he did not immediately step back, bringing them very close to each other. She could not help but look directly into his eyes.

"Yes, of course—you and the other marine and your lovely companions; you were at the other table. I guess you could say the gentleman I was with simply didn't know the meaning of no. I...I never had the opportunity to thank you."

Anna had that same feeling in her stomach again. Her legs felt a little weak.

He was looking directly into her eyes; unless she looked elsewhere, she couldn't do anything except look directly into his. They were the same color as those dogs. The ones from Siberia—what were they called?

"My name is William Schott. My friends call me Billy."

She saw his insignia and remembered her father's dissertation on the ranks of various services.

"I'm pleased to meet my rescuer, Captain Schott. My name is Anastasia Bore-isha."

Malamutes, she thought. He had the same color eyes as a Malamute!

"Please call me Billy, Ms. Boreisha. How did you come to work at the Far East Cabaret?"

His eyes were boring right into her now, and she was sure he could see exactly how vulnerable she felt.

"Oh no, Captain Schott, I don't work there!"

"It's Billy...I thought you were one of the hostesses!"

"No, Sergei Hovans...he's the proprietor. He invited me as his guest."

"His guest?"

"Yes," she answered.

She explained the circumstances of their meeting and said, "I guess it was naïve of me, but before I knew what was happening, he had made arrangements for me to be a companion to that Japanese gentleman you confronted."

She wondered why, all of a sudden, it became so necessary to explain her circumstances to a complete stranger.

Billy said, "Did I hear you speaking Japanese to him?"

"Why yes," said Anna.

There was a pause, and Anna noticed a quizzical look on the handsome officer's face.

Billy said, "Well, as far as I am concerned, this is all very fortunate for me."

"Fortunate?" Anna said.

"Why yes, Ms. Boreisha...had it not been for your being pawed by that guy and me intervening, I wouldn't have had much of an excuse to speak to you today, now would I?"

Anna smiled, looked him squarely in the eyes and said, "Surely, you are resourceful enough to have figured another way...am I not right, Captain Billy Schott?"

Billy put both hands on his hip, cocked his head and said, "Ms. Boreisha: we marines *are* supposed to be up to any mission. I am certain, in any event, I would have found some excuse to come over here and speak with you. What are you doing at the Park, Ms. Boreisha?"

She said, "My friends call me Anna, Billy, and I'm here on business. I work for CNAC, the Pan American Chinese subsidiary.

"CNAC…what do you do for them?"

"I am what my boss calls a traffic representative. I meet passengers…help them with their transfers, translations, that sort of thing."

"Oh Yeah…and what brings you to the Park hotel today?"

"I am to meet Mr. and Mrs. Juan Trippe and their guests. Mr. Trippe is Pan Am's boss and founder, from New York. They are here as part of the celebration inaugurating mail and passenger service from the United States to the Orient. He is taking a tour of CNAC's routes to evaluate the operation."

Billy said, "Yes, I read about it in today's newspaper." He continued, "Jeez, Anna, I am fascinated with what's going on in aviation! If you have time, would you let me buy you a refreshment? I would love to hear more."

She looked at her watch and said, "I have a little time, Billy…sure, why not!" She wondered how she sounded to an American using slang with her slight Russian accent.

Billy beckoned to the maitre d'. He took Anna by the arm and escorted her to a table far enough from the dance floor where they could speak without being overwhelmed by the string ensemble. He held her chair as she sat down just as the musicians began to play. Two couples stood up made their way to the dance floor and began dancing the tango.

Billy asked, "Do you tango?"

"No, I'm afraid not," she said.

"You must allow me to teach you some day. It's a beautiful, romantic dance. But enough of that, tell me about CNAC, and how you happened to get a job with them."

Anna told of their going to the airport and meeting with Mr. Bond. She told of her friend Saul getting a job as a radio operator apprentice, and she as a traffic representative.

"So tell me about Pan Am and CNAC."

She explained, "Pan American's transpacific service now terminates in Hong Kong. It should terminate here, but the Chinese government is reluctant to grant Pan Am direct rights beyond Hong Kong to Shanghai even though it's obvious Shanghai is the logical terminus. Because of extraterritoriality, they would be obliged to open the country to the airlines of any other country, including the Japanese, if they granted rights to Pan Am. The Chinese don't want that to happen."

"Ah yes, the Japanese. Besides commerce, what do you think the Japanese want in China, and how did you come to learn the language?"

"I don't think there's any question," she said, "They want everything! They've illegally held Manchuria since '31 and their ambitions for China are totally transparent. As for Indochina, and the rest of South East Asia, it's only a matter of time. They are a small island nation, have very few natural resources of their own, have succumbed to a militaristic government condoned by their Emperor and have an appetite for more raw materials: oil, tin, rubber...all the stuff of war."

"My, my...aren't you a smart cookie. Where did all those thoughts come from?"

Anna explained her father's educational regimen including the learning of Japanese. Billy Schott continued to ask her questions about her family, and what she knew of the political climate of China, and Shanghai in particular.

After a while, the dance orchestra switched to a more traditional foxtrot, and Billy again asked Anna to dance. She looked at her watch and towards the far side of the lobby. Still seeing no sign of the Trippe party, she said, "All right, I think I have time for just one and then I have to be off."

He pulled her chair and escorted her through the tables to the dance floor. As he put his arms around her, she felt that feeling in the pit of her stomach again; unsure or what it meant, she decided to enjoy the moment.

As tall as she was, she could not see over his shoulder so she turned her head to one side and he to the other.

Billy said, "When you were with Hovans, did you by any chance run into his side kick chauffeur...a guy named Ostafii Rabin?"

"The man is a pig, Billy! After I left Akimoto, I went back stage to the dressing room to get my clothes so I could go home. He came back there saying Hovans wanted me to spend the night with that guy. When I refused, he slapped me and that was too bad for him!"

"Slapped you? What did you do?"

"Yes...slapped me and I hurt him...rather badly, I think! Now that you mention it, he's outside right now...parked in front of the hotel, in Hovan's limousine."

Billy stopped dancing and held her at arms length and said, "Outside...now?"

"Yes: he was there when I came in."

Billy's face took on a look of concern. "Anna, unless he knew for sure you would be here, I don't think he was here because of you. I think he was here because of me!"

Anna looked at him astonished and said, "What do you have to do with Rabin and Hovans."

Billy was just about to speak when Anna saw the Trippes step out of the elevator and walk toward the concierge.

She said, "Excuse me Billy; I have to go. That's the party I am supposed to meet."

She was starting toward the concierge's desk and the Trippes when Billy caught her and thrust a business card in her hand. "Please, Anna, don't think me presumptuous, but I really would like to see you again."

He followed her across the lobby.

"I'm so busy now!"

"Whenever you have a chance, please call, any time...I really want to see you again," said the young captain.

Anna knew she would, but didn't answer immediately as she started toward the Trippes.

Half way across the lobby she turned and shouted, "O.K., I'll try!"

CHAPTER 52

▼

TRIPP'S PARTY

Shanghai
November, 1936

Anna's journal
1936, 15 November

So much has happened in the last weeks I have not had time to journal my thoughts. Since the day Mr. Trippe, his wife, and his party arrived from the United States and Hong Kong my life has been carried along by a whirlwind of events I could have never foreseen.

First were the receptions and banquets in Shanghai celebrating Mr. Trippe's great achievement in bringing mail and passenger service to the Orient. I never dreamed that people lived and dined in such splendor as I have seen in the last weeks!

No sooner were the Shanghai celebrations over than Mr. Bond enlisted me to serve as translator for his party's inspection of CNAC routes; this gave me the opportunity to fly for my first time, and fly we did! Mr. Bond and the others were able to act as travel guides in flight, as they had traveled these routes many times before. Most of my duties were spent translating on the ground. In flight, I spent almost the entire time looking out of the window with a map in my hand trying to identify the rivers, valleys and towns. It was absolutely breathtaking, and for the first time, I was able to understand why people who fly love it so much.

It has been almost a week now since our return and the Trippe's departure for Hong Kong. From what I understand, he and Mrs. Trippe will fly west-bound around the world by air! Oh what a marvelous thing that must be for them. Maybe some day!

Regardless of the Trippe visit, so much has been happening in my life that I don't know where to begin, but I think it necessary to journal these thoughts so some day I can look back over these words and perhaps be able to see what happened from a different perspective. Maybe I will even learn something about myself.

After the incident with Sergei Hovans and that pig Rabin, I expected the worst kinds of recriminations from my parents, especially Papa. Instead, they were more understanding than I had reason to expect.

I described to them the fascinating flight with the Trippe party and the exciting things we saw along the way. Papa was ever so pleased when I told him that my language skills helped a great deal.

I didn't tell him about meeting Marine Captain Billy Schott, though. Although highly regarded, the American Marines have a reputation among Shanghailanders as being womanizers and of frequenting estab-lishments around "Blood Alley." If Papa knew I knew of his indiscretions, I really don't think he could use that argument very well.

I still have Billy's card from that day we met at the Park hotel—should I call him? He has no way of contacting me so it is really up to me if I want to see him again. I know I will—it's simply a matter of getting the nerve and finding the time....

Anna walked into the telephone exchange and presented the business card Billy Schott had given her to the operator. She said to herself, "Anna Bore-isha...this is 1936, and you are simply not going to wait and see if Billy Schott will just happen to run into you again. Seeing him at the Park was serendipity, and the chances of that happening again are too small to imagine."

She paid the clerk who in turn pointed her to one of the many wooden booths. Anna pushed herself through the throng of people and picked up the heavy black receiver. A voice with an accent she could hardly understand said, "Fourth Marines, Gunnery Sergeant Maxwell Priddy speaking; how can I help you?"

Anna said, "My name is Anna Boreisha. I am trying to get in touch with Marine Captain Billy Schott, sir."

"Yes ma'am, I'm sure you are! He gets a lotta calls from the ladies. He's at his house right now…off duty. Can I take a message for ya miss?"

"Does Captain Schott have a telephone at his house?" She asked.

"Yes ma'am, he does…but I'm not allowed to give out that information."

"Would you please tell Captain Schott that Anna Boreisha called? Please tell him he can meet me at the CNAC hangers, at Lunghwa airport, tomorrow, at 5 p.m."

"Lunghwa airport, CNAC, 5 p.m. O.K. ma'am. Could you spell your name for me please?"

"Just tell him Anna called, Sergeant."

Without waiting for a reply, Anna hung up the heavy instrument and left the booth, disappointed.

The next day Anna was busy learning about CNAC's frequent business travelers. It would be her job to make sure these clients were well taken care of and that they would continue to use the airline for their travel needs.

While combing through the names of those customers it occurred to her that many other businesses in Shanghai probably had the need of CNAC's services but simply had not considered flying for their business travel. She explained her thoughts to Mrs. Woo, Mr. Bond's secretary, who agreed. The rest of the afternoon the two of them combed Shanghai's telephone listings and business publications searching for the names of likely prospects.

When she left the hangar, Anna was still deep in thought thinking the best way to approach potential clients. She was so absorbed that she failed to notice the black Buick Century coupe sitting just outside the CNAC hangar gate.

As she walked through the gate, Captain Billy Schott opened the door of the big car and shouted, "Anna, hey Anna…it's me, Billy!"

His voice broke her concentration. When she saw who it was, she broke into a broad smile as she recognized it the handsome marine. He wore the same khaki uniform as he had at the Park, and as he walked toward her with his wonderful smile, she thought him even more handsome than she remembered. For a moment, she forgot she was a mature eighteen-year-old and almost skipped like a child before regaining her composure and slowing to a walk to meet the marine.

"Captain Schott, you got my phone call after all, didn't you?"

Billy said, "Hi ya beautiful! You had to scram so fast the other day, you didn't let me know how I could ring you up. Looks like that card I had made up did the trick, though…sorry, but it was the only thing I could think of at the time except maybe joining you with the rest of those swells."

Billy motioned toward the Buick and said, "Come on…hop in! I'll give you a lift to wherever you are going. It will give us a chance to finish our conversation."

"Oh Billy, that would be swell! I was just on my way home. When I called I spoke with someone I could barely understand…I'm so glad you got the message."

Billy held the door of the Buick and as she slipped into the passenger seat he said, "Yeah, that would be Sergeant Priddy: he's from Louisiana…I have a hard time understanding him myself sometimes."

Billy started the car and turned into the traffic. Anna said, "Billy, you never finished telling me how you happen to know Mr. Rabin."

"Well, let's just say it's one of my jobs to keep an eye on that bird Hovans and Rabin, that personal torpedo of his. Thing is, I think he's on to me now and instead of me keeping tabs on him, he's keeping his peepers on me. I've caught him tailing me a couple of times now."

Anna asked, "Why would a United States Marine want to know anything about the likes of Hovans and Rabin, Billy?"

Billy was silent for a minute and said, "Let's just skip that for awhile, Anna. How's about us stopping at the Cathay for a little while? I'd like to introduce you to a couple of friends of mine that stop by there for drinks about this time of the day."

"That would be swell, Billy…if we aren't too long. My parents are expecting me home soon, but since I'm getting a ride with you, maybe I'll only be a little late."

Billy stepped on the accelerator and made good time through the farmland just outside of Lunghwa airport. As they approached the Old Chinese City, traffic got worse and caused them to slow for bicycles, carts, farmers with carry poles—every possible conveyance. Soon they were on the magnificent "Miracle Mile" of the Bund, representing the best and the worst of Western capitalism in China. Captain Schott brought the flashy Buick to a stop in front of the Cathay where an attendant opened doors and dutifully parked the car. Billy took Anna by the elbow and ushered her through the revolving door.

Anna had never been to the Cathay before and marveled at the opulent use of marble in the beautiful lobby. The dominant colors were rose and grey punctuated by enormous marble pillars and art deco frescoes on the walls. At ten stories, the Cathay was the tallest building on the Bund and just happened to be the home of its owner, Victor Sassoon, who occupied the entire tenth floor. Overlooking the Whangpoo River, most Shanghailanders agreed it was also the most elegant building on the Bund.

Billy, and his friends who could afford it, preferred the Cathay to meet for drinks, especially in the summer. It was one of the few places that had air conditioning and a respite from Shanghai's heat and humidity—a true luxury. The bar had an excellent view of the Whangpoo. Sampans, junks, river steamers and steamships from every port were moored or anchored along the river's banks. Then, there was the *Idzumo*—the huge Japanese battle cruiser moored just outside the Cathay and a constant reminder of the power held over Shanghai by Imperial Japan.

When the couple entered the revolving door to the bar, another marine captain and a lieutenant let out a long whistle when they saw Billy's companion.

"Captain Schott…this time you've really outdone yourself," said the lieutenant.

Billy said, "At ease Lieutenant. Anna, allow me to introduce you to Captain Ron Howell and Lieutenant Nick Allen, both these guys are from my regiment."

Anna had no doubt that Billy had brought her here to show her off. For the present, she was thoroughly enjoying it. She said, "So nice to meet you Captain Howell…Lieutenant Allen."

Anna looked around the room. It was just like the American movies. Businessmen, world travelers, maybe even movie stars. The hotel was magnificent and to think only weeks before she was just another jobless Russian going to the movies with mere children.

She focused on the conversation. From their suggestions, it was clear she wasn't the first woman friend Billy had taken to this "watering hole," as he called it, and no doubt not the last. Moreover, they made mention of a Mae Lin and a Suzy something or other…probably those two that she had seen Billy with at the Far East Club. She had hoped she was the only one, but what could she expect, she thought.

He offered her a cigarette even though he knew she did not smoke; he lit one for himself as the bartender set her squash and his scotch on the bar in front of them. As Billy chatted with his friends, she looked at his profile. The man was truly handsome without being pretty. His facial features seemed almost sculpted. He had well defined cheekbones, a fine nose, broad mouth and good teeth. He was indeed a beautiful male. It was also obvious the other soldiers regarded him highly. At this point, however, she didn't know if it was because of his personality, leadership or simply rank. Time would tell on that point, she thought.

They hadn't been there long when the two Chinese women she had seen Billy with at the Far East Cabaret came into the bar. They both wore the ubiquitous

Chi-Pao though different from the ones they had worn at Hovan's cabaret. Anna wondered if it was normal for Chinese women to come into a bar un-escorted.

Billy was at first surprised and then seemed a little annoyed. The other soldiers obviously knew the girls. He introduced them as Mae Lin and Suzy Liu—no doubt English adaptations of Chinese names.

He looked at his watch, pulled out a money clip and peeled off enough yuan, or mex, as the Americans called it, for the round of drinks and a handsome tip. He leaned over to Mae Lin and whispered something in her ear. She simply looked ahead and did not smile. Billy then said, "Gotta go gang! Anna has to get home...see you all later."

Anna was glad that he decided to leave but did wonder why the sudden hurry. When they were back in the Buick she said, "Thanks for the drink and introducing me to your friends and keeping it short. I really do need to get home. Drive south on the Bund and take Avenue Eduard VII...it's faster this time of day."

Billy said, "I really didn't expect to see Mae Lin and Suzy Liu today. They are really just friends that occasionally do things for me."

"Do things? What kind of things?" asked Anna.

"It's kind of hard to explain. Sometimes they can get some information I need for my job that I can't get myself. The government, ah...the Marines pay them for it. It's a pretty good thing for them, and it helps me a lot."

"And you take them to the Far East Cabaret as a reward?" asked Anna.

"Yeah, it works something like that. I need to be there, sometimes, to check up on who's in town. They make good companions. Nothing serious, though. They're really good eggs."

Anna looked at Billy with a dubious smile and said, "Good eggs, huh?"

Billy said, "Look, it's nothing like that. We are just friends that help each other out every now and then. In return, I let them earn a little money."

"If you say so, Billy."

They turned on Avenue Eduard VII, drove past the race club and left onto Nanking Road. Anna then gave Billy street by street directions to her parent's apartment in the French Concession.

As they neared her home, Anna saw her father's Packard parked in its usual place and said, "Oh...my father is home already. Why don't you come inside for a minute and meet my parents?"

Billy said, "Nah, I really need to get going, Anna...maybe some other time."

As he pulled to a stop, she said, "Nonsense...it will only take a minute and I would like you to meet them. You know, my father was an officer in the Russian Army. Come on, now...it will only take a minute."

Billy began to protest and then saw how animated Anna was at the prospect of showing him off to her parents and said, "Oh, all right…but just for a minute."

He grabbed his garrison hat, scooted across the seat behind Anna and closed the door. She took him by the arm with both hands and walked with him across the small courtyard to the front door of the Boreisha's modest apartment.

Her mother was off in the small alcove that served as a kitchen making tea. Her father was sitting in the modest living room reading a local Russian newspaper. Having removed only his tie, Peter Boreisha still sat in his suit pants and dress shirt.

When Anna came in with the big marine, he stood, and folded the newspaper in front of him, distracted by the unannounced visitor.

Lilia Boreisha heard the door close. She saw Anna coming into the apartment with the tall soldier and began to take off her apron and smooth her hair.

Billy looked around at the small but neatly furnished living room of the Boreisha family. One wall was almost entirely covered with books in open cases. The other had a sideboard with glass doors displaying a few dining room treasures, probably from their old life in Russia, he thought. An ornate tea set sat on a silver serving tray. On the wall, above the bookcases were several pictures. One was a family portrait with Anna's father and mother standing behind their daughter. Anna looked to be about five or six. Her father was in military dress uniform, complete with sword. Her mother wore an elegant dress with puffy sleeves and oversized shoulders made with what appeared to be large quantities of lace. Her hair was piled high in an elegant style that must have taken some servant hours to put just so. She looked much younger and self assured than the woman just entering the living room.

There were others, but before he could focus on them, Anna was making introductions.

She said in English, "Billy, This is my father, Mr. Peter Boreisha. Father, This is Captain Billy Schott of the United States Marine Corps."

Peter Boreisha placed the folded paper on the end table by his reading chair and extended his hand to the young officer.

"I am pleased to meet you, Captain," said Peter Boreisha in heavily accented English.

"Anna, if we knew you were bringing someone home with you, mama could have prepared something for Captain Schott."

Anna's mother said in Russian, "Anna dear, you should have told us you were bringing a guest home."

Anna made the introductions, translating where necessary. Peter spoke passable, but highly accented English. Lilia spoke none, and Anna was careful to make sure she followed the conversation. Billy noticed her mother was more subdued than Anna's father and barely recognizable as the aristocratic woman in the portrait. He suspected their change in circumstances had been much more difficult for her than for Anna's father.

Anna said, "Captain Schott is the officer I told you about. He is the one that came to my rescue at the Far East Cabaret."

Her parents both nodded their heads as they remembered their daughter's revelations of her night at the cabaret.

Billy was surprised that Anna had told her family of the incident and made a mental note as something that might be important in the future.

"And what did you think of the Far East Cabaret, Captain Schott?" asked Peter Boreisha.

"They have fine food and entertainment, Mr. Boreisha. Anna told me of the circumstances that brought her there…it sounds like a complete misunderstanding on her part to me. Those places are always looking for hostesses like your daughter. There's no doubt that bird Hovans lured her there under false pretenses and took advantage of her once she was there."

With a raised eyebrow Peter asked, "What brought you there, Captain Schott?"

"Business and pleasure alike," said Billy. "Like I said, the cabaret has excellent food and entertainment. In my capacity with the Marine Corps, we have to keep tabs on some of the other governments' officers and officials. The clubs and cabarets are where many of them go, so that's where I go…but that's not to say I don't enjoy the clubs, Mr. Boreisha."

"So you are in the intelligence gathering business, Captain Schott?"

"All marines are in the intelligence business, sir. It's part of what we do."

Peter Boreisha nodded his head in a knowing way and said, "Of course Captain Schott, of course."

Billy was glad when Anna changed the subject and said, "I ran into Captain Schott again at the Park hotel a couple of weeks ago. It was the day I met the Trippe party. Today, Billy picked me up at Lunghwa field and gave me a lift home."

Lilia Boreisha said, "Captain Schott, I have just made evening tea. Would you please join us?"

Anna translated and Billy said, "Oh no, Mrs. Boreisha…as I told Anna, I have an appointment. I really have to be on my way."

Anna pleaded for a moment to no avail. Billy paid his compliments to the Boreishas, said goodbye, and left.

He had no sooner gone than Anna turned to her parents and asked, "Well…what do you think of Captain Schott?"

Anna's mother was first to speak. "He is a very handsome man Anna, but you know the reputations of those American soldiers."

Lilia looked briefly at Peter and then back at Anna. "They have reputations for frequenting the bars and brothels of Rue Chu Pao San, my daughter."

"Yes, I know mama, but I think he must be different."

Anna couldn't help but think of Mae Lin and Suzy Liu. Certainly, as elegant as they were, they couldn't be taxi girls.

Peter Boreisha said, "Anna: you be very careful! You are smart and intelligent, but you are very young and inexperienced. I saw the look on your face with Captain Schott. You glowed like a beacon, but I think that man will break your heart if you let him."

"Oh Papa, Billy has been a complete gentleman…just like the Americans in the movies. He wouldn't think of hurting me."

Anna's father closed the two steps between himself and his daughter, put his arms around her, and drew her close in an embrace. "Anna, darling, your mama and I love you so much…we just don't want to see you hurt. Please think with your head as we have taught you, and not with your heart."

The following day Billy called and asked if he could see her after work on Friday evening. He took her home where she changed into her new business suit dressing it up with a few pieces of costume jewelry to serve as eveningwear. After dinner at Maxine's, Billy asked if she would like to come to his house for a nightcap.

He parked the Buick in front of a low wall with a small gate. He opened the car door for Anna, took her hand and helped her out. A young Chinese urchin appeared out of nowhere and said, "Ain't got no mama, ain't got no papa, ain't got no goddam chow! Me watch car plenty good! No much little mex!"

Billy said, "This kids been hanging around the marine barracks too long. He followed me home and now he hangs out around here." He thrust several Yuan into the boy's hand knowing full well, if he paid him in full now rather than in the morning, the boy would be gone as soon as they were out of sight.

Billy put his arm around Anna, opened the gate and ushered her through. On the other side of the gate was a garden with ornamental lamps and a small fountain. Behind the garden was a house with tiled roof and wooden ornamental fretwork surrounding a heavily carved wooden door.

He opened the door. They were greeted by classical music on a phonograph and a Chinese manservant Anna guessed to be forty or fifty.

Billy said, "Anna this is Chang Chu, he has looked after me for the whole time I've been in Shanghai."

Anna greeted him in Mandarin. Chang Chu bowed, took their top coats and asked if they would like refreshments. Billy asked for a scotch for himself and a lemon squash for Anna.

While the manservant was going for drinks, Billy excused himself and took off his uniform blouse, Sam Brown belt and necktie. He folded the tie into the blouse, and laid them over the back of the couch. While he was doing this, Anna strolled around the living room wondering about the dichotomy of a man who could be versed in the art of war, conversant in the modern slang, and still interested in classical music and the pieces of art she saw around her.

The house was decorated with an eclectic collection of Chinese art. On the walls were landscapes from the Song dynasty. There were also several lacquer bowls and a Ming vase. The house had beautiful hardwood floors partially covered with oriental rugs of a type Anna had seen only in the homes of some of her father's more wealthy clients.

Contrasting heavily with the artwork was a little wooden box, with a hinged glass top. Inside the box was a military medal that seemed to be contrived rather than struck. At the end of a colorful ribbon was the caricature of a Chinaman pushing the ubiquitous "honey cart" and on the periphery, engraved in bronze, was "Soochow Creek, 1932."

Anna asked, "Billy, what is this medal for?"

"Oh, back in 32, on my first tour with the Fourth Marines, we stood nose to nose with the Japanese across the creek from Chapei."

"That was just after their invasion of Manchuria, right?"

"Yeah, that's right. Everyone except the Marines shrugged it off as insignificant. So, a lot of the marines got together and made themselves a medal as kind of a joke. I thought it was a gas, so I had a little box made for it."

When the manservant returned with the drinks Billy said, "Thank you Chang, that will be all for the evening."

Chang bowed with his arms crossed in the typical Chinese fashion—each hand tucked into the arm sleeve of the other. He turned and left.

Anna gestured to some of the artifacts around the room and asked, "How did you become interested in Chinese art and the music…isn't that somewhat out of character for a marine?"

Billy laughed and said, "Yeah, I guess so. My profession is an ugly one some-times. Some of the men under my command are pretty tough cookies, and we see a lot of ugly things. We practice the best way to kill other people. We hear a lot of loud noises and have to deal with some very bad people."

"Like Rabin and Hovans?"

"Yeah...Like Rabin and Hovans."

"I guess it sort of gives some balance to my life. I need beautiful things in my life like these things...like you, Anna...especially you."

That peculiar sensation she had felt the first time she saw him ran through her body again. Billy took her hand in his. "Come on," he said. "I'll show you the rest of the house."

To one side of the living room was a short hallway that led to a kitchen, much larger than the one Anna's family had in their small apartment. The room on the far side of the kitchen, Billy explained, was Chang's sleeping room.

Another hallway led off of the other side of the living room. The walls were decorated with more artwork of lesser quality than she had seen in the living room, but nevertheless tasteful and no doubt expensive. On one wall were pic-tures of a handsome middle-aged couple that Billy explained was his parents. Off to one side of the second hall was a full bathroom of the type Anna had only seen in the luxury hotels and in the movies.

Billy explained, "Yeah, I had that head shipped all the way from the states. I just couldn't deal with the hole in the floor that came with this place. Same with the tub and shower...cost a bundle, but to me, it was worth it."

Anna asked, "Head? You call the toilet a head?"

"Yeah, it's a marine and navy thing...for hundreds of years it has been the term used for a toilet on a ship."

At the end of the hall way was the bedroom. Billy opened the closed door and showed Anna in. It was a little austere compared to the rest of the house—thor-oughly masculine, she thought. The furniture was beautiful. It consisted of a large carved wardrobe, a dresser, one straight-backed chair, night tables on both sides of what Anna considered a very large bed and the ubiquitous overhead fan. She wondered if Billy had shared it with one, or both of his beautiful Chinese companions from the Far East Cabaret.

Anna said, "You must be quite wealthy...nice house, good car...are all marines as rich as you?"

Billy laughed and said, "No...not at all. In the United States, I'm what they would call a 'trust fund baby'. My grandparents left me enough money so I really didn't have to work if I didn't want to. When I finished college, I didn't want to go into textiles, the family business, so I gave the Marine Corps a try. I liked it, and have been with them ever since."

Anna sat down on the American contemporary looking sofa and said, "Handsome and rich too! You would be quite a catch for Mae Lin, Suzy Liu, or a poor little Russian girl like me, wouldn't you?"

As Billy held his iced scotch in one hand he said, "Would I now? Maybe until the first time I was sent to some fourth-world Godforsaken jungle…then you, or they would be gone like a shot!"

Anna said, "They might not all have fine cars and a house like this, but most of the marines I have seen in Shanghai always seem to have enough money to spend…not like some of the other troops in the International Settlement."

"It might seem our soldiers are rich, Anna, but really they aren't…not by U.S. standards. It's because we are paid in dollars. When dollars are converted to mex with such a favorable conversion rate, even the enlisted guys are able to live very well here in Shanghai. In the rest of the Corps, being assigned with the Fourth Marines is considered the best duty there is, and as you probably know, many of them do have Russian or Chinese girl friends."

Billy took two black and red lacquered coasters from their matching rack on the coffee table. He placed his scotch glass on one and sat besides Anna on the sofa. He said, "Anna, unless you stop me, I'm going kiss you. It's something I've wanted to do since the first time I saw you in the bar at Hovan's cabaret."

He took her squash and placed it the other coaster besides his own. He turned and faced Anna's ever-present half smile that changed to one of quizzical expectation. She was about to say something, but decided not to, as Billy encircled her waist, back and shoulders in a full embrace, and pulled her gently towards him.

She responded to Billy's embrace and kiss in a way she did not think herself capable. As her lips met his, and she felt her breasts against his chest, that wonderful feeling in the pit of her stomach spread its warmth to her whole body. While continuing the embrace she felt one arm slip under her legs as Billy lifted her effortlessly, stood and carried her into the bedroom.

As Billy carried her down the hall, things like parents, pregnancy and morality flitted through her consciousness with the last shards of logical thought, but at that moment, they ranked a distant last as she succumbed to unrestrained passion.

CHAPTER 53

▼

ON BEING A WOMAN

Shangai

Anna's journal

> *Last night I found out what it was to be a woman. I had no idea there were so many ways for a man and woman to make love. Billy is a good and patient teacher, and I have no illusions that I am his first student. I am consumed with desire for more of him, and I am counting the hours until I can be with him again. Only now can I appreciate all that has been said in words, music and poetry about love and all that surrounds it. Does every woman feel as I after her first time? I think not. I don't know if it is Billy, me, or the combination that makes me feel this way.*
>
> *Billy drove me home at just past four and I am still wondering if Mama and Papa heard me come in....*

The holiday season came and went and winter turned to spring and summer. Anna's life moved from the wonderment of adolescence to the knowingness of a woman. Work and Billy occupied every waking moment. Only occasional sessions with Cheng Tu, learning the art of broadsword combat, interrupted her two obsessions. Regardless of the changes in her life, it did not quell her tremendous curiosity in world events her father's teaching regime had instilled in her.

Because of her family's background, she couldn't help but be fascinated by events taking place in Spain. She thought both of the clashing ideologies seriously flawed. There was no doubt in her mind that regardless of who won the contest between the Fascist and the Communists the people were sure to lose.

When she tried to discuss the subject with Billy, he was much less interested in the ideologies than the tactics and military hardware both sides brought to the conflict. He pointed out that the mass bombings by the German Luftwaffe probably augured a whole new role for the airplane in bringing terror to civilian populations in war.

In March, Amelia Earhart disappointed Anna when she crashed on takeoff in Hawaii, postponing her "first woman pilot around the world" attempt.

Only one month after Pan Am's first successful scheduled mail flight to Hong Kong the German zeppelin Hindenburg incinerated itself, and probably the future of dirigibles, at Lakehurst, New Jersey. More and more, the airplane was proving to hold the future for international aviation. It was in July, however, that Anna's life, intertwined with world events, and began to spin out of control forever.

CHAPTER 54

▼

PERFIDY

July, 1937
Shanghai

Mrs. Woo said, "Miss Anna: where are you?

"What?" Anna thought, am I so transparent?

Mrs. Woo continued, "That's the second listing you placed in the wrong pile. How will we ever get these businesses in the right order if you don't pay attention?"

Anna snapped out of a wistful reverie—her half smile more prevalent than usual.

"Excuse me Mrs. Woo; I don't seem to be able to keep my mind on my work this morning."

"Well you had better, Miss Anna. I told Mr. Bond of your scheme and he liked it very much. He wants the list in his office tomorrow. We have much work to do, so you keep head out of clouds...O.K.!"

Anna smiled and returned to sorting the files.

For the next three afternoons, Billy picked Anna up after work at CNAC. Each rendezvous was the same. It was a mad dash to see how fast they could get to his house, dismiss Mr. Chu, strip their clothes and fall into bed. After the first night, they had agreed that for appearances she would be home no later that ten o'clock. Anna used the subterfuge of working late on the advertisement scheme, and her parents seemed to understand. She felt a tremendous guilt.

Anna remembered—it was around 9 p.m. on a Friday when Billy asked her. They had been making love for hours. She knew she had to get home, soon. It was April, and already they were having a hot spell. He was lying in bed, smoking a cigarette, and contemplating the slowly turning blades of the ceiling fan. Anna was exhausted and half-asleep after a week of working all day, and making love most of the night.

"Anna love—I want you to do something for me."

Anna rolled on her side; she lazily looked at Billy and with a smile said, "For you, my love, anything."

"I want you to go back to work for Hovans, at the Far East Cabaret," Billy said.

"Back to work for Hovans…but why," she asked.

Billy continued to contemplate the smoke curling from his cigarette, wafting its way toward the oblivion of the ceiling fans gentle breeze and replied, "We need information. We have reason to believe he is working for the Japanese and something big is cooking. You would be doing me, my government and China a big favor."

He rolled on his right side, away from Anna, and took longer than necessary to snub his cigarette in the ashtray. Anna was silent.

Billy rolled around, propped his head up with his left hand and faced Anna. He wasn't smiling. His expression was serious. She was staring at him in disbelief and when his expression didn't change she said, "You are serious, aren't you?"

Billy said, "Yeah, babe, I'm as serious as a heart attack."

"But Billy…you know what monster's he and that Rabin are! Why would you ask me to go back there! They expect me to have sex with their customers. How could you ask me to do that?"

"I wouldn't, except there is no other way. You are tough, smart, and have what it takes. More important, he likes you, and you have the language skills."

Tears began to well up in Anna's big brown eyes and she said, "Is this the only reason you have been with me Billy?"

He tucked one arm under her head and the other around her waist and pulled her close to him. With his head over her shoulder and his face out of sight, he said, "Of course not, babe! I wouldn't do that to you. I'm not that kind of a guy." He released her from the embrace, pushed back a little way and said, "Anna: this is very important. We…the Marines and the Navy…know Hovan's palm is getting greased by the Japanese, and we know it's just a matter of time until they make a move on the International Settlement. We need to find out what he is doing for them and what their intentions are. I never intended for this to come down to you, but you're perfect for this…otherwise, believe me, I wouldn't ask!"

Anna continued to look at Billy with a look of misery and incomprehension. Uncontrollable sobs and tears replaced her perennial half smile.

Billy continued, "Darling, I'm in the information gathering business. It's called intelligence, and the U.S. government is willing to pay if you work for us. I know you wouldn't normally do this for money, but there *is* money to be made…so why not?"

Anna said, "I thought it was just me you were interested in Billy, but in reality it's only what I could do for you; isn't that true?"

"Of course not, darling! You know what we have together. You know what you mean to me."

"Do I, Billy? Answer me honestly. Do Mae Lin and Suzy Liu work for you too? You said you pay them for their services just as you pay prostitutes for theirs'! Do I mean no more to you than that?"

Without answering, Billy sat up on the bed with his back to Anna and reached for the pack of Camels on the nightstand. He tapped out a cigarette, put one in his mouth, and lit it.

"How many girls do you have working for you in your *intelligence business*, Billy…how many?"

Billy said, "It's not my intelligence business, Anna…it's the Marine Corps'…it's…it's what I do! Mae Lin and Suzy Liu are professionals. They do this for money."

Billy rose from the bed, cigarette in his hand and turned to face her in his full nakedness that only moments before was the focus of Anna's every waking thought.

Billy said, "Damn it Anna, no…that's not it at all. It's just that we need to get this information and you are the perfect one for getting it. Just forget I ever asked, will you? Just forget it!"

Anna got up from the bed. She walked to the chair where she had tossed her clothes some hours before and began to dress. For the first time she felt dirty and wanted to shower—but not here; she wanted to go home.

Anna said, "Billy: please ask Chang Chu to drive me home."

CHAPTER 55

▼

TRUTH

Shanghai

Anna's journal

> *Now I have a small appreciation for alcoholics, drug addicts and their addictions. I think my addiction is sex! Every waking moment is one of desire. I spend every moment waiting for the next time with him, and I hate myself for it.*
>
> *I never thought it possible that someone who loved you would ask you to do something as odious as ferreting information from Hovan's Japanese clients. I know that his marines have put him under extraordinary pressure to obtain information about the Japanese, or Billy would not have asked me.*
>
> *My logical side tells me he could not love me and still ask that I do these things, yet I hope that by doing so he will love me even more. For the first time in my life, I feel stupid and unable to do anything about it! I will enlist Tanya to help me. Can I trust her? I must give it a try.*

Mrs. Woo ushered Anna into the upstairs hangar office of the operations director. When she entered, Bond stood, and walked to the front of his desk with his hand outstretched and said, "Miss Boreisha, Mrs. Woo tells me that you have been busy in the months you have been with us."

Anna forced a smile even though recent events did not make her feel in the least bit happy.

Bond shook her hand and said, "Please sit down and tell me the scheme you have for canvassing potential CNAC customers."

Anna forced the fatigue and pending return to the Far East Cabaret from her mind. Preparing for the meeting, she had used Cheng Tu's technique of clearing the mind of extraneous information by visualizing her immediate goals, much as she visualized her boxing postures and maneuvers before executing them. She found the exercise to be very useful any time she had to clear her mind of distractions. Now, she focused on the one page management summary she had typed for Bond.

Her scheme explained what type of business client was most likely to use air travel and her ideas for selling them on using CNAC for their transportation needs.

Bond said, "Anna: I like your idea. What you are suggesting is business 101 back in college, but the truth is, I am ashamed to say, we haven't been doing anything of the sort here. Tell you what, though…starting tomorrow I would like you to work with Mr. Sun, in our marketing department, and help him develop some sales materials that would convince the business people on your client list that they should use our services. What do you say to that?"

Anna was ecstatic that her idea met with Bond's approval. In the back of her mind, though, clouding everything so promising with her new position was the decision she had made regarding Billy's needs. She would have to gain Hovan's trust through subterfuge and spy on his clients. She tried to convince herself she was doing it for love—that it would help Billy with his career, and that he would love her even more for doing it. All the while though, her inner voice, her pragmatic self, kept telling her she was being used.

On the one hand, she was happy that after such a short period of employment, her efforts at CNAC were being recognized. On the other, it was the first time she could ever remember holding herself in low esteem.

C H A P T E R 56

▼

DECADENCE REDUX

Shanghai

Anna's journal
The Far East Cabaret

July has been a horrible month. First, there was the distressing news of Amelia Earhart and Fred Noonan being missing near a place called Howland Island, somewhere in the South Pacific. At the same time while they were searching for any sign of her aircraft, the Japanese and Chinese were at each other's throats again, supposedly over a missing soldier at the Marco Polo Bridge, not far from Peking. Right after that, they occupied Peking and Tientsin. Can Shanghai be far behind?

It has been several weeks now since I returned to work for Sergei Hovans. At first, he seemed suspicious. I explained to him that my parents were having a hard time making ends meet with only papa's chauffeur business, and that I needed a second income to help. (I didn't explain that papa spent a good portion of his earnings on a Russian whore!)

As expected, Hovans paired me mostly with his Japanese clients. So far, most have been diplomatic personnel; to date I have learned nothing except that they are like most other men and enjoy a female companion that speaks their own language. I think he does it mostly as a sort of bonus he offers a client for doing business with him—whatever that might be. Some only want companionship. Others make it quite clear that they want *sex. So far, I have been successful in excusing myself using any number of excuses. Usually, by the time the cabaret closes they are quite intoxicated, and it's easy to fend them off.*

Hovans hasn't insisted; at least so far, that is. He has always found another girl more than willing to spend the night with them.

I have recently begun to renew my old friendship with Tanya. When we were growing up together, the farthest thing from our minds was political intrigue. Tanya won't admit it but for all practical purposes, she's a prostitute. If that is so, though, what does that make me?

Yesterday, we had tea together before we were assigned guests for the evening. (She poured vodka in hers from a little flask). I asked what she thought about her Japanese guest, and she was non-committal, saying it was part of the job. When I asked about the buildup of their troops in Northern China, she didn't seem to care one way or another; she said that the plight of Russians wouldn't change regardless of who was in charge.

Then, I asked if she was making enough money with Hovans. She just laughed. She said almost all of it went to pay back Hovans for the clothes. When I suggested there might be another way that we could both make more money she seemed interested. She asked for more information, but I told her I would tell her more when the time came. I'm sure she thinks I will suggest prostitution on the side, and then holding out on Hovans. The prospect of selling our bodies on our own seemed not to bother her in the least; it was only that such an enterprise, if discovered, would mean a certain visit form Rabin…

As the month progressed, Anna found herself more in the company of the sales department located in CNAC's downtown offices on the Bund. For the past week, everyone was speaking of the hostilities that were sure to come. Added to the anxiety was the August heat and humidity that mixed with the smells of the Whangpoo producing a miasmatic hell. Her clothes stuck to her as if in one of the steam baths frequented by the Russian men on Bubbling Well Road.

This evening, Anna arrived at the cabaret at 8 p.m. She was a little later than normal. All day she had worked with Mr. Sun in CNAC's marketing department. He seemed to be fixed on traditional advertising methods: colorful banners, perhaps with a picture of a DC–2, or Loening, and the like. Another idea he had was a simple brochure of text suggesting how flying their personnel or cargo could be efficient and modern. Anna had other ideas, but she knew anything she suggested would be a delicate matter coming from a foreigner—especially a foreign woman. She would have to and make any ideas she suggested appear as Mr. Sun's own.

Anna was thinking of these things when she arrived at the Far East Cabaret. She had taken two steps up the entrance to the cabaret before she noticed Rabin, standing with arms akimbo, blocking her way at the top. Regardless of their mutual animosity, she was determined to maintain a semblance of peace with the thug. As she reached the top step, Rabin still had not moved. Remembering Cheng Tu's admonition, she simply looked into his fat face and said in English, "Good evening Mr. Rabin."

Rabin dropped both arms to his sides. Anna noticed his fists were tightly clenched as one part of her mind reviewed the appropriate postures and maneuvers she would use should he become physical. Instead, Rabin stepped to one side and said in Russian, "I am watching you, you little Tsarist bitch...your day will come!"

Anna said, "I am sure Mr. Hovans will be very interested in your comments, Ostafii."

As she passed, Anna did not look directly at him. Peripherally, though, she could see Rabin's fat face turn crimson with rage as he clenched and unclenched his ham hock fist. There was no doubt in Anna's mind, that given the chance, he would try to kill her.

Passing the bar on the way to the dressing room, she noticed Mr. Akimoto, the diplomat, another Japanese gentleman and a Caucasian man standing at the bar. The three of them were in animated conversation with Sergei Hovans. Akimoto motioned towards Anna as she passed and made some comment to the impresario.

Already late, Anna began to change as soon as she reached the dressing room, but even in her haste, she couldn't help but wonder what Billy was doing tonight. Last night had been a night of love making that had left her sexually satiated, and physically exhausted, but yet unfulfilled. It was then that Billy had given her the small German camera and showed her how to use it.

The other girls shot enviable glances at her, as she stood naked before them changing into underwear suitable for evening clothes. She went to the group closet room needed for a moment's privacy. Just as she had finished wiggling into a chemise, Tanya came into the room and kissed her on both cheeks.

"Anna, darling...that figure of yours has the rest of these tarts green with envy. How do you keep it so?"

"Working all day for the airline, then all night for Hovans with only about three hours of sleep helps a lot, Tanya!"

In former times, her practice with Cheng Tu and Saul provided good exercise and a trim figure. That now seemed a luxury from a distant past as she silently longed for a return to a simpler life.

Without waiting for a reply Anna asked, "What's up out there tonight? When I walked past the bar I saw Hovans holding court with Akimoto and a couple of other uppity-ups."

"Yeah...I heard there are several foreign swells in town tonight. Akimoto and another guy from Japan, and some swell from Germany. I think they said he was one of those Nazis."

Anna thought...Billy had said that he was interested in any Japanese officials. Two of them together with a German visitor should be very interesting to him and his superiors.

She contemplated her reflection in the mirror. The chemise showed her figure to good advantage. She thought that she indeed might be a little thinner...probably, like she said, from all the work, no sleep, little time to eat and of course, the marathon love making that she hadn't mentioned to Tanya. She felt that familiar tingle run through her body at the mere thought of Billy's body next to hers.

As usual, she put on just a little lipstick as her only compromise to makeup. Her naturally long eyelashes and eyebrows required no mascara—a custom she thought carried to extreme by so many of the girls at the cabaret.

She was just putting on the finishing touches to her makeup when Hovans strode into the dressing room. Some of the girls looked furtively in his direction—none making eye contact. Others simply continued what they were doing. None bothered with modesty. It was his cabaret and a normal thing with him.

She saw Hovan's reflection in her makeup mirror as she continued finishing her face.

"Anna: Akimoto, the gentleman you kept company with your first night, several months ago...he's here again with some other guests. These people are very important to me and I want hostesses for the show and afterward...anything they want...understand?"

"No, Sergei...I will not go with him...he's a drunken bore."

Hovans hissed sharply at her, "In front of the other girls you call me Mr. Hovans, Anna! Now listen: I want you and Tanya to keep them company tonight. He and the Japanese gentlemen he's with like Russian girls. I don't know about the German. Akimoto asked for you in particular. I told him no assignations with you...that you had other commitments! He said O.K. He just wanted you to sit and translate for them tonight. Other girls would do for later. You work it out with Tanya. Get as many girls as they want, and do anything to keep them happy...understand?"

Ignoring Hovans comments Anna said, "Sergei...that brute of yours, Rabin, tried to intimidate me again tonight. If you want me to entertain your guest, I will, but tell that beast to stay out of my way or I'm out of here...do you understand? As for Tanya and other girls, I'll work it out. I'll make sure your guests are happy...all right?"

A hush fell over the dressing room as the rest of the girls heard Anna talking back to Hovans about Rabin. All pretended not to hear and continued with their dressing and makeup. Everyone knew about Rabin. Those that had not been directly intimidated or beaten by him had heard of his violent behavior.

Hovans pointed his finger at Anna and was about to reply when he became aware of the unusual silence in the dressing room. Looking around he saw the astonished looks on the faces of the girls, thrust his hands into the pockets of his dinner clothes and stormed out of the dressing room. At the door, he turned, and said theatrically, "You make sure they are well taken care of, Ms. Boreisha...I'll be watching!" Anna did not reply.

CHAPTER 57

▼

SPYING

Shanghai

Several rounds of drinks had come. The first floor show had finished and the second had begun. Anna was translating Mr. Akimoto's comments regarding the Anti-Comintern pact into English for the German, Hermann Römer, as he spoke the language with little facility.

Their group occupied a table for six. They sat three on a banquette, three tiers above the stage and orchestra pit. Facing the group, Anna sat at the far left separated from Akimoto by a briefcase he kept close to him on the banquette. Natasha was Hermann Römer's companion for the evening. She sat between the German and Akimoto. Tanya was on the other side and sat with a Commander Cato. He was introduced as the new Naval Attaché to Shanghai.

Even as Akimoto sat in the hospitable atmosphere of the Far East Cabaret, Anna could not help notice he kept his right arm draped over the briefcase at all times. It was as if he wanted to assure himself that it was still there. If he raised his arm in a toast, she noticed he was always quick to return it to the case, much as some men would occasionally tap their billfold pocket to insure it was still there. Anna had never had training in such things, but she had always been a keen observer of human behavior. Akimoto considered something in the briefcase to be very important. Even as the diplomat slipped into an alcohol induced camaraderie he continued to assure himself that the case was still there and had not been compromised. As she speculated on the contents, she crossed her legs—more conscious than ever of Billy's small camera taped high on the inside of her thigh. If Tanya had come in the group closet one second earlier, she would have seen her taping it in place. Uncomfortable as it was, it was still only inches from being visible under her short sequined chemise. She considered the probabilities of being able to use the camera to photograph the contents of Akimoto's briefcase somewhere between slim and none. Improbable as it seemed, though, she felt exhilarated by the challenge.

Anna said, "Yes, Mr. Akimoto suggests that about the only thing Chiang Kai-shek, the Japanese and Germany agree on is their mutual hatred of the Communists." Everyone laughed with great conviviality as Anna again beckoned for a waiter to fill any champagne glasses that were less than full.

She continued to translate for Mr. Römer. "Mr. Akimoto says, 'he was only too happy when his nation signed the Anti-Comintern pact last November."

Römer said nothing but, "Ya ya." He raised his glass in yet another toast to the Japanese and the best wishes his government had for Japan's future. He said, "I was in the bar of the Cathay this evening before coming here. All of the talk was about the Japanese soldier that was shot by the Chinese Air Force officer today. Will the Japanese government stand for that?"

This time, Commander Cato answered.

"In the next few days the forces of Chiang Kai-shek will be severely punished. Japanese soldiers will never suffer dishonorable death at the hands of the Chinese. Even now our Blue-Jackets are preparing their response!"

After uttering the last sentence, Cato seemed to realize he had said something he wasn't supposed to. From one second to the next he changed his demeanor from one of bombast to diffidence.

The news she just heard came as a surprise to Anna. In the last days with all of her efforts in Billy's behalf, Anna had not kept up with the news.

Alcohol soon tempered Commander Cato's bluster. Tanya grabbed his hand—more to keep it from reaching between her legs than in intimacy. Anna had seen her in action before and thought there was a good chance that that would come later.

Anna had picked Natasha, the German's companion, for her appearance more than any other reason. Other than dutifully filling her glass, Hermann Römer almost totally ignored her. This caused Natasha to glance first at Anna and then at Sergei Hovan's table. She knew he would be extremely unhappy with her if Römer even hinted dissatisfaction. It might even mean a visit by Rabin as a measure of Sergei's displeasure.

Glancing back at Römer, Anna noticed that most of his attention was directed at the six piece orchestra three tiers down from where they were sitting. Following the Nazi's gaze, she determined that the object of his attention appeared to be a slender young man with extremely long fingers playing the clarinet. He continually tossed the long hair falling across his face much as many girls would do. Anna smiled inwardly to herself as she gleaned this new intelligence about their German guests.

Anna definitely did not want to promote the amorous attentions she experienced the first time she was Akimoto's companion. Nevertheless, she went ahead with a small test she had planned. She reached across the briefcase to hold the diplomat's hand. He smiled with pleasant surprise and said something she did not understand. At the same time, she lifted the briefcase with her other hand and placed it on the floor by the diplomat's foot and said, "Mr. Akimoto, we can never let a briefcase come between us even for a brief time, now can we."

Even as she said it, she could feel him move his legs to place the briefcase between his feet. Yes, she thought—there is something in that case that he doesn't want anyone to know about.

The second act finished, the dinner dishes were cleared, the orchestra paused, the curtains were drawn and the stage was cleared in preparation for the next performance. It would be several minutes before their attention returned to the stage when Anna suggested in English: "Why don't we all go to the Parisian? I understand they have some really naughty acts with an all male review...now wouldn't that be fun?"

The two Japanese perked up at the suggestion, and the German responded with "Ya Ya...that voud be sehr interessant! We do not have such things in the new Germany! It is verboten!"

As Anna translated, Akimoto saw his Nazi guest's phlegmatic disposition change to one of exuberant enthusiasm. He hesitated only a second before saying to Anna, "Tell Herr Römer we will go at once!"

Tanya and Natasha threw up their hands in mock modesty as Anna translated their intentions to the rest of the group.

As Akimoto called for the bill, Hovans came to the table and asked if everything was all right. Anna told him in Russian that the group was on their way to the Parisian. Still speaking in Russian, she tossed her head toward the German and said, "Our guest is interested in seeing the all-male-review."

All the while smiling at Akimoto and the German, Hovans nodded knowingly and said, "Do what's necessary to keep them happy. These people are important business contacts. Do not disappoint me, Anna!"

Anna didn't respond and excused herself to freshen up prior to their departure. She only had a few minutes to make the arrangements she had in mind, and instead of going to the rest room, she went instead to the kitchen.

As they exited the cabaret, Ostafii Rabin was standing by Hovan's Bentley. He made a point of not looking at Anna as she and the rest of the group stepped into the limousine. She could only surmise that Hovans had told him to save his sadistic perversions for the others, and to leave her alone.

The Parisian presented no surprises for Anna and the other Russian girls. They had all been there several times with other clients from Hovan's cabaret. Anna was grateful that so far none of their guests, except Cato, had given any hint as to what they expected later on.

The Nazi and Akimoto followed the show with rapt attention. Akimoto switched from champagne to sake and Römer to schnapps. Both were now engrossed in the all male review. Commander Cato was interested in Natasha.

Akimoto put his briefcase between his legs and sat transfixed by the onstage exhibition. Anna sat close to him and continued to hold his hand. Römer's attention was on the male performers when Anna said, "You know, Herr Römer, private showings are available after the main show. They take place in a private room separate from other guests and performers. We would be separated by a one-way mirror...you can see the performers, but they cannot see you."

Anna could see that the suggestion of further indulging the German's peccadilloes was working. Hermann Römer said, "Ya...I would like that very much!"

She translated Römer's interest to Akimoto and Cato. They agreed, and asked Anna to make the arrangements to start as soon as the main show was over.

Anna withdrew from the group and motioned for Tanya to come with her. Tanya excused herself. Straightening her dress she walked unsteadily to where Anna was standing near the rear of the club.

"Tanya, do you want to make that extra money I spoke with you about?"

Tanya said, "Are you crazy? Hovans knows we are out with these guys...if we even think of holding out on him he will turn loose that animal Rabin on us!"

Before she could continue, Anna put her finger in front of her lips and said, "No, Tanya, listen to me carefully! It has nothing to do with holding out on Sergei...I only want to look at the contents of Akimoto's briefcase. There are people in this city that are very curious about what Japanese diplomats carry in their brief cases. I simply need to have him distracted for a few minutes to take a look...that's all!"

In her half drunken stupor, Tanya eyes tried to focus on Anna and comprehend what she was saying. She said, "Well how do you expect to do that, and what's in it for me?"

Anna said, "Help me do this and I'll give you fifty dollars U.S.; If we get caught, you get nothing!"

At the mention of the unbelievable sum of fifty dollars, Tanya seemed to come awake. She said, "Where in the hell are you going to get fifty dollars?" Anna replied, "Never mind where I get it…do we have a deal?"

Tanya said, "What do you want me to do?"

She explained her plan and arranged for a *private exhibition*. Then, she asked the girl at the coat check stand if her package had been delivered; reassured it had, she rejoined the group.

The private room was as Anna remembered the only other time she had been there; there were three couches with end tables forming an open "U" facing a window approximately two meters in width and covered by a flimsy velvet curtain about one meter high. Mercifully, the dingy room was dimly lit with fake electric candles on two opposing walls. Music from a phonograph played through a tinny speaker on the entrance wall to the viewing room.

Another round of drinks were served to their group by a scantily clad waitress. Tanya used the distraction to excuse herself to go to the ladies room. The German sat staring at the covered window, tossing down schnapps, waiting for the curtain to be drawn. He was still ignoring Natasha who had now switched her attention to Mr. Cato with Anna's promise of five dollars before she left.

Anna continued to translate while managing to dispose of one drink after another in a spittoon by one of the end tables. She refilled her glass with water from a pitcher left by the waitress. Alcohol was beginning to have its effect on Akimoto. As before, he was trying to grope her breasts. Warding off his advances as well as she could, she suggested he remove his dinner jacket to be more comfortable for the coming performance. She took the jacket, folded it, and placed it on top of his brief case on the floor just in front of the end table.

Tanya timed her return to coincide with the opening of the curtain. The whole party focused what limited attention they had left on the multiple machinations of naked bodies in front of them. Only Anna was aware Tanya had returned to the room, closed the door, and slipped her package forward under the end table as planned. A quick glance confirmed her accomplice at the Far East Cabaret had done well.

Anna had paid a busboy to get a good look at Akimoto's case as he cleared the table back at Hovan's cabaret. After work, he had gone to an address she had given. It was the shop of a case maker frequented by her father's clients. Although he had closed for the evening, an offer of double the normal price by the busboy persuaded the proprietor to open his store. It was almost an exact replica. Moreover, the heft of the bag confirmed the case had been filled with papers to approximate the same weight, just as she had ordered.

Tanya came to the front side of the couch and sat between Akimoto and the German. On seeing the stage action Tanya let out an exaggerated yelp, and as planned, thrust her hand between the diplomat's legs. Still watching the action, he predictably groped for Tanya. His attention diverted, Anna shoved the real briefcase to the rear and at the same time pulled the substitute forward.

While the diplomats were distracted by Tanya, Anna picked up her clutch purse as if to go to the ladies room. On her way out of the darkened room, she picked up the briefcase she hoped was full of intelligence useful to Billy. The little noise of her exit from the exhibition room was masked by the pathetic music coming from the tinny speaker. She glanced at her watch. It was four minutes after two a.m. Two Englishmen and two Chinese women were just entering another room for their own *private viewing*. They paid no attention to Anna as she made her way to the ladies room. Besides providing a distraction for those so inclined, she had specifically chosen the Parisian because the ladies room provided private stalls with enough light to accomplish her task.

She opened the door of the room and was again in luck. For the moment, it was unoccupied. She stooped and looked for feet and legs under the three stalls. All were empty. She chose the one closest to the door that was illuminated by a bulb just over the stall. She stepped inside and immediately began to work.

First, she placed the briefcase and her clutch purse on the floor, lowered the toilet lid, and sat down. There was no doubt Akimoto considered the contents secret. She opened her clutch purse, took the key from the substitute briefcase and held her breath. She had no idea if it would work or not. She fingered the latch and exhaled a breath of relief as it sprung open with a click—she hadn't needed the substitute, and reasoned Akimoto must have lost the original. Without hesitation, she pulled back the leather strap and opened the case. There were three sheaths of papers clipped together in booklets. She pulled the first one out—it was written in Japanese. Anna looked at her watch. It was seven minutes after two.

Anna hiked her skirt and winced in pain as she pulled the tape in one quick movement to free the miniature camera. Billy had told her the film was the fastest available for the little device and would work well with very little light. The little instruction Billy had given her was almost redundant as she was already familiar with the art of apertures and speeds from using her father's Leica. She knew exactly what she needed to do.

She smoothed her chemise, angled both knees to one side of the stall to take maximum advantage of the little light available and placed the first sheath on her lap. She set the aperture full open, set a very low speed and bracing the camera against her chest methodically began to shoot, one page at a time.

When she finished the first sheaf, she replaced it in the same slot. Just as she began to shoot the second, the door to the rest room opened to the laughter of two women speaking in Russian. They were comparing notes on their escorts for the evening. Covered by the noise of laughter, Anna scooted the briefcase as far back in the stall as possible in case one of the women tried to look under the door.

Anna glanced at her watch. It was 12 minutes past two. Water was running in a sink. At lulls in conversation, Anna held her breath. When the girl talk resumed she continued to turn the pages as quietly as possible hoping the running water would mask the buzz click of the low shutter speed. Each time the women resumed their prattle she would advance the film and shoot another page.

Then, one of the women asked in Russian, "You O.K. in there honey?"

Thinking quickly, Anna let out a pitiful moan at the same time looking at her watch. She hoped the performers wouldn't run out of variations of human copulation for another few minutes. "Yeah...guess I had a little too much to drink tonight! I think I'll be all right in a few minutes."

"O.K. honey...you just stick your finger down your throat...It'll all be better, then. Just stick it in and let it go...you'll be glad you did!" More laughter.

"Yeah...O.K....just a few more minutes. I'll be O.K."

Still laughing, the two women clicked toward the door in their high heels. One departing voice said, "Bring it all up, honey!" The other woman continued to laugh.

As soon as the door shut, Anna continued to shoot. She ran out of film with two pages left in the last sheath. She taped the camera back to her leg, closed the briefcase and stood up. It was 22 minutes after two!

Anna picked up the briefcase and her clutch purse, stepped out of the stall, opened the door to the ladies room and looked both ways in the dim corridor. No one!

In seconds, she was again standing before the door of their private viewing room. Luckily, it was very dark in this part of the hall.

Anna held the briefcase behind her and began to twist the door handle. It made no sound against the background of the tinny speaker. Soon, the door was open enough for her to see that the exhibition was still in progress. The music from the pathetic speaker was loud enough to mask any sound she might have made, and Anna slipped through the doorway, appreciating Tanya's efforts only a half hour before.

When the door was closed, there was only the light from the stage on the other side of the one-way glass. Her heart almost stopped when she could see only Cato's, Natasha's and Römer's silhouettes against the light of the stage. No one turned around.

Anna closed the few feet to just behind the couch, knelt silently, shoved the briefcase forward under the end table and pulled the other case to the rear. Reaching under the end table she again covered the case with Akimoto's coat. Holding her breath, she took her substitute case and pushed it under the rear skirt of the couch. Placing each hand on the backrest, she raised her head over the back of the couch.

Staring her in the face was Akimoto, lying down the couch, flat on his back. Tanya's face was in his lap.

Without hesitation, Anna said in Japanese, "You naughty boy...I go to the ladies room for a few minutes and look what happens!" Akimoto did not reply.

Hermann Römer left with one of the young men from the review. Anna begged illness and took a rickshaw to her home. The rest left with Rabin who had waited outside as Hovans ordered.

CHAPTER 58

▼

THE IDZUMO

Shanghai

Anna's journal

I cannot believe the depths of depravity I have been willing to sink to—all for the love a man who seems incapable of loving me except for what I can do for him. I will do it no more! Before I did this, Billy suggested the end was justified. I do not believe it is—at least not for me! The end might be justified for him, but the means for him is I continuing to do more of the same. I cannot! I will give him the film today and it is over—I cannot, and will not, pretend to be a whore to gather information anymore.

I had breakfast this morning with Papa before we both went to work. Mama was there too, but only made small talk. Papa looked at me and must have known I was sick with fatigue. I know he sensed I was heartbroken with Billy. "Anushka," he said, "I think you knew all along that American marine would break your heart, but you wanted love so much, you listened only to your heart, and not to your head as I have taught you to do."

He told me I was a grown woman now and had to deal with it in my own way. He told me what I already knew—that he and Mama loved me very much and that they were always there to help in any way they could....

It was 6:30 a.m. when Anna left the apartment. She had slept only a little over an hour and had dressed in a light flowered summer dress knowing what she had to do. Even at this hour of the day, the heat and humidity of August caused the lightweight dress to cling to her body. She went to the kiosk to catch the streetcar to Lunghwa airport. She bought the *North China News* and folded in under her arm.

The specter of imminent conflict claimed the entire front page. War was breaking out over the whole world. The lead story chronicled the Japanese soldier shot by a Colonel in the Chinese Air Force. The article confirmed Commander Cato's vow of the night before: "The death of a Japanese soldier would not go un-avenged." Also claiming space on the front page was more news of the ongoing Spanish Civil War. The article spoke in ominous tones of how last spring hundreds had been killed in a place called Guernica, and it went on to speculate on the thousands more likely to die as the opposing forces vied for power.

She scanned the front page to find if there was any more on the disappearance of Amelia Earhart. Only a small segment of one column mentioned anything at all. "No wreckage was found and there was some suspicion in the United States that her plane was intercepted by the Japanese, and either shot down, or forced to land."

Flipping to the second page, she found news of yet another Russian girl's apparent murder. She looked at the small picture and sat bolt upright on the streetcar bench. The body photographed lying with its head at an un-natural angle was wearing the same tawdry little dress Tanya was wearing the night before. The article went on to say, "So far the victim was unidentified. There were no suspects."

Anna was certain, though—it was Tanya Federenko!

Anna knew it was Rabin and knew it had something to do with last night! Rabin had picked up everyone at the Parisian except her. She had taken a rickshaw. She was sure he would have dropped the two Japanese off at their hotel first. The Nazi had left with one of the actors. That left Tanya and Natasha; both lived in the French Concession.

The whole world was going mad! War breaking out everywhere, Tanya was dead, the loss of Earhart and Noonan, China on the verge of war—what more could happen, she thought.

Anna arrived at the CNAC hangers still in shock over Tanya's murder. Before going to Mrs. Woo's office, she went to the radio room. Saul had on headphones; he was copying a message when she entered. He broke into a wide grin and held one finger in a gesture that said, "Be with you in a minute."

When he was finished, he pulled off the head set and stood to greet her. Before he could say anything she said, "Saul: Tanya's dead…I think I know who did it, but I can't prove it yet."

She told Saul about the night before and what she knew about their childhood friend. Before she left, Saul said, "Anna, don't you wish things were like they were before?"

"Saul, dear friend, I'm afraid nothing will ever be the same again."

She left Saul standing with his hands in his pockets staring disconsolately at the floor.

When Anna came into the office, Langhorne Bond was waiting for her. He said, "Anna: I'm driving to the downtown office in a few minutes. I need you to come along and help with some traffic matters. Would that be O.K. with you?"

Anna answered, "Of course, Mr. Bond…please…just give me a minute."

She made her way to the ladies rest room. She grabbed the sides of the sink with both hands and looked at herself in the mirror. Only with great effort was she able to stifle the sobs welling in her bosom. She said to herself, "I will not become that kind of woman! I won't…I won't!"

She splashed some water on her face and regained her composure before returning to the front office.

Bond waited patiently as Anna used Mrs. Woo's telephone. The call was answered by the Sergeant with the Louisiana accent. She said, "Please tell Captain Schott that Anna called and that I have the package he is expecting. If he wants it, I will meet him at the Cathay Hotel at five o'clock."

"I'm ready to go now, Mr. Bond…sorry to keep you waiting."

When they drove off Anna was silent. Bond looked at her and said, "Anna, are you getting enough sleep? You look all fagged out!"

Just able to hold back tears she said, "It's nothing, Mr. Bond…I have some personal problems I'm dealing with. I am in the process of putting them behind me, now."

Changing the subject Anna said, "Tell me sir, with everything that's happening in the world, what do you think will become of CNAC…to China?"

"You must be reading my mind, Miss Boreisha. That is the very reason I want you with me today. I expect a full Japanese onslaught within the next couple of days. CNAC is finished in Shanghai, and I have no doubt the city will fall to the Japanese within the next couple of weeks. We have maybe six months for Nanking and a year at best before Hankow falls. I want to inform the employees of my plans to save as much of the airline as possible. After Shanghai falls, interior

China will have almost no communication with the rest of the world. CNAC will be more important than ever."

Anna said, "Is it as bad as all of that?"

"Yes, Anna…it's that bad."

After they arrived at the Robert Dollar building Bond spent the rest of the morning pointing out to employees the records and supplies he wanted removed. The plan was to move the base of operations to Hong Kong—officially, a British colony, and China's only real remaining link to the sea. Nanking and Hankow would be kept operational as long as safety would permit. Bond called the employees together and told them of his ominous predictions and his plans to save the airline. They would begin wrapping up operations here today.

It had been an arduous morning for everyone. Almost all of the Chinese clerical staff suddenly realized they were about to be unemployed. If they were to keep their jobs those associated with direct flight operations were faced with uprooting their families and moving to wherever CNAC needed them. The rest would be left to their own devices.

Bond explained his first order of business was to keep the Chinese Air Force from commandeering their airplanes and flight crews. He had an appointment that afternoon with the ministry of transport to try to ward off that probability.

Just before noon, Bond invited Anna for lunch at the Cathay. He said he had a matter he wanted to discuss with her. The heat and oppressive humidity were unbearable. A blast of frigid air greeted them with instant relief as they walked through the doors of Victor Sassoon's contribution to unrestrained opulence.

Many things weighed on their minds. William Langhorne Bond was trying to save an airline that was needed by the Chinese now, more than ever. Fatigue, Billy, Tanya's murder, that brute Rabin, the camera still in her purse, her parents and her own tolerance of her depravity—all hung like a heavy weight on Anna's spirit. She had endured it all, betrayed her parent's confidence—all that for a love she realized was never to be.

Bond had his hand held high trying to get the headwaiter's attention.

Most of today's clientele were noisy newsmen trying to cover the impending war from one of the few air-conditioned places in Shanghai. Anna felt total empathy as her thin flowered dress stuck to her tired body like a wet dishrag. Even with everything on her mind, though, she still couldn't help notice that unless they were carrying a tray, everyone in the restaurant was white. This state of affairs could not long endure, she thought. Someday soon, all of that would change.

One of the reporters shouted, "Hey Carter! My Nanking office says Chiang Kai-shek is sending the eighty-seventh and the eighty-eighth divisions…ain't that the best they've got?"

The guy called Carter yelled back, "Yeah and when they get here, what the hell you think the nips will be doing with the guns on that baby?"

Anna turned toward the voice and saw the guy called Carter pointing through the restaurant's huge plate glass window at the Japanese cruiser that had become part of Shanghai's landscape. For some time now, Anna had been vaguely aware of the *Idzumo's* presence on the Whangpoo, but until now, she had paid it little attention.

Anna again thought about Commander Cato's vow regarding Japanese honor the night before. Was that only last night?—It seemed such a long time ago.

The maitre d' seated Bond and Anna. Although they sat several tables back from the window, they still had an excellent view of the Bund, the Whangpoo and the *Idzumo*. After the waiter took their drink and lunch orders Bond came to the point. "Anna, I need you to go to Nanking and help out with traffic. God only knows how long we can stay there, but I need you there right now. I know it's on short notice but in my judgment you are the perfect one to handle the traffic end of the job there."

Anna looked at Bond in disbelief. She couldn't believe the confidence he was placing in her after such a short time with CNAC.

She said, "Mr. Bond: this is so sudden; I'm only just now learning the job."

Bond said, "The events of the last couple of days are sudden too, Anna. I know you are new, but I need someone up there right now. The operations people are already in place. There is a wonderful Chinese national up there to help you by the name of Chung Si; he is our accountant and fills in as our traffic representative. He will show you the ropes, and the rest will be what you are more or less doing here: translating, problem solving for the airline and passengers—that sort of thing. In addition, there will be an increase in your salary commensurate with your increase in responsibilities."

Anna stirred the ice in the orange squash the waiter had just brought, looked at Bond and said, "I would have to leave my family, Mr. Bond."

Bond said, "Yes, you would…I am asking everyone to make sacrifices and change. One way or the other, though, everyone's life will be changing very soon. The decision you make now is probably one of the most important you will ever make. Is there someone else besides your family, Anna?"

"There was…but not anymore."

Bond said, "Look: I think you are the perfect one for the job, but I need an answer now. I'm leaving for Nanking tonight. After that, I have to go to Hankow. I would want you to leave on tomorrow's steamer…it might be the last. We have already flown most of our planes out, and steamer space is getting scarce."

Anna looked up from her squash and was about to answer when she heard a muted thrum—thrum—thrum coming from the direction of the *Idzumo*. Everyone turned in the direction of the sound just in time to see an explosion on the Bund just short of the Japanese battle cruiser. Bodies were flung into the air like rag dolls in a hell of flame, asphalt and dirt. Before anyone could react, the entire plate glass window that had only seconds before insulated the privileged from the reality of the world outside, came crashing in on the diners with a deafening roar.

Anna found herself under the overturned table. Bond was on the other side. The cool peaceful atmosphere of lunch at the Cathay was usurped with the muffled screams of diners cut to pieces by the falling glass. She could hardly hear—her head hurt and her ears were ringing.

Anna tried to stand but the table held her down. Diners and waiters alike were running about, some seemingly with no purpose. Some were trying to help the wounded, others in panic. "*When in danger, or in doubt—run in circles…*" Her head hurt. She couldn't remember the rest of the ditty—"*run in circles, scream and shout!*" Was it Kipling?…No, the Canadian…what was his name? It described the scene perfectly…Lawrence…Peter Lawrence…yes!

In just seconds, she felt the table being pulled off of her. "Miss Boreisha! Anna! Are you all right?" Bond sounded far away—his voice was weak, as if speaking from a tunnel.

Anna shouted, "Yes…yes, Mr. Bond…I'm O.K. What happened?"

Bond said, "I don't know, but it looks like the *Idzumo* opened up with her anti-aircraft batteries just before the blast."

Diners were crawling from under tables when she heard the man named Carter shout to anyone who might be listening, "Stop the presses! News flash…The battle of Shanghai has just begun!"

Bond grabbed Anna's hand and led her away from the window and into the lobby of the hotel. Anna's head still hurt and her ears were still ringing, but her hearing was returning. As they made there way toward the door Bond said, "That reporter back there—I think he's right."

He looked at his watch, gestured at the devastation and said, "Look: after this, it's going to be even harder keeping our aircraft out of the hands of the Chinese Air Force, but I've got to try. I'm going to go right now and keep that appointment with the Transport Ministry. I'm afraid the job will be doubly difficult, now."

Anna nodded in agreement.

Bond continued, "I'm leaving on tonight's steamer. You go to your family. Don't worry about going back to work. Let me or Mrs. Woo know by four o'clock if you want the assignment...Anna, I really need you in Nanking!"

Bond waved over his shoulder as he hailed one of the rickshaws making its way around the bomb craters on the Bund.

Anna stood in the hotel entrance trying to decide what to do. She went to the ladies room, washed her face and cleaned up. Her hearing had returned and her head didn't hurt so badly now. It was only 11:30 and the pre-arranged meeting time with Billy was 5 p.m. She wondered how her parents were. She reasoned her father would be with clients—her mother probably at home. So far as anyone was able to tell, the only explosions were those in front of the Cathay. The buzz in the lobby was that Chinese bombers were trying to hit the Idzumo, and missed.

No one had heard any explosions from the direction of the French Concession. Not immediately concerned for her parents, she ran back into the hotel lobby and dialed Billy's number at the marine barracks. Another marine answered this time with yet another accent. "No ma'am...Ain't nobody here. The whole regiment...they is taking up positions along Soochow Creek...just like they done in '32."

Anna decided to go home and check on her parents. The streets were clogged with masses of people trying to leave Chapei, the area North of Soochow creek where everyone suspected the conflict would begin. The Marines and other armed contingents would be massing south of the creek to protect their respective concessions from the combatants.

Anna saw her father's Packard in front of their apartment as her rickshaw pulled up in front of their apartment. She noticed the coolie was dripping with perspiration after the long jog from the Cathay. After paying, she offered him something to drink before going on. He looked at his passenger with incredulity and handed her the flask hanging on the side of the rickshaw. Anna surprised both of her parents with her early arrival, made a greeting in Russian and went to the kitchen to fill the vessel. While filling the flask, she explained to them what had happened at the Cathay. She returned the flask to the coolie, and closed the door as they all continued to speculate on the cause of the latest explosions to the north.

So much had happened since last night. She tried to tell them all at once. When she got to the part about Tanya's murder, the events of the last days overwhelmed her, and she began to cry.

Bond's offer of Nanking and greater responsibility had brought things to a head, and she decided to tell her parents everything that had happened over the last months. She told them everything—of her affair, her return to the Far East Cabaret for Billy, his suspicion of Hovans, his collaboration with the Japanese and her espionage for the Marines. Then she told them of Tanya's death, probably at the hands of Rabin. All during her discourse, Peter Boreisha paced the floor only stopping her when he did not understand a point.

When she had finished, she told her parents that CNAC would no longer be in Shanghai and of Bond's offer of a position in Nanking with more responsibility and more pay.

"If I stay in Shanghai," she said, "There will be nothing."

Peter Boreisha did not speak of the marine captain. He knew he had broken her heart. When the time was right, he reasoned, she would tell him, but now was not the time.

"Anushka...Your papa wants you to go Nanking...Mama too."

He looked in Lilia's direction and she nodded her affirmation. He said," You will be safe. It will be a chance for you to be something you otherwise could not. This Mr. Bond sounds like a good man. Aviation is a business that will only grow in importance...especially with the war. My daughter...this Bond sees something in you. He is giving you a chance that will not come to you again. Take it! Go to Nanking! Mama and I will be all right."

Anna threw her arms around her father first, and then her mother, thanking them for their understanding and confidence in her. She said she had one last appointment this afternoon at the Cathay, with Billy. Then it was over. She would go to Nanking and start her new life.

Peter Boreisha volunteered to drive his daughter to the Cathay in the Packard. The roads were clogged with people and every manner of conveyance. As he inched through traffic on Eduard VII, Peter rolled down his window and hailed a man with a pushcart. "What's going on," asked Peter.

The man wailed, "Bombs at the International Entertainment Center! Bombs from the air! Thousands have been killed! There's blood running in the streets!"

With the help of pedestrians acting as traffic wardens, Peter managed to turn the big car around. They inched back along Eduard VII, back through the Russian sector, and turned right onto Route Pere Robert, then north, across Bubbling Well Road and past the country club. Father and daughter sat silently, each with their own thoughts as Peter Boreisha turned right onto Peking Road, toward the Bund and the Cathay Hotel. Just after the turn, their progress was slowed by long columns of soldiers from all of the concessions.

As the Packard inched along, they came upon a column of marines. Anna rolled down the window and shouted, "Is there a Captain Schott in your group?"

The soldier shouted back, "No ma'am…but could be he was already up along the defense perimeter, on the south side of Soochow Creek."

The closest they were able to get to the Cathay was two blocks away. Not surprisingly to either of them, the local police had already cordoned off most of the Bund. Peter said he would stay with the car and Anna set out on foot for her rendezvous with Billy.

Already, hundreds of coolies were filling in the bomb craters in the asphalt, returning the Bund to the elegant splendor the city's masters had come to expect. Anna could not find an empty chair in the lobby as many of the correspondents had decided to continue their coverage of the imminent war in the air-conditioned Cathay rather than on the front lines.

One, and then two hours passed—still Billy had not shown up. At 3:30 p.m., she waited in line for a telephone and was finally able to get through to Mrs. Woo. She asked her to tell Bond that she would accept the Nanking assignment; she would be on the steamer the next day.

Anna had only been on the phone for a few minutes when an impatient man behind her tapped her on the shoulder saying, "Hey sister…you gonna tie up that phone all day?"

She hung up the phone and turned as a deep voice said, "Hey buster, that's no way to speak to a lady…wait your God-dammed turn!"

Both Anna and the reporter turned to see Captain Billy Schott in modified battle dress. He wore one of those olive-drab steel derbies; it was much as the British soldiers wore, except it had the Marine Corps globe and anchor fixed on the front. Over his summer kaki uniform, he wore leggings, full web gear, a canvas holster with a Colt 45 automatic pistol and ammunition clips. Slung over his shoulder was a Thompson sub-machine gun.

Anna wondered what her reaction would be when she next saw him. Now she knew. She did not feel hate or even animosity. It was a feeling one might have if they had lost a good friend, she supposed. She said, "Billy, my friend Tanya is dead! I am sure it was Rabin who murdered her."

Billy's first response broke her heart even more than it already was. Billy said, "Did you get the information?"

"Yes, with Tanya's help. I photographed the entire contents of Akimoto's briefcase."

"Can I have it?"

"Yes, but it will cost you one thousand dollars."

"A thousand dollars?"

"Yes, one thousand dollars!"

"How do I know the information is worth it?"

"You don't, Billy…but then again, you didn't know that when you asked me to get anything I could, now did you?"

"Anna, baby…I don't have a thousand dollars!"

"Then you aren't going to get the film or the camera."

"Anna…don't do this to me! The ONI isn't going to authorize a thousand dollars for information that may be worthless."

"Then, they don't need it that much Billy. Listen…I risked our lives to get that information. Tanya lost hers!"

Billy asked, "How did she die?"

"I thought you would never ask!"

She took the newspaper clipping from her purse and showed it to Billy.

Anna continued, "She was murdered right after Rabin dropped Akimoto and Cato, the Japanese Naval Attaché, at their hotel. Her neck was broken. As for the German, Hermann Römer, he left with a boy from the Parisian."

"Did you say Römer…Hermann Römer? He was with you and the Japs here in Shanghai? Why didn't you say so? What did they talk about? What did he do?"

"When I get one thousand U.S. dollars I'll tell you what I know, but you don't have long. I'm going to Nanking on CNAC business, Billy. I'm leaving on the noon river steamer…tomorrow. I don't know when I will be back."

Billy was distracted and kept looking around. He was aware people were staring and lowered his voice. He looked at his watch and then at Anna.

"Anna, darling: we have something together…we are a team."

"Not any more, Billy. You were my first love, you know. I'll never forget you for that. I didn't prostitute my body for you, but I did prostitute my self-respect. I'll never forgive either one of us for that. Another thing…I am sure Tanya was murdered for the part she played to get that information…so be careful Billy."

Billy said, "You don't know that, Anna. You don't even know that Tanya was murdered by Rabin…all you have is a newspaper article, for Christ sake!"

"Billy, Rabin murdered Tanya just as sure as you and I are standing here. She was very drunk when I left her. I could hardly blame her. If I lived like she did, I would probably stay drunk all the time. If she told Rabin anything about what I did, I'm next...don't you understand?"

"But why one thousand dollars, Anna?"

"When you treat a lady like a whore, sometimes she starts acting like one. I want that thousand dollars, Billy. Chalk it up to the compromise I made when I prostituted my self-respect. Prostitutes do what they do for money, don't they Billy? Besides, I had expenses. I paid Tanya fifty dollars U.S. to help. She did her job. I also paid for a very expensive, look-alike brief case, so I could photograph the contents of Akimoto's case while Tanya kept him busy. There were other expenses too, Billy. Because Tanya might very well have compromised me, I have to leave. If the information is worth anything to you, meet me at the steamer tomorrow."

"You photographed what was in his briefcase?" Billy grabbed her by the shoulders and said, "Anna...baby...listen to me."

People continued to stare.

"Let go of me, Billy...I have to go."

The marine watched her as she went through the revolving door. He wanted to call the ONI, but he didn't trust the Shanghai operators. They, like almost everyone else in Shanghai, were on somebody's payroll.

CHAPTER 59

▼

LEAVING SHANGHAI

Shanghai

Anna's journal
Leaving Shanghai

When the steamer moved out into the Whangpoo, I took a picture of the Bund, Shanghai and Billy as he waved goodbye. Even though he is a beautiful man, standing there in his uniform, waving to me on the dock, he looked somehow pathetic. Before we even reached mid-stream, Billy stopped his desultory waving, turned and walked away. I kind of feel sorry for him. He's one of those many people incapable of being passionate about anything for very long. I don't think he is a bad man—he's just one of those that simply doesn't care much about anything.

Rabin was there too. Just after Billy traded me an envelope for his little camera, film, and the report on what I heard, I saw him. He held a U.S. fifty dollar bill close to his body and snapped it repeatedly, shooing away anyone that stood between us. He wanted me to know. I am certain it was the fifty-dollar bill I had given to Tanya. With his malevolent scowl, he kept snapping the bill between his hands as I went up the gangway. Billy saw him too. He noted the exchange, but he didn't say or do anything. Maybe then, he knew I was right about Tanya, but it didn't matter now.

I pleaded with Mama and Papa not to come to see me off in case Hovans or Rabin were there. As much as I had wanted them to be there, I did not want to take the chance their safety might be compromised. I think my fears were justified.

When the steamer started down the river, I took several more shots of the "magnificent mile" and the only home I had ever known. Soon, the Bund, the Cathay, the Idzumo—everything disappeared behind Pootung Island. For the first time in my life, I was truly alone.

Papa gave me his wonderful Leica as a going away present. It was given to him by a wealthy client in appreciation of his good service; it was his most prized possession. He only asked that I take many pictures of the new and exciting places he and Mama would never be able to visit. I said I would. Besides the Leica, he also gave me his Russian officer's map case. It was from his time in the Tsar's army and later the Whites. He knew, that since I was a little girl, I had always admired the case, and it does make a truly grand, if unfashionable shoulder bag.

In the privacy of my cabin, I opened up the envelope Billy had given me and began to count the money. There were twenty fifty-dollar bills. I remember it made me feel kind of cheap. Stuck under the rubber band that held the bills together was the military medal that said, "Soochow Creek, 1932." It was the medal I saw my first night at Billy's house, and I remember him saying that the medal was struck by the Marines as "kind of a joke." I can't help but wonder if that was the message he tried to give me along with the money—that our affair had been "kind of a joke."

CHAPTER 60

▼

NANKING

Nanking
December, 1936

Anna's journal
Nanking
1937, 13 December

> Chung Si is busy gathering up the last of the ledgers and documents we
> want to take with us. The two of us are the only remaining CNAC employ-
> ees left in the city. We have been working around the clock for the last
> several days trying to salvage only the most important airline records, and
> now we are almost finished. As soon as this is done, we will follow Mr.
> Bond to Hankow.
>
> Mr. Bond has been extremely busy trying to get CNAC on a wartime foot-
> ing and outside of the control of the Chinese Air Force. He is certain that if
> the air force is put in charge of the airline, it will only be a matter of time
> until CNAC ceases to function as an effective transportation system. It
> seems I have played the role of Pied Piper. In fewer than four months, the
> whole Japanese army has followed me here from Shanghai! Although I
> came to Nanking to work as a traffic representative, the advance of the
> Japanese has been such, that other than some government officials, the
> only traffic in this city has been outbound. Everyone having had the
> opportunity has gone.

The day before yesterday, the Japanese dropped leaflets encouraging inhabitants of the city "not to resist." They said the civilians and cultural relics as well as troops who surrendered would be treated well, and those that resisted would be harshly dealt with. The Chinese army is retreating pell-mell on both sides of the river. Perhaps they mean it, but Chung Si and I will not be here to see if it is true. We will be gone within the next hour.

The city is being bombed almost non-stop now. By listening, I am getting better at determining how close the bombs will fall. The ones falling now are about three blocks away, and here I am, writing away like a fool instead of hiding in a basement while Chung Si finishes. As soon as he is ready, we are to join the rest of the American refugees on the American gunboat, Panay. It has been a symbol of American power in China for years and now is anchored just up river from Nanking to insure it will not be accidentally bombed by the Japanese. Mr. Bond knows the ship's captain. We will join them should we not be able to leave by other means.

Since arriving in Nanking, I have been staying at the Metropolitan Hotel and have had the good fortune to meet Hamilton Carter. He recalled seeing me at the Cathay the day the Chinese Air Force tried to bomb the Idzumo, in Shanghai. Now, Carter is here covering the Japanese advance on Nanking. My journalist friends assured me they would not let the Panay leave without us (as if they would remember once the bombs began dropping). Anyhow, Bond, being the quintessential operations man, has made contingency plans for Chung Si and I in case the Panay could not wait. True to form, he has prepared maps, set up dates and times and left me instructions on how to proceed in the eventuality they have to leave without us.

The only thing left for us to do is to make sure the Nanking employees are paid and to collect what Chung Si considers the most important records and then to leave the city. The bombing and shelling yesterday were intense but nothing compared to what has been going on in the last ten minutes. I still think we have enough time left to get our jobs done and get out of here....

The sound of the next stick of bombs told Anna that they would be very close. They began to fall several blocks away and stitched their way closer; still, she was not overly alarmed. She gathered the traffic records and her journals, put them into her map case and slung her Leica over her shoulder when she heard the droning of aircraft almost directly overhead—still, she found no reason to hurry and simply shouted over her shoulder to Chung Si that it was time to leave. Just as she was opening the door, a bomb landed in the square fewer than twenty meters from the CNAC office. The concussion blew her back into the building, knocking her flat on her back.

"Miss Anna! Miss Anna! You have to get up plenty quick." The voice came from far away. Faint at first and then louder. It was the Cathay Hotel all over again. "I hear shooting plenty close. We have to go! We have to go!"

Even though Chung Si realized Anna spoke English, and almost fluent Mandarin, he spoke to her in pidgin as he did with many white people who expected it of him. In his terror, he had reverted to the pidgin he usually reserved for foreigners who could not grasp the concept that most educated Chinese spoke English as well as they. For a moment, just like the day at the Cathay, she could not hear; then it came rushing back, this time accompanied by the sound of cannon and machine gun fire. Again, like at the Cathay, an intense throbbing in her head remained as she struggled to grasp the situation.

"Dammit Chung Si, speak English or Mandarin!" This seemed to register with the otherwise calm accountant.

"Sorry Miss Anna, but you have been unconscious for a long time. The Japanese are inside the city walls and there is shooting everywhere."

Anna struggled first to her knees, then crouched and crawled over to the window in the front of the office. The throbbing in her head was intense and there was still a ringing in her ears. As she peeked out of the lower corner of the window, the first Japanese tanks flanked by soldiers on both sides were entering the square outside. Some curious Chinese citizens stepped from the entrances of several businesses and were immediately machine gunned by the tanks. Others were shot by infantry soldiers. An armored car with a large mounted loud speaker followed closely behind the tanks blaring the message that resistance was futile, and anyone caught harboring Chinese soldiers would be shot.

Anna pulled the Leica out of her map case and took several shots of the random shootings taking place outside. She turned to the accountant and said in a calm voice, "We cannot go out the front. Do you know another way?"

Chung Si said, "There is the back alley Miss Anna, but if I were a Japanese commander, I think I would have those covered. I think we had better go upstairs and try to make our way across the roof tops."

Anna asked, "Do the roof tops lead in the direction of the International Safety Zone?"

"Most of the way Miss Anna…at least once…maybe two times, we will have to come down to street level, cross over and again go to the roof tops."

"Let's go then," said Anna, "They seem to be checking every building." She took one more picture of the Japanese slaughter and followed Chung Si as he led the way up the steps.

Just as they reached the second floor, they heard the bomb-battered front door crash in as the Japanese entered the office below. Anna took off her shoes and motioned to Chung Si to do the same. There was much shouting and the sounds of opening and slamming doors coming from the first floor as the soldiers looked for people seeking refuge from their blood lust. Anna heard boots on the stairs below, as first the accountant and then she, made their way to the third floor and the last flight of stairs to the roof.

Chung Si led the way and reached a large hatch leading to the roof. He pushed on the hatch with his arms as he reached the top of the stairs. It wouldn't budge. He then moved his feet up one stair and pushed again with his arms. Suddenly, the hatch gave a few inches with a teeth-numbing screech from rust frozen hinges that had not seen oil since the day they were made. He stopped and looked at Anna in horror. Anna got very close to him and whispered, "Get in position to lift the hatch with your back the next time there is shooting or noise from below!"

Chung Si climbed up one more step, turned, and facing down the stairs squatted with his back against the hatch. Ten or fifteen seconds passed with only moderate noise from the office and the street outside. Then there was a long burst of machine gun fire from the courtyard below and Chung Si lifted the hatch with his legs and back. The noise from the hinges was deafening in the confined space of the small stairwell. Anna's heart pounded in her chest as she and Chung Si looked at each other waiting to hear anything that indicated they might have been discovered.

They scrambled through the trap door knowing that they must shut the hatch or risk discovery of their escape. "Miss Anna...you look the other way for just a moment."

Anna opened her mouth to speak and Chung Si said, "Please, just for once, don't argue! Just do as I ask!" Puzzled, Anna scrambled to the edge of the roof to see what was going on in the streets below. On hands and knees, she slowly raised her head to get a better view.

The square their office faced had now been cordoned off by tanks and armored cars. Patrols were fanning out to reconnoiter the streets not yet occupied. Behind the tanks, troops were rounding up Chinese men of all ages and descriptions. They were binding their hands behind their backs. Anna took all of this in at a glance.

She unslung her Leica. While continuing to crouch behind the rooftop parapet, she estimated the f-stops, speed and focus, held the camera over the parapet's edge and recorded the scenes below.

She turned around and saw Chung Si lowering the hatch with hardly a sound. Both hinges were wet with the only lubricant the young accountant could find on short notice. Anna grinned at her friend's resourcefulness.

The two joined near the center of the roof and made their way from building to building keeping about a block ahead of the advancing Japanese. As they moved along, they saw that many of the people trapped in buildings had also fled to the rooftops. At first, there were just a few. Approaching the last building in their block's row the few turned into many. Anna had a sudden fear that they would all be trapped in a stairwell, in the last building, all trying to get out at once. They would be unable to get to the street and escape the encroaching army.

Anna said, "Chung Si, you know this city much better than I. What is the quickest way to the International Safety Zone?"

"We are very lucky Miss Anna. We are headed in the right direction. If we can cross the street at the end of this row of buildings and keep going the way we are, we should come into the zone in about six blocks."

Anna ventured another look over the buildings parapet and saw that the patrols were delayed rounding up prisoners as they went along. Some were roped to the lengthening prisoner chain, while others, seemingly without reason, were either bayoneted, or shot. They were now only about a 100 meters ahead of the patrols.

Anna said, "Chung Si, let's try to open the next roof entrance we come to. I am afraid if we wait until the end of this row of buildings; we will be delayed by everyone else up here trying to go down a single stair case."

"But Miss Anna, the patrols!"

Anna said, "This time, you listen to me! Their advance is being delayed by their taking prisoners. We are about 150 meters ahead of them now. There is no time to argue! Let's open that door coming up and try to get to the street as soon as we can."

Chung Si half laughed, "If you were a Chinese woman, you would be beaten as a shrew for such obstinacy!"

They both grabbed the ancient door and pulled in tandem. After several tries, Anna was convinced it was either stuck or locked from the inside. Without hesitation, she snatched two poles from a clothesline and handed one to Chung Si.

"Use the pole as a lever under the edges of the hatch!"

The two positioned the poles under the hatch and lifted in unison. With a groan, the hatch gave way and opened to a point where both of them could lift it the rest of the way without a lever.

It had only been moments since she last looked into the streets below, but still, they had no idea of what sort of reception awaited them at street level as they clambered down the ladder onto the third floor.

Several rooms opened off of the landing leading to the roof exit. There was no one in the hallway. Anna shot another glance at the street below and saw that the patrols had not advanced from their previous position. She motioned to Chung Si to keep moving.

On the second floor, mothers and amahs clustered in groups, their arms around each other and terrified children. Several old people were staring into space trying to comprehend what was happening to their city—their lives.

The ground floor was vacant. It was as if the inhabitants somehow thought that since the enemy were in the streets they would be safe if only they stayed inside. Anna looked first out of the back of the building and then the front. The patrols on both streets had advanced to about the same position. She guessed they were clearing one building at a time, coordinating with the patrols through the building on the next street over. She judged the soldier's caution would slow them down enough, but only just.

"Chung Si! The patrols have advanced to about the same place on both streets! That street do you think will be the quickest route to the Safety Zone?"

"The front, Miss Anna…the front!"

They were just about to step onto the street when Anna noticed several white cotton rolls of cloth that had been made up for bandages. She grabbed two of the bandages and rolled them out onto the table. She reached into her shoulder bag, took out her lipstick and made a neat red cross on the bottom border of each one. She then took a fountain pen from her map case and inked in "International Safety Zone" above the cross. The ink hadn't run too badly, and she thought the armbands would suffice. She handed one to Chung Si and said, "Quickly! Tie this on my arm!"

Anna did the same for the accountant and said, "You are now my Red Cross assistant!"

Anna grabbed Chung Si's hand and stepped out onto the street. Like themselves, dozens of people ran from doorways on both sides of the street, fleeing for their lives.

The patrols looked as if they had progressed to one or two more offices in their block. They were approaching the intersection when both heard shouting in Japanese. "Halt, halt!"

Anna said, "Continue walking at the same pace; do not look back!"

They were only about ten meters from the intersection and temporary safety of the corner when a short burst of machine gun fire ricocheted and fragmented the stone building immediately to their right. She felt a sharp sting on her right arm and turned to see two men and a woman fall to the street just as they rounded the corner, out of the field of fire.

She grabbed her right arm and looked at the spot where she felt the pain. It wasn't bad, but already a little blood was starting to come through her sweater. Before she could inspect the wound, a Japanese officer rounded the adjacent corner on the parallel street followed by a patrol of six soldiers. He had his automatic pistol leveled at her and Chung Si.

Before the officer could say anything, Anna spoke in English. In an authoritative but level voice she said, "Thank God, an officer! My name is Anna Boreisha, and I am a member of the International Safety Committee of Nanking. My assistant and I were looking for foreign nationals to escort to the Safety Zone when your troops began firing on us! Please sir, as an officer of the Imperial Japanese Army would you be so kind as to escort us to the Safety Zone before your troops kill us?"

The officer appeared to be in his late twenties. He was quite a bit shorter than Anna, and she wondered, as in so many negotiations with the opposite sex, if this somehow intimidated him, affected his ego, or self-image. He appeared interested in the armbands she had fabricated for herself and Chung Si, and she wondered if he knew what she had just said. He hesitated a moment and lowered his pistol. He bowed slightly at the waist and said in an educated, but highly accented English, "Madam, the Japanese Army has no ill will toward foreign nationals or non-combatants. We are looking for Chinese soldiers and renegades; we are taking them into protective custody."

He barked an order to one of the soldiers telling them to lower their weapons.

He said, "Tell your assistant that we must see his papers."

Anna said, "My assistant speaks English and understands your orders sir." She did not indicate that she had understood the Japanese order.

Chung Si handed the officer his papers, written in Chinese, indicating he was an employee of CNAC. The Japanese had not had time yet to issue identity cards to Nanking's conquered citizens.

The seemed to be satisfied, jotted something in Japanese on a piece of paper and said, "I cannot escort you to the International Safety Zone now as my duties will not permit it. I have prepared a document granting you both safe transit to the Zone. If any one should try to stop you, please show them this document. Until you receive instructions from the occupational authority, I would suggest you do not leave the Safety Zone again."

Anna looked down the street and saw that the patrols had almost completed their searches of all the offices in the block and were getting close to their position. Many more Chinese, old and young alike, had been rounded up. As before, the soldiers had bound their hands and were herding the prisoners in the direction of the Yangtze River. Anna and Chung Si thanked the officer and set out in the direction of the Safety Zone, this time at street level.

For the next twenty minutes, Anna followed Chung Si at a good pace. Bomb craters and rubble from the constant aerial bombardment slowed their progress as they made their way around the devastation. Chung Si complained of thirst when it occurred to Anna that she too was thirsty, but she was determined to reach the Safety Zone before they stopped.

Even as the noise of the occupying army behind them began to recede, the two began to hear the sounds of war in the direction they were walking. She suspected the Japanese were attacking the city on several fronts. "Chung Si…how much farther to the Safety Zone?"

"Only about two more blocks."

The sounds of engines got louder as the two made their way around the remains of a bombed out building. Emerging from a large pile of rubble, they found themselves facing an armored car and another Japanese patrol. They were shouting at a tall Western woman who appeared to be in charge of a group of Chinese civilians.

CHAPTER 61

▼

THE GIRAFFES

Nanking

The woman was dressed much as Anna. She wore a long woolen skirt, matching waistcoat and a white blouse. The blouse was fastened at the neck with a broach. In spite of the wartime conditions, the woman was impeccably groomed. She wore an armband much as the one that Anna had fashioned for herself and Chung Si.

This time, there was no officer present. The soldier who appeared to be in charge yelled in Japanese and motioned with his bayoneted rifle for Anna and Chung Si to join the tall woman and her small group.

Anna turned toward the accountant and said in Mandarin, "Chung Si, he is telling us to join the other group. Don't look at him...just follow me!"

She walked toward the tall woman, smiled and extended her hand. In English she said, "So nice to find you here! I and my assistant were unable to find any other foreign nationals as you requested, so we were returning to the International Safety Zone."

The tall woman didn't betray her surprise at the fabricated armbands. "I'm so sorry dear, but with all that has been going on, I have simply forgotten your name."

All this time, the Japanese soldier had been shouting for the small entourage to be quiet and show their papers while being ignored by the two *giraffes*, of women, as they called them, who paid no attention to his orders. With this, he began to prod Anna in the back with the bayonet on the end of his rifle.

Anna reached into her pocket and withdrew the document given to her earlier, turned, and held it out in front of the Japanese soldier. She used the authoritative voice that had worked so well for her earlier and said in Japanese, "Put that weapon down this instant and write your name and unit on this document!"

The tall woman's rejoinder checked the soldier. Before he could speak again she said, "This party has been granted safe passage by an officer of the Imperial Japanese Army! You are in violation of this order. Instead of safe passage, we are being detained and assaulted by you and your troops. I insist you and your men escort this party to the International Safety Zone, immediately!"

At Anna's rebuke, the soldier actually came to attention and muttered something to the effect that the order would be obeyed right away. As much as he resented being spoken to like that from a foreigner, especially a foreign woman, the rigid discipline instilled in Japanese soldiers made questioning the authenticity of an order from an officer out of the question.

For the next few seconds no one spoke. Only the sounds of war could be heard as a background in this isolated confrontation. Then, the soldier in charge barked an order for everyone to fall in. The conscript handed the note from the Japanese officer back to Anna without affixing his name and started marching in the direction of the Safety Zone. Without further word, Anna and the tall woman exchanged knowing glances and motioned for their charges to fall in behind their new escort.

As they marched, the tall woman turned to Anna and said, "My name is Wilhelmina Vautrin. Please call me Minnie."

Without looking at Minnie, Anna introduced herself and Chung Si. Before Minnie could respond Anna said, "Do not shake hands please—we are supposed to know one another."

"Yes, of course, Miss Boreisha."

Minnie continued, "I find myself in charge of the Ginling Women's Arts and Science College as most of my superiors have had the good sense to leave. I gather from the armband you and your assistant are wearing, you are aware of the significance of the Safety Zone. I must congratulate you on your resourcefulness. As you probably know, the college has become the center of about a two and one half square mile zone where non-combatants are safe—at least for the present; it's the only place of refuge left in the city. I, and about twenty other Westerners have elected to stay in Nanking, and it has fallen to us to be as much in charge as one might, considering our Japanese visitors. Right now we have been trying to find non-combatants and bring them into the safety of the Zone."

Minnie asked, "How did you know about the armbands?"

"I made an assumption. For the last few days, I have been staying at the Metropolitan Hotel. I knew the people in charge of the Safety Zone would have to identify themselves somehow and guessed most Japanese would not know an authentic armband from a fake this soon."

"Good guess, Ms. Boreisha, good guess!"

With the Japanese escort walking along on both sides of their small group Anna said, "Ms. Vautrin, you have an American accent!"

"Yes, I am an American."

"How did you come to be associated with the Ginling College?"

"I've been in China for years. When I first came out, I fell in love with it and never left. My people back home think I'm crazy, and perhaps I am…but my destiny is here, now…this is my home."

When they approached Ginling College, they began to pass other troops beginning to surround the area; Minnie Vautrin began to point out the boundaries of the secure area within the zone. When they arrived at the college, the group saw a large American flag laid out on the winter grass. Minnie explained it was her idea to help identify the Safety Zone from the air and maybe keep them from being bombed. Already, the college appeared filled to capacity, and the Japanese had only just begun to occupy the city.

Within sight of the college entrance the Japanese soldiers that had assumed duty as their escort stopped to converse with other soldiers surrounding the zone. Anna and Minnie Vautrin's small group were also forced to stop. The Japanese exchanged cigarettes and boasted of their units' successes that day, gesturing to a group lined up against a nearby building. Like the others Anna had seen, their hands were tied behind their backs, and to each other, in a string, making flight and resistance impossible. Already, they had heard enough of the conversations to understand that some of the unfortunates were soldiers that had been caught trying to elude capture by trying to get to the Safety Zone disguised as non-combatants.

Anna was intrigued by the overall expression on the faces of the captured soldiers. Rather than defiance, most, if not all seemed resigned to whatever fate awaited them. They looked like frightened sheep going to slaughter with no sign of resistance left in any of them. Before she could give her observations much thought, the Japanese sergeant in charge of their group barked the order for them to resume their march.

Just as their escort departed, Anna, Minnie and their entourage heard them say that as soon as all the Chinese soldiers were rounded up they could concentrate on finding girls! They all gave a knowing laugh, tossed their cigarettes into the street and left the small group without further comment.

Minnie said to Anna, "We haven't a moment to lose! We will take quick refreshment, notify the others and get back into the streets as soon as we can. The Safety Zone is the only hope for what those soldiers are looking for."

Minnie led Anna to her rooms in the college and invited her in to take some lunch with her. She said that she and Chung Si were welcome to stay at the College until arrangements could be made for them to get out of the city.

While the educator was fixing tea and rice, she told Anna that she was from a small town in Illinois. After graduation from the state's university, she decided on missionary work as her life's vocation. For her first assignment, Minnie had been sent to teach at a girl's school in Anwei province. It was there she had learned to love this land, and with the exception of brief trips back to the small town she came from, she had never thought of going back.

Wilhelmina Minnie Vautrin had never married. She was one of those rare women who carried herself with the calm poise of a person who knew exactly who she was. She was a striking beauty, and on doing the arithmetic, Anna estimated Minnie to be in her late forties or early fifties.

As the two women were hurrying to finish their meager lunch, one of Minnie's assistants entered the room and told them that Mr. John Rabe, Mr. Charles Riggs and Professor Miner Bates had returned from the streets. They were ready to go out again when Madame was ready. The two got up; still sipping their tea, they left their dishes in the sink, and joined the other Westerners.

Minnie introduced Anna and Chung Si to the group. After a brief discussion, it was agreed that it would be safer if only Westerners went out in the streets to negotiate safe passage with the Japanese for non-combatants. Chung Si said in English, "I'll be OK Miss Anna...you go; I will stay here!"

Anna told the group she would be more than happy to help with their patrols, but only for this afternoon. She explained the arrangements her boss had made for safe passage aboard the *Panay*. Tomorrow morning they would go on foot up river to a place he suggested would be safe to board the gunboat. Everyone was unsure whether their CNAC credentials would insure safe passage, but with no more commercial transportation available, it was their only option.

Anna was astonished to find out that the leader of the International Safety Committee was a not only a German, but a Nazi, complete with the red, black and white swastika armband. She remembered Hermann Römer from that degrading night in Shanghai and thought how different the two men were. The paradox did not escape her. Here was a German belonging to one of the most tyrannical groups in the world leading a humanitarian effort that put his life at risk to save innocents!

Rabe unfolded a detailed map of Nanking's streets. They decided it would be better for them to patrol individually to be able to cover more territory with the little manpower at their disposal. Each was assigned an area. Regardless of circumstances, they were to return to the college no later than 4 p.m., or when they had too many non-combatants to escort safely. Although it was late in the day, the small group still managed to escort hundreds back to the safety of the zone.

The same day word came that the *Panay* had been attacked by Japanese aircraft and sunk. Everyone in the International Safety Committee was shocked at the news. Everyone was certain the United States would now come to their aid.

Now, Bond's meticulously laid escape plan was the only way out, but it did not go into effect for another ten days, and she still had no idea how she and Chung Si would be able to get to the rendezvous point some twelve miles up the Yangtze River. She talked it over with the accountant. They decided it best if they passed the time in the Safety Zone, help out, and hope the Japanese army's fervor over their easy victory would soon pass.

CHAPTER 62

▼

THE KILLING FIELDS

Nanking

The next day John Rabe organized patrols of two members each from the Committee. They were to go out in the city's streets and try to save non-combatants from the fate of being rounded up with the remnants of the Chinese Army. Today, Chung Si insisted on going with Anna to help. Anna and the accountant were to cover the Chungshan North Road, to the Ichang Gate, the river and return. Professors Charles Riggs and Searle Bates went east, toward the Chungshan Gate. As before, everyone agreed to be back in the zone no later than 4 p.m.

Anna and Chung Si hadn't been gone from the college more than five minutes when they came upon yet another string of Chinese, this time being herded in the direction they were going. Some wore Chinese army uniforms. Others were in any manner of civilian dress. Anna stepped up her pace to be in step with the lead Japanese guard. Chung Si trailed behind. Armed with nothing more than her International Safety Zone armbands and, still walking, she asked the guard, "Where are you taking these prisoners?"

At first, the Japanese guards said nothing. None of the prisoners even looked up, shuffling forward like herded animals. Anna tried using the commanding voice that had worked for her in the past. Ignored, she tried to make eye contact with the soldier and was just about to speak, when she tripped over one of the many bodies left at random on the street. She recovered her composure, caught up and said, "Sergeant, I am a representative from the International Safety Zone."

The soldier turned and yelled at Anna and Chung Si. "You have no authority here! If you continue to interfere with our duties, you will be severely punished!" Anna fell back to walk with Chung Si. He had his finger in front of his lips and whispered, "No Miss Anna…not these guys. They will hurt us if you continue."

They slowed their pace and let the guards and prisoners move ahead. The two continued to follow at a distance where they could keep the formation in sight.

In time, other prisoner trains converged onto the Chungshan North Road. The growing procession was joined from cross streets and alleyways swelling the group they were following to hundreds. Bodies littered the procession's path at random intervals. There seemed to be no reason or pattern that led to the murders except that they were *just there*. No one stopped to move them out of the way. After a while, as the procession grew even larger, guards and prisoners alike paid no mind to the dead except to avoid tripping on them.

Soon the horde narrowed and slowed. Unable to turn around even if they wanted to, Anna and Chung Si were swept through the gates of the ancient walled city. As they came out on the other side, they were herded north towards the expanse of fields adjacent to the Hsiakwan wharfs. When the procession finally stopped, they found themselves in the middle of wholesale murder of unimaginable brutality.

To her right, prisoner strings were being herded into graves pre-dug by its present inhabitants. First, some were unbound and given shovels and forced to dig at bayonet point. When the new grave was finished, the laborers were bayoneted and either kicked or shoved into the graves. The others, left bound behind them, were then ordered into the excavation and shot. In the adjacent excavations, soldiers were practicing bayonet lunges on their live charges. The same scene was being repeated for hundreds of meters beyond where they were standing.

Anna and Chung Si stood, mouths agape, trying to comprehend what they were witnessing. Again, she could not understand why the thousands of prisoners, certain of their fate, stood docilely by simply waiting their turn. Their sheer numbers could have easily overwhelmed their captives killing many before being killed themselves. She wondered if the captive's behavior exacerbated the already obvious contempt the Japanese soldiers had for their prisoners.

Anna turned in the other direction to see the backs of a crowd of soldiers observing some activity she could not see from her vantage point. Over the heads of the on-lookers what she could see were dozens of raised swords swishing through the air accompanied by the indescribable sound of blades striking human flesh and followed by shouts of "Banzai" from the crowd. Several were photographing the spectacle. She dragged a reluctant Chung Si a little closer. He said, "Miss Anna, we have to get out of this place!"

"Just a minute, Chung Si!"

Anna reached through the cutouts in her coat pockets and manipulated the lens of her camera to protrude between two buttons on the front of her coat. The line of soldiers was about fifty meters long and five to ten meters deep. Anna was taller than all but a few and could look over their heads and see some of what was going on. Incredibly, she saw ceremonial swords lifted and descending all along the line. It took only seconds for the two to comprehend what they were seeing.

Anna's height gave her a better view of the spectacle than the lens of her camera at waist level, but it was the best she could do without being discovered. She continued to shoot, manipulating the film advance as fast as she could.

The wary accountant grabbed her arm and began pulling her back toward the gate they had just come through. "Miss Anna, we've got to get out of here—now!"

She looked back at the gate through which they had just been swept. It was still disgorging trains of linked prisoners. She knew there was not a chance of returning through that gate to the city.

Until now, the soldiers had paid no more attention to Anna and Chung Si than they would a tree. Then, all of that changed. A senior officer on horseback noticed the tall female Caucasian and her unbound, obviously Chinese companion with the Safety Zone armbands. He said something to a subaltern and in seconds, several soldiers grabbed Chung Si and Anna and shepherded them in front of the general.

"Who are you people, and why are you here," he said in a calm but authoritative voice. "You are interfering with operational duties of the Japanese Army!"

Anna paused a moment before she answered the officer. From her experience in Shanghai, she knew she was standing before an important general. In a controlled voice and pointing to her armband, she answered in English repeating the litany that had worked so well for her in the past, "I am Anna Boreisha from the International Safety Zone Committee. My assistant and I are on a mission to find non-combatants and assist them in getting to the Safety Zone. We were swept up by your soldiers and their prisoners and forced to this place against our will."

The subaltern translated what she had said to the general. He turned to Anna and Chung Si and said, "The general does not believe you! You are spies! You are interfering with Imperial Japanese Army operations."

The officer turned to one of the soldiers holding Anna. "Take these two suspects to Captain Kobuyashi for interrogation. Tell him we found them spying on our cleansing operations. Tell the captain to report back to me immediately after he obtains the truth from them!"

Not betraying her knowledge of what was said, Anna said in English, "If we do not report back to the Safety Zone promptly, at 4 p.m., our absence will be reported to the International Community!"

The subaltern translated what she had said, but the general turned his horse away signifying the matter had been dealt with. Chung Si looked at Anna as if he was certain that this time she had gone too far.

The soldiers bound their hands behind their backs in the same way the Chinese prisoners had been bound on their way to this field to be murdered. Both were surprised that they were not searched.

It did not take long to reach their destination. They were taken to an ancient municipal building that had been turned into a special military police station.

The noisy reception room was full of the same fearful faces that in the last days Anna had come to think of as the norm. After reporting in at the central desk, it was only moments before they were shown to a holding place to await their fate.

A guard slammed the door closed to the small holding room. They were alone. For a moment, it was dead quiet, the clamor from the reception area shut out by the door. It was then they heard the agonizing cries from somewhere deep in the bowels of the building. Anna turned to see her co-worker trembling in fear. She took his hand and said, "Have courage my friend…somehow I'll get us out of this!"

The trembling Chung Si said nothing but looked at Anna with little hope in his eyes.

It seemed that they had been waiting for hours. Anna looked at her Elgin surprised that only minutes had passed since they were ushered to the little room. As if reading her thoughts, one of the Japanese soldiers who had brought them to the police station came into the room. He left the door open. Through the door, Anna saw several members of the International Press Corps at the reception desk they had just visited. She recognized one as Hamilton Carter, from the Cathay, the day of the attempted *Idzumo* bombing, and late of the Metropolitan Hotel. She shouted as loud as she could through the open door. "Carter!…Hamilton Carter! It's Anna, Anna Boreisha from the Metropolitan Hotel. Quick, take my picture…take it now before they take me away!"

Not knowing what she said, the guard looked first at her and then the reporter. Hamilton Carter understood what Anna wanted. Without hesitation, he lifted one of his chest slung 35mm cameras, aimed, and shot several times before the soldier could stop him. The guard slammed the door, grabbed Anna roughly by the arm and slapped her several times while yelling for her to obey and to be quiet!

Anna commanded her inner-self to be calm and consider the consequences of anything she might do in the next few seconds. She hung her head in submission and did her best to effect a deportment of resignation she had seen in the Chinese prisoners. Their guard seemed satisfied and left her alone.

Presently, a Japanese officer came into the room. From her Shanghai days Anna recognized his uniform to be that of the feared Kempeitai—the Japanese Secret Police. The officer perceived the tension of the last moments and demanded an explanation from the guard. The soldier snapped to attention. Like an automaton, he spoke in short staccato sentences and gave his explanation of what had happened. At no time did Anna let on that she understood the exchange.

This Kempeitai officer turned to the still open door to see the group of journalist observing the exchange. He slammed the door and paused for a moment. Anna knew he was weighing the importance of any intelligence she and Chung Si might have gathered against the ramifications of the meddlesome Press Corps reporting the detention of two Safety Zone officials. No doubt, he was also considering making those same members of the Press Corp *disappear*.

Then the officer asked the conscript soldier why Anna and her Chinese companion were there to be interrogated. Still standing at attention the soldier reported that the two prisoners had observed the purging of the Chinese criminals outside the city walls. They were suspected of being spies by his commanding general. They were ordered to this place for interrogation. The officer turned to Anna, and in English asked why she was outside of the city walls. Anna told the officer the same story she had told the general.

The Kempeitai officer reached into his pocket and withdrew a folded list. He again asked her name. Anna said, "My name is Anna Boreisha. My colleague is Mr. Chung Si. Both of us are working under the authority of John Rabe who is a senior official of the International Safety Committee."

The Kempeitai officer looked at the list but made no comment. He folded it, and paced back and forward in the small holding room. After a short time, he opened the door and barked an order to a subaltern in the outer room. When the soldiers arrived, they were told to unbind the two and escort them to Ginling College. Under no circumstances were they to stop until they were returned to the Safety Zone.

The officer walked out of the room and did not say another word. Anna was stunned. Chung Si looked to her to see what was happening. She understood the orders given to the subalterns but gave no evidence she understood. As they walked out of the room, she simply held her finger to her lips much as Chung Si had done earlier.

After the officer was gone, Anna whispered to her companion that they were being escorted to the college. He looked at her in disbelief as if she was somehow trying to shield him from their true fate of torture and an agonizing death.

Soon, they were back into the streets. The hundreds in the parade of death towards the river had now grown to thousands. The difference this time was that she and her assistant were walking in the opposite direction.

Their escorts took a secondary street back to Ginling College so as not to interfere with the sea of prisoners being herded toward what Anna had come to think of as *the killing fields*. After walking only a few blocks, their party came upon an army truck backed to the front of a building. The truck was flanked by several soldiers smoking cigarettes and chatting among themselves. From the canvas-covered flatbed, the soldiers had placed a plank that led to the top of the entrance stoop leading to the building. Even at a distance, Anna and her party could see that much as sheep were loaded and taken to market, the plank was being used as a ramp to load young women and take them to a fate worse than that of any animal.

As they got closer, one of their escort guards seemed to understand what was going on in the building. He broke from their ranks and ran yelling to the soldiers on the truck. The others yelled back and pointed to the building. Immediately, he headed for the open door already unbuckling his web gear and bandoliers of ammunition.

When they were almost to the truck, Anna could hear the screams of women coming from the building. She pulled loose from her guard and ran to the place where the plank was placed on the stoop of the building. A young woman on the ramp looked at Anna as though she was insane. Through the terror in her eyes, she seemed to plead with her not to interfere, as if anything she might attempt would bring even more pain than she had already endured.

Just as she put her foot on the bottom of the stoop, one of the truck guards threw down his cigarette and blocked her way with his rifle and its fixed bayonet. When she took another step up the stoop the soldier brought the butt of the rifle across Anna's left cheek knocking her almost to the ground. She tried to ignore the pain in her jaw and reverted to her commanding discourse of whom she was and why she was there. The tall woman speaking English sounded very official to a conscript conditioned to obey all forms of authority.

Their remaining escort ran forward and told the soldiers in the truck that they had been released by the Kempeitai. They were escorting them back to the International Safety Zone, and they were under orders not to harm them in any way.

Anna of course understood, so she continued in English demanding that she be given access to the building. The guard who stuck her looked confused; he found himself in direct violation of an order that carried severe consequences in the Japanese army.

Still rubbing her cheek, Anna stepped through the doorway that opened into a medium sized room. The first thing she saw was five, no six Chinese women in various stages of undress being raped and systematically beaten by soldiers. She looked quickly around the room and determined these were the only ones remaining that had not been loaded in the truck. The floor was covered with blood. In the corner closest to the entrance lay the crumpled body of one of their victims. Her throat had been cut.

For the first time Anna spoke in Japanese. "By the authority of General Asaka Yasuhiko you are ordered to cease this brutality this instant!" She fervently hoped that these conscripts would not know the name of all of their general officers as she had just made this one up. At the invocation of a general's name, the soldiers ceased ravaging the girls. One of the rapists was their escort from the Kempeitai police station. He told the others that, yes they were being returned to the Safety Zone under escort. Yes, she had previously been seen with a general outside of the gate to the north.

All of the soldiers but her guard hastily pulled on pieces of uniforms and equipment, picked up their rifles, and ran out the door. They jumped on the rear of the truck, dropped the plank and sped off down the street with their female captives. Their own guard began to dress.

Anna spoke to the Chinese girls in their own language and told them to dress quickly and to wash themselves as best they could. She would take them to the Ginling College where they would be safe.

The girls looked at Anna as if they could not believe they had been delivered from their hellish nightmare. They gathered up what few belongings they had and followed Anna, Chung Si and their escort the rest of the way to Safety Zone.

The next day was much the same as the first. It seemed that most of the Chinese soldiers who surrendered without a fight had already been herded to one of many killing fields and murdered. The army now seemed focused on rape, plunder and the murder of innocents. It was as if they were trying to replace Genghis Khan as the preferred metaphor for unrestrained barbarity.

They didn't seem to discriminate. They raped any female ranging from grand-mothers to sub teens. Most were herded into trucks and taken to God knew where, never to be seen again. Minnie Vautrin, Professor Bates and Riggs saved many by escorting them to the zone. John Rabe and others in the International Committee performed miracles saving hundreds from forced prostitution as *comfort women* until they were killed or otherwise used up.

CHAPTER 63

▼

INFAMY

Nanking

On the eighth day, Anna was exhausted. They had just returned with five young girls from what everyone now called the "Rape Patrol." Thinking they were finished for the day, Chung Si had gone to find something to eat. It had just turned dark when Anna heard the voices of drunken men shouting in Japanese behind her.

Pushing the girls in front of her, she hurried her charges through the vestibule and into the annex of the college's main dormitory. She shut the heavy door and shot the bolt behind her.

Minnie had shown her the annex only the day before. It was a small room, perhaps only four by six meters. It was used to process new girls before giving them refuge in the college, now overflowing with refugees. The shouts following her from the outer courtyard seemed to be receding at first—like dogs on a hunt that had lost a scent. Then, at some distance, the voices stopped moving away and remained constant for awhile—then louder again as they realized their quarry had eluded them. The shouting—it was that boisterous kind—the kind jacked up by alcohol that blustered to their comrades: *they had found new prey!* It was the kind she had come to know all too well in the last days.

Anna did not even have time to learn the names of the five girls she had just rescued from the street. She simply said in Mandarin, "Quickly, follow me, follow me...do not speak!"

The four soldiers—she thought there were only four—were again in the college courtyard. "Sit very quietly on the floor, backs to the wall, and face the center of the room," she told the girls. She stood and flattened herself against the wall hoping the soldiers had been instructed not to come into the college.

The voices stopped just outside of the vestibule. Anna willed herself to inch towards the shutters just enough to get a quick look. There were five—not four as she originally thought. Anna saw that one wore a junior officer's uniform. The others were conscripts. The officer had a sword and pistol at his side. The conscripts were all armed with rifles with the ubiquitous fixed bayonet.

In the past, she thought, her International Safety Zone armband had been her aegis against the marauding invaders, but this time they were in the courtyard, they were not observing the Safety Zone. She understood enough Japanese to know they wanted women—girls—they had the rape lust, and they were drunk. This time, the armband wouldn't even protect her, much less her five terrified charges.

The soldiers paused in the foyer between the main orphanage and the annex. She listened for some sort of intelligence in their yammering, but couldn't make out what they were saying. For a moment, she thought the soldiers had decided not to enter either of the buildings. There was, after all an officer with them. She hoped they were considering the consequences with their superiors if they persisted with the intrusion.

Her optimism was shattered when she heard boots just outside on the wooden vestibule floor. Then, someone tried to open the door. A soldier shook it violently. Maybe the old bolt would hold, she thought. There was a pause—more shouting of which she could only make out a few words, and then a tremendous crash as a heavy object was rammed against the annex door. There was a second, then a third crash before the bolt gave way, and the ancient door flew open. The four conscripts saw the girls sitting against the annex wall and immediately dropped the heavy wooden bench they had used as a battering ram.

When they picked up the bench in the courtyard, the four conscripts slung their rifles, bayonets fixed, over their backs using the weapon's sling. Such was their lust that three of the soldiers pounced on the girls, rifles still slung. The soldiers turned rapist, started to rip the pajama pants and tunics from the terrified girl's bodies, even though the protruding bayonets made their slung weapons exceptionally cumbersome inside the confines of the small annex. The fourth soldier unslung his rifle as if he somehow expected resistance from the sub-teen girls. The Japanese officer followed him into the room. Both turned and saw Anna at the same time.

Anna tried using the militant voice that had worked so well for her in the past. She said, "Stop this instant! You are on the protected soil of the International

Safety Zone! Your commanding general has decreed that this zone, and the non-combatants of all nationalities, shall not be compromised by your army in any way as long as they remain in this zone!"

The three marauding conscripts stopped molesting the sub-teen girls, stood, and waited for some cue from their officer. The fourth conscript, mouth open in shock at the tall female barbarian's outburst, brought his bayoneted rifle to the ready when the officer stepped between the soldier and Anna. Anna was breathing heavily, her bosom rising and falling from her exertions—her senses bombarded with the smell of alcohol and sweat. For several seconds, the officer stood trembling with rage looking first at Anna's heaving bosom and then at her face. Then, he slapped Anna so hard across the face that it staggered her. Only days before, she had been stuck in the same place with a rifle butt. Before she could recover, the officer ripped open Anna's cotton blouse, exposing her brassiere, and slapped her again on the other cheek. It hurt terribly but focused her attention. He yelled in Japanese, spittle flinging into Anna's face—"I am an officer of the Imperial Japanese Army! You will not speak to a soldier of the Emperor in this manner! You will kneel and beg forgiveness this instant!"

Anna felt a sudden calm. This time there was no one to save her. Cheng Tu's counsel of flight was not an option. There was no alternative. Already her mind was on the offense autopilot already responding to the disciplines she had practiced so many times before in what she now considered those halcyon days in Shanghai. Her mind and body reacted as one—with the fluid postures and movements practiced and visualized for all of those years under Wu Master Cheng Tu.

It was done so quickly, the officer had no time to react. She turned away from him at the same time hiking her skirt and spiraling down into her offensive crouch. Using the momentum of her feint, and still turning, she extended her right leg while pivoting on her left. As she reached 360 degrees of turn, her foot struck the officer at knee level knocking his feet out from under him as with no effort at all. While continuing her pivoting sweep, Anna reached with both hands for the handle of the officer's ceremonial Samurai sword withdrawing it from his scabbard in one fluid movement. At 720 degrees of turn, the officer was on his back; Anna was now on both feet, knees bent, and swinging the sword in a perfect horizontal arc in the same plane as the closest conscript's neck. At the completion of the turn, Anna had risen to full height adjusting the blade's path to accommodate the beginning of a much too late feint by the rapacious soldier. His head came off as neatly as a cabbage chopped during summer harvest.

The prostrate officer had just begun to move his hand toward the Nambu semi-automatic pistol in his belt holster as she chopped the thick heel of her practical shoe into his larynx. Without taking her eyes off of the other conscripts there was no doubt in her mind the officer had slapped his last female. She didn't even stop to look as she automatically assumed a new attack posture and kicked the closest of the three remaining soldiers in the chest knocking him into the wall as he fell. The two remaining rapists were trying desperately to un-sling their rifles, but they didn't even come close. Before they could bring the weapons to bear, she eviscerated them with one slashing cut drawn across both their mid-sections. The conscript she had kicked to the ground looked incredulously as Anna reversed her grip and grasped the handle of the sword in both hands high over her head, blade vertical, and plunged it through his heart. She again reversed her grip and returned to the defensive posture she had practiced so many times before until she realized there was no more imminent threat.

The only conscripts left alive were the two to whom she had delivered the single slashing cut. In shocked disbelief, they stared at their viscera as they were rapidly bleeding to death. One was whimpering for his mother. With two aimed merciful thrusts, Anna quickly ended their misery thinking that if he had thought about his mother first, maybe he would have eschewed raping pubescent girls.

For the first time, she looked at her wards. It had been only seconds since she had yelled at the Japanese officer, and now there were five dead soldiers in the annex. From what she had seen in the last weeks, it was not at all inconceivable that five human bodies could yield so much blood. As gruesome as it was, it did not compare with the gutters of Nanking's streets that ran with the blood of innocents. The girls looked at Anna and the scene around them in disbelief. They hugged each other in shock and began to sob in inconsolable gasp.

Anna's brain was still on automatic pilot. She stooped to the floor, picked up the Nambu pistol and two clips of ammunition and dropped them into the large pockets of her woolen skirt. She knew she must dispose of the bodies before they were missed and hoped no other soldiers had seen them enter the compound.

Pieces of a plan began to form in her mind, but first she had to have help. She turned to the girls, and knew she could not leave them in this charnel house by themselves. She told them they must be quiet; she would take them to a place that was safe from the Japanese soldiers. They were to hold hands and to follow her back out through the foyer and into the courtyard. She told them they must be brave, and that they must not cry.

Having learned the fate that awaited them at the hands of the Japanese, hundreds of Chinese soldiers had fled to the Safety Zone in the last days. Minnie and the others could not turn them away and accommodated them as best they could. They exchanged their uniforms with what clothing they had and hid them in an empty college storeroom knowing it was in direct violation of their agreement with the Japanese.

Now, every square foot of the courtyard was filled with refugees. Everyone was huddled together seeking some respite from the December night and the city's marauding hordes. When the drunken soldiers followed the tall Russian and the five girls into the Annex, most chose *not to see*. They simply turned their heads, trying to look as inconspicuous as possible. When Anna came out with her charges, and no soldiers, they looked at the small group in total incomprehension.

She turned to no one in particular and asked in Mandarin if anyone had seen Madame Vautrin. An old woman stared at her torn blouse and anxiously said, "She had come in from the streets with several refugees, left them in the courtyard and gone to her rooms."

Anna pushed her way through the crowd pleading with the refugees make way so that she and her five charges could pass. Finally, she reached Minnie Vautrin's rooms and knocked on the door. Minnie opened the door, saw that it was Anna and asked her and the girls in. Minnie was so used to seeing distress in everyone's eyes during the past days, the terror on the young girl's faces did not give her undue cause for alarm.

Anna gave them tea and told the girls to sit down and try to remain calm while she explained what had just happened. When she was finished, Minnie sat, hands on both cheeks trying to consider the ramifications should the dead soldiers be found. Before she could respond Anna said, "Ms. Vautrin: I am sorry for the terrible danger I have brought to the Safety Zone, but there was nothing else I could do. Now please listen a moment. I have a plan that will be better for everyone, but before I tell you, I want you to order the following things."

CHAPTER 64

▼

THE CHARNEL CARTS

Nanking
December, 1938

"Send someone to clean up the mess in the annex. Have them strip all of the soldiers of their uniforms. Take them to the incinerators and burn everything, then, take all of their weapons and bury them. While this is being done, send someone with good sense from the clean up crew to the place you have stored the Chinese Army uniforms. Chung Si and I will meet them there. Have them take good measure of the size of the dead Japanese soldiers, find uniforms that will fit, and bring them to the annex. Have them dress the soldiers in those uniforms and leave the bodies in the annex until I return."

Minnie began to speak but Anna said, "No, Minnie, please…hear me out! Over the last days you and I have seen the bodies of thousands of murdered Chinese being carted to the river for disposal. I want you to find someone to contact one of the poor wretches pushing those death carts. Promise U.S. dollars if they will help. It is important that he have orders to push the cart to the river and not one of the many other places they are disposing of bodies. My plan is to load the dead Japanese soldiers side by side with those already on his cart; Chung Si and I will also be on that cart posing as dead Chinese soldiers."

Minnie moved her hand in front of her mouth. Before she could speak, Anna silenced her again and said, "Ms. Vautrin, it is the only way. You have been very kind to us. You have also been instrumental in saving thousands of lives. Even though there was no other alternative, I have put the entire safety zone in danger by my actions. Chung Si and I must get to the river tonight in order to effect our escape plans. I cannot tell you more than that so that you will have deniability should the Japanese find out we are missing and question you."

Before the siege, Anna had been staying at the Metropolitan Hotel where she had left most of her possessions. She had nothing with her but her father's map case, her journals, her Leica, some money and a tin of undeveloped film from photographs taken since Shanghai. She had no idea at all if these were the only visual records of what had happened in Shanghai and Nanking, but she did know she was going to do everything in her power to get this visual evidence back to freedom and make sure the world knew what happened here.

Anna asked if Minnie had any waterproofing material. The best she could offer on short notice was the oil treated checkered tablecloth off of the breakfast table in her small kitchen. She tore off a square, laid her journals in the center, and gathered up the excess to make a waterproof package. Anna twisted the ends tightly while Minnie bound the bundle with brown merchant's string.

She decided not to take a picture of Minnie so she would not be implicated, should she or Chung Si be captured. With what remained of the tablecloth Anna wrapped and taped her Leica inside its leather case and hung it from her neck. Minnie and Anna waterproofed the CNAC ledgers much the same way and gave them to Chung Si to carry.

It was almost seven o'clock when Anna and Chung Si returned to Minnie's room dressed in threadbare, bloodstained, Chinese Army uniforms. Anna took the precaution to jab their coats with a bayonet and to smear the gashes in the uniforms with blood from the vestibule. Each had brought a musette bag to carry essentials. They were the type used by Chinese troops in the field, and in each, they placed two bags of rice and dried pork. In hers, she also placed the map case with her journals, film and other essentials. In his bag, Chung Si placed the CNAC ledgers together with the food. To cover their faces, both smeared them with ash from Minnie's stove and pulled on standard issue quilted caps complete with earflaps and bill.

Anna put the quilted field jacket on over her Leica, dropped the Nambu pistol and ammunition into the large cargo pockets and slung the musette bag over her back. Chung Si did the same.

A little after 7 p.m., a man knocked at Minnie's door and said that at any minute the coolie would arrive with the cart. He cautioned the two tall women that the man was required to follow a route prescribed by the Japanese, and it would be necessary for him to deviate two blocks out of the way in order to pick them up. He could only wait for a couple of minutes; he had to get back on his route before it was discovered that his cart was missing.

Anna stood for a moment, not quite sure of how she could say goodbye to this remarkable woman. Minnie, anticipating her dilemma, closed the distance between them, gave her a big hug and said, "I have never met anyone quite like you, Anna Boreisha. I sometimes wish I were like you. If more women were, perhaps the world would be a better place. You are one of the few who would rather be dead than a victim. You also have the will and facility to keep it from happening. Go now, there is no time...God speed and good luck!"

Anna and Chung Si hurried to the side entrance where the coolie was to meet them. The refugees in the courtyard looked on in wonderment as the tall Russian and her companion, dressed in their blood-smeared uniforms, made their way back to the annex.

When they came out of the annex, they were accompanied by a work detail carrying the dead Japanese soldiers stretched out on planks. They, like Minnie and Chung Si, were dressed in Chinese Army uniforms.

The little party had waited for about ten minutes when a young boy ran up to them saying, "The man with the cart was just moments away!"

Presently, they saw the coolie pushing his cargo of death through the gate. The handcart was typical of thousands throughout China. The difference with this one was, that instead of being stacked with produce, cordwood, or other items for market, it was stacked with bodies—the frozen bodies of Chinese soldiers who had surrendered, been bound together, taken to the killing fields and shot, bayoneted, decapitated, buried, tortured or brutalized in some other way, until they died. No one could ever forget such a sight. It was a sight that Anna had recorded on film and in her journal. It was a record she had to get to the free world.

In the dim light of a lantern it appeared the bodies she and Chung Si would be traveling with had been shot or bayoneted, and were being carted to the Yangtze for disposal in God knew what manner. It only took a moment for her to decide the best method of concealment. The hardest part was trying to focus on the job before her and not to think about their grisly surroundings.

Anna directed that all layers of bodies be removed from the center of the flat bed cart. She and Chung Si would crawl on the next to the bottom layer: heads and faces down. The other bodies would be placed on top of their own. She directed they be placed face down and concealed with the quilted hats.

Chung Si looked at the void created by the work party where he and Anna would have to lay down. He then looked at Anna and said, "Ms. Anna, is there any other way?"

Anna said, "Chung Si, we have already been through a lot together, but this time I don't see any other way. Sooner or later, the soldiers I killed are going to be missed. If we stay here, we are endangering the entire Safety Zone. If you come with me there are no guarantees, but I am not going to stay here at the mercy of these barbarians. Now make up your mind—there is not a moment to lose, and it's time to go!"

Chung Si nodded, climbed on the cart, and with a grimace, lay down next to one of the Chinese corpses. Anna said, "Now keep your face turned down all of the time; do not look up for any reason!"

"Okee Dokey Miss Anna…I just hope I don't puke!"

Anna couldn't help but laugh and said, "If you do, it will probably be your last bodily function, ever. Now you lie still…I'm going to crawl in at a different layer so our body heat doesn't draw too much attention should we start to steam in the cold. Remember: don't make a sound until we reach the river; wait until you hear from me!"

"OK, Miss Anna…good luck!"

Anna directed the work detail to fill in where the bodies had been removed and then crawled on the cart herself. All the time the coolie was saying to hurry up, hurry up! He had to return to his route or they would miss him at his next checkpoint. She agreed and handed the coolie a wad of bills.

Anna felt the bodies being loaded on top of her until she thought she couldn't stand it any longer. Each new one crushed her more heavily onto the one below. She thought to herself that this gave new meaning to the term "dead weight" as she tried to squirm into the least uncomfortable position.

At once, the coolie hastened to return to his assigned route before he was missed. Right away, the jostling from the cobblestones compacted the bodies on top of her into her own, squeezing the breath out of her. For a second she thought she heard a cry from Chung Si, as he was no doubt suffering the same discomfort. As the bodies settled in around her, she was glad she had thought not to be on the bottom layer. The weight of the extra layer on top of her, and the absence of any cushioning, would have been too much to bear. Looking for anything to be optimistic about, she thought of the insulation the bodies around her gave against the bitter December night. At least the cold helped assuage the smell of death all around her.

In what seemed to be an eternity of jostling, crushing, and near suffocation, the cart finally came to a stop. Without turning her head, she could see little. Anna heard shouting in Japanese. From her limited field of vision, facing downward, she could see the leg of a soldier from about the waist down. He was moving back and forth in the vicinity of their cart, but she couldn't tell what was going on. Every time she breathed, steam came from her breath; she couldn't help it. She tried to slow her breathing and hoped Chung Si was doing the same. She dared not turn her head. The cart remained motionless as the soldier continued to shout. With the shouting came the memory of the officer's shouting, the slapping, and the spittle in her face. She had been so busy coping with survival and escape, it was the first time she had thought about the incident. Only hours ago, it seemed like days. She felt guilt—not at killing the soldiers, but at her total lack of remorse. She knew that was not normal. In the moments it took for all of this to flash through her mind, she made a promise to herself that she would not think about it again until they were safe. Instead, she tried very hard to concentrate on a hot bath with her favorite salts.

The shouting stopped, and once again, her cart began jostling down the cobblestones. She tried thinking about anything to take her mind from discomfort and again reflected on the shouting and slapping. She had seen it in Shanghai and now in Nanking—so many in the Japanese command structure shouted. Brutality toward anyone lower in the hierarchy was institutional—especially towards conscripts. She was almost certain the brutality had an effect on the way their soldiers treated their captives.

After what seemed forever, Anna began to see nets, fishing gear, small boats and other trappings of river commerce. They were getting close to the Hsiakwan wharfs, on the Yangtze. Away from the soldiers, she turned her head. Now she could begin to see the immensity of the murders. Everywhere were piles of bodies, stacked like so much cordwood. Their cart stopped. She saw another coolie start pulling bodies off the other carts in her small field of vision. Then, they were at theirs! She felt the weight of the soldier on top of her being moved and hoped it was one of their coolie's companions and not a soldier. With no warning, someone grabbed her arms and another her feet. She tried to remain limp. Two swings, and she was falling on top of yet another pile of bodies. She recognized Chung Si staring up at her just as she was dropped on top of him.

The coolie turned and said in dialect, "You safe for a little while! Japanese soldiers out looking for gasoline to burn bodies. No one down by river right now. I go now! May your ancestors be with you missy!"

CHAPTER 65

▼

CHENG FAT

Nanking, Hsiakwan wharf
January, 1938

Before she could respond, the coolie was gone. Anna had no doubt that when he and his companions were finished with their grisly task the Japanese would have no more use for them, and they too would join the others on those piles of bodies.

First, she looked up and down the Hsiakwan wharfs. Hardly able to move from the stiffness, she disentangled herself from the bodies in the pile and asked Chung Si if he was O.K. He said he was. She grabbed his hand and began backing down to the waters edge, careful to keep the body piles between themselves and the Japanese soldiers higher up on the banks. Soon, they were at the waters edge, creeping along the ruin of junks and sampans destroyed during the siege.

Anna cupped her hands to her mouth and began to call into the wrecked boats. She tried each of the dialects she knew. "Is anybody there? We are an American and Chinese! We need help! We can pay in U.S. dollars for help!"

Anna thought an appeal from an American would carry more weight than from a Russian.

All the while, Chung Si kept an eye further up the riverbanks toward the wharves. He was certain that was where the guards would be. Anna kept calling as they worked their way through the derelict workboats. After a while, she thought she heard something moving at the waters edge beside a wrecked junk broken almost in half by some kind of ordinance. She motioned to Chung Si to be quiet.

Presently a young girl peered over the bulwarks of a derelict sampan and motioned for Anna and Chung Si to follow. The threesome stepped gingerly over the wreckage, all the time working themselves farther out in the river on boats rafted together far out into the Yangtze.

When they stepped out onto the last sampan Anna noticed that unlike the others, this one tipped suggesting buoyancy. She judged it about thirty feet long, and it looked just like the other sampans lying derelict along the banks. It had arched matting stretched on a bamboo frame over the stern, a small mast and sail near the bow and a large sculling oar lying between a worn oar chock on the stern.

This one was floating; it was not just sunk in the mud like the others. The young girl took one last look around—first toward the wharves and now burning body pyres, and then up and down the Yangtze. Satisfied no one was watching, she reached down and opened a one-meter square hatch near the bow of the sampan and dropped silently below. With head and shoulders still at deck level, she motioned for Anna and Chung Si to follow.

In the hold of the sampan, Anna could not see a thing. As she dropped to the sole of the boat below, however, she sensed life all around her. When Chung Si dropped through beside her, the little girl slid the hatch back in place. Someone struck a match and touched it to the smallest of oil lamps.

Anna looked around her and saw there were no ports from which the light below could betray their presence. The dim lamp revealed the faces of what appeared to be ten, maybe twelve terrified faces sitting in a huddle. The faces peered back at them horrified at the sight of what looked like two filthy Chinese soldiers covered in blood. There was very little room to sit in the confines of the small craft. Anna surmised the group comprised at least two families—the kind one saw working the sampans up and down any river in Asia.

For the first time, the little girl spoke. Anna heard her say to no one in particular that she found them while she was foraging for snails and clams on the banks of the river. Pointing to Anna, she said in half dialect and half pidgin, "I heard this one call out asking for help. She said she was Mellican, and that one was Chinese. She say they pay for help with Mellican dolla, and I bring them to you father!"

The little girl's summary complete, Anna unfastened her earflap string and pulled off her quilted cap. There were hushed murmurs from the small crowd as they saw that this *foreign devil* was a woman. A middle-aged man rose from the customary Asian squat and approached Anna. He was a good foot shorter than she was, and had one of those beards that consisted of about three long hairs.

Even in the dim light, the man's teeth betrayed a lifetime of betel nut addiction. The man raised his hand for emphasis and said to Anna, "These people are my family and the family of my brother who was killed today by the yellow dwarfs. It is my job to protect and care for them. You cannot stay! Japanese patrols are everywhere! They have patrols on the riverbanks and boats on the river! We have only stayed rafted up to these other sampans because the yellow dwarfs do not know anyone is aboard, and it looks to them like my boat has been abandoned in the mud. We have only a little rice and very little water. If we try to move our sampan, the Japanese patrol boats or soldiers on shore will know we are not a derelict. They will capture us and kill us all!"

"My name is Anna. This is my colleague Chung Si. We work with the Chinese company that sends airplanes into the air for Chiang Kai-shek's government. Maybe you have seen them flying up and down the river into Nanking. We are trying to get to a place just this side of Wuhu, where we will be able to get help from our friends in the sky. It is only about twelve miles from here. I will pay good Yankee dolla if you can help us get to this place."

The group looked unimpressed. The spokesman said, "My name is Cheng Fat, and missy, you crazy! We move sampan, yellow devils see us...not think we sunk and kill us all!"

Anna said, "There are too many soldiers at Hsiakwan wharf. They will be busy here for the next several days disposing of the bodies of your countrymen they have murdered. If you stay here you will soon be found, and all of you will certainly be killed. We must find a way to leave this place, or there will be no chance for any of us!"

Before the spokesman could respond she asked, "How often does the patrol boat come by?"

The river man thought a moment and said, "They run two patrol boats, one up river...one down river. One passes about every twenty, maybe thirty minutes most." As if on cue, they heard diesel engines in the distance, and after a few minutes felt the wake from a passing vessel.

Anna asked, "Before the next one passes by do you think you could work the boat up-stream for twenty minutes, pull into where the other boats have been wrecked, and look like you do now...aground, or just another derelict?"

The spokesman fingered his scraggly beard in thought. He said, "No can do! Yellow dwarfs see us and kill us all!"

Anna asked, "How long do you think it will take them to find you if you stay here?"

The spokesman continued to stroke the scraggly hairs as the rest of the group looked on. "You right missy, we stay Hsiakwan wharf and we all meet our ancestors before sun sets tomorrow!"

Before Anna could respond, the captain was giving orders to his family and crew. He appointed himself to the sculling oar and posted two of the young men as lookouts. He directed that the oil lamp be put out. The two young men moved the hatch to one side and climbed out into the frigid night.

Anna stayed below with Chung Si and the rest of the family. She knew nothing of sampans and decided she would only be in the way. In the dark hold, they could see and hear nothing. In a few minutes, Anna thought she felt motion through the water. She rolled up the sleeve of her Chinese army jacket and looked at the luminescent dial of her wristwatch strapped high on her forearm to avoid detection. It was just after eleven at night. She hated the inaction and wished she could be on deck and see what was happening.

A middle-aged woman with a weathered face lit a small oil stove; in a short time, she was passing tea to everyone in the hold. Someone worked their way toward the stern of the boat and passed tea through a hatch to the three on deck.

After about twenty minutes, Anna felt the boat ground. One of the boys slid the hatch back a few inches and called down for everyone to move all the way to the stern of the boat. Anna and the others did as they were told. Presently they felt the boat being pulled through the mud, up onto the banks of the Yangtze.

As soon as they grounded, Anna felt the boat careening over to one side, stopping at about a forty-five degree angle. No sooner had the careening stopped than those topside scrambled down through the hatch and dropped below.

Anna asked the captain, "What's happening?"

In the darkness Anna could hear slight laughter in the captain's voice as he said, "We sculled close to the river bank so we could beach the boat in a hurry if we saw a patrol boat coming. When yellow devils come, boys careened us next to some wrecked junks. My sons take sail halyard from top of mast…make fast to next junk…pull boat over in mud. Maybe we lucky and look wrecked too!"

They were careened over so far that now everyone sat on the sides of the hull. Even so, Anna marveled at Cheng's ingenuity. When the lamp was lit, Anna took out the map that Bond had drawn for her describing where they would be picked up the following night. The captain looked, and immediately understood where Anna wanted to go. He said, "If we lucky, maybe we there by morning…then we wait all day in reeds till night! We go to spot on map after sun go down! If not lucky, make no difference…we all be dead!"

It wasn't long until they heard the patrol boat's engines and felt the passing wake in the shallow water. Cheng, the boys and Anna, noted that this time the interval between the patrol boats was farther apart. They reasoned it was probable that since they were farther away from Nanking, the boats patrolled this area perhaps only every other time. Soon, the chug of the diesels faded and the little crew scrambled out, released the halyard, brought the little sampan upright and poled off into the river. In minutes, the little sampan was again sculling up river in the freezing darkness.

All night Cheng and his sons continued to work his small boat upriver. When the wind was fair, they used the sail giving those below respite from the constant groaning of the sculling oar in its lock. Sailing made it easier to hear approaching engines. Each time they anticipated the patrol boats they poked their bow as far as possible on to the banks disguising themselves as one of the hundreds of wrecks destroyed by the Japanese.

At around three a.m. Cheng Fat called below that they were passing the American gunboat, *Panay*. Anna and Chung Si pulled themselves out onto the deck to see what remained of what was to have been their way out of Nanking. As they crawled on the deck, the shock of the December night bit through their clothes like a sharp knife. It took a few moments for their eyes to adjust to the darkness, and then they saw it. All that remained above the surface of the shallow Yangtze was the shot up superstructure. Anna thought, "Gunboat Diplomacy" had fallen to the diplomacy of total war. Japanese aircraft had strafed and bombed the *Panay* until she sunk—so much for the symbol of American might, she thought. She wondered how many people had been killed in the attack and whether anyone had been able to escape. The thought crossed her mind that she might be the only person alive, besides those Japanese soldiers in the "killing fields," that had photographic evidence of what happened in Nanking. As she dropped down to the relative warmth below decks she thought maybe some time in the near future "Gunboat Diplomacy" would have to give way to Battleship Diplomacy with the United States and England. She wrapped herself in the army overcoat and fell asleep thinking of the events of the last two days.

The next thing Anna remembered was someone shaking her awake. She opened her eyes in the below decks gloom of the sampan. She recognized the captain's voice as he was trying to tell her that they had arrived near the place on Bond's map. First light was beginning to show through cracks in the overhead hatch. The plan was to hide in the reeds until darkness the following evening. Even at this distance, the glow of the fires in and around Nanking gave Cheng and his sons enough light to guide their small craft into the thick reeds growing far out into the Yangtze. The boys on the bow of the boat continued to sound the mud bottom of the river with a long bamboo pole until it was shallow enough for them to jump into the water and continue to pull the shallow draft vessel far into the natural camouflage. The crew whispered back and forth estimating the distance that would make them invisible to river traffic, but still far enough away from the shore to remain unseen by passersby on the river's edge. His sons were careful to pull the reeds parted by the boat's passage back in to place so as not to leave a tell tale trail. As they moved deeper into the river's natural camouflage, Cheng Fat and his family pulled reeds, gathered mud, and other growth, camouflaging the boats decks and top sides. Like everything else in China, teamwork, and many hands accomplished the task in little time. Everyone, including Anna and Chung Si, worked tirelessly until Cheng's floating home was hidden from the air patrols that were sure to begin after first light.

Just before sunrise, Cheng judged the sampan hidden as well as possible and ordered everyone below. Blue with cold, the two boys scrambled back aboard the boat. The rest of the family rubbed them down with burlap and cotton to warm them up. Already, Cheng Fat's wife and daughters were preparing tea and the little rice they had left before settling in for the day's hiding.

As Cheng's wife and daughter began to boil the water for their breakfast of rice and tea, Anna reached into her musette bag, retrieved the cloth bags of rice and dried pork she had taken from Ginling College and gave them to Mrs. Fat. Chung Si did the same. It was the first time Anna had seen Cheng's family smile. His wife poured some of the grains into an iron pot of boiling water on the small oil stove. She estimated that by rationing, their meager gift would be enough to feed the family for a couple of days—at least until they could safely re-supply. The first portions were fed to the two boys to help offset their numbing cold.

While they were still thanking their respective gods for getting this far from Nanking without being discovered, Cheng watched Anna as she took off her musette bag and quilted coat. Mostly, they marveled at the Nambu pistol that this strange female took out of her pocket and stuffed in her belt. They knew that only Japanese officers possessed such weapons.

Anna took her map case out of the bag and withdrew a wad of U.S. dollars. She counted out fifty dollars in one-dollar bills and handed the fortune to Cheng Fat. She said in Mandarin that tomorrow night they might not have time to give Yankee Dolla that she had promised.

Cheng Fat bowed and thanked this strange foreign female devil once again. Where most foreigners brought only grief, he was beginning to think that maybe, just maybe, this one might bring "good joss."

She reached into her case, took out the map Bond had made, and spread it out on the sole under the dim light of the sampan's oil lamp. Cheng showed her where they were. After sunset, he estimated it would take no more than two hours travel to reach the rendezvous point.

She explained that their rescue plane was to land as close to midnight as possible. Bond had emphasized that the amphibian could not, and would not wait more than ten minutes once it landed. It would be far too dangerous. Anna remembered his words, "One—the patrols were bound to hear, even if they couldn't see him land. Two—the pilot would have to cut the engine as soon as possible after sailing to the pickup point near the river's edge. To leave the engine running would invite discovery. Three—after shut down, he would have to anchor. With only the pilot aboard to handle the airplane and the anchoring, the swift running river would make that task tenuous at best."

Everyone slept soundly for the first hours of daylight. Cheng's sons took turns standing watch under blankets on deck. They were able to whisper down a ventilation hole if they saw or heard anything. Once they heard airplanes flying close by, but none flew close enough to be a threat to the camouflaged vessel. After the first few hours of rest, the boys became impatient to be under way. Even though it was dangerous, they preferred action to idleness, and they pleaded with their father to leave. Cheng cautioned patience and helped pass the time by telling them stories passed down by his ancestors.

Anna took her active diary from her map case. She shoved the Leica in its waterproof pouch into one of the coat's large cargo pockets. Then, using the overcoat as a cushion, she leaned against the hull and gave considerable thought to all that had transpired since arriving in Nanking. As everyone else slept, the forced idleness gave her the first opportunity in many days to organize and journal her thoughts.

In time, she dozed off—sleeping for the first time since the night before their escape. She was unaware that the two boys had once again slipped into the freezing waters of their backwater haven and began the numbing work of towing their craft back to the swift waters of the Yangtze. It wasn't long before Cheng was again sculling the small sampan toward their rendezvous point. Anna slept, exhausted from the events of the past days.

At about ten o'clock, she was awakened by the now familiar sound of the sampan entering reeds. About the same time, one of Cheng's sons slid the hatch back and said that they were to come on deck with their things as soon possible. Chung Si was already on deck and Anna was still struggling to overcome the sluggishness of waking up. As she tumbled out onto the deck, the sampan had already been poled very close to the bank. This time the boys would not have to enter the water to tow the boat. When they were just scraping bottom, Cheng Fat said it was as close as he could get. They must go quickly!

In the darkness, Anna and Chung Si said quick goodbyes and thanked the waterman again. Although they couldn't see, they sensed the waterman's smile as he wished them good joss. The two survivors slipped waist deep into the river, where Anna was shocked instantly awake in the freezing water.

CHAPTER 66

▼

MOON CHIN

The Yangtze River
January, 1938

They waded out of the river onto the banks looking both ways for Japanese patrols. The only light was the reflected glow in the night sky from the distant fires still burning in Nanking. Sculling away from the light, Cheng Fat and his family were already swallowed up by the night. Anna and Chung Si stood motionless, listening carefully for any sound; there was nothing—nothing except for the winter wind blowing through the reed field. Right away, they started looking for a sheltered vantage point where they could wait for CNAC's amphibian to take them to safety.

Not far from where they came out of the water, they found a gully that no doubt was a raging torrent during monsoon. It offered limited protection from wind but gave them a good vantage point to hear and see an amphibian when it arrived.

Anna looked at her watch. The luminous dial said eleven o'clock. With any luck, they had only a little over an hour to wait. After they settled into the least uncomfortable vantage point, the ever-resourceful Chung Si pulled some long grasses from the overhanging banks of the gulley. When he had a significant pile, he pulled them up over their lower extremities giving them a little camouflage and at least some protection from the piercing wind. The two huddled closely trying to promote as much heat as possible from their wet legs and torso. When

Anna put her arms around Chung Si for warmth, she felt the musette bag over his uniform coat.

In shock she remembered! In her sleep fogged mind she had not put her father's map case back in the musette bag on her back. The map case—her journals, the film, everything was still on Cheng Fat's sampan! The only thing she had was her Leica, what money was left, and the pistol. Although she tried, she simply could not hold back her tears of remorse. All of the risks she had taken to record what she had seen were for nothing. All her hopes of being able to deliver a visual record of the unimaginable bestiality she had witnessed was lost.

Chung Si was shocked seeing his paragon of courage crying and asked, "Miss Anna...Miss Anna...what is the matter?" In that moment, all of the courage and resolve of the last weeks left her. She held her gloved hand over her mouth trying to stifle her uncontrollable sobbing as she tried to explain to Chung Si what had happened. He didn't know what to say. Chung Si held her and said, "It will all be all right Miss Anna, It will be all right...you will see, you will see!"

Finally, the misery of her failure gave way to piercing cold. Time dragged as slowly as the blood flowing through their frozen bodies. The longer they sat, the colder they got and the less they could feel their lower extremities. Chung Si kept one of the ear flaps from his army hat pulled half way back to hear the aircraft and to give early warning of any foot patrol. At first, he thought it to be a patrol boat moving down the river. Then, he heard the distinct sound of a Loening Air Yacht's engine coming from the southwest. Chung Si shook Anna and lifted the earflap on her hat; then, she too acknowledged the approaching plane. Both tried to stand on their frozen legs and began plodding down the gully to the river's edge.

The amphibian displayed no lights. They heard the ship turn back into the wind flying up river. The noise diminished as the pilot retarded the power and began his approach onto the pitch-black Yangtze River. They heard, but did not see the approximate touch down point of the amphibian. Trying to run on the frozen stumps of feet, Anna could just make out the spray from the plane as it splashed down. When the plane, now boat, began edging toward the shore, it appeared the craft was coming directly toward them. It must have been sheer luck, she thought. The pilot maneuvered directly into the reed fields not far from where they stood.

With the darkness and the reed field for protection, the single engine craft was almost invisible. Besides hiding the amphibian, the reed field was also helping the pilot hold the aircraft from being swept downstream in the rapidly moving river. At first, the two refugees could not find the airplane or the pilot, and they felt certain that anyone within a mile of their position must have heard the Loening as the plane maneuvered for its landing. Anna and Chung Si tried to hurry through the mud on their frozen stumps doing their best to be quiet.

They had no idea whom the CNAC pilot was that had come for them. Freezing, and in desperation, Anna cupped her hands to her mouth so that her voice would be more directional. In a muffled voice she yelled, "Pilot!...Pilot!...It's Anna from the Nanking Office!"

There was no response. Again, she called, "Pilot!...Pilot!...It's Anna from the Nanking Office!" After a short pause, a voice came back.

"Miss Anna, is that you? It's Moon Chin! You stay there and I will come to you."

After a few moments, Anna heard the reeds being pushed aside and then saw Moon Chin. He was dressed in a full length, fleece lined coverall, winter flying hat, and goggles. He seemed to have difficulty walking in the mud in the bulky flying gear. He said, "Miss Anna, am a glad to see you! Did you see me land?"

Anna through her arms around the pilot and said, "Moon Chin...are we glad to see you! We heard you coming and saw the spray from your splash down. We lost you in the reeds."

Moon Chin said, "If you saw and heard me, there's a good chance a Japanese patrol did too! We must takeoff immediately! I believe I saw lights moving on this side of the river just before I splashed. It could be a Japanese patrol, but with luck it's from the lights of curious farmers."

At that moment, Chung Si touched Anna on the shoulder and held his finger to his lips. "Shhh, I think I heard shouting!"

Faintly at first, and then louder, Anna too heard voices. The language was Japanese! "Moon: how long will it take us to get out of here?"

Moon said, "We can leave plenty fast Miss Anna, but I don't want to start the engine until we are out of the reeds! I'll pull up the anchor, turn the nose around and help push out until I have to get in to start the engine. You two keep pushing until you are chest deep; then pull yourself in as fast as you can! The river is running swiftly here. With this wind, we will start to drift right away. I will have to start the engine to keep from drifting back into the reeds again."

Anna thought, at least the wind is blowing *from* the direction of the Japanese patrol and it won't be as easy for them to hear us.

Moon had weighed the Loening's anchor that he had dug in the riverbank to keep the nose of the airplane in the reeds. While stowing the anchor, he tried his best to avoid metal against metal. All three helped turn the plane around. Then, they began to push the amphibian out of the reeds and into the river. The shouts of the patrol became louder. It was not long until they were waist deep in the muddy water. Moon pulled himself onto the hull and climbed up the side into the cockpit; Anna and Chung Si continued to push. Soon they could no longer stand and were armpit deep in the freezing water. The breeze caught the Loening's tail and began to weather vane the airplane into the wind. Anna said in a quaking voice, "Chung Si, pull yourself aboard; we aren't helping any longer!"

When Chung Si was almost aboard, Anna rapped on the hull to let Moon know they were coming aboard and to start the engine. Anna heard the whine of the starter as the three bladed propeller began to turn. She heard a chug, then a cough and smelled raw gasoline as the four hundred and fifty horsepower Hornet tried to catch. Moon stopped turning the engine, pulled the mixture control all the way off and again pressed on the starter. The engine continued to turn with more coughs and puffs of smoke. All the time the amphibian drifted tail first towards the reeds near the waters edge. Anna was still not aboard. Her limbs were so cold they refused to function. Though she willed her body to move, it would not respond. Chung Si had managed to climb into the cabin. Lying on the floor, he grabbed Anna by the scruff of her quilted coat and pulled her aboard. The propeller continued to turn as the fabric rudder of the Loening began to strike the reeds pulling the nose of the amphibian down river.

With her teeth chattering Anna managed to say, "What's wrong?"

Moon yelled, "I flooded the damned thing!" He continued to turn the engine several more turns before moving the mixture control to rich. The engine fired, flooding the river's calm with the unmistakable roar of a radial engine. With the cabin door still open, Moon headed straight out into the center of the Yangtze at half throttle. Anna and Chung Si were still pulling themselves into the cabin. It seemed almost quiet when Moon pulled the throttle to idle and turned the amphibian into the wind. It was only just then that they managed to pull the cabin door closed. The Loening turned to what Anna believed parallel to the river's bank, and then, just as suddenly as the engine noise subsided, it returned with the un-muffled roar of a radial engine at full power.

Chung Si shook Anna by her soaking coat and pointed toward the shoreline. Just abeam their position, she saw lanterns and electric torches twinkling on the bank as the Loening gathered speed. The amphibian skipped once, twice, became airborne, and banked hard, climbing away from the muzzle flashes as the patrol made their last desperate attempts to bring them down. In seconds, they were climbing into the black December sky highlighted only by the fires of Nanking still burning in the distance as Moon Chin set a course for Hankow and freedom.

CHAPTER 67

▼

THE PENINSULA HOTEL

Hong Kong
November, 1994

Stephen stood and stretched his legs. With the last journal in his hand, he walked to the window and looked out at the city, thinking about what he had just read.

He thought about the time covered by the journals he had just recovered. They covered 1936 through the early part of 1938. The China Diaries he had always had began in the middle of 1941, and ended in 1942. For a moment, he wondered about the gap between the two sets and what had happened to account for the lost time between 1938 and 1941.

Not focusing on anything, he stared out of the hotel window, trying to assimilate everything he had just read. He was physically and mentally exhausted. He still had trouble realizing he was reading not a novel, but a personal account of his mother! The hotel alarm clock on the end table showed twenty minutes until five on its digital display. Still thinking about the diaries, he pulled off his clothes, let them drop on the floor and fell into bed.

CHAPTER 68

▼

KAREN HARDISTY

Hong Kong
November, 1994

Stephen woke from a restless sleep. He had been dreaming. The last shards of the dream were fleeing from consciousness. He had Anna's picture, the one where she looked like Garbo; he was showing it to Chinese peasants and no one recognized his mother. He looked at the clock on the night table and wasn't surprised to see that it was past ten in the morning.

Stephen completed his morning toilet and his exercise disciplines. Finished, he reached into his flight case, dug for his address book, flipped it open to Karen Hardisty's new entry and dialed her work number. For reasons he could not explain he felt the need to tell her what he had found out about his mother in the missing journals.

"Miss Hardisty? Stephen Cannon...I just wanted to thank you for the work you did with the translations yesterday. You...you really helped pull the whole thing together for me."

Stephen could hear telephones ringing and people talking in the background.

Karen said, "I was glad to be of some help, Stephen. Somehow, I felt...how can I put it...as if I were helpful in linking the past with the present. That mother of yours sounds like some lady!"

"Yeah...some lady all right! I sat up most of the night reading the diaries. It's like I am being introduced to someone very important in my life, except...except, it's like I'm meeting her for the first time...which is more or less true, I guess.

After what I've read I have a much greater insight into the type of person she is, or was, but still have no idea what happened to her."

Karen said, "Maybe you would like to talk to someone about it...I'm a good listener; how about giving me a try?"

"I was thinking the same thing, and I was going to ask if you would do just that. Is it possible you could join me at the Peninsula for a late lunch...maybe the Verandah restaurant?"

"Yes, I'd like that. How about one o'clock?"

"That's fine...one o'clock then...see you at the Pen."

Stephen was having a cup of coffee when Karen walked into the Verandah. She was dressed in a smart raw silk suit that looked good on her. She was the kind of woman who made clothes look good, rather than the other way around. He hadn't paid attention the day before, but today he noticed she wore no wedding ring. They exchanged greetings and sat down. Both picked up the luncheon menus, but instead of looking at the fare, Stephen snatched glances of Karen over the top of the menu.

She had that thick hair that most women would kill for. It was short and feathered naturally to the shape of her face. It really looked good on her. She had blue eyes, full lips and a dynamite figure—he wondered what she did to keep so fit, and why she wasn't married.

Karen said, "I think I'll go with the soup and half sandwich...so what do you think? Are you any closer to finding out what happened to your mother?"

"I think I'll have the same. And yes, some...more than where she is though, I gained a lot of insight into what kind of person she is."

Karen said, "Go on."

"She had a strong father...pushed her really hard, but in the good way...you can tell from her entries there was a lot of love. The truth is, or was, my mother was almost a self-made woman. They didn't have very much at all, and her whole education came from home. My God, in her late teens she knew several dialects of Chinese, English, French and had a good working knowledge of Japanese. She knew geopolitics, geography, and guess what else?"

"What, then?"

"She was a martial arts expert! That father of hers didn't want her to be a victim...ever...and it paid off in spades! In Nanking, she took on a group of Japanese soldiers molesting some young Chinese girls."

"Just her...what happened, Stephen? Was she hurt?"

"Oh no, Karen. She killed them...killed them all...five of them...with their own officer's sword!"

"Killed them…with a sword?"

"Yes…Their soldiers were drunk and into lust. Karen, from her descriptions of what they did in Nanking, they made Genghis Kahn look like boy scouts. In your line of work, you've probably heard the stories about Nanking. Their officer was attacking her…in the act of tearing her clothes off, not to put to fine a point on it. Somehow, she got hold of his sword and killed them all!"

"My God!"

"It was after that she embarked on that remarkable escape that Cheng told us about yesterday. It's an incredible story. You really must read it for yourself to get a feeling for what she went through. You just can't imagine what she saw during the Japanese siege of Southern China—especially Nanking…just how she got to the banks of the Yangtze will amaze you even more than the river story we heard from Mr. Fat. Get this…she and her Chinese companion played *dead soldier*. They somehow persuaded someone to divert one of the hundreds of carts the Japanese were using to move their murdered victims to the Yangtze for disposal. She and the Chinese guy we heard about last night lay down among the corpses! When they unloaded the cart, they tossed them with the other bodies piled up for burning and disposal in the river; that's when they got away and ran into Cheng Fat and his family.

"Get this Karen. It was pitch black when that pilot landed to pick them up. I was trying to figure out just what he had to do to pull that rescue off, and think I've got it."

Stephen took the silverware and put it end to end to indicate both sides of the river. Like most pilots, he used his hand to indicate the amphibian in flight.

"At that time of night, there weren't a lot of lights on the ground. This guy must have put what lights there were on both sides of the airplane, flew parallel between them, and made a controlled let down into the black place he knew had to be the river. He set up a rate of descent and airspeed that he knew would result in a good touchdown attitude, and he flew that way until he hit the water! Can you imagine that?"

Karen said, "I'm not a pilot, but I get the idea. Nothing electronic to guide him at all, was there?"

"Not a thing. He did it all with the seat of his pants and a lot of horse sense. As he made his descent, he noted the compass heading he was on…he knew he wouldn't be able to see the lights once he was on the water, so after he stopped, he just turned ninety degrees to that heading and timed how long it took to reach the river bank. When he left, he just reversed it, turned ninety degrees again and took off…hard to believe that something so simple could work. These days it would take several million dollars worth of electronics to pull off the same stunt."

Karen was a good listener and didn't interrupt as he told the story. The technical problem he described didn't mean that much to her, but she could feel the tremendous empathy he had for this fellow pilot from a lifetime ago that saved his mother from the Japanese.

"You know, Karen, before last night, I knew very little about my mother. After reading the missing diaries, I know her much better. I can't believe what she had to overcome just to live. She must have been a very strong person…with an iron will."

Karen said, "Was there anything in the diaries that gave you a clue to how you might find out what happened when your parents returned to China?"

"I think Shanghai holds the key…Shanghai and CNAC! Shanghai was where she grew up. CNAC was the Chinese American airline she worked for."

Their brunch came, the waiter poured more coffee from the pot, and left.

Alex continued, "I was thinking, there just has to be some people left from the old airline that made it through the war…probably some in China, maybe Shanghai, and no doubt some are living in the U.S."

"Why don't you try the internet? The Web…It's catching on like wildfire in the last few years. I would imagine there must be an alumni organization, or at least a website out there."

Alex said, "Good idea! I brought my laptop and I noticed the hotel has direct connections. I'll work on that this afternoon."

"I'll be interested to hear what you find out. If you have to speak with anyone in Shanghai, maybe I could be of some help?"

"Do you have any plans for this evening? Maybe we could have dinner…I'll fill you in on what I find out."

Karen said, "I would like that on the condition that I get to choose. After all, I'm the Chinese speaking resident."

"You're starting to sound like my mother in the diaries! What time?"

Karen laughed, "How about seven? I'll meet you in the lobby."

Stephen stepped off of the elevators and went to the same sitting area he and Matsumoto had used the day before. He wore his usual travel outfit of slacks, polo shirt and sports coat again. Looking around the lobby, he recalled his parent's description of the hotel on the day the war began. It was here that all of those people had gathered trying to leave when escape became impossible for all but a few. It was here that his parents decided to marry, and it was probably in this hotel where he was conceived!

December the eighth was still on his mind when Karen came through the hotels' front entrance. She wore the perennially fashionable Chi-Pao that showed off a woman's body as only that unique Chinese garment could. It was black with large floral prints and the traditional high collar. The modest slit on the side of the dress showed legs that complemented the rest of her figure. She had her hair in a twist with an ivory comb holding everything in place. The entire effect was stunning.

Stephen stood and extended his hand. When she reciprocated, he drew her close to him, kissed her on the cheek in the European manner and said, "Karen, you look magnificent!"

"Why thank you! In that we are going to a famous Chinese restaurant tonight, I thought I would dress traditionally."

Karen asked, "How did your day go? Any luck with the CNAC website?"

"Very much so!"

Karen said, "I don't want to sound trite. I know this is very important for you, but this is starting to have all of the signs of a good mystery."

He proffered his arm and said, "Come on, take me to dinner and I will tell you about it on the way."

The doorman hailed a taxi and Karen simply said, "Jumbo Restaurant." The driver nodded in understanding and drove off in the direction of the Kowloon public pier and ferry.

Karen said, "So, what did you find out?"

"Well, just as you supposed, there was a web site for CNAC on the internet. I shot off an e-mail and told them my story."

"Any reply yet?"

"You bet…I hit the mother load! I asked the webmaster if any of their members might remember my mother, or maybe even my father who left Pan Am to join CNAC in late '42. I used her maiden and married name when I asked for information reasoning there were probably more people who knew her under her maiden name. It seems one of the CNAC association members knew Saul Abrahamson from before the war. Saul figures prominently in the diaries I got from Cheng. Since the PRC took their foot off everyone's neck, he, and a CNAC radio operator in Arizona, have been corresponding on a regular basis by snail mail. They want to set up an amateur net, but the government still has a hard time with long distance transceivers and the like…e-mail is catching on, though. The guy's name is Tom Weiler. Best of all Weiler e-mailed me Saul's address in Shanghai…seems he has been there since the war."

Karen asked, "What's next then?"

"I guess the next logical step is to go to Shanghai and speak with him. Chances are, he knows nothing, but right now he's the only link to the past we have."

Karen reached over and put her hand on his. It was a spontaneous and sincere gesture. "You really must go to Shanghai Stephen! You have only been here two days, and already it has taken you so far."

Her touch was electric. Since reading the missing diaries, Stephen felt a strong need to confide in this woman. Until this moment, though, the thought of this becoming other than a business relationship had not entered his mind. The usual feeling of panic of *getting to close* wasn't there—yet! It would come though—it always did.

"Yeah, it sure looks like Shanghai is in my immediate future," he said.

Karen sensed something negative and withdrew her hand.

"This Jumbo Floating Restaurant is standard tourist fare. It's like living in Washington or San Francisco, though…you never do those things yourself until you have visitors…besides, I like all of the lights."

Stephen laughed and said, "I've never been there…sounds like a fun thing."

The cab driver weaved in and out of the traffic congestion, and soon they came to the pier.

There was almost no wait for the ferry. Soon they were marveling at the thousands of lights that festooned the pagoda looking Jumbo Floating Restaurant. Stephen reflected on his mother's account of crossing Kowloon Bay on the first night of World War II and only could wonder at the emotions they must have been feeling.

The waiter showed them to tables and brought the menus. Both ordered a Tsingtao beer.

Karen asked, "You want to do the tourist thing and go pick your dinner from the fish tank?"

"No, don't think so…the menu will be just fine."

"Well not me; I want to go shopping. I want to see the little sucker that's going on my plate."

Before Stephen could stand, Karen pushed her chair back and walked off toward the fish tank. Stephen watched her as she gave her instructions to the waiter. He guessed she was in her late thirties, maybe early forties. Beautiful woman, intelligent—everything going for her. He wondered if she was ever married.

As the waiter turned to go toward the kitchen, Stephen saw a familiar face on the other side of the floating dining room. It was Shigao Matsumoto sitting with another man. He didn't appear to be aware of Stephen's presence.

When Karen returned from selecting her entree Stephen stood, pulled out her chair, and looked again toward Shigao's table; the two did not appear to notice him.

"You are a relic from the past, Mr. Cannon. I can't remember the last time a man pulled out a chair for me, but I like it."

"Last of a dying breed, my dear. Could you excuse me a moment...I see someone I just met and just want to say hello."

"Yes, of course!"

Stephen walked over to the table where Matsumoto and his companion were having their drinks. It appeared they too had just arrived.

Stephen stood with both hands hanging loosely at his side and said, "Mr. Matsumoto! What a coincidence meeting you here. I thought this place was only for tourists, like me. Do you dine here frequently?"

Matsumoto stood up. He looked genuinely surprised and said, "Oh, Mr. Cannon...how nice to see you again. Let me introduce you to Mr. Otani. He is an associate of mine from Japan. He is here in Hong Kong on...on business."

The other man stood but said nothing. Stephen guessed him to be in his late twenties—no older than thirty. He was wearing a grey suit, white shirt and tie. Stephen couldn't help but notice tattoos on his wrist showing from under his shirtsleeves. He was powerfully built and did not smile but did give the traditional Japanese half bow.

"Mr. Otani has never been to Hong Kong before. He has been called in to handle...to handle a special business problem. He is...how do you say, 'a facilitator'. I thought I would show him some of the sights of the city while he is here."

"How nice of you, Mr. Matsumoto...running in to you twice in as many days is really quite a coincidence, wouldn't you say? If it happened again, one would wonder if it really was a coincidence, wouldn't one?"

Matsumoto contemplated the floor. Before he could say anything Stephen said, "Mr. Matsumoto, Mr. Otani, I hope you both have an enjoyable evening."

He looked up, but before he could answer, Stephen turned and walked back to his table. Karen asked, "Who was that?"

Stephen described the meeting with Matsumoto in the hotel lobby. She looked over at their table where the two men were in heated conversation. Karen said, "Do you think these guys are following you?"

Stephen told her of the meeting in New York with Cheng's grandnephew, his explanation of the revisionist and the Ultra Nationalist. She said, "Do you think it's really possible there could be a concerted effort to suppress a nation's history?"

"If there isn't, why was my house burglarized, and why did Matsumoto try to buy me off? Just look at our own country. I don't know if it's intentional or not, but it is happening. Ask any high school graduate about how the U.S. got into World War II, and they only just might be able to tell you it was because Pearl Harbor was bombed. Ask anything about our history as a country, and most couldn't tell you more than who the first president was, a little about the War for Independence, maybe a few things about the civil war, and not much else. Other than history majors, college grads aren't much better. Actually, it doesn't surprise me."

"Do you think these guys are dangerous?"

"If they are zealous enough to burglarize someone's house it does make you wonder just where they would stop. Offering twenty grand to suppress my mother's diaries when they don't even know for sure what it says is pretty damned radical, don't you think?"

Karen said, "It's really amazing the extent some people will go to suppress the truth. You know, it works though...just look at the Turks. Hardly anyone in their own society knows about the Armenian massacre."

"Yeah...I was thinking about that very example just a short time ago."

Karen said, "You know, I'm glad the internet idea worked out. When I went back to work this afternoon, I poked around and found out there is a central registry in Shanghai that has quite a bit of information. They don't seem to be computerized, though, and it looks like you would have to ask through official channels. Either way, from past experience with the PRC, getting information will be tedious at best."

"You didn't have to do that, Karen...You really are going out of your way to help, and it really means a lot to me. Why don't you let me pay you for your time?"

"Don't worry, you are! You're paying through the nose! You bought lunch, and even though I brought you here, you're paying for dinner and later, maybe even dancing," Karen said.

"Dancing! Dear lady...do they really let embassy employees dance?"

"Are you kidding? Every level of State Department employee dances from the top right down to the bottom! Why they dance around every issue that ever comes before them just for the practice. Ever seen a diplomatic negotiation?...same thing. Now down at my level we have to dance around the bureaucracy just to make anything happen. Do we dance? What a question."

"Can I take that as a yes?"

"Yes you may…but unfortunately, all the dancing at work usually exhausts me to the extent I don't know of one place to go in Hong Kong, except maybe the hotels."

Stephen said, "I was hoping you might want to do something, so I asked at the Pen. The concierge took one look at me, and probably didn't figure me for the 'rave scene' so he recommended the Felix, right there in the hotel…says it has a spectacular bar with a great view and if we feel like dancing afterwards there's a place called the Crazy Box."

Karen smiled and said, "Then the Pen it shall be!"

Their dinner came. Stephen picked at his dim sum and Karen at her fish. Both were distracted by the intrusion of Matsumoto and his *facilitator*.

Stephen motioned towards the two men and said, "Let's forget about those two and the diaries for awhile, and try to enjoy the rest of the evening."

"Not to worry…I really enjoy the mystery of it all. It's like I'm a character in a detective story."

The view from the Felix bar was everything the concierge claimed. Karen ordered a DuBonnet and Stephen a Campari. Both were admiring the Hong Kong skyline when Stephen asked, "Karen, have you ever been married?"

"Yes…when I lived in Washington."

"What happened?"

"It didn't work out…Michael, my husband, was one of those men who had to continually prove he was attractive to other women. I couldn't live that way, and I guess came out here to forget about it, start a new life and indulge my lifelong fascination with the East. That was almost five years ago. What about you?"

"No…never."

"Any particular reason?"

"I don't know, Karen…There have been a few *almost*, but I couldn't go through with it. I've been trying to figure it out for a long time now. It might have something to do with this notion, up till now anyhow, of being abandoned by my mother…not knowing why she left. It is hard to put in words, but I think it has something to do with trust, or lack of it."

"Have you ever tried to speak with someone about it…a professional?"

"Once…It was a bad experience…left a bad taste in my mouth about the profession. Maybe it was just that guy, but I'll never go back."

Stephen continued. "You know…filling in these gaps in the China Diaries…the whole odyssey…it's kind of cathartic. So far, it's turning out different than what I expected. Already I feel like a large stone is being lifted from my chest. Regardless of the reasons my mother left, I can't help but admire the kind of person she was. Enough of this! Let's see that State Department light fantastic you told me about."

The music had just stopped, and the only other couple on the dance floor was leaving just as they arrived. Stephen led Karen by the hand, walked over to the lead musician and handed him a twenty-dollar bill. "Any chance of playing something that gives me a chance to hold this woman in my arms rather than standing ten feet away?"

"You got it mister."

He turned in time to see Karen's face slightly flushed and said, "That O.K. with you, Karen?"

She said, "Yes, I would like that Stephen."

CHAPTER 69

▼

FINDING SAUL

Shanghai
November, 1994

It had been a short flight from Hong Kong, and they still had the rest of the day. The cab driver wove his way through the sea of bicycles and taxicabs in Shanghai's teeming traffic. Neither Stephen nor Karen had been to the city before. Stephen couldn't describe how he felt. All he knew was something was different. He knew neither one of them had meant it to go that far; it just did. They held hands, but neither one said anything about what happened the night before.

The cab driver found Saul's apartment building with little difficulty. It was much more modern than he had expected. They took the elevator to his floor and found his apartment. A tall, slightly stooped man greeted them in English. Stephen was not surprised. Saul was simply an older version of the boy Anna had described in her diaries almost sixty years ago.

He would have been about the same age as his mom…about 75 or 76. He was about Stephen's height and slightly bent over, probably from arthritis, but Saul had the look of one in good health. If it were trimmed, the speckled beard would have looked good on him. Introductions were made, and he invited his guests to sit on a somewhat modern sofa. Saul offered them tea that they both accepted.

"Mr. Cannon, I am so glad you had the good sense to see if there was anything about CNAC on the web. Tom and I have been writing for years and without your resourcefulness, I wonder if you would have ever been able to find me?" Saul was easy to understand. He spoke good, if somewhat accented English.

"That was Karen's idea. She works for the U.S. State Department in Hong Kong; a good deal of her time is spent trying to re-unite families in China with relatives in the West."

Saul said, "Mr. Cannon, there is hardly a day that goes by that I have not thought about Anna...ah, your mother."

"Anna's fine, Mr. Abrahamson. I have the same problem. Since I've never met her, I find it difficult to refer to her as mother...please call me Stephen if you like."

"You know," Saul said, "I was always in love with her, and in a way, I felt she always loved me too...not romantic love you know, but like a brother."

Stephen said, "You guessed right; she knew it, and spoke of it in the China Diaries. That's what I call her journals. And yes, she loved you as a brother. It's kind of hard to think of a mother you never knew as a tease, but she definitely knew she had you wrapped around her finger. I guess when you are seventeen or eighteen, that sort of thing goes with the territory. You know, there was also a marine...before my father. From what I can gather those two were her only romantic loves...she didn't hold much back from those journals."

"Yes, I knew about the marine," Saul said. "She left Shanghai about that time. I think he broke her heart. I didn't know about your father, or about you, until she returned to Shanghai in early '43."

Stephen said, "That period...after she returned to China...that's still a mystery. When Anna and my father fled Hong Kong in '41, they brought all of their journals with them. They started in '41, and went right up until late 1942, when she disappeared. Up until a few days ago, they were all I had. The ones I told you about in Hong Kong filled in the gap between '36 and '38, and it's in those that I found out you were such a large part of her life. That's how we got the idea to contact you."

"You have all of those journals, Mr. Cannon? That would make some interesting reading, I think. Remember, the last time I saw your mother was in 1937...just before the Japs took Shanghai. It was during that time that that she had the falling out with the marine. She went to Nanking with CNAC, and that's when I lost track of her, until '43.

"Please wait here. I have something for you."

Saul left the living room and went to what Alex assumed was a sleeping area in the rear of the apartment. Soon, he returned holding a metal box. He pried the lid off, and inside were two very small cardboard bound notebooks. Both were filthy; they had dog-eared pages that were brown with age. Saul handed the notebooks to Alex. Karen shifted her position to the edge of the couch so that she could see Anna's ancient writing.

Saul said, "Anna gave these to me the last time I saw her."

Almost reverently, Stephen turned to the first page of the book. He was struck with the fact that it was hand printed in a text so small as to be barely readable without the aid of a magnifying glass. He flipped to the middle and then to the end. There were ten, maybe fifteen pages left in the first journal indicating she had never finished it. The second contained about the same amount of pages with no entries near the end.

Saul said, "Before you read either one, maybe it would be better if I tell you everything I know and how I came by this journal."

"Sure, go ahead, Saul."

"When I first heard from your mother, it was by CW."

"CW...You mean Morse code?"

"Yes, that is correct. Back then, of course, Morse was the only technology available for long-range radio communication. As you know, I was a radio operator for CNAC. Right up to the time the Japanese occupied Shanghai, I worked in the radio room at Lunghwa airport. It was CNAC's home base until the invasion."

"Go on."

"After the occupation, the Japanese shut down every radio except those under their control. They found out I was an operator for CNAC and put me to work in one of their field radio repair facilities. After awhile, I gained the commander's confidence and convinced them that I could work longer hours, and repair more radios, if they would let me work out of my old apartment in Hongkew. As you know, I lived in the French Concession, but all Jews and Chinese were forced to move either to Chapei or to Hongkew. I moved to Hongkew. Their commander was under a lot of pressure to increase production, so he authorized my experiment. It worked! I was able repair more radios. He looked good, so he left me alone. Every day he had broken sets dropped off at my apartment workshop and picked up the repaired ones to return to the field. Later, he even authorized a small truck for me. That way, when I finished, I brought the repaired ones to the depot and picked up more broken ones."

"How were you able to get away with that?"

"Like I said, I made him look good. Working alone, I was able to *liberate* parts from their field radios and make a transceiver. I hid it in the wall of my old apartment, not far from here in Hongkew."

Stephen asked, "Didn't they ever check you?"

"Only occasionally...the main thing their commander was interested in was how many radios I repaired."

"Before we were occupied, I and some of my HAM friends in free China set up contact times. We were certain it was only a matter of time until we were overrun, so we set up a frequency and time schedule so we could stay in touch. We had to keep our transmissions very short. We knew the Japanese had mobile listening posts, and if we weren't careful with our transmissions, they would have located my station in no time.

Later, some of my contacts with CNAC ended up with the Nationalist, some even went with the Communists. When the war was finally won, we had no illusions that the Communists would probably rule the new China, so we gave intelligence to both. As time went on, I became one of the only keys left in Shanghai. That was how I came to know that Anna had married and gone to the United States. It was also how I found out she came back."

"How did you find out?"

"When she returned to China in late '42 I heard of it from Roger Chang. He was the guy that helped your mother, and I get a job with CNAC...one of the old flight keys...you know...airborne radio operators. He flew out of Shanghai up until '37. He got out with the rest, when Bond moved the operations to Hong Kong. By '42 he was flying the hump to India.

"I knew his 'fist'. You know what I mean by that?"

"Yes," said Stephen. "It's a kind of signature for a radio operator using CW. Everyone operates the key with a rhythm unique to them. Kind of like a finger print...you could tell who was sending regardless of who they said they were...is that about right?"

"Yes...exactly!"

"How did you go about authenticating Roger and making sure he wasn't under the control of the Japs?"

"We had to be very cryptic. We had no codebooks at that time; we had to be very careful to make only short transmissions to keep the Japs from finding our transmitters. The Kempeitai were tenacious in finding clandestine nets. They used direction finders on trucks. So, when Roger made his first contact, I asked him a question that only Anna could answer. He came back with the right answer so I had the authentication I needed."

"What did you ask?"

"I asked: 'how smelled the breath of the master?' It wasn't long until he came back with 'Dog breath.' I knew then it had to be your mother."

"Dog breath?" asked Stephen.

"Yes…We both took martial arts together and referred to our Taijiquan master…behind his back of course…as 'dog breath.' Anna always said, 'If he can't knock you down with one of his moves, he can always breathe on you.'"

Stephen and Karen laughed. "We always assumed it was because he ate so much garlic, mixed with the betle nut he chewed. It was very distinctive, to say the least! Anyhow, the next transmission was his last, but it assured me it was your mother. It simply said, 'how are my parents?' I replied, 'as of last month, OK!' That was the last I heard from her until we met."

Saul continued, "Your mother returned to Shanghai in late winter, 1943…It was March fifteenth to be precise. 'The ides of March'…I'll never forget that night. I was in my Hongkew apartment…where I repaired the radios. It was about three o'clock in the morning."

CHAPTER 70

▼

SAUL'S APARTMENT

Japanese occupied Shanghai
March, 1943

The last burning embers of the coal he had stolen from the repair facility did little to keep the chill from the air. Before he went to sleep, he noted he had only five chunks left and would have to go to the post tomorrow to scrounge what he could. Fully clothed, all he could do for now was burrow into the cotton quilts that covered his bed.

Saul was sound asleep when the knocking at his door awakened him with a start. He sat bolt upright. The rapping was incessant. He assumed the worst. He had been too careless! They had triangulated the source of his transmissions and had found his location.

It was a guaranteed death sentence to have a transmitter. For a second, he thought of running. There was the rear door, but he was sure any Kempeitai patrol would have covered all exits. The best he could do was open the door and feign innocence.

Fully clothed, he had only to put on his felt boots that keep his stocking feet off of the cold wooden floor.

Expecting the worst, and shaking in terror, he opened the door. The bitter wind shocked him fully awake. There was a light snow falling.

A tall figure stood before him clad in the ubiquitous quilted parka with a traveler's bedroll slung over her back. Regardless of the winter cap with earflaps and bill, Saul knew who it was.

"Anna! What in God's name are you doing here?"

Saul took a step in the street and looked both ways. There was no activity—no one there! He glanced across the street at Wan Soo's apartment. Saul had long thought him a collaborator. Although only a watchman at a large warehouse, he always had plenty of coal and never seemed to lack for something to eat.

"Come in, come in quickly! You can't believe how many people would report your visit to the Kempeitai for a bowl of rice!"

As Anna stepped through the door, he shut it behind her and shot the bolt. Before he could say anything, she wrapped both arms around him, drew him close to her and kissed him on both cheeks.

"Saul, my wonderful Saul…It's so good to see you. Thank God, you are all right! Other than being a little thin, you look almost the same."

Anna pulled off her mittens and let them fall. They hung on cords from her neck, like a small child's. She untied the bedroll and began to work on the string ties that secured the earflaps under her chin.

Before she had finished Saul asked, "How long have you been out there? You must be freezing!"

Anna took off the cap and shook her short, lustrous, raven-black hair free. Saul looked at her; her cheeks were radiant from the cold night air. She looked the same but somehow more mature—more strained than he remembered.

"Only for a few hours…I have been on the river for the last few weeks making my way to Shanghai, so I'm used to it. The Yangtze…it's not the warmest of places in the wintertime. You know, the river…it's the same way I got away from Nanking, in '38."

Saul picked up two of the five remaining chunks of coal, opened the door to the small iron stove and carefully placed them on the remaining embers. As he poked the coals around the new fuel he said, "The river, huh…I always wondered.

"Anna, What in God's name are you doing here…why on earth did you come back?"

Anna stared at the floor. She seemed to be weighing something before she spoke. Then she looked at Saul with her signature smile as if about to speak, but instead, simply looked at her old friend.

Waiting for her answer, Saul slapped the sides of his quilted trousers with his coal dust covered hands and said, "Until your radio message, all I knew about you was that you made it to free China, then Hong Kong. Roger said you escaped from Hong Kong, married an American aviator and somehow got back to the

United States. When I heard you had returned, I knew it must be for a good reason. Why in God's name did you come back here, Anna?"

Anna continued to look at Saul, still weighing what she would tell him. She said, "It's a long story old friend. I'll get to that. Right now, our old boss, Bond, thinks I'm in Kunming with my husband. He already thought I was crazy for coming back to China. The Japanese think I came here to see my parents, which is true. As a matter of fact, they arranged for my transportation…but I have other business here too. You remember Sergei Hovans, don't you? He's my control in Shanghai. He's the guy I worked for in '37."

"Of course I remember him, but control…what do you mean *control*? Why did the Japanese help you come visit your parents? Hovans! Dammit Anna— Hovans is working for the Japanese!"

Anna still smiled with her private secret thoughts, looking around Saul's small living area. She strolled over, regarded a picture of his parents on the wall and said, "Saul, how are your parents?"

"There're dead, Anna. They were killed by a fucking bomb during the initial siege. Wrong place wrong time…Did you hear me say Hovans works for the Japanese?"

Anna said, "Oh Saul…I'm so sorry about your parents. I know you weren't that close, but they were the only family you had."

"Anna…forget about my parents; they're gone…you said you worked for the Japanese."

"Yes, that's right old friend. Hovans and the Japanese both think I work for them."

"You…you work for the Japanese?"

"Yes, so they think, but I am also working for the Americans."

"Anna: are you out of your mind? Have you forgotten, these bastards are ruthless…they play for keeps! Bonds right…you are crazy!"

"Saul, did you know I have a baby?"

"A baby? No! When…in the States?"

"Yes…Alex, he's my husband; we have a new baby boy. His name is Stephen. He's living with Alex's parents, in Maryland, in the United States. Alex returned to China in '42; he's flying the hump. The Army Air Corps wants him, but right now, he's flying for CNAC, out of Kunming, mainly to India…Dinjin mostly, in Assam province. I worry about him so! The flying is treacherous…the mountains, weather, and of course the Japanese. We see each other when we can, but it's sporadic at best."

"I had no idea! So you came back to be with him?"

"No...not just for that. Hovans has people in Chongqing and the United States. One of his spies in Chongqing...the guys name is Li Shih, spotted Alex and I when we went through there on our way to the U.S. He contacted one of their agents in the United States. The man's name is Arnaud DeRuffe. He runs a spy ring for the Japanese there. DeRuffe came to me in Maryland, the day my son was born. He demanded that I return to my job with CNAC, in China. If I didn't, he threatened the safety of my parents in China, my husband's parents and my baby in the States. They knew that in my old position with CNAC, I would be in a perfect position to pass them information regarding personnel, shipments, overhear high level conversations...the lot."

"Yes, I'm beginning to see."

The room began to warm perceptibly. Anna removed her coat as she continued speaking.

"I've been feeding them enough plausible information to be believable...stuff that they could check, and confirm to be true, but nothing that would compromise anything the Allies are doing. What is passed on to them is coordinated with the OSS."

"The OSS...what's the OSS?"

"It's short for the Office of Strategic Services. It's an American organization, but they use nationals from any country that can get the job done. They are just getting started here, but they have been active in Europe for some time. Their purpose is to gather information about the enemy any way they can. They are also very good at spreading confusion and misinformation to confound the enemy. It's very much like Britain's commando outfits and intelligence services all rolled into one."

"And you, innocent little Anna, are working for them?"

Anna looked absently at the fire flickering in the stove and said pensively, "I'm afraid I haven't been innocent for quite a few years now; but yes, dear Saul...yes I am."

Saul took a dented teakettle and filled it with water from an urn.

With his back to her Saul said, "What will you do now that you are here? What are your plans?"

He sat the teakettle on the iron stove and turned to Anna. She paused a moment, looked at Saul, and then said, "First, old friend, you and I are going to set up an organized radio network that can't be compromised, right here in Shanghai. Then, we are going to set up an intelligence network to gather information from and confound the Japanese."

Anna pulled a small book out of her pocket and put it on the table.

"This is the key," she said. "My friends working the other networks have the same thing. You will receive a new one from time to time. Do you still have that old 1933 Webster's dictionary you used for your lessons?"

"Of course...I would never get rid of that!"

"Good! I thought you would. I was hoping it wasn't confiscated. I remember that dictionary from when we used to study together. I told our people in Chongqing to use that for a start. We can change when needed."

"What are you going to do about your child...your parents?"

Anna looked directly at him. "All I can say now, Saul, is I will do what I can. It's best I don't say anything else in case either of us is compromised. That way, they won't be able to get anything out of us to use on the other."

Saul said, "Anna, I've stopped all transmissions from here. As I said, the Kempeitai have mobile DF; they are patrolling all of the time. They must already have it narrowed down to this part of the Hongkew. If I keep it up, they will find me for sure."

"Then you need to have more places to transmit from, Saul. We need to set up multiple transmitters, or better, multiple fixed antennas camouflaged to look like ordinary objects. My OSS friends say we could hide some antennas and camouflage others...like a dipole, disguised as a clothesline on top of an apartment building, or a sloper permanently attached to a building, or a tree, and then stretched tight when we hook up the transmitter. What do you think?"

"I think you have learned a lot from your American friends!"

Anna nodded.

"Yes...multiple antennas could work. I would have to develop excuses to move the truck around the city...maybe to pick up and deliver the repaired radios directly, rather than through the warehouse. I could hide the transmitter in their own truck; no one would suspect me! If we did that, I could use the truck's battery as a power source. Hooking up to the antenna so that no one knew what we were doing could be dangerous though."

"I knew you would come up with something," Anna said. "How safe is it for me to meet you here?"

"Not safe at all. We really need to come up with something else. Do you remember Asher Swartz, the tailor?"

"Yes I remember him. Is his shop still in Hongkew?"

"Yes...he has indicated he would like to do something to get back at the Japanese. I'm sure we could use him as an intermediary."

"Good—you work on that."

"Anna—what are you going to do about Hovans?"

"I don't really know yet. As far as he is concerned, I'm under his complete control. As I said, it was because of his contacts in Chongqing that they knew I was returning to the States. I would really like to break that hold they have on us, but I have to be very careful. When I left Hovans in '37, we weren't on the best of terms. To say the least, I won't be one of his most trusted associates."

Saul and Anna had their tea. They talked of all of the changes that had taken place in Shanghai since the Japanese occupation—about their old friends.

"You know Saul—the last time we really talked together was during those days in the fall of '36 when we were both still just kids, really. Remember? We could talk about the movies, the characters, the leading men and ladies, the American slang…we could talk about those things for hours. It seems a lifetime ago, doesn't it?"

Saul said that the last he had heard of their friend Irina was that she and Wan Ting had gone to Chongqing, but then, she had dropped out of sight.

"I met Irina on a few occasions, in Chongqing, when I first arrived there, after leaving Hankow…just after I fled Nanking in '38. I met her coming out of Colonel McHugh's office and got the impression that she might have been working for the Americans, but she wouldn't say. I asked if she knew of Wan Ting's whereabouts. If she did, she did not say. She wouldn't say much about what she was doing, either, only that she was living in Harbin, and occasionally her business, whatever that was, brought her down to Chongqing."

They spoke of Cheng Tu, their old Taijiquan master, and asked each other how they had been able to practice their postures and exercises. Both confided they had little time for that anymore. Anna kept looking at her watch knowing that first light would soon replace what little safety the night provided. She wanted to be gone before the neighborhood began to stir. Reluctantly, she stood, embraced Saul, put on her heavy parka and bedroll and left the same way she had come.

CHAPTER 71

▼

HOVANS

Japanese occupied Shanghai
March, 1943

It was dawn when Anna crept out of Saul's apartment. So as not to attract attention, Anna walked through the cold morning until she was several cross streets away. She woke a half frozen coolie sleeping under his rickshaw with only a thin blanket to cover him. Glad to have any fare and the chance to warm his blood, he rose, did several squats and pulled the tall female devil back to the ferry terminal. She got off near the old customs house. She knew that Hovans, and his friends from the Kempeitai, would be aware of the arrival times of any public transportation. They would want to account for all of her time since she had arrived the previous evening.

She found a place on the riverbank where many refugees slept in the open. No one paid much attention to just one more homeless person looking for a place to sleep. Anna was exhausted after the long river trip and then being up all night with Saul. She un-slung her bedroll, spread it out in cobblestones, lay down, and went to sleep surrounded by workers and refugees. If Hovans kept to his old habits, he wouldn't rise much before noon.

After a few hours sleep, she woke to find that she was by herself. Almost all the homeless were busy looking for work or foraging for food. The rest were gone. She rolled up her blanket in a tight roll, attached the carrying cord, slung it over her back and made her way to the telephone office where she called the Far East Cabaret. She asked to speak to Hovans saying that it was Anna Boreisha, from

Chongqing. After a few minutes, Hovans answered the phone and said, "Mrs. Boreisha, or do you prefer Cannon?…So good to hear your voice!"

He was as full of it as ever, Anna thought. She explained she had spent the night at the ferry terminal.

"Li Shih said you would be along about now," Hovans said, "You remember my man, Ostafii Rabin, don't you? I'll send him along to pick you up in front of the customs house!"

In about thirty minutes, the same limousine she had last seen in 1937 pulled up in front of the customs house. Sure that Rabin would not recognize her peasant clothing she walked up to the Bentley and rapped on the window. Rabin turned to what he thought to be one more begging refugee. A look of irritation turned to one of malevolence as he recognized Anna. He didn't leave the drivers seat, but instead, gestured with his thumb to the back seat.

For the first couple of blocks Rabin weaved the Bentley in and out of the now sparse wartime traffic of Shanghai. It was one of the few private automobiles that hadn't been converted to burn charcoal gas. After several blocks, Rabin said in Russian, "I've thought about you often since you left in '37, and I'll bet you thought about me more than once, didn't you chickie."

Anna didn't say anything. Rabin continued. "You remember your little friend, Tanya, don't you? Before you left, we had a little chat…you know, the night you two were with those Japos and that Nazi homo!"

In the back seat Anna's heart all but stopped.

Rabin continued. "I thought I would have a little heart to heart conversation with your little friend about what *really* went on that night so, to be more persuasive, I stopped the car and got in the back seat with her. Oh, chickie…how I remember that moment. *The fear on her face was like a tonic!* 'It was only business' she cried, and that 'Hovans had ordered your bunch to do whatever it took to keep those guys happy.' Well I didn't believe her…not for a fucking minute. Hovans…me, we both knew you were fucking that marine. Even back then, we knew he was snooping around…trying to get the goods on what we were doing with the Japs. We kind of figured you were working for him just like those two chinks he used to hang around with. I knew she was lying. That's when I went through her purse and I found that fifty-dollar bill."

Anna still wore her peasant hat with earflaps. She could see a portion of his fat face in the rear view mirror, but still she was silent. Only her blink rate changed as she continued looking straight ahead.

Rabin was warming to his subject and continued, "Yeah—the little bitch said you gave her the fifty dollars all right…imagine that…so I asked her: Why was a little Russian whore like you giving another little Russian whore like her fifty dollars? She kept saying she didn't know, and it was just that Hovans had told you to do everything to keep that bunch happy…it was your payment for doing a good job. I knew she was lying, so I started to knock her around a little to get the truth out of her, and the first thing I knew her fucking neck was broken. She just sat there, on the back seat of this car, sitting right where you are—looking like a little fucking rag doll…beady little eyes staring straight ahead, kind of how you look right now, chickie."

Anna didn't answer. Rabin snatched glances of her in the rear view mirror. She appeared to be in a trance. Rabin looked at the road ahead and said, "Tsarist bitch…snooty as ever, aren't you; except this time we got you and that chink you used to work with right where we want you!"

To a casual observer Anna appeared to be staring at the fat rolls on the back of Ostafii Rabin's huge head. In reality, however, she had cleared everything from her mind. As he began his rant, she was visualizing the defensive postures of Master Cheng Tu's, Wu style of long-range boxing. During this exercise, though, she did not miss a thing he said. When Rabin told her of killing Tanya, she began to visualize the offensive postures and continued to do this until the car pulled up in front of the Far East Cabaret.

Rabin opened the driver's door and got out. When he looked through the back window, Anna was still sitting, staring straight ahead, still in her peasant hat and parka. He pulled the rear door open and jerked his thumb toward the cabaret door. He said, "What in the hell is wrong with you, chickie…Mr. Hovans is waiting."

Seeming oblivious to Rabin's invective, Anna blinked several times, turned to face him with her "Mona Lisa smile," and, still saying nothing, got out of the car. Rabin glared at her in confusion. He was speechless at the woman's demeanor. Not knowing what to do he cursed her in Russian and followed her up the steps to the cabaret.

Rabin led Anna down the hall to Hovan's office. She had only been there a few times before. Things had changed little since the last time she was there. Still standing, she took off her hat, gloves and parka.

Rabin said, "Wait here!" He went out into the hall and closed the door to the office. She heard his heavy footsteps receding down the hallway.

Anna looked around the office. She had to admit: Hovans had taste. His office was much as she remembered from six years ago. A huge ornate desk, probably from Tsarist Russia, dominated one side of the room. Pictures of Bolshoi prima donnas, celebrities and valuable paintings hung on the opposite wall. Below the paintings was an ornamental safe with a combination lock.

She thought of the crash course in safe cracking she had received from one of America's foremost criminals. The OSS had borrowed her tutor from prison; they made a deal with the authorities for leniency if he would train some of their agents and keep his mouth shut. She wondered if she would have the opportunity to try out her new skill.

She didn't think the opportunity to plant her trap would have come so soon, but here it was. There were no footsteps on the hardwood floor of the hallway. With no wasted time she knelt down, felt up under the ornate desk for a ledge and found what she was looking for. She judged by the mass of the desk that it would not be readily moved for cleaning. Anna stood and with rapid movements, untied the drawstrings to her quilted pajama like trousers, dropping them to the floor. She pulled the long underwear she had worn for the cold river trip down over her hips. Should anyone come in the next few seconds, she was naked below the waist. She pulled at the adhesive tape that held the miniature camera and the small tube of documents the OSS had provided her. The camera was identical to the one she had used for Billy Schott, that horrible night in 1937. Like that night, she had both pieces taped high and slightly forward on her thigh to avoid chafe.

The camera free, she used the same adhesive to tape the tube and camera together. She kneeled down and placed it out of sight on the ledge under, and on the front of the desk's frame; she used what tape was left to hold it in place. Unless someone was lying on his back, looking straight up, her little package was completely out of sight.

She pulled up the long johns and fastened only the top button. Even as she tugged at her trousers, she heard footsteps coming down the hall. They were much lighter than before. Anna knew it had to be Hovans.

As he entered the room, she feigned "fiddling" with the drawstrings of her trousers when in actuality she was still tying them back in place. Her heart was pounding so hard she was sure he could hear it from the office door.

Hovans didn't just come into the room; he made an entrance. He paused, or more accurately, posed for a second as he observed his guest fidgeting with her trouser drawstrings in apparent nervousness.

"Anna my dear…it's so good to see you again," he said. "You left so quickly the last time I never had the opportunity to say goodbye!"

Anna smiled and said nothing, as she knew that Hovans, ever the actor, always on stage, was still in the first act. He had only just begun to gloat over his prize.

"My dear girl—what a dreadful costume! Li Shih told me of your plan to deceive the Americans. Very clever indeed...pretending to fly off to Kunming to be by your husband's side, and then disembarking at the last moment and making your way here by steamer. Yes, very clever indeed, but then again you have always been very smart, haven't you, my dear?"

"I came to see my parents."

Hovans ignored her statement.

"I know you had to be as inconspicuous as possible. It's really quite difficult for a beautiful woman like you to blend in with the riffraff...but really, darling, don't you think you went too far with those peasant clothes you're wearing?"

"Sergei...cut the crap! I've been sending you and your little friends a lot of good stuff. I've kept my part of the deal. DeRuffe guaranteed you would make sure my parents were O.K., and that I would be able to see them. That's the only reason I'm here, you know, to see my parents. I want you to keep your part of the bargain."

"Yes, Li Shih said you made that quite clear...no more information until you see your parents."

"When will I be able to see them?"

Hovans said, "In good time, Anna...in good time. They are being brought to Shanghai just for your visit. You do realize just how difficult it is to keep my friends from the Kempeitai from indulging their passion for brutish behavior, now don't you?"

He turned and raised the finger on one hand for effect and said, "Remember, my dear, you are not in an advantageous bargaining position. Don't forget, we have all the cards. The well-being of your family, here, and in America, depends on your cooperation my dear; but enough of that! First, let's get you cleaned up, fed and rested. When you are ready, I'll have one of the girls take you shopping. These dreary Japanese have really made it so difficult to buy anything with style anymore. All of the good Chinese and Jewish tailors have been forced up into Hongkew and Chapei. On top of that, good material is almost non existent...and we do want you to look presentable for your parents, now, don't we?"

"Sergei, did you know that Ostafii Rabin killed my friend, Tanya?"

"Tanya?...Oh, your little friend you worked with, way back in '37. Yes...I remember...unfortunate business. Ostafii has a way of being excessive when he thinks he's on to something. Was he on to something Anna? There was that marine you were seeing, you know...and he did have an inordinate interest in me and my clients now, didn't he?"

Anna said, "No, Sergei…there was nothing going on. He was simply a friend that I met that first night at your cabaret; nothing more."

"Don't give me that, my dear…not that it makes much difference now. We know you were much more than simply friends…we had the two of you followed ever since you met; you see…we know you were having an affair with him right up until the time you left; so don't play me for the fool, Anna!"

Hovans continued, "You know, Captain Schott…that was his name, wasn't it…was with Marine Intelligence in Shanghai right up until they left in '41. Oh I remember it well…bands playing and the Marines, smart as ever, boarding the U.S.S *Harrison* on the Bund…too bad the way it turned out for them, wasn't it."

Anna remembered only too well. She was in Chongqing at the time. She knew Hovans was leading to something.

"Well, it occurred to me that after that pathetic defense of Manila and Corregidor, almost all of those very same marines were either killed…they were the lucky ones you know…or interred in one of those dreadful prisons, like Changi, here in Shanghai, or Cabanatuan in Luzon. Then, I thought, in honor of your arrival I would have my friends look through their records…they do keep very meticulous records, you know…and see if maybe Captain Billy Schott might have survived any of those appalling ordeals. I was thinking that if he did survive, wouldn't it be a nice surprise for you two to meet again?"

Anna's father had always taught her to pause and think before answering serious questions. This time she didn't.

"Sergei: Captain Schott dumped me. He's a son of bitch! I couldn't care less if he turns up or not."

Hovans looked at her in mock disbelief and said, "Anna: Dumped you?…Dumped you my dear? If he is that stupid, it is no wonder the Americans are losing this war, now is it?"

Anna thought about Mitchell's raid on Tokyo, America's success at Midway and Guadalcanal, but she was playing a dangerous game. If she were to survive, she would have to continue to play by his rules, at least for now.

"Sergei: How about that bath you were speaking about? I'm really filthy and tired. Then, I do need to buy some clothes before I see my parents."

Hovans opened the door to his office and yelled down the hallway, "Mae Lin! Mae Lin!" Anna stiffened at the name. It must have been Mae Lin that Rabin had been ranting about. She had not even thought of Billy's beautiful Chinese informant since 1937. She did not have long to wait to see if indeed it was the same woman.

When the girl came through the door, she noticed that Hovans was looking straight at her to gauge her reaction. He knew! He just wanted to see Anna's response.

Anna said, "Mae Lin…long time no see! It doesn't look like the war has treated you so badly…how have you been?"

Mae Lin's first reaction was of no recognition at all. Then she said, "You were Billy Schott's friend…the one that worked for the Chinese airline, weren't you?"

Anna said, "The very same, Mae Lin. I think the last time we met was at the Cathay hotel, in '37. I was having drinks with Billy and some of his marine friends. You were with another girl; I can't recall her name."

With no emotion, Mae Lin said, "Her name was Suzy…Suzy Liu; the Japanese killed her in '37."

After the initial exchange, Anna noted that Hovans paid no attention. He hadn't seen the reaction he expected; he had lost interest and was looking at papers on his desk.

"Mae Lin," Hovan's said, "I want you to take Anna to the Excelsior. I've cleared it with Major Matsumoto of the Kempeitai, and it's O.K. Anna needs to get cleaned up and get some rest. After that, I want you to take her someplace to get some decent clothes. When you are finished, I want you to bring her back here…understand?"

The two left Hovan's cabaret and took a rickshaw to the Excelsior. On the way, she asked how she came to work for Hovans. Mae Lin explained that she had worked for Billy right up until the Marines left. After their departure for Shanghai in 1941, Hovans remembered the work she had done for them. He offered her a job much as any businessman would hire the competition's good people if their employer went out of business. One of the conditions, of course, was Mae Lin would have to tell Hovans all of the information she had collected, their sources, and the techniques they used. Susie Liu wasn't so lucky. The Kempeitai raped and killed her before they understood her value.

After helping Anna check in and sign the hotel register for the Kempeitai, she went with her to her room. When they closed the door Mae Lin said, "You can be glad that you had a respectable job with CNAC and never got into the spy business. It's a sordid, despicable enterprise."

Anna wondered if she were on a fishing expedition. She also wondered how much the girl really knew. She asked Mae Lin, "Were you and Billy lovers?"

"Once—more for recreation than anything else; how about you?"

Anna said, "He was my first lover. It lasted from about the time I first met you until I left Shanghai, in the summer of 1937."

"Hovans said you married an American, went to the States and then came back here to be with him and also work for the Japanese; is that right?"

"Yes, I didn't have much choice. If I didn't cooperate they threatened my child and my parents."

Mae Lin looked at Anna with a melancholy, pensive expression. "It is a very hard thing for me to work for Mr. Hovans, but I too have no choice. They have killed so many Chinese…my family, Suzy, so many of my friends…It is hard for me to express how much I hate these people."

Anna reached for Mae Lin's hand and held it tightly in both of hers. All she said was, "I know Mae Lin, I know!" She still did not know if she could be trusted.

Mae Lin waited until Anna had finished her bath. She had but one simple dress rolled up in her bedroll and put it on with her peasant's coat. They went to the lobby, left her key, stepped out in the street and hailed a rickshaw.

Anna said, "When I was here last, there was an excellent tailor in Hongkew. He did some work for me a couple of times…do you think we could go there so I could order some decent clothes to see my parents in?"

Mae Lin agreed, and Anna gave the rickshaw man directions to Asher Swartz's shop in the Hongkew district.

CHAPTER 72

▼

THE TAILOR

Japanese occupied Shanghai
March, 1943

The coolie padded to a stop in front of the simple shop. The sign over the door said, Asher Swartz, Tailor. The advertisement in the window showed a woman's caricature in an American suit that Anna guessed was probably in fashion just before the war.

They paid the coolie and entered the dressmaker's store. There were no other customers. A small bell on the back of the door rang as they stepped into the shop. An elderly gentleman came out of a room in the back of the shop, and somewhat diffidently approached the two young women. Few Caucasians, and fewer Chinese, had visited his shop since the war began. He was stooped, wore a black suit, vest, yarmulke and pince-nez glasses on the tip of his nose. With an almost saintly smile he introduced himself as Asher Swartz, proprietor, and asked what he could do for the ladies.

Anna told the tailor her requirements. She only needed a *"simple spring suit,"* she said. "Those three words spoken by a Russian woman were his cue that she had been sent by Saul Abrahamson. Asher only blinked. He didn't think it would have been so soon.

"Choices of material were few, so it didn't take Anna long to select a fabric. While Mae Lin was browsing on the other side of the store, she cautioned the tailor that Mae Lin was not reliable by waving her finger back and forth making sure the gesture was hidden from Mae Lin's view. As he took and wrote her measurements in his order book he said, "Ms. Cannon, I will be very careful and see to your requirements personally. I will send word to you at the Excelsior when your suit is finished."

The two women said goodbye and opened the shop door to see Ostafii Rabin leaning against the door of Hovan's Bentley.

CHAPTER 73

▼

TURBULENCE

The Hump
March, 1943

The DC–3's rate of climb indicator had dropped to just under one hundred feet per minute, and he still wasn't on top. It didn't give Alex any more concern than at other times except for the shape of the cumulus clouds obscuring the mountain peaks today. These had sharp, clear edges and indicated the probability of a lot of ice. Hovering over the peaks were well-defined lenticular clouds, a good indication of strong winds and turbulence. On this trip, he carried the usual load of fifty-gallon drums of aviation gasoline destined for Kunming and Chiang Kai-shek's war machine. His DC–3 was not overloaded any more than usual, but at the present rate of climb, he was sure they would not be able to top the clouds when they began to thread their way between the mountain peaks. At least they had just confirmed their position crossing the Mekong River before they went into the clouds, he thought.

Alex had made dozens of round trips over the Hump, and by now, he knew the hazards. It looked like he would have to deal with the ice and turbulence one more time. The co-pilot looked at his worn, creased and almost unreadable chart. He confirmed the new heading to Alex. With the good visual confirmation of their position less than a minute before he went into the clouds, he wasn't too worried. Regardless of the visibility, they knew the heading on the chart would take them between the peaks, just as it had so many times before. As he turned to the new heading Jian, the co-pilot, punched the elapsed time clock and began timing the next leg.

Just as the first wisp of clouds flew by the DC–3's window, Alex remembered the radio message he had received from Anna two weeks before, in Dinjin. He hadn't seen her for more than three months, and now, in fewer three weeks, they would be together in Kunming, and then home!

Somehow, she had managed leave from her CNAC office in Chongqing. Furthermore, she had finagled priority transportation for both of them to the States—for two whole weeks! He looked forward to holding her in his arms and hearing just how she pulled that one off. It would be the first time that he would see his new son. Alex pushed the throttles the rest of the way to the stops as the overloaded airplane struggled to get a little more altitude before being totally engulfed in cloud.

CHAPTER 74

▼

MASTER CHENG TU

Japanese occupied Shanghai
March, 1943

Hovans seemed to have lost interest in her, but still kept her under surveillance with Rabin and Mae Lin as her ever-present watchdogs. On two separate occasions, she had stopped by the cabaret to arrange a meeting with her parents, but still they had not arrived in Shanghai. Time was getting short, and she wanted to make sure they were OK before she alerted Saul, through Asher, to send the message that would spring her trap. To be safe, she had to be well on her way back to Chongqing by then. There wasn't much time left, and she still had a lot of loose ends to pull together to make it all work.

Three days later Asher Swartz called the Excelsior and left word that her suit was ready. Again, they traveled by rickshaw. As before, there was no one in the shop but Anna, Mae Lin and the tailor. The fit was perfect, and Anna wondered how the old tailor stayed in business with so few customers. After she returned to the Excelsior, she read the note he had pressed into her hand. The note said Saul had erected two more antennas, and received a message from the OSS that they wanted her back in Chongqing as soon as her mission was accomplished.

Ever since she arrived in Shanghai, Anna pleaded with Hovans for permission to see Cheng Tu, whom she described as an old friend of the family. On her third try, Hovans granted her permission, as long as Mae Lin and Rabin accompanied her.

Cheng Tu was very happy to see his old student. Anna introduced him to Mae Lin and Rabin in Mandarin. When the three began conversing in the Mandarin, Rabin lost interest and went back outside to the limousine to smoke, assured that Mae Lin would report anything untoward during the meeting.

With Mae Lin present, Anna told Cheng Tu as much as she could about her life since she had left Shanghai. She confessed that she did not practice the postures and maneuvers as often as she would have liked, but her job, and later motherhood, precluded routine practice. At every opportunity, however, she visualized the postures and maneuvers as he had taught her to do. With Mae Lin present, what she failed to tell Cheng Tu was that during her short training session with the OSS she was able to train daily using his Wu style of boxing against the OSS instructors. Her old master would have been very happy to know that his prize female student acquitted herself very well against some of the best in the world.

Anna thought of what Mae Lin had told her about her feelings toward the Japanese and decided it was safe to tell Cheng Tu about Nanking. Not only would it be a good test of Mae Lin's allegiances, she reasoned, but even if Mae Lin told Hovans about her revelations, he would not tell his Japanese colleagues at the risk of losing such a well-placed and lucrative informant.

She began by telling her old teacher that she had not always been able to refrain from using the skills she had learned from him. She told of witnessing the murder and rapes of many thousands of Chinese soldiers and non-combatants in Nanking. She then told of the drunken soldiers and defending the young girls. Her old master listened without interruption as she described in technical detail how she had dispatched the five soldier-rapists. Cheng Tu nodded and asked how she lived with this burden. Anna told him, "Master: at the time I did not think anything about it...I just reacted as there was no other choice, and to this day do not understand why I feel no regret. I still feel the end was justified. My worst fear is that with this deed I might have become a little less human...a little less civilized."

Anna was astonished at Mae Lin's reaction. "Oh Anna, if only I could have done that! I would feel no remorse at all. Girls like me have spent our whole lives being victims. I would do anything to change that."

Anna said, "What really disturbs me is that these feelings have not left me. Mae Lin, you may not know this, but Rabin, that pig just outside killed a friend of mine in '37. It was the Russian girl, Tanya...she worked for Hovans at the Far East Cabaret when I was there. Master Cheng, you might remember when I told you of the man who assaulted me in 1937. I described the incident to you the next day. It is that man outside, and I am certain when I am of no more use to Hovans, he will try to kill me too. I will not let that happen."

Cheng Tu stood and walked to the door of his home and looked out to where Rabin stood leaning on the limousine. Unseen, he observed the man carefully and said nothing for almost a minute. He turned to Anna and said, "Child, do not concern yourself with that man. If it becomes necessary, I am sure you will make the appropriate decision."

It was only then that Cheng Tu felt confident enough to tell the two young women that he was part of a secret organization doing everything possible to undermine the Japanese. He asked Anna and Mae Lin if they would be interested in helping. They both said they would. Anna explained that she would only be in the city for a few more days but she would put him in contact with others who, because of their technical skills, could be very helpful to his organization.

CHAPTER 75

▼

ICE

The Hump
March, 1943

The last gust threw Alex's head against the cockpit's side window. The two pilots had to shout over the continuous noise of ice thrown from the propellers into the fuselage. Both pilot's windshields were completely frozen over.

Alex shouted to the co-pilot, "Hey Jian...un-latch that Aldis light! Wedge it between the glare shield and my windshield...then turn it on."

Jian looked at Alex without comprehension. Alex shouted, "The bulb...it gets hotter than hell! It just might melt a hole in the ice so we can see when we break out of the clouds. Right now, even if we did break out we can only see out of the sides!"

Jian nodded in understanding.

Alex looked out of his side window. It was still partially clear of ice, but he couldn't see beyond the wing. The wings and engine cowling had about an inch of ice build up. He had probably waited a little too long, he thought, but he didn't want to turn the de-icing boots on too soon and create an igloo over the boot and under the ice. The timed cycle function on the switch was inoperative today. He would have to use manual cycles. He actuated the de-icing boots. Most broke off the wings, but as soon as he turned the boots off, the ice began to build again.

"Hey Jian! The timed cycle on the boots is inop! I might get busy on the gages...so how about using your elapsed time clock and pulsing those boots every five minutes or so."

"O.K., Skip!" Jian started the elapsed time clock on his instrument panel.

In a few minutes, the controls began to feel different taking Alex's attention immediately back to the airspeed indicator. So far, the carburetor heat was keeping the intakes clear but the trade off was they were robbing valuable engine power. The turbulence was causing the airspeed to fluctuate wildly—plus or minus twenty knots. The airframe ice had resulted in a loss of almost twenty knots. As he fought for control, the trend in airspeed continued downward.

Airspeed was everything now. If he let it get much slower the wings angle of attack would increase, and the ice would build rapidly on the bottom of the wing where there was no de-icing gear.

Ice made the airplane heavier and distorted airflow around the wing. Both increased the airplane's stall speed. He did the only thing he could; he began a slow descent trading altitude for airspeed; regardless of the ice and turbulence, he had to keep the airspeed up.

The turbulence was so great, the instrument panel and whiskey compass were almost unreadable. Alex concentrated on the artificial horizon, airspeed and the gyro heading. With the bouncing whiskey compass, he couldn't see a heading accurate enough to reset the directional gyro. He would just have to hope the DG hadn't precessed too far. He lowered the average pitch attitude ever so slightly. That brought the airspeed up about 10 knots with full power on and resulted in a rate of descent of about 150 feet per minute. He couldn't ignore the slowly unwinding altimeter.

Jian yelled, "Alex we're through 12,000 feet!"

"Yeah...I'm on it," Alex shouted. "Take a look at that chart of yours and see how much air we have below us before running into cumulo-granite."

Jian Quan pulled the chart out from where he kept it under his thigh. He studied it in the bouncing airplane and yelled back, "I dunno for sure Alex...depends on the wind. From the flight plan we should have about, let's see...about 2300 feet under us right now and that of course depends on if we are on course and in the right valley!"

"I don't want to hear that, Jian!"

The co-pilot replied, "Under 10,000 feet, no guarantees, and again, that's if we are on track! The peaks on both sides are thirteen to fifteen thou."

The Aldis light was making a little headway on the windshield ice. In spite of the severe turbulence, Alex was holding the flight plan heading within 10 degrees on the DG, or directional gyro. He called back to the radio operator. "Hey Mac! You have anything on the direction finder?"

"Not a thing, Cap!...the fucking loop won't turn...I think the whole thing is frozen up!"

Alex said, "OK guys...we can't trade altitude for airspeed forever. Much as they need this gas in China, we've gotta lighten the load. I'll try to keep us on the road. You two take the machete, cut the straps and start kicking drums...right now!"

CHAPTER 76

▼

PETER AND LILIA

Shanghai, Hongkew district
March, 1943

The next day Hovans again sent Mae Lin and Rabin to the Excelsior to pick up Anna in the Bentley. Hovans didn't come. They drove to Hongkew where the Kempeitai had sequestered Peter and Lilia Boreisha. As they pulled to a stop, Anna noted they were not far from Asher Swartz's shop. Mae Lin stayed with Rabin in the car. When she stepped out, no guards were apparent.

Since the war began, the Japanese had confiscated almost all of the homes in the French concession and the International Settlement. The former occupants not sent to prison camps were forced to live in the already overpopulated Hongkew where it was not uncommon to find several families living in one apartment. The temporary room provided by Hovans for Peter and Lilia was no different.

Anna walked up one flight of stairs to the apartment number given to her by Rabin and knocked on the door. Her father opened the door. For a moment Peter Boreisha just stood, looking at his daughter. Then, he opened his arms and said, "Anushka! Anushka! Is the war over? Lilia, come quickly...it is our daughter, Anna. They told us we would not see you again until the war was over!"

Anna wore her new suit. Although very modest, from her parent's perspective of abject depravation, she looked well and affluent. Anna dropped the few things she had been able to purchase on the black market with American currency on the only table in the room. To her parents, the gifts were indescribable treasures:

A few cans of meat, rice, milk, aspirin, tea, some sugar and a few other things. She also brought mufflers and gloves for both of them. Hovans had allowed only one hour—no more.

She began by saying she was married to an American, that they had a grandson, and his name was Stephen. She told them of her flight from Nanking to free China in '37. She did not mention any particulars and very little about her life until she moved to Hong Kong. She then told them of her continued employment with CNAC, how she and Alex had met just before Pearl Harbor and how they were able to escape to the United States by Clipper. As she was speaking, she produced a picture of both of Alex and their grandson. She explained that her husband was flying between India and free China, and their grandson was living with Alex's parents in a beautiful house overlooking the Chesapeake Bay, in Maryland.

Peter and Lilia had tears in their eyes, partially of joy and partially of envy of the other grandparents. It was as if their daughter were telling them a fairy tale rather than the story of her life. When Anna was finished, she explained that she came back to China and CNAC to be with Alex. She planned to return to her son just as soon as she had taken care of some important business in Shanghai.

Peter Boreisha asked how she was able to visit them in Shanghai and still return to Chongqing, in free China. Anna simply said, "Father: do not worry; trust your daughter to conduct herself as you have taught her. It is best if I don't say anything else just now."

Anna had already made up her mind that she was not going to say anything about DeRuffe, the baby's or their own safety. She wouldn't tell them of her pact with the Japanese. What good would it do, she reasoned? It would unnecessarily burden them with guilt. They would blame themselves for the trap and their daughter's plight. Instead, she spent the rest of the time talking of Shanghai and old friends.

When she left, she asked Rabin to drop her and Mae Lin at the tailor shop to make adjustments on her new suit.

"Mr. Hovans directed that I have suitable clothes," she said.

Hovans had been emphatic that he accommodate the Russian girl's wishes. He told Rabin and Mae Lin he wanted to know where she was interested in going and with whom she met while still in Shanghai. He wanted any information that might give him leverage with her in the future. It was during this last visit to Asher Swartz that she passed the message to Saul telling him to send the message in *three more days*.

CHAPTER 77

▼

THE CANYON

The Hump
March, 1943

Alex thought he could feel the airplane getting lighter. In spite of the extreme turbulence, Jian and Mac were slashing the straps holding the gasoline barrels to their pallets and muscling them through the jettisoned door as rapidly as they could. Alex's head slammed against the window with yet another gust.

"Fly the airplane...fly the airplane," he said to himself.

A glance at the almost unreadable altimeter showed them descending through 10,300 feet. Even though the plane was getting lighter, and the engines were developing just a little more power at the lower altitude, the ship didn't feel right. That last recovery had taken a lot of aileron and rudder.

With Jian in the rear helping with the barrels, all of Alex's concentration was on the bouncing instrument panel.

"Fly the airplane," he repeated again.

The Aldis light was still wedged where Jian had left it, burning a feeble little hole through the ice-shrouded windshield. Alex's concentration on the instruments was broken by a sudden change of light in his periphery. There was a sudden change from the bright opaqueness of being inside a snow-filled cloud. He chanced a quick glance out his side window and was terrified to see snow covered boulders flashing by so close he felt he could touch them. Worse, the leading edge of the wings and engine cowling were completely covered with ice. No wonder the ship was so sluggish! He reached quickly for the de-ice control and his heart lurched in his chest. The dammed switch was already on! Jian had left it there when he had to help with kicking barrels. With his concentration on the instruments, he hadn't noticed. Rather than letting the ice build up and then breaking it off with a manually controlled pulse of the boot, the boots had pulsated continuously! A bubble had been allowed to form under the ice, and now the leading edge of the wing was deformed. The wings no longer had the shape the Douglas engineers had designed, and that was why the plane was so sluggish.

He thought that there was no way in hell he was going to shed that ice.

For the umpteenth time he tried pushing the throttle forward, but as before, they were already at the stops, where they had been for the last forty minutes.

Alex yelled at the top of his lungs, "Dump the drums as fast as you can!"

He heard a yelled reply but could not understand it. He thought, "How could I have let this happen!"

Alex looked at his airspeed again—well above normal stall but who knew what the *real* stall speed was with all that ice? He reached for the Aldis lamp and repositioned it six inches to the left. It had worked! He had a little hole about eight inches round! The shadows in the cockpit changed again. They were breaking out! He could see straight ahead and the ship was feeling lighter. Then he saw it—straight ahead—a large jagged boulder sticking obscenely out of the snow-covered valley. Alex didn't think; he only reacted. He pulled back on the yoke and banked to the right trying to coordinate the turn with rudder. Immediately the entire airplane shuddered. He leveled the wings and relieved the backpressure on the control column lowering the nose just as the bolder flashed by the left cockpit window. He scooted as far forward in his seat as his seat belt would allow, trying to look through the little viewing hole on his windshield. He breathed a momentary sigh of relief. The DC–3 was flying under the clouds now. The snow covered valley he was in looked clear straight ahead, but for how long, he couldn't tell.

A glance left and right showed they were in a valley a little less than mile wide. His compass showed he was on the approximate flight plan heading only he couldn't explain why they had bottomed out some 500 feet higher than when they should have. Even if the altimeter setting were off, it wouldn't be off by that much. Then it hit him—they had to be in the wrong valley!

Along their route, several valleys in their mountainous route ran parallel to one another. The terrific winds must have set them enough so that when the ice forced them to descend they had flown down into one of the adjacent valleys. God only knew how close they had come to the peaks and how high the bottom of this new valley really was.

Alex heard the fifty-gallon drums still being manhandled to the door when the end of their valley began to come into view. He quickly glanced right and left for an escape path. There was none. If he tried to turn around there wasn't enough room, and the iced up airplane would certainly stall in any steep bank. He thought of Anna and then of his son that he would have seen next month for the first time and once more pushed the throttles where they refused to go. The airplane started to shake uncontrollably as he tried even a slow climb. He knew they wouldn't make it but he had to try. The last thing he remembered was the control yoke jerking back and forth in his hands and the entire aircraft in uncontrolled buffet. It was hard to say whether Alex and the other crewmembers were crushed by the remaining drums of gasoline, or died from the explosion, as the DC–3 plowed full stall into the far end of the canyon wall.

CHAPTER 78

▼

THE OSS MESSAGE

Saul's apartment, Shanghai
November, 1994

Saul stood looking at Stephen and Karen. "I got the message from the OSS in Chongqing that your father had been lost. To this day, I question their judgment knowing that Anna was already stressed to the limit with her mission. What harm would it have been to wait until she returned? Anyhow, when the weather cleared, they used regular flights on their way to and from Dinjin to look for wreckage. They found what was left of his burned airplane several hundred feet below the rim of a canyon. There were so many lost flying the Hump…everyone just assumed it was weather related."

Karen took Stephen's hand in both of hers wondering what he was thinking. Stephen asked, "Did my father know mother was coming to Kunming?"

Karen couldn't help but notice that in the last days Stephen was using the term, "mother," much more than when they first met.

"Yes…Chongqing had sent a message to Dinjin saying your mother would be joining him in Kunming. Some arms were twisted and somehow she had swung it. She had managed to convince CNAC and the OSS that she and Alex needed a couple of weeks in the States with their new son before she could continue. As soon as she returned, they would have had transportation chits with the Army's ATC, round trip to the States. I am sure she did not intend to return to China once her business with Hovans was finished. Her effectiveness as a spy would

- 429 -

have been lost, and she knew DeRuffe and Hovans would no longer be a problem by then."

Alex asked, "How did my mother know that Hovans and DeRuffe would no longer be a threat?"

Saul said, "Here's how it happened."

▼

CHAPTER 79

THE TRAP

Japanese occupied Shanghai
March, 1943

Anna was preparing to go to the steamer docks and pick up her ticket for her return trip to Chongqing the next day when the hotel phone rang. "Madamn Cannon: front desk here—your man from the tailor is here. Shall I send him up?"

Anna was shocked. There was nothing in their plans that called for Asher to come to the hotel. It must be an emergency, she thought. Soon there was a knock at the door. She opened it and there stood Saul—valise in hand. Anna said, "Saul, what are you doing here…I am watched at every moment!" She stopped speaking when she saw he held a finger to his lips for silence.

"Good afternoon, Madamn Cannon—I am Mr. Swartz's apprentice. He has sent me over to adjust your suit and to show you these new samples."

Saul closed the door and went over to where the radio was playing. He turned up the music in case the room was bugged. He was dressed in black, and carried a small bolt of cloth. In his valise was a measuring tape, chalk, scissors as well as straight pins and needles. If detained, he wanted to look like one in the profession.

In a voice louder than necessary, he said, "First let me check these measurements."

Saul whispered in Anna's ear. "Anna I have some very bad news…The message you brought for transmission…it was sent today!"

Anna whispered back in exasperation. "Today! Saul...what the hell happened? The trap wasn't supposed to be sprung until I was in the clear...on the steamer...on my way back to Chongqing! It wasn't supposed to be sent for two more days! The Kempeitai are supposed to think I'm one of them to make it believable! Unless I can get out of here, I'll be swept up with Hovans and his gang!"

"Anna—I...I gave the message to a new operator. I wanted it to be sent with a new fist in case they recognized mine. He made a terrible mistake! In his eagerness, he didn't read the date and time it was supposed to be sent and instead, sent it right away. I just found out a couple of hours ago...we have to get you out of here!"

The OSS had prepared the damning message. Anna had carried it with her to Shanghai. It was to be sent using a code they knew the Japanese could break. It was to appear that someone in Hovan's network had sent the message. It was the perfect sting operation.

The substance of the OSS message referred to payoffs Hovans was expecting from the allies. It even referred to an operation that the OSS knew the Japanese had knowledge of through their spy network in Chongqing. Knowing that the Kempeitai would immediately pounce on Hovans, and everyone associated with him, they had Anna plant a camera, complete with compromising pictures and documents, all certain to confirm the Kempeitai's suspicions regarding the intercepted message. His entire network: Hovans, DeRuffe, Li Shih—all would be suspect and no longer of any use to Japanese intelligence. There was no doubt in anyone's mind that Hovan's agents in China would be rounded up, tortured, questioned and executed. The Allies knew nothing they could say would mollify the paranoid Kempeitai. Other agents would murder DeRuffe and anyone in the States associated with him. Anna's family would have no more value to them. Their hold on her would be gone. All had gone as planned except that Anna was still in Shanghai instead of on a steamer returning to Chongqing.

"Anna: there is more bad news."

Anna looked at Saul as if wondering what could be worse than what he had just said.

Saul said, "Anna, your husband is dead. They say his plane crashed in the mountains flying the Hump from Dinjin to Kunming. Probably weather. CNAC has positively identified the wreckage. Anna, I'm so sorry, but no one survived."

For a moment, Anna stood speechless gasping in muffled sobs and grasping her stomach. "Oh Saul, Saul...It can't be true! It just can't be true!"

Saul threw his arms around her and held her tightly as she sobbed uncontrollably. "Anna…my dear, dear Anna…I'm so sorry."

Just then, the door burst open. Ostafii Rabin lunged into the room with his pistol drawn. He closed the space between them in two quick steps, yanked Saul from their embrace and brought the heavy revolver down hard across Saul's head.

As Saul was dropping to the floor Anna grabbed Rabin's weapon hand, twisted, and at the same time kicked obliquely at his knees while holding on to his hand and arm. The big man fell to the floor in a heap and was just beginning to yell, "You Tsarist bitch," when she twisted, turned and broke his wrist at the same time pinning him to the floor with her foot on his neck. As he howled in pain, Anna looked at the now helpless sadist and said in a low guttural voice, "Was the fear on Tanya Federonko's face really *'such a tonic'* for you, you insufferable pig? Was it Ostafi?" The big Russian began to comprehend her question about the same time he realized his certain fate. Before he could finish processing the thought, Anna killed him with a heel chop to his larynx.

Saul stared at the huge man on the floor. "Jesus Anna, we've got to get out of here."

"No, Saul, you've got to get out of here. You haven't been compromised…I have! They will be looking for me any moment now. Leave…quickly…by the side street entrance. When they get here, they will be interested in Rabin and me. The desk clerk will have forgotten about you…now go!"

CHAPTER 80

▼

THE BRIDGE HOUSE

Saul's apartment, Shanghai
November, 1994

Stephen asked, "What happened then?"

"I had no sooner left than the Kempeitai arrived. I felt impotent…unable to help. In a few minutes, they came out the front. They had tied her hands in front of her and pinned her arms with a bamboo stick between her elbows, behind her back. From the time the Kempeitai came for her, and the time I saw her next, there is little information. I do know they took her to the Bridge House," said Saul.

"Bridge House…what's the Bridge House?"

Saul regarded the two Americans drinking tea on his couch with quizzical faces. It never ceased to amaze him how uninformed the rest of the world was about what went on in Shanghai during the war, but then again, it was a world war, and people had a tendency to only pay attention to matters close to home.

Saul said, "The Bridge House was a notorious prison where the Kempeitai held and interrogated their prisoners. Many who were taken there simply disappeared."

Karen asked, "Aren't there any records?"

"Other than personal accounts of those who were lucky enough to be released, little is known. When the allies finally came, the Kempeitai burned all their records, took off their uniforms and blended in with the rest of the Japanese waiting to be repatriated."

"Was anyone allowed to visit her at the Bridge House," asked Stephen.

"It was in fact encouraged," said Saul.

"The Kempeitai wanted to see who visited as visitors became suspect and fell under their scrutiny."

Stephen asked, "Were you able to visit?"

"I went once...it was in the fall of '43. It was the last time I saw her. She wasn't at all well. They had her dressed in what I think you call a smock...she was filthy and had lost so much weight that at first I almost didn't recognize her.

At first, she seemed disoriented. She was so weak she could hardly stand; she just stared blankly at me with no recognition. Then, with that half-smile of hers, part of her old self came through. She knew it was me."

Saul turned away from Stephen and Karen. He had to struggle to regain his composure before going on. He motioned to the dirty little notebook in Stephen's hand.

"How she kept that journal from them, I will never know."

Saul took a sip of his tea and looked the other way when next he spoke. In a barely audible, quaking voice he said, "The bastards tortured her too, you know. She admitted working for Hovans knowing full well that DeRuffe was doomed and that you would be safe.

Then, there was that Marine Captain: Billy Schott. They found him at Cabanatuan, in Malaya. They took many of the prisoners captured at Corregidor to that prison. Before Anna sprung her trap, Hovans had him brought to Bridge House to use against your mother. As it turned out, the Kempeitai tried to use the marine to get information from both of them. By then, though, with the passing of time, Billy didn't have intelligence of any value.

When they were sure they had gotten as much information as they could they beheaded all of them...Hovans, his cronies, the marine, all of them. Your mother said the officer in charge of interrogations forced her to watch the whole thing. I'll never forget the bastard's name...it was Major Matsui Matsumoto."

Stephen asked, "Did you say Matsumoto, Saul?"

Saul looked up—surprised at Stephen's question. "Yes...you will see him mentioned a lot in that little journal. Why, Mr. Cannon?"

"It's a long story, Saul...I'll tell you later. What happened to my mother...my Russian grandparents?"

Saul said, "Cheng Tu and Asher Swartz had become part of our unit by then. Between the three of us, we managed to recruit quite a few others. Mae Lin was able to escape their net, joined us and helped immensely. We were able to move your grandparents to safety in case the Kempeitai took out their revenge on them.

We hid them with a Chinese family in a village just to the north of Shanghai. Word came that your grandfather died just before the allies liberated Shanghai. Without your grandfather, your grandmother just seemed to give up. She died a short time later."

Stephen waved the little journal that Saul had given him earlier and asked, "What's in here, Saul?"

"Mostly about prison life and people she met in there," said Saul. It was brought out by another childhood friend of ours who visited her once...a girl named Irina Federenko. She was in Cheng Tu's martial arts classes with your mother and me. I have reason to believe she also worked for Allied intelligence, but have no idea how she came to be here, or why. The last I heard, she had been active in Manchuria trying to uncover some secret Japanese operation up there.

"Stephen, there's a letter to you in that journal I think you should hear. Saul held out his hand for the book and turned to the part he was looking for. Let me read you one passage that should be very important to you."

CHAPTER 81

▼

THE LETTER

Shanghai, the People's Republic of China
November, 1994

Saul opened the journal to the page he was interested in and began to read.

My dearest Stephen:

I have no way of knowing if you will ever receive this letter, but if you do, I am asking your grandparents to read this letter to you only when you are old enough to understand what I am about to say.

If you are reading this letter without me now, it is because circumstances are such that I cannot tell you personally all of the things in my heart that I so much want you to know. Most importantly, I want you to understand that it was only something terrible that threatened all of you that could have forced me to leave and still keeps me from being with you now.

When this terrible war began, my Mama and Papa became trapped in China by evil people from a culture once respected by the whole world. Just as zealots in Germany convinced an entire nation of honorable people that aggression was justified, so have the militarist in Japan convinced their citizens that savagery perpetrated on others was necessary to protect their heritage and their future. Those same men threatened to bring harm to all of you in the United States and my parents here in China if I did not do as they ordered.

I want you to know that your mother has made sure that those evil people who threatened you can do so no more, but in making sure you were in no more danger I have come into circumstances that make it impossible for me to return to you until this war is over.

By the time you read this, I am sure you will have heard from your grandparents that your wonderful papa is no longer with us. He was lost to us doing what he loved and did best as his part in defeating these evil people. It is impossible to describe to you what a fine man he was, how much I loved him, or the sadness that his loss has caused me. Except for a photograph, your father never even had the opportunity to see what a handsome boy you were, and I only wish that I was there to be able to tell you how fortunate we were to have him as your father.

Even though you will learn a lot about your papa from Zachary and Charlotte, I am afraid your grandparents knew me only for a short time, and that you all will have to wait for my return to get to know your mother, as you were only a little baby when I had to leave.

Stephen, I want you to try to remember me from the pictures I left with your Grandma and Grandpa. Every time you look at those pictures, know they are images of your mother who loves you more than life itself. It has been difficult for me here away from the ones I love. If this war is over soon and I am able to leave this terrible place, I will come home to you as soon as I can, but I am afraid I won't look like the mother you see in those pictures.

I look ever so much to the day that I can return and watch you turn into a young man. Until then, know that your mother misses you terribly and loves you more than anything in this world.

Your loving mother, Anna.

"Stephen, there's one more letter," Saul said. "This letter was delivered to me from Irina Federenko in 1944. By that time, the first B–29's started bombing Shanghai, and not even the strongest filtering by the Japanese propaganda machine could hide the Allied advances from anyone in Shanghai."

Dear Saul, if you read this letter it is probably because the advance of the allies was not soon enough to save me. With the loss of my beloved husband, I have also lost much of my pluck, but I am trying to sustain myself as best I can by the thought of seeing my son and parents again. I am afraid that even if I do survive, I will never again be quite the same.

Love, Anna

Saul finished reading the letter that told more about prison life, her tormentors, Billy and the others she saw die at the Bridge House.

For a moment, Stephen just stared ahead focusing on nothing. Then he said, "Please excuse me for a moment."

He walked across the room, opened the door and stepped outside on the balcony. Karen stood up as if to follow. Saul shook his head, and she sat back down.

After about ten minutes, the door to the small apartment opened again and Stephen stepped back in. He was devastated. His eyes were red and it was apparent he had been weeping. He said, "I'm very sorry; I had no idea…no understanding…no idea at all of the kind of woman my mother was. Here…here I thought that all these years she had abandoned me either to be with my father or for something more important to her in China. My God, I feel so guilty…I've been a fool…Christ! My mother gave up her life to save me, her parents and my grandparents."

CHAPTER 82

▼

THE PENINSULA HOTEL

Hong Kong
November, 1994

Before they left, Stephen asked if Saul would give him the honor of being his guests in the United States making it clear that everything would be at his expense. He explained he would need a little time to take care of some unfinished business and would soon be in touch.

On the plane back to Hong Kong, Stephen sat lost in his own thoughts; he spoke to Karen only perfunctorily. Karen knew that he was wrestling with the prejudices of a lifetime and respected his silence. After arriving in Hong Kong and clearing customs, they caught a cab. Stephen dropped Karen off at her apartment thanking her for her help and support—he said he would be in touch before returning to the States. From his demeanor, Karen had no idea if she would ever see or hear from him again.

On the second day of their return, Stephen called Shigao Matsumoto and asked if he would meet with him in his room at the Peninsula. He asked him to come alone as he had some important information to tell him regarding the China Diaries.

Shigao arrived late in the afternoon. He was certain the first mission for his cell had been a success; that the American had, as expected, succumbed to the offer of money to suppress the slanderous material from his mother's journals.

Even now, he could imagine his colleagues' reaction when he returned to Kyoto. He would be venerated! He had visions of the celebration sure to ensue.

Just as his father in the past, he would be the honored guest, drinking toast and speaking of the future—of a time when their ideals would be embraced by a grateful nation.

Stephen shook Shigao's hand, took his coat and asked him to sit down; he offered him some tea or coffee he had ordered from room service. The handsome Japanese accepted the offer of tea and set the cup and saucer on the coffee table in front him.

"Mr. Matsumoto, I asked you to come so I could read you the information you are interested in directly from my mother's original journals. The passages that I think will interest you were written in 1938, another two in 1943."

Stephen went to the luggage sideboard, opened his mother's Russian map case and took out the last journal from 1938 left aboard Cheng Fat's sampan. He also withdrew the two small notebooks given to him by Saul. Shigao Matsumoto picked up the cup and saucer placed before him and began to sip the tea. Stephen continued to stand and said, "Mr. Matsumoto, I would appreciate it if you would not say anything until I have read these passages in their entirety; then, I would like to hear any comments you might have before I tell you what I have decided to do. If that is satisfactory with you, I will begin to read…if it is not, I would appreciate it if you would leave, now."

Shigao was surprised at the way the meeting was going. He replaced the cup on the saucer, put it back on the coffee table and regarded the American standing before him. He realized that with the way the conditions were presented, he didn't have much of a choice, if he were to find out the content of those journals he was willing to buy sight unseen. The only other way would be to use Mr. Otani, their *facilitator*, and that would mean he had failed in his mission.

He said, "That will be satisfactory, Mr. Cannon. I will save my comments until you are finished. Please continue."

Stephen opened the 1938 journal and began to read. He slowly paced back and forth in front of the coffee table as Shigao Matsumoto sat and listened. He read of Anna's return to Nanking, the bombings, the courtyard shooting of civilians as the Japanese entered the city, their fleeing across the rooftops, the Japanese officer, Minnie Vautrin and the International Safety Zone Committee.

Shigao showed only little discomfort at this point. He remembered the stories his father and their colleagues told of how brutal the war was and how their warrior's code called for ruthless action to achieve glory for the emperor.

Stephen continued to read. He read his mother's entries regarding the roped prisoners, what she had witnessed during the committee's "rape patrols," and then their presence at the killing fields, the bayonetings and the mass beheadings.

During this time, Shigao became visibly uncomfortable, first wringing his hands and making small gasping noises, then crossing and uncrossing his legs. He had completely forgotten his tea. At one point Shigao, much as a child in a classroom raised his hand to speak. Without looking at him, Stephen held his hand up, palm out, like a traffic cop, shook his head and continued to read. He read of his mother's encounter with the soldier rapists at Ginling College, how she had dispatched all of them and of their flight into the Japanese created nightmare of charnel carts and stacked corpses, of meeting Cheng, and their escape on the Yangtze.

Stephen shut the 1938 journal with a soft snap and again held up his hand to remind Shigao of their agreement. Shigao was staring at the opposite wall trying to assimilate the story he had just heard into some logical order that would fit the remembered versions from his father and his friends.

Stephen then picked up the first of the two covertly written journals and turned the filthy brown pages to the one that began his mother's letter to him, and began to read. Before he finished, Shigao Matsumoto was visibly weeping, his face in both hands. Without pausing, he set it aside and began reading from the last of the little journals written not for him, but for Saul, as perhaps the only written account to leave the Bridge House.

"Mr. Cannon: I want you to know...."

Stephen paused still holding the pathetic little journal in his hand. He was weeping and said, "Mr. Matsumoto...remember our agreement!"

Stephen skipped over his mother's accounts, the torment of prison life and torture, and turned to the pages he was intent on reading.

> *Major Mitsui Matsumoto made it his personal goal to break me. From Hovans, he knew of my relationship with Captain Billy Schott.*

"No...that is impossible!" Shigao looked up in horror. Stephen again held his hand up and continued.

> *Major Matsumoto knew that Sergei Hovans ordered Captain Schott brought to this tragic place even before the Japanese discovered Hovan's duplicity.*

When I first saw Billy, it took some time for me to recognize him. He was less than half his former physical self, and yet his stomach had swollen to hideous proportions from the effects of starvation and beriberi. Because of my own pitiful condition, it took Billy some time before he recognized me.

I was in my cell with some sixty odd other wretches suffering as I. It was July. The temperature was well over a hundred making the usual miasma of unwashed bodies and feces more overpowering than usual. Then, they sent for me. Two conscripts came and dragged me out into the midday sun that nevertheless felt wonderful compared to the hell of that prison cell. I was in a small courtyard surrounded by a wrought iron fence. I was taken there every time Major Matsumoto wanted me to witness an execution. Hovans and Li Shih came to their ends in this place as I expect I too will in time.

He made me kneel, and asked me once again to tell what I knew of the spy ring. I told him I had nothing more to add to what I had already said. He then had Billy dragged out, his hands behind his back, bound together with thin wire and bridled to his neck so that if he failed to hold his hands painfully high on his back he would choke himself. He made him kneel next to me and as he had so many times before, Matsumoto asked him to tell what he knew. Once again, Billy said he knew nothing more. He looked at me with those beautiful malamute eyes, and with that look, he said goodbye. I had seen Matsumoto do it many times before. It was a ritualistic ceremony with him. I tried to turn my head away but the Major made me watch. He withdrew his sword in one swift movement, held it high over his head, shouted the same incantation he had every time he used that accursed blade, and decapitated that once beautiful man.

As part of the ritual, he normally put the sword back in his scabbard in the same swift movement it was withdrawn. This time though, his ritual was interrupted. Matsumoto had swung the sword with such force that it carried though and struck the wrought iron fence breaking off the tip of his prized murder weapon. He was furious to the point of apoplexy, and I thought surely that he would vent his fury on me. I thought of Alex, my newborn son, my family, and realized I would never see them again. That time, however, it was not to be. It seemed that the two guards found his swordsmanship the subject of their amusement and were doing their best to suppress their mirth. Matsumoto turned his fury to verbal abuse on the soldiers and stomped out of the courtyard, forgetting me, at least for the moment. I was thrown back into that hell of depravation I had endured all these months. I don't know how much longer I have, but I do not think the war will be won soon enough to deliver me from this place.

Shigao was weeping inconsolably, still listening to what Stephen was reading. Stephen said, "Mr. Matsumoto, there are many more references to murder and torture of civilians at the Bridge House in my mother's journal, but I have read to you the passages I thought pertinent for my purpose, which is to ask if you still believe your country was not complicit in war crimes."

Shigao Matsumoto tried desperately to regain some composure. He stood and walked to where Stephen was standing, knelt down before him, and looking at the floor said through his sobs, "Mr. Cannon…please forgive me and my country for what we have done."

Stephen reached down, grabbed Shigao under the arms and pulled him to his feet. He placed his arms around the smaller man's back and between his own sobs of misery said, "Mr. Matsumoto, we are to blame for the sins of our ancestors only if we allow them to be repeated. Whether they are German, Japanese, American, radical Islamist, Africans or whomever—whether in the name of religion, politics, nationalism or some goddamned *ism* we haven't heard of yet, we must never again allow the zealots of the world to coerce nations to do their bidding. It is up to us as citizens of the world to expose the truth and make sure this never happens again.

The next day Alex called Karen and asked if she would see him. At lunch, he told her of last evenings meeting with Shigao, and asked her to forgive him for being so cold.

That evening, and for the rest of the week, Stephen spent as much time with Karen Hardisty as possible. Several times, he met with Shigao and the two of them discussed what part each might play to counter the revisionist.

Before he left for Maryland, he asked Karen if she might consider coming back to the States. Maybe she would consider working in the Washington area so that they could continue see one another. She said she would think about it and be in touch.

When Stephen landed in New York, he telephoned Charlie Fat and told him what he had found out about his mother. Stephen asked if he would be his guests for a weekend at his Maryland home so that he might thank him properly, tell him about the great-uncle he had never met, and show him the journals. Before he hung up, he told Charlie that he and a Japanese friend from Hong Kong would both be interested in helping his organization spread the truth of what really happened in the war.

The End

Some Thoughts and Acknowledgements

Except for historians, history buffs and people old enough to remember, very few people know that there was a war raging in China for ten years before the United States entered World War II. There are many books on the subject, but except at the graduate level, little, if anything, is taught regarding those events. Today, as then, not many people care. Re-enforcing that notion, I read that in a recent poll, fifty-two percent of Americans do not even know whom we fought in the war. Even if they did, for most Americans World War II began with the bombing of Pearl Harbor on December 7, 1941.

It was not as if the world was not aware of what was going on in Europe and China in the thirties; it is just that it was not happening to them. Yet. In America, people were much more worried about the Great Depression, and events at home, rather than what was happening half way round the world. Moreover, horrific events such as the rape of Nanking lacked the impact of instantaneous graphic images on TV. Instead, people had to rely on the verbal descriptions of a radio news commentator, their newspapers or Movie Tone News for visual images. Much of the national sentiment was that if we somehow kept out of it, it wouldn't affect our security at home. (Sound familiar?)

Both at home and abroad, our institutions were governed by isolationist sentiment. They failed to take significant action until it was too late; the result was World War II and the loss of over fifty million lives.

Today, we don't have the same excuses. We are prosperous, and we have history to show what happens if aggression and genocide are tolerated. To the extent we haven't tuned it out of our lives, we also have the ability to examine world events through the microscope of twenty-four hour non-stop news cycles complete with instantaneous pictures. Could it still happen again? I'll let the reader be the judge.

What is even less known than the events that led up to Pearl Harbor is the part played by one of America's airlines during those fateful years. Beginning in 1935, the now defunct Pan American World Airways pioneered air travel to the Orient. On the day the war began, four of her famous Clipper flying boats fell into harm's way.

China Diaries encompasses both of these themes. While the book is a fictional story set in the actual surroundings of the years and days leading up to America's entry into the war, there are many factual accounts of those times on which I have drawn for the story. For the Pan Am part of the story, there is the excellent *An American Saga* by Robert Daley and *the Pacific Clipper, the Untold Story* by Albert S.J. Tucker, Jr. and Matthew W. Paxton IV and Eugene J. Dunning. In addition, there is *Wings for an Embattled China* by W. Langhorne Bond and edited by James E. Ellis that tells the story of CNAC, Pan Am's subsidiary in China. Credits for the Pan Am part of the story would be incomplete without mentioning the two volumes of Jon E.Krupnick's *Pacific Pioneers* and Bob Gandt's *China Clipper*. For the story of what occurred in Nanking I relied on many accounts, most notably Iris Chang's bestseller, *the Rape of Nanking*. For those interested in learning more about aviation and China during this period I would recommend all of these books.

Many of the characters in *China Diaries* were actual people who lived during that time and accomplished the deeds described in the novel. In those cases, I have tried to characterize their accomplishments and exploits as closely as possible to written accounts. While trying to remain as true as possible to what these pioneers did and said, let me be clear that all of the dialog of actual and fictional characters is from the imagination of the author. In addition, the flight from San Francisco to Cavite beginning in chapter six is purely fictional and in no way representative of any particular crew or individual.

I would like to thank my good friend Ted Christ for his tireless assistance as copy editor supreme and my lovely wife Carol for her infinite patience. In addition, I would like to thank Charles Brown and David Craig, two "ex-marines" (if there is such a species) who lent their expertise on the uniforms and activities of the China Marines of that time.

0-595-32600-5

Printed in the United States
26014LVS00006B/85